Zane Presents

Déjà Vu

Dear Reader:

It is my pleasure to present *Déjà Vu*, the story of Angelica Barnes, who is struggling to lead a normal life in the middle of chaos and danger. Author Suzetta Perkins has established herself as a provocative, engaging novelist of the new millennium.

After doing a five-year stint in prison, Angelica finds herself trying to become re-acclimated to society. That is not easy for a convicted felon with no support system. She decides to move to New York City but instead of the life she dreamed of, she ends up working as a stripper.

Like most people, Angelica has trouble escaping from her past and when a demented ex-boyfriend takes her captive and starts murdering people in the name of his love for her, she has to fight for her life or concede to becoming his next victim. Readers will be sure to enjoy this thrilling offering and recommend it to all of their fellow avid readers.

Thanks for supporting the work of Suzetta Perkins, one of my authors under Strebor Books. I appreciate you giving this book a chance and if you enjoy it, I hope that you will read the author's other books: *Behind the Veil*, *A Love So Deep* and *Ex-Terminator: Life After Marriage*.

Peace and Many Blessings,

Zane

Zane
Publisher
Strebor Books International
www.simonandschuster.com/streborbooks

ZANE PRESENTS

DÉJÀVU

SEQUEL TO *BEHIND THE VEIL*

Suzetta Perkins

SBI

STREBOR BOOKS

NEW YORK LONDON TORONTO SYDNEY

SBI

Strebor Books
P.O. Box 6505
Largo, MD 20792
http://www.streborbooks.com

ISBN 978-1-59309-259-7
LCCN 2009924329

First Strebor Books trade paperback edition August 2009

Cover design: www.mariondesigns.com
Cover photograph: © Keith Saunders/Marion Designs

10 9 8 7 6 5 4 3 2 1

Manufactured in the United States of America

For information regarding special discounts for bulk purchases, please contact Simon & Schuster Special Sales at 1-866-506-1949 or business@simonandschuster.com

The Simon & Schuster Speakers Bureau can bring authors to your live event. For more information or to book an event, contact the Simon & Schuster Speakers Bureau at 1-866-248-3049 or visit our website at www.simonspeakers.com.

DEDICATION

To everyone who's ever loved someone and lost—
this is for you.

ODE TO ANGELICA

My life has been floating on a cloud
Drifting from one bad place to another.
Now I have a chance to get it right
To show the world that I have arrived.
But now that I've taken that step
I realize I've been this way before.
But I've got to find my way
My way to freedom.

—SUZETTA PERKINS

ACKNOWLEDGMENTS

I don't have the words to express how wonderful I feel and how thankful I am for all the blessings God has given me, enabling me to utilize my gift of the written word to reach out to others. It's still an amazing journey, and to the readers who've expressed so eloquently how much they've enjoyed my work, I thank you.

My family remains the springboard from which I fly, as they continue to support me in my endeavors, forever giving me encouragement as I continue to pursue this dream of mine. To my Dad, Calvin Goward, Sr.; my sisters, Jennifer and Gloria; my brother, Mark, thank you for taking every step of the journey with me. Your enthusiastic praise and support has meant the world. To my daughter, Teliza—We thank God for bringing your hubby, Will, home from war to a *changed* United States with its new black President, Barack Obama, and First Family in the White House. God is awesome. Kiss my granddaughter, Samayya. And last, but certainly not least, to my son, JR, who graces the cover of this novel, your unwavering support of my writing and all I do is so much appreciated. You said you wanted to be on one of my book covers, and I've delivered. I hope we sell as many books as you predict we will. LOL

To my sisters-in-law, Celeste, Gwen, and Dolly, especially my mother-in-law, Lavada, and my niece, Candace, thank you for sharing the love and singing my praises from California; Raleigh,

North Carolina; to the family reunion in Columbia, South Carolina. We sold some books at the family reunion, but it was fun because I shared it with you.

Whether out to sea in the Mediterranean or onboard ship, my niece, Carla, has always been an inspiration and a great supporter of my work. Thank you, sweetie, for sharing my work with the Navy.

This journey wouldn't be what it is without the special people who I've been blessed to meet along the way, those who've made my dreams possible, those who've given me a path accessible to readers, and those who just reached out and gave me love. To Maxine Thompson, my agent, I couldn't have done what I've accomplished without you. Our marriage was meant to be, and I love you. To the helm of Strebor Books, Zane, you made my dream possible. You never cease to amaze me as you move from one level of success to another, while helping others share their written works with the world, to your own work that now boasts a primetime series on CINEMAX, *Zane's Sex Chronicles*, based on your own book. Thank you so much. To Charmaine, the other powerhouse at Strebor, thank you for all that you've given unselfishly to help me be successful. To Curtis Bunn, founder of the National Book Club Conference, it was an amazing ride being a featured author last year. Although I've attended this conference since its inception, 2008 will always have a special place in my heart. Thank you for the opportunity. To Shunda Leigh of *Booking Matters*, thank you again for giving me the forum to showcase my work.

To Yvonne Head, Mary Farmer, Marsha Jenkins-Sanders, Lissa Woodson, and Emily Dickens, each of you have been an integral part of my journey. Yvonne—thank you for the warm bed and good eats each time I came to or passed through Columbia; Mary—thank you for your unwavering support and your good word that helped me to land that spot at NBCC; Marsha—thanks, roomie, for all of your hard work putting the Between the Sheets Tour together; Lissa—thank you for a first-class ride at the Cavalcade each year and because of you, I LOVE CHICAGO; and Emily—thank you for being one of my strongest supporters and believing in me enough to invite me to speak at the Alpha Kappa Alpha Women's Networking event.

The book clubs continue to be my strongest allies on the journey. I'd like to thank all the book clubs for their continued support, especially the Sistahs Book Club—Val, Bridget, Donna, Tara, Bianca, Bianco, Jean, Latricia, and Melody; The Angelou Book Club—Debra, Alice, Sheila, Ernestine, Janine, Star, Jessi, Latoya, Elma, Myra, Norma, Robin, and Patricia; Let's Talk Book Club—Carolyn, Desdy, Daisy, Lyndelia, Charlene, Mavis, Sharon, DeSandra, Barbara, and Paula; Sisters Unlimited—Patricia, Priscilla, Dail, Freddie, Mary, Gwen, and Tina; and the Imani Book Club—Angela, Mary, Pam x2, Denetrice, Teaner, Bernadette, Stephanie, and Charlotte. I must give a special shoutout to Motown Review who always show up and show out in full force in support of me—Jeanette (thanks for the spiritual experience), Sherri (for the great drink you fixed when you hit Fayetteville), Francine (smile), Yvonne (where is my gold blouse?), Roberta (thanks for my bag), Valerie (have your flat iron ready the next time I hit Detroit), and Yvette. While I didn't meet with them this year, I would be remiss if I didn't thank Sister Circle for their support—Mary, Pamela, Jo, Rhonda, Alberta, Derian, and Lenora.

Thank you Simon & Schuster/Atria for another wonderful year. And to all the readers who have read my work and enjoyed it, thank you from the bottom of my heart for letting me come into your homes, your vehicles, on your stress-free vacations to entertain you, wow you, and give you an exciting read. God bless.

1

"Hey, hey, hey. What's all the commotion about?"

Twenty-five occupants of dorm "L" dressed in prison blue moved back from the two inmates who were in an intense shoving match as the plump corrections officer in a starched, slate-blue uniform and curly Afro wig approached the quad, giving everyone a once-over like she owned the joint. The two women continued to push and curse each other until one of them got in a lucky punch and knocked the other to the floor, but then offered a hand to help her up.

"I said, what's going on in here?"

The two women stood erect and glared in defiance at the intruder. The inmates were serving five years to life, and Ms. Macy didn't scare them. In fact, no one liked Ms. Macy. She had a mean attitude. She was Sgt. Macy at the control desk but was Ms. Macy to the inmates. Some speculated that Ms. Macy had endured a tough life…that someone had done her awfully wrong. Others thought Ms. Macy might have served time in prison, too, because she looked like a cold-blooded killer.

Ms. Macy swung her arm out and pierced the air with her long finger, stopping short of one of the inmates' faces.

"You don't have to say anything—none of you. Somebody will snitch you out. But I better not catch none of you passing another lick because you'll be mine, if you get my meaning."

The twenty-seven women stared at Ms. Macy who had her nose stuck in the air like she hadn't said a word. She was "Big Bark" to them because they knew Ms. Macy wasn't going to do anything, that is not if she expected to reap any sexual favors from "her girls" while the others kept quiet.

"Sgt. Macy, please report to the control room immediately," said the voice over the loudspeaker.

"Barnes, I'll be back for you in a minute," Ms. Macy said. "We've got to go up the hill to see the warden."

Angelica pushed her nose as high as Ms. Macy's and nodded her head. The other women crowded around Angelica. Ms. Macy looked on, and then turned abruptly and left the quad.

"Hey, sister. Getting ready to get up out of this joint, huh? Tell that fine brother of yours to do what he can to get me out of this hellhole."

"I'll do what I can," Angelica said.

"I'll miss you, Angel," another inmate said. "You are the only sane person around here. I appreciate all you did to protect me from Ms. Macy. I don't know what will become of me once you're gone."

"Don't worry. Ms. Macy is not going to touch you. If she does, let me know. There are ways to take care of the big, bad wolf."

"It's just that the other corrections officers are so nice and Ms. Macy is so full of hate. She makes it her business to see that we suffer anytime she's around."

"Like I said, don't worry about Ms. Macy. My brother is an attorney, and even though he couldn't save me, Ms. Macy wouldn't want to face him in a court of law."

Angelica looked around at the place she had called home for the past five years. Sharing a room with twenty-six other inmates dressed in seasick blue didn't compare to the cozy home with the moat around it that she had left. Her mansion was a gift to herself made possible by a messy divorce from ex-husband Hamilton Barnes. Hamilton was serving a life sentence at Central Prison a stone's throw away from where Angelica lived at the North Carolina Correctional Institution for Women. She had been a model prisoner, and now her time here had expired. Angelica was ready to get her release papers, which lay between where she stood and the outside world.

"Barnes, let's go," Sgt. Macy shouted on her return. "I'm taking you to out-process."

Angelica stopped to hug the few women she had befriended. It had been tough on her, but these women made her time bearable.

She had had very few visitors in her five years at the prison, but what saddened Angelica most was that the one person she thought would come didn't. Margo Myles was her best friend once, and the cost of betrayal was too high and painful to think about. But Margo had forgiven her, or so Angelica thought. Margo's name was on the visitor's list, but not once in the five years Angelica was in prison had Margo shown up and signed in, which seemed to confirm what Angelica didn't want to believe to be true.

"I'm ready."

Sgt. Macy eyed Angelica from head to toe. Angelica's hourglass figure made Sgt. Macy squeeze her hand like she was holding a glass of chocolate milk that she was about to consume. She licked her lips for emphasis, and her breathing intensified every time Angelica took a step.

"I can hook you up on the outside—get a place for you to stay, if you like," Sgt. Macy whispered, her voice raspy and deep.

"And why would I want you to do that, Ms. Macy?" Angelica

said, turning around to look at Ms. Macy with contempt in her eyes and heart.

"Because you don't have nowhere else to go? I hear your brother had to sell your place to pay your attorney's fees."

"What's it to you?" Angelica barked, her finger pointed at Ms. Macy's nose. "You need to keep your nose out of other people's business. I do want to make one thing absolutely clear, though. There is nothing you can do for me."

Ms. Macy grabbed Angelica's arm and gripped it tight. "Don't play with me, girl. You ain't even all that anyway. You just sugar with some paint on it. Good riddance."

"Whatever. Now take your hands off me."

"You'll never be far. I hear that your ex-husband and boyfriend are at Central Prison."

Angelica flinched. The last time she saw Jefferson, he was being placed in an ambulance after the shootout at the courthouse. It was also the last time she saw Margo. She had tried to see Hamilton, but his family made sure that she had no access to him.

"Process me out, Ms. Macy. Today is a new chapter in my life. If prison taught me anything, it taught me to be strong, to be tough, and let nobody change who I am, no matter what is dangled in front of me. I am who I am. I'm ready."

Ms. Macy wrinkled her nose and rolled her eyes. "You'll be back before Christmas. You can't survive by yourself. Let's get you out of here."

The clerk at the property desk handed Angelica her belongings. There wasn't much—a North Carolina driver's license, a tube of lipstick, two hundred dollars, and a diamond ring that her ex-boyfriend Robert Santiago had given her. Funny, she had not thought about Santiago the entire five years she was in prison, but looking at the ring made it all come back to her. So vivid was the image, it made her shudder.

Santiago was a vicious person. As head of Operation Stingray, an underground group that purchased weapons stolen from a military base to sell to Honduran rebels, Santiago had ordered her ex-husband Hamilton and good friend Jefferson Myles killed. In fact, Angelica was in the car with Jefferson when he was gunned down. She and Jefferson miraculously survived the hit, although Jefferson was partially paralyzed from the waist down and was now spending time in jail for his part in Operation Stingray. Angelica had no idea where Santiago was and she didn't want to know. Simplicity was what she craved, and anonymity is what she prayed for.

An old-gray bus approached and stopped directly in front of her. *S-c-r-e-e-c-h.* The door flew open and a portly middle-aged man dressed in a blue uniform flagged Angelica in.

"Going to Fayetteville?"

"Yes," Angelica half whispered.

"Well, get on. I have another stop to make and we'll be on our way."

Angelica stepped onto the bus and ignored the bus driver's stare. The bus was nearly empty save for two other gentlemen who were asleep in the front of the bus. Angelica moved to the back and didn't respond to the bus driver's attempt at conversation.

Sleep tried to overtake Angelica, but the noonday sun, familiar streets, and the roads she once traveled beckoned her to stay awake. It was a perfect March day, although she was certain that March winds had visited earlier in the week, with all the broken branches scattered across lawns. The bus stopped outside of Central Prison. A lone black male with braids got on the bus. He noticed Angelica sitting in the back, but when it was obvious that Angelica wasn't interested in sharing prison stories, the gentleman took a seat near the front, looking out the window as the bus started to take off.

A sigh escaped from Angelica's mouth. Her heart began to palpitate. Thoughts of the forbidden were choking her mind. She was back in the car with Jefferson as the bullets rained down on them and she had left him to die. Angelica wondered what Jefferson was doing behind the walls of Central Prison and if he thought of her at all. She knew it would be suicide to try and contact him, but she couldn't release the feeling that gripped her heart.

What was it with her and Jefferson? Did she have feelings for him or was it the high she got whenever she and Jefferson came together in the heat of a moment? Margo would never trust her again. After all, Angelica had betrayed Margo—the one person who loved her unconditionally and treated her with decency and respect. Why couldn't she leave alone the one thing Margo loved dearly—Jefferson? It made no difference that she and Jefferson were never in a real relationship. Angelica was lost in her thoughts.

She jumped. She must have dozed off. She sat up straight and stared up at the man who had moved into her space. His braids were natty and his face unshaven. He wore an old Army field jacket that was two sizes too big.

"Hey, Miss, you going to Fayetteville?" the man with the braids asked.

"Ain't none of your business, and I don't feel like talking."

"You ain't got to be like that. Look, you don't have to say a word; I'll do the talking," he said.

"Suit yourself."

"What's your name?"

Angelica got up in the man's face. She wrinkled her nose and moved back quickly. His breath was stale. "I said, I don't feel like talking." Angelica closed her eyes.

"All right then. My name is Walter Hopkins. I did time for armed robbery and attempted murder."

One eye flew open, and Angelica took a good look at the man who wouldn't shut up.

"Yeah, I killed a man once, but never was convicted of the crime. I was a hired gun—got paid real good, too. Tried to get me to kill a cop."

Angelica sat up straight, measuring every word her seatmate uttered. Walter had taken the liberty of sitting in the seat in front of her while he entertained her with sordid details of his destructive life.

"Bad cop. Killed a sistah because he claimed she saw some mess he was involved in. Killed a white man too. He was tough on the outside, but that fine brotha ain't nothin' up against the real hoods in Central."

"Wha…what is the cop's name?"

"Oh, you want to talk now?"

"No, I remember a cop in Fayetteville who was put away about four or five years ago for murder and accessory to an arms deal scheme." Angelica leaned back in her seat.

"Yep, that's him. Hamilton Barnes. That pretty boy got it hard. The boys are spanking that behind. Bee-sides, nobody like a cop that ain't got no respect for anutha brother. So, pretty thang, did you say you were going to Fayetteville?"

"I didn't say."

"What were you in for?"

"Walter, I don't feel very hospitable right now. I should be happy, but I'm not. And I don't feel like talking."

"I was thinking that maybe you and me could hook up."

"When I get off of this bus, Walter, it's just me and me—no you."

"Umm, had you pegged wrong. Ain't you one of Macy's girls from the women's prison?"

Angelica sat bolt upright and looked straight into Walter's eyes. She bore a hole deep into his soul.

"Who are you, and what do you know about Ms. Macy?"

"Sgt. Macy, ahhh, she comes by the prison on occasion."

"To do what?"

"How do you expect me to know? I was locked up like you."

"Funny, you were offering her up like you were handing out government cheese."

Angelica looked at the braid-wearing brotha in the wrinkled T-shirt, Army field jacket, and tattered blue jeans with renewed interest. He knew something that he failed to share—something that had to do with Ms. Macy, Central Prison, perhaps her ex-husband or maybe Jefferson. Angelica wasn't sure, but there was one thing she was sure of—Walter struck a nerve with her. She would have to extract as much information as she could before the bus arrived in Fayetteville because entertaining the likes of Walter Whatever-his-last-name was strictly out of the question whether she had a place to stay or not.

Angelica sat back and crossed her legs as Walter fidgeted and searched for what he was going to say next.

"Look, ahh…I never caught your name."

"Don't have one. My number is 656933."

"Cute. Well, I think I'll go back up front and sit."

"No need to go. I'm interested in talking about Ms. Macy."

A frown crossed Walter's face. Angelica watched as Walter sized her up, his eyes lingering too long on her breasts that filled out the pink cotton stretch blouse she wore. He didn't look half bad. A good washing and scrubbing would probably make him presentable.

"Look, I figured a good-looking woman like yourself had to be one of Sgt. Macy's girls. See, Sgt. Macy is well known in these parts. It's no secret that she likes the little girls and the grown ones, too. No big deal. That's prison life."

"Walter, what are you trying to tell me? I was never good at riddle games."

"Ain't trying to tell you nothin', sugar. Just makin' conversation to pass the time." Walter stood up and bowed. "Excuse me if I interrupted your…sleep. I'll let you get back to it."

Angelica sat staring at Walter as he walked to the front of the bus. The last twenty minutes were bizarre, and no further information would be forthcoming. She wracked her brain for the meaning, but nothing came and she fell asleep.

"FAYETTEVILLE," shouted the bus driver an hour later.

Angelica wiped her mouth and collected herself. She stood up and looked toward the front of the bus, but the man in braids had disappeared into the brightness of the day. She got off the bus and looked around at the few patrons who waited for buses to take them as far away as New York. Angelica hugged her few belongings and sat on a bench, wondering how far the money she had in her pocket would take her and who the man in braids was.

3

Angelica collected her thoughts and decided to call a cab to take her to one of the motels that dotted Eastern Boulevard. She was disappointed that her brothers weren't around for her release. She realized the importance of their jobs—her brother Edward, the attorney, and brother Michael, the doctor, but thought they should have been there for her, although she suspected they were putting distance between her and their prominent images.

Several cars passed by and the occupants tooted their horns. Angelica frowned and turned her back, hoping the cab would get there soon. The blast of the horn made her curse, but she was happy when she looked up and saw the cab sign on top of the car.

The ride took less than fifteen minutes as the cab hurried down Eastern Boulevard. Angelica paid her fare and entered the motel.

Angelica tossed her belongings on a chair and fell down on the double bed. She looked up at the ceiling as her mind went into overdrive. This place was a far cry from her fabulous home outside of Fayetteville, and this certainly wasn't the welcome she had hoped to receive.

Images of Margo bombarded her head—the adoring friend, the angry friend, and the forgiving friend. Without notice, an image of Ms. Macy replaced Margo. Ms. Macy was watching her with eagle eyes, like Angelica was a prize Ms. Macy was trying to win. Angelica felt Ms. Macy's breath on her, whispering in her ear about what she'd like to do to her. Angelica shook the vision from her mind, but before Ms. Macy disappeared the man in braids appeared, looking between her and Ms. Macy. And then Ms. Macy was gone, and the man in braids stood over her with a sawed-off shotgun.

Angelica sat up quickly. She held her chest as she tried to catch her breath. Sweat poured from her face as she tried to shake the image that was so real to her. The man in braids scared her, and suddenly the thought of being in the room by herself made her feel unsafe.

The phone nearly fell as Angelica reached out to grab it. Her hand shook violently, and she clasped the other one over it to calm the shakes. She dialed her brother's law office and was about to hang up on the fourth ring when she heard a voice say, "Thompson, Smart and Fisher."

"Yes, is Edward Thompson in? This is his sister, Angelica Barnes."

"Ohh, ahh, yes, Ms. Barnes. Just a minute."

Angelica hated waiting, but she had no choice. Before long, she heard a familiar voice at the other end.

"Hey, Sis. You out?"

"Thank you for nothing, Edward."

"Don't be that way, Sis."

"You act as if I murdered someone, chopped their body to pieces, and stuffed it in a refrigerator in someone's basement."

"I know it's not as grim as that but, Angelica, you've done some awful things. I get tired of carrying you. You are this great big burden on my shoulder that I need to lighten."

"Where's my money? I won't need you, Edward, once you give me my money. Consider your burden gone...*forever!!*"

"Look, the money is locked up in trusts."

"Then write me a check…a cashier's check. You knew I would be getting out today and would need a place to stay and a little something to get on my feet. But I guess you and Michael call yourselves fixing my behind. I got news for you; Little Sister ain't playing no games. Give me what is due me, and you two don't have to worry about me ruining your images that nobody cares about."

"Come on, Angelica. I didn't mean to sound so harsh. I love you, Sis, and I want what's best for you."

"What does that mean, Edward?"

"Look, why don't you come to D.C. for a while—find yourself?"

"A minute ago, you said I was some kind of burden."

"That was tactless of me. You still mad because I lost your case?"

"Edward, I did the crime and I served the time. It is water under the bridge now. I'm ready to start fresh—a new beginning. The sins of the past are behind me. I try so hard to be this person everyone would love, but somehow I screw things up. Why couldn't I have been like you and Michael?"

"Don't be hard on yourself. Everything's going to work out fine. I'll drive down there day after tomorrow, and we'll get you situated. How's that sound?"

"Much better than before. I heard you sold my house."

"It was for the best, Sis. Your money is collecting interest. Your furniture and clothes are in storage. Used some of the money for your court costs."

"And attorney fees, I'm sure."

"Pro bono, Little Sis."

"Yeah, right." Angelica and Edward laughed. "Thanks, Edward. I love you, too. I was hurt that you and Michael weren't here, but

I feel better now. I'll be looking for you on Saturday. And tell Michael he can call me."

"I will. Take care, Sis."

"You too."

Angelica placed the phone in the cradle and fell back onto the bed. Things were going to get better. She needed a job and a place to stay. The money that Edward had put away for her from the sale of her house would probably keep her for a year or more, but she wanted to do more with her life, and she wanted respectability. She closed her eyes and fell asleep.

4

Bzzzzzzzzzzzzzzzz. Angelica peeked from under the comforter at the alarm clock. She stretched her arms and saw the sun beaming through the window. She smiled and sniffed at the freshness of her brand-new condo. Edward had come to town as promised and helped Angelica settle into her own place.

Edward was accommodating. He made sure Angelica's utilities were turned on, and she had food in the fridge, and later helped place the furniture where she wanted it. Edward did not leave town until he found a suitable car for Angelica to drive—nice, but nothing that would draw attention.

Today was Sunday. Angelica wasn't sure what she would do. She promised herself that she was going to turn over a new leaf, and she couldn't think of a better way to start than to go to God's house. There were so many churches in Fayetteville, but it struck her as what she should do. It was eight o'clock—plenty of time to make it to an eleven o'clock service.

There had only been one color in the one suit that Angelica had worn the past five years—blue. Now she surveyed her closet with excitement. She probably had enough suits to go around for all the women in her prison quad two or three times. Angelica tugged at each suit, lifting each hanger to get a good look until she settled on the one she would wear to church. She decided on the white suit. It was first Sunday and, more than likely, all the women would be dressed in white. Looking through the two hundred pairs of shoes that were held captive in their boxes, Angelica decided on a three-inch white Italian leather pump to accompany the rest of her ensemble.

Next, Angelica walked into the master bathroom. The room was painted a deep rich, mango orange that was soothing to the soul. It lacked in decorations, which she would attend to next week. Angelica was thankful that she wasn't on the street or in some motel passing the time.

Angelica let her robe slide down the length of her arms, stealing glances of herself in a large mirror. She smiled at her image, patted her buttocks, and cupped her breasts as if she was on display. Satisfied, Angelica eased into her bathwater that filled the tub to the brim with foaming bubbles, and then stopped to pick up a few and blow them into the air.

With one leg raised, Angelica took her sponge and squeezed water over her legs and arms, admiring the legs most men thought were beautiful. She flexed her toes and then brought her leg down, only to repeat the sequence with the other. Tina Turner had a nice pair of legs, but Angelica's were to die for—insured value easily one million dollars. Angelica relaxed in the water, letting the jets in the tub massage the lower part of her body.

It would be nice to have a strong pair of hands to massage all the places I can't get to, Angelica thought. Angelica and Hamilton had often taken baths together—him scrubbing her back while they relaxed and talked about what made their world revolve. The feel of a man's hands would take away some of the tension and maybe chase her blues away. It had been too long since strong arms held her close, although Ms. Macy tried, but Angelica would have gone to death row before she allowed Ms. Macy to touch her the way she had touched the other women in Dorm L. Angelica was lonely, and she needed her best friend.

Bath over, Angelica hurriedly dressed, checking herself once— no, twice—to make sure her hair was in place and that her make-up complemented her almond-shaped, hazel eyes and blended well into her caramel-colored skin. Angelica used warm, cool colors that made her look as if she was chiseled out of the earth. She looked radiant, and her medium-sized lips gave the mirror a parting smile.

It was a gorgeous day. Angelica slipped on her sunglasses and raced to her car, an apple-green Nissan Altima, and hopped in, excited about the prospect of seeing her friend Margo. *What if Margo rejected her? Surely not in the House of the Lord.* Bouts of doubt began to cloud Angelica's mind, but she was determined to see her. No one could soothe a broken heart like Margo.

She and Margo had shared many wonderful moments together. Quiet as it was kept, there were moments that Angelica kept hidden from her best friend, a time in history when Angelica's self-loathing heart had cajoled her into seducing her best friend's husband. And there were other moments that she was not proud of— moments that led her to where she was today. Angelica drove on.

A medium-size white church hugged the corner. Angelica recognized it right away. She had accompanied Margo to this place of worship many times. The choir could sing! The music would be jamming and every now and then it would make Angelica stomp her feet, sway her shoulders from side to side, and get in with the groove. The atmosphere was one of love, and they had a preaching, teaching pastor who exuded it.

Angelica found a place to park and turned off the ignition. She sat a moment hidden behind her shades, but the heat in the car caused her to get out before she was ready. Friendly faces smiled, and Angelica smiled too, her eyes darting back and forth searching for a glimpse of Margo.

The sanctuary filled fast. The elder mothers of the church sat off to one side, and the deacons sat on the other. All were dressed in white, and Angelica smiled. She took a seat near the back—not quite on the last row, but far from the front.

She scanned the sanctuary again. There was no sign of Margo or her children. Angelica sat on the edge of her seat the moment she saw him. Malik, "Mr. Hot Buttered Soul" they had called him. He was still handsome in a taupe-colored suit with a burnt-orange dress shirt and designer tie. Margo came in behind him. *Strange*, Angelica thought. *Where was Malik's fiancée, Antoinette?*

Tambourines were clicking and people were clapping their hands as the praise singers led the first part of the service. But Angelica couldn't keep her eyes off of Margo and Malik. Margo looked well in her white-knit suit with ostrich feathers around the collar. Too much for Angelica on a Sunday morning, but any other day of the week, watch out.

The music was uplifting, but Angelica wasn't feeling the glory of the Lord. In fact, the good feeling she came with had all but evaporated. Angelica had been there all of thirty minutes, and while she had spotted Margo, no one even knew she was in the sanctuary.

"If you are visiting with us for the first time, will you please stand," the announcer said.

Angelica looked around her to see if anyone was going to get up. Before she knew what she was doing, Angelica was on her feet.

"I'm happy to be here today, even though I'm no stranger to

your church. My name is Angelica Barnes, and I feel blessed to be in your midst," Angelica lied. "Pray for me."

Angelica sat down. When she felt brave enough, she looked up into the shocked faces of Malik and Margo. Margo turned away when she realized Angelica was looking her way. Yes, Angelica had surprised Margo good. Margo probably felt guilty for not coming to see her.

The friend Angelica came to see did not come to church. Angelica felt robbed. She needed Margo, but Margo didn't wave or acknowledge her presence. Margo's utterance of forgiveness that last time she saw her meant nothing, and the pain stabbed Angelica in the heart. The pastor was in the middle of the sermon that Angelica didn't hear, and eventually she got up and walked out. Neither her soul nor her longing would be fed today.

Angelica hurried to her car and began to back out.

"Oh," Angelica said, stepping on the brake. She rolled down the window to see who had walked into her path.

"Hello, Angelica."

Angelica stared in disbelief. "Malik...I could have hit you."

"You weren't going that fast."

Angelica couldn't believe this handsome, muscle-bound man stood next to her car calling out her name. She tried to pick her lip off the floor, but those dreamy eyes were to die for.

"I'm glad I didn't hit you," was all Angelica could say.

"When did you get back in town?" Malik asked, walking up to the car window.

"Earlier in the week. My brother came down from D.C. to help me get on my feet."

"So why Third Baptist?"

"I'm desperate to change my life, Malik. I've had a lot of time to think about what I'm going to do with the rest of it. I want a new start, and I couldn't think of a better place to be than right here.

"To be honest, Malik, I missed Margo. I missed my friend dearly. I know I've caused a lot of heartache and grief, but Margo is the one good thing that has happened in my life. I wanted to be where her spirit was because Margo always had a calming way about her that made me feel safe."

"It's good to see you, Angelica," Margo said. No one saw her come up.

Angelica turned off the car and got out. She tried to speak, but she was having difficulty letting the words come out. Finally, she found her voice.

"It's good to see you, too, Margo. You're one of the reasons I came here this morning, and the other is that I need Jesus."

Margo smiled. "Come here."

Angelica fell into Margo's outstretched arms and hugged her. She squeezed Margo and held on tight until Margo pushed back gently.

"I was surprised, no, shocked to see you standing in the sanctuary this morning. It was like déjà vu. Do you remember when we first met at my real estate office? It was that kind of moment."

"Yes, it was a moment I'll never forget. I met my best friend there."

There was a moment of silence.

"I won't hold you up."

"Where are you staying?" Margo asked.

"I have a place not too far from here. My brothers sold my house, and I'm using the proceeds to help me get started again. I've got to figure out what I'm going to do. Nobody's interested in hiring a felon."

"I'm sure there's something out there for you," Malik said, offering nothing more.

Malik was so fine and every woman's dream, but Angelica felt his disdain for her. She had no idea why he felt as he did, but it no longer mattered. Anyway, the last she heard, Toni was his woman.

"Well, I hope it won't take long for me to find it. How's Toni?"

A frown replaced concern. Malik dropped his head and then looked up at Margo for reassurance. He blew air from his mouth and prepared to speak.

"Did I say something wrong?" Angelica asked before Malik could speak.

"You wouldn't have known. Toni and our unborn baby were killed in a car accident almost a year ago."

Angelica drew her hands to her mouth. "Oh my God. I'm so sorry, Malik. I'm so sorry. I didn't see her, and…"

"It's okay, Angelica. When you mentioned Toni's name, it was like reliving that tragic day all over again. Toni and I got married four years ago, and we were living our lives to the fullest. We were going to have a family," Malik reflected, "but our dreams…my dreams ended tragically. If it wasn't for Margo, I don't know what I would have done; she's why I joined the church. You said something earlier, Angelica, about Margo having that calming spirit. She was the person I went to in my hour of need."

"Margo, what would we do without you?" Angelica asked.

Margo smiled. "It's nothing but God, because if it wasn't, I can't begin to tell you where I would be and what I'd be doing."

Angelica didn't want to know. This was her cue to leave, and somehow Angelica knew that although she had settled down into her new condo, eventually she would have to lose this town.

"Maybe we can get together sometime," Angelica said.

"I'd like that," Margo said. "How about this week?"

Angelica wasn't sure, but she said yes anyway.

5

F resh plants made the condo come alive. It had taken three days to make the place feel like Angelica, and now she sat back and smiled at what her magic had done. Her brothers were coming down for the weekend, and she wanted everything to be in order before they arrived.

Angelica brushed the back of her head and rubbed her neck to release the tension she was feeling. She looked at the phone several times before gathering enough courage to pick it up. She couldn't bring herself to dial and hung up the phone.

Walking away, she suddenly turned back and dialed the numbers quickly before the voice in her head instructed her to hang up. On the first ring there was an answer, and Angelica was petrified.

"Hello."

"Margo, this is Angelica. Just calling to see how you're doing and perhaps interest you in lunch."

There was some hesitation in Margo's voice. "Sure. I'm on my way to show a house, but why don't I pick you up? We can eat after I've finished showing the house, and we can catch up on the past five years."

For Angelica, there was nothing much to tell. She was surrounded by prison bars, unable to touch, smell, or look into the faces of those who meant something to her.

"Okay. That will be fine."

"Give me some directions, and I'll be there in a few."

Angelica gave Margo directions and hung up the phone. She went from room to room, picking up pillows and straightening up things so that everything would be in place when Margo arrived. Nerves started to replace the calm she felt when the day had started, but it was only Margo, the one person she could talk to about anything.

"Maybe I should call and cancel," Angelica said aloud. "No, that's the coward's way out."

With her hands on her hips, Angelica stopped short. Images of Malik crowded her head. *Were he and Margo having a thing in Jefferson's absence? She could love a man like Malik—a strong and intelligent man.* Her head was confused. One minute she was thinking about Jefferson, the next Malik. But Malik was available and unattached, or so it seemed. Somehow, Angelica would have to find a way to ask Margo about it.

Angelica's head jerked at the sound of the doorbell. She couldn't believe Margo was already here. The mirror on the wall said she was a sharp-looking diva, and Angelica ran to the door before Margo rang the bell again.

"Hey," Margo half whispered. She wasn't sure if a hug was in order.

"Hey, yourself," Angelica replied. "Come on in. It's not much, but it's home. I would have called you to help me find a place if I wasn't in such a hurry."

"Don't worry about it. Commission isn't everything."

Angelica wasn't sure if that was a slight or an attempt to make light of things in their awkward moment.

Margo glanced around the condo. She nodded her head in approval and stopped to pet the plants. "Nice place. Have you found a job yet?"

"No, I'm looking," Angelica lied. She was going to enjoy getting up late and watching the news stories, the soap operas, and *Oprah*. When the time came for her to look for work, she would.

"Malik has an opening for an office assistant at his computer store." Angelica perked up then thought, *Funny, Malik hadn't mentioned it yesterday*. "He is so talented," Margo continued. "He builds computers for his customers, and he makes good money."

"Is Malik dating, again?" Margo frowned at her. "With Toni's tragic death, I thought he might be…"

"Lonely?"

"Did I say something wrong? I'm not interested in Malik, if that's what you think. I'm so out of the loop, and…"

"I'm sorry. I'm a little overprotective when it comes to Malik. He's like a brother to me and I tend to react irrationally sometimes when it comes to his well-being."

Tell me anything, Angelica thought to herself. *Margo knows she wants to hit that; everyone else does, including me. No man in five years or at least she's pretending like she's had no one. Like a brother—humph.*

"I'll give Malik a call to see if the job is still available."

"I think we should go. I'm supposed to meet this couple in twenty minutes to show the house. If you want, I can take you by Malik's while we're out."

It wasn't what Angelica had in mind, but it might be the right introduction for the start of her new life.

"Sounds like a plan."

It was amazing to watch Margo create a thing of beauty, taking her clients on an Alice-in-Wonderland adventure as she shared all the wonderful intricacies and secrets of the homes she showed. It was almost as if she had a magic wand in her hand and, with a tilt of her wrist, she would have the client clinging to her every word, glancing about the room as Margo waved the wand because the client didn't want to miss any attribute that Margo thought most worthy of description. Angelica would have bought every house Margo showed if she had the money to do it.

Margo had a bite, and it was about to be her lucky day. A smile crossed Angelica's face as she watched the husband and wife go back and forth until they finally settled on the house they wanted. Life was all about decisions—especially the right ones.

Margo cruised down Bragg Boulevard. Bottoms Up, The Dollhouse—Angelica cringed. Memories of a time she would rather forget flooded her mind. Her best friend Margo had no idea she used to pole dance for a living. That is where her ex-husband Hamilton found her, giving it up to a pole because it was the easiest money she ever made.

They fell into their seats at the restaurant. After placing their orders, there was an awkward silence. Angelica tapped the table lightly.

"Look, Angelica," Margo said. "Let's try and relax."

"I'm all for that. I want you to know, Margo, that…"

"There's no need to rehash bitter moments."

Angelica placed her hand over Margo's. "Margo, Jefferson and I did not have a relationship. I had gone to warn him about the hit on his life. I'm guilty of turning my back on Hamilton and Jefferson with the mob boss."

"Why, Angelica?"

"I know I was selfish. Hamilton had degraded me to nothing. Every detail of our bitter divorce was in the newspapers, and when Santiago approached me offering a life of grandeur and enough jewelry to keep a sister happy for life, I fell for it. I can't say that I was proud of what I'd done, but I waited too late to redeem myself."

"That's quite a story, Angelica. I want to believe you, but it's past tense."

"But, Margo, if we are to get past this, I need you to know the whole story—the truth."

"I've forgiven you."

"Yes," Angelica sighed. "I don't take that lightly. But Margo, you and I...you and I were more. We were friends. You were the first real friend that I had." Margo smiled. "It's sad. I know that it took thirty-eight years of my life to finally meet someone I could totally confide in and feel that they would lay down their life for me."

"I would have, you know. What about you, Angelica? Would you have laid down your life for me or taken mine from me?"

Angelica released her hand from Margo's. The truth hurt. While Margo had forgiven her, the wound was still there.

"All I can say, Margo, is that I'm sorry."

"Have you told me everything? I do want to believe that, but let's have lunch since it has arrived, and we'll discuss this later."

The waitress placed their meal on the table. Angelica fingered her food and stifled a tear. She felt like a stranger with her best friend.

"How's Jefferson?"

Margo laid her fork on her plate and looked into Angelica's eyes. "Jefferson is doing fine. We are working through our issues."

"You know he was on his way back to you when I told him about the hit," Angelica added quickly. Margo stopped chewing her food and stared at Angelica. "He told me he had made a mistake with Linda, and that you were the best thing in his life. He loved you without a doubt, and he had to make you understand."

Margo sighed. "It would have been nice if he had told me himself."

"He thought that he might not get the chance to tell you."

"I'm glad to hear this." Margo began to choke up. "Angelica, I have loved Jefferson from the first day I met him. We were a team; we were one. There isn't anything that I wouldn't do for him or he for me. I don't know what went wrong, but I still love him and always will.

"I bore this man four beautiful children whom we have nourished and given the best years of our life together so they would be good people. It was the family I always dreamed I would have. Things happen in life, but I wasn't ready for Jefferson's indiscretions and illegal activities. Linda was one thing but you, my best friend, are another. I couldn't digest it, but I hope you've been upfront with me today. You've paid your dues, and now I'm looking forward to the day Jefferson comes home."

"I pray that you and Jefferson will heal from all that has happened to you." Angelica looked up and smiled at Margo. "Thank you for giving a girl a second chance."

"We still have a long way to go on our friendship, but welcome back, friend. Now let's eat."

Angelica smiled again and squeezed Margo's hand. She had her friend back.

∞

Malik was busy explaining the ins and outs of the computer system his customer was picking up. When he looked up, his eyes shifted between Margo and Angelica. Surprise registered in his eyes, and he lifted a finger and mouthed one minute. Malik helped the customer take the computer to his car and returned.

"So, what brings you two to SuperComp Technical Solutions?" Malik asked, directing his question at Margo.

"Angelica is in need of a job," Margo began, "and I think you told me you needed office help."

It was soon clear to Angelica that, while Malik might have an opening, she wasn't going to be the recipient of it—Malik's body language said as much.

"I do, and I've already interviewed a few ladies for the job."

"What if I donated my time?" Angelica spoke up. "It'll keep overhead down."

"It's not that, Angelica."

"It's because I'm a felon. Is that it, Malik?"

"Okay," Margo interrupted. "Bad idea. We'll go."

"When can you start?" Malik asked.

Margo smiled.

"Tomorrow," Angelica said, not wasting another precious moment.

"The hours are nine to six, and don't be late. If it works out, maybe we can think about permanent."

"It's a deal."

"Margo, what you fixing for dinner tonight?"

Angelica looked between the two of them. She knew there had to be something going on.

"Malik, there isn't going to be any cooking at my house tonight. Angelica and I are going shopping and we're not sure what else the night holds."

"Nine o'clock," Malik said to Angelica.

"Gotcha, brother. I will be here on time."

There was something about Malik that Angelica couldn't put her finger on. He always deflected her advances, even when he was a serious, single bachelor. He was Jefferson Myles' best friend, but that could not have been it. Angelica was sure Malik didn't want her around, but she planned to be all up in his face.

6

ngelica was up early. She was like a schoolgirl in love. The thought of being with Malik for eight or nine hours excited her. Maybe Fayetteville had something to offer after all.

She picked out a lime-green, lightweight suit. The skirt hit an inch above the knees, and the jacket had a fly-away collar that buttoned just below her cleavage. She found a pair of two-and-a-half-inch heels so she could look up into Malik's eyes. It was going to be a good day. She could feel it.

Malik smiled when he saw Angelica standing at the front door, waiting to be let in. She smiled back and moved away from the door so he could let her inside. His cologne was intoxicating, and she fought the urge to run her hands through the curls in his hair.

"I am *so* ready to get started," Angelica said, trying to cut through the slight strain or whatever it was that settled over the office.

"Make yourself comfortable. I'll show you where you'll be working after I put on a pot of coffee."

"Let me make it, Malik. That's one thing I'm good at."

"Okay, help yourself."

Angelica felt Malik watching her. She made sure her best side was in view at all times. Although Malik was turning on computers and setting up for the day's business, his eyes were trained on Angelica.

The morning passed quickly since business was a little slow. All receipts were filed and inventory entered into the system. Angelica waited for Malik to give her further instructions.

"Lunch time," Angelica said heartily.

"I brought my lunch. I rarely get a chance to get away from the shop, except to deliver computers and help with setups. We can share a sandwich, if you like."

"No, that's all right. I'll go out and get something."

Malik walked to where Angelica was sitting, took a chair and sat down. He ignored the smile on Angelica's face or the legs that extended beyond the short skirt she chose to wear.

"I'm not sure what your agenda is, Angelica, but I hope it doesn't include hurting Margo."

"Why would you say that? Of course not," Angelica said with a frown.

"I want to believe you. Margo has been through enough without having to look over her shoulder every moment to make sure that she hasn't made a mistake by letting you back into her life."

"Are you and Margo seeing each other?" Malik's eyes widened. "You were always friends, more Jefferson's than Margo's," Angelica continued, "but I'm wondering if all the preoccupation with Margo is because you are more than a big brother."

Malik got up out of his seat. "I don't know what you're talking about, Angelica. Margo loves Jefferson, and that's where her heart is."

"What about yours? I see how you look at her."

"You've got it all wrong. There's nothing between Margo and me except friendship. She's my best friend's wife and I happen to care about her and want to make sure she's all right."

"Whatever. You can tell me what you want, but I know what I see."

"Draw your own conclusions. Fact is fact."

"Look, I appreciate you letting me help you out, Malik. While I'd rather get paid, this will do for the moment. I'm going to be real with you. I want to get on with life, and hurting Margo is the last thing I want to do. I missed her very much. If I was half the woman…" Angelica stopped, lowered her head and then raised it. "If I was half the woman Margo has been, my life wouldn't have turned out this way."

"I appreciate hearing that, Angelica. You are beautiful."

Surprise registered on Angelica's face. "Thank you. Where did that come from?"

"Just stating what is."

"I'm a little confused. All the times I've tried to get you to notice me, you've never given me a moment's glance."

"How do you know?"

"I'm stating what is."

"Let's say I thought about taking you on a road test."

"A road test? You say that as if I was a piece of meat that you take out of the freezer if you get a little hungry."

"I didn't mean it like that, Angelica. I apologize if it sounded harsh."

Angelica got up from her seat and stood directly in front of Malik. "What is it that you don't like about me? I know you think that Jefferson and I were together when he had the accident. We weren't together the way you think; I had gone to warn him about the hit on his life."

"So you've never been with Jefferson?"

"No," Angelica said too quickly.

"Well, Ms. Angelica Barnes the Beautiful, my frat and best friend Jefferson must be a liar."

"What are you talking about, Malik?"

"Why don't you tell me? You're turning over a new leaf. The truth might set your soul free."

"Okay, Malik, this is over. I'm going to get some lunch, finish out my day, and decide whether I'll be back tomorrow."

Malik gently grabbed Angelica by both wrists. "Look into my eyes and tell me you and Jefferson haven't been together."

"Let go of me. Now. I don't know what you're talking about. Jefferson and I have not been together."

Malik released her arms. "You haven't learned your lesson yet, and you'll never be the woman Margo is."

"Funny, Jefferson said the same words to me." Tears formed in Angelica's eyes.

"See, I know all about how you seduced Jefferson while you were married to Hamilton. I know all the sordid details. Jefferson didn't leave a seedy detail to chance. That's what frats do. They share everything—their joys, their toys, and their conquests. Yes, it even got me to thinking about hitting on you, but I'm not the dog Jefferson is. He's my boy, but I didn't agree with half the things he did, especially where it concerned Margo. Margo has been his whole life, and I hate that I hold the kind of secrets that would hurt her to the core."

"I believe my day here is done."

"I will never tell Margo, you know. She never needs to know that her best friend is a pole-dancing ho who laid with her husband."

"I hate you, Malik." Angelica pointed her finger at herself. "You will never get to road test this because you're not good enough. It takes a real man to handle Angelica Barnes. Ask Jefferson."

Angelica turned on her heels and started out the door. She turned around and looked back at Malik with tears in her eyes.

"Thank you for nothing. I expected you to be more of a man than Jefferson. I guess I was wrong."

Malik watched her walk out, stop, and then run back into the shop.

"What is it?" Malik asked with concern written on his face.

Angelica's chest heaved in and out. "Oh my God!"

"What is it, Angelica? What happened out there?"

"I saw the guy who was on the bus with me when I left prison."

"It's probably a coincidence. Anyway, why would he be after you?"

"No, Malik. It was the way he stared at me. He was in jail for armed robbery and attempted murder. He told me things about Hamilton—some terrible crap that these guys are doing to him in prison, things only someone on the inside would know. But the frightening thing is he doesn't even know me. And then he mentioned Ms. Macy."

"Who's Ms. Macy?"

"One of the corrections officers at the women's prison. I have a weird feeling about that man. I can't put my finger on it, but I don't feel good about it. If you don't mind, I'd like to sit here a minute, and if you're still offering half of your sandwich, I'll accept."

"Sure. You can have the whole sandwich; I'm not that hungry."

"Malik, whatever you think of me, I'm not the same person you once knew. Yes, I am guilty of the things you accuse me of, but that was then and this is now."

"What things?" said the familiar voice. "You need to get a bell in this place, Malik, so nobody walks in on you."

"Margo, what are you doing here?" Malik blurted.

7

"Why are you both looking at me like that? Angelica? Malik? What are you guilty of, Angelica?"

"Margo, Malik and I were talking about how I let you down as a friend."

"We've talked about it, but I thought we've agreed to move ahead with our lives."

"I plan to do just that, and the only way to do that is to get a real job that pays."

"Malik, can't you pay Angelica? I was wondering why she would opt to do it for free."

"I'm not sure that Angelica wants to be hemmed up around computers all day," Malik said.

"Right. I don't think anyone's going to let me be a buyer for their store, but maybe doing a little retail, which is my love, would better suit me," Angelica said.

"You can cut the charade. I don't know what happened between you being excited about working for Malik and this very minute, Angelica, but whatever it is, it's on you. I was going to ask you both out to lunch—I just sold a four-hundred-thousand-dollar house—but since you're being so secretive, I'll take myself to lunch."

"But…" Angelica tried to say. Margo held her hand up, palm side to Angelica.

"No, no. You and Malik continue your little conversation. You know that everything hidden eventually comes to the light."

Silence. Margo swung around and looked from Angelica to Malik. "It will come to the light." Margo turned and left, swinging her purse over her shoulder.

Malik moved to within an inch of Angelica. "You have opened old wounds. Margo is not going to rest until she finds out what we were talking about."

"If I'm not going to tell her and you're not going to tell her, how is she going to find out?"

Malik pondered the question for the moment. "You have to leave Fayetteville. You are a constant reminder of the past and, as long as you remain, Margo is going to want to know what we don't want her to know."

"So, Mister I've Already Got This Figured Out, you're going to tell me that I have to pack up my belongings and get out of Dodge so you and your girlfriend can live a peaceful life without having to dance around me and worry about me being up in your face? You know you want this, Malik."

Angelica removed the top button, then the second button on her jacket. "Mighty tempting, don't you think?" She teased Malik while he stood staring at her breasts, which were encased in a lime-green plunging, push-up bra.

"You're not going to trap me in your web, Angelica. I kill spiders, especially black widow spiders with the venomous spot on their heart. You can take your spindly legs and try to wrap them around me, but you don't want to mess with me."

Angelica looked up into Malik's eyes. Her movements were sensual and slow as she lifted her mouth to his and planted a gentle kiss on his lips. She removed her lips and saw that Malik's eyes were closed, his lips poised for another round. She tasted his lips again while slowly pawing her way down the front of his plush knit shirt. Angelica waited for him to open his eyes while she stared, daring him to resist her.

Ashamed, Malik threw his hands out and moved back suddenly. Angelica continued to stare at him with eyes that were like magnets, drawing Malik closer the more he resisted.

"You're fired."

"Was never on the payroll. You want me to leave?"

"Yes," Malik said weakly. "Please put your clothes on and don't bother to come back."

"Jefferson also found me irresistible, you know. He fought the urge like you're doing, but it didn't take much encouragement to lure him in."

"I'll never be one of your victims, Angelica. You can count on that."

"Oh, on the contrary. You enjoyed the touch of my lips on yours. I was taking you to the brink, and you know you wanted to test the water, brother. But it's all right."

They turned when they heard the bell. Angelica's eyes grew large at the sight of the man in braids. He wore the same tattered jeans but had on a white, loose-fitting, crinkled shirt that buttoned down the front. His feet were curled up in a pair of brown sandals, and he wore a cap that partially covered his hair.

"Hello there, missy. I thought that was you when I passed by a minute ago. Look different all dressed up in a suit and some high heels."

"Can I help you, sir?" Malik asked.

"No. Just thought I recognized the pretty lady. She and I rode the bus to Fayetteville last week. We have some common interests."

"Is that right? Well, I think you make the lady nervous."

"You her man friend?"

"No. I'm looking for a job," Angelica spoke up. "Are you following me?"

"No, in fact, I was headed to a job interview myself. I guess I better be going. Miss, you should close your jacket before another customer comes in." The man saluted and walked out the store.

Angelica had all but forgotten that her jacket was unbuttoned. She pulled it together and fumbled with the buttons until she had them all fastened. With a slight tremble in her hand, she held onto Malik's arm for support and then let go. It could not have been coincidental that Walter, the man in braids, happened to be on the same street at about the same time. Malik may have hit the nail on the head. It was time to go—to leave Fayetteville—because the town gave her very little room to start a brand-new life.

8

She bought a one-way ticket to New York. The city made Angelica feel as if she belonged. Bright lights, tall skyscrapers, and the vast city with its millions of people seemed to welcome her with open arms. Lady Liberty waved her torch while the Empire State Building stood alone in the middle of Manhattan without the support of the Twin Towers.

The plane circled the city and eased onto the runway at New York's LaGuardia Airport. A surprise phone call from Hamilton's cousin, Donna, had made leaving Fayetteville an easy decision for Angelica.

Donna Barnes Reardon had established herself as one of New York's notable fashion photographers. Having graduated at one of the top schools of the arts, her portfolio was a collection of rich and flamboyant designs modeled by Donna's exotic friends from Brazil and Trinidad that she'd met years earlier while a student. There were trips to the island beaches of Jamaica and Bermuda where Donna took advantage of all she learned to advance a career that was in need of a jump-start. It didn't take long for Donna's work to be noticed and then for her to be hired by a well-known modeling agency.

Donna needed an inexpensive subject for a personal project she was working on and remembered how excited her cousin's wife, Angelica, had been about her work. Angelica loved fashion, which was evident by her love for the fashion retail industry. On a chance that Angelica might accept, Donna invited Angelica to come to the Big Apple and, much to Donna's surprise, Angelica was available and on her way.

This was going to be the new life Angelica craved. Far away from the place that swallowed her up and advertised her sins on a billboard 24/7, Angelica was grateful and flashed a full set of teeth, so beside herself was she at her newfound fortune.

Hailing a cab, Angelica instructed the driver to take her to Manhattan. She sat in the back with the window down and let the breeze flow through her hair. Tranquil blue water from the East River separated Queens from Manhattan and the drive across soothed Angelica's nerves.

Much to Angelica's disappointment, Donna was out on a shoot when the cab arrived at the high-rise condo. The phone call had been simple and abrupt with instructions for the doorman to let Angelica in. Angelica had expected red-carpet treatment on arrival with Donna talking a mile a minute about the new project, where she was going to take Angelica for dinner, who the who's-who in town were and what fabulous stars they would be cozying up to. With no welcome in sight, Angelica sighed, put her hair into a ponytail, and willed her body from the cab along with her three pieces of designer luggage and her Hobo handbag.

The doorman was an attractive, middle-aged Greek whose graying temples made him look distinguished. His cap sat atop a crop of thick, wavy curls that dropped below the hairline. His maroon and black doorman's jacket fitted him like an Armani garment, custom-made for a movie star's body.

Silence engulfed the elevator during the ride to the twenty-fifth floor. The doorman stole glances at the tall, statuesque beauty.

Four-inch stilettos adorned her feet, while a green three-quarter-sleeve, retro cotton and linen jacket sat on top of a sheer, green-and-black, cheetah-print, short-sleeve silk blouse. White wide-leg cotton and spandex pants completed her look. Their eyes connected, and Angelica forced a smile when the doorman winked.

The doorman let Angelica in as Donna had instructed. He placed her luggage in the foyer and stood back by the door. Angelica fumbled around in her large Hobo handbag, but when she finally pulled the money out, the doorman had already gone. She would have to get his name in case she needed someone to talk to.

Angelica's jaw dropped as she walked through the foyer and gazed around the room. It was a penthouse suite decorated for the rich and famous. Angelica walked through the huge living room/dining room with its mod furniture in colors of tangerine, chartreuse, blue, banana yellow, and coffee brown. The walls were painted custard yellow with off-white baseboards and trailer boards running the length of the rooms. The room was airy and light, but the highlight was the tremendous view of the city with a generous view of the Hudson River to the West and Central Park to the North.

Museum-quality art hung on the luscious walls. On further investigation, she found that huge blown-up photographs of Latin-looking women done in black and white, probably Donna's work, adorned the walls of another large room that was most likely Donna's studio. Angelica fingered the work as if she were appraising it for auction. She went from one portrait to the next, admiring what everyone in New York already knew—an award-winning photographer lived here.

Angelica walked around until she doubled back into the living room. For the first time since her arrival, she stepped into the stainless-steel jungle with the white and black tile running the length of the floor. Opening the refrigerator, Angelica had not expected to find it bare. A lonely, four-pack wine cooler that looked to be off limits sat in the back next to a block of cheese. Angelica took one of the coolers, went into the living room and sat in the chair closest to the window to take in the view.

"Angelica."

Angelica jumped at the sound of Donna's voice that was deep throat with too much "put-on." It had been a long time since she had seen Donna, but to a casual observer, Donna looked like a young woman in an old person's body. Too much make-up and her perfume was overpowering. Donna's cocoa skin was beginning to show cracks—a sign that she was letting the industry suck her under.

How long was Angelica asleep? She wiped her mouth and noticed that the wine cooler still sat on the coffee table where she had left it.

"Donna."

"Have you made yourself comfortable?"

Angelica wasn't sure if that was a slur about Donna finding her asleep on her best chair or if she really meant it.

"Exhausted. Since I left Fayetteville so abruptly, I had to get someone to take care of my condo, my car, and stuff like the mail. I was so excited about getting away and coming to New York, I threw a few things together and caught the first thing smoking."

"You'll come to love New York like I do."

"I think I already do," Angelica said as she casually got up from her seat and stood in front of the window to peer out of it for the umpteenth time.

"Well, I have an exciting project that I'm sure you'll enjoy. The pay's pretty good and, who knows, you may end up on the twenty-fifth like me."

"I'm intrigued."

"Have you eaten? If not, I know this great little jazz club in SoHo. We can have a bite to eat and talk about the project."

"Sounds great. I would like to know, Donna, why you called me. We haven't spoken in a long time. Frankly, since Hamilton and I are no longer together, I thought I'd be the last person you'd call."

"My cousin, Hamilton. He's probably getting what he deserves, sitting in that rotten prison. He's my blood, but I've seen too many lives ruined at his hands."

"I wish someone would have told me before I married him."

"I understand he met you in a strip joint."

Ouch, that stung like a cattle rancher's brand, Angelica thought. *Where is this woman coming from?*

"Yes, Hamilton met me in a strip club. Haven't you had some hard times? That's why I was there." Angelica moved away from the window and stood face to face with Donna.

"Didn't mean to offend you, Angelica. Just ironing out some facts. Let's get started on the good foot. Give me some love."

Angelica didn't feel like giving any love. She could feel her days being numbered at the penthouse, but she would go along with the program until something else came along. Right now, she was far away from Margo and Malik, and ready for a new adventure. She reached over and gave Donna a hug. "Thank you."

"As soon as I change, we'll be on our way," Donna said. "I think we'll take the subway."

Angelica smiled. "Can't wait."

9

The doorman opened the door as Donna and Angelica approached. He gave Angelica another once-over as she glided past him in a flirtatious way, she turning slightly to see if he had noticed. Angelica still wore the outfit she had arrived in while Donna had slipped into a pair of tight-fitting jeans and a cream-colored satin blouse with a high collar and plunging neckline.

"You trying to make a move on Ari?"

"Of course not, Donna. I was being playful my first day in New York."

"Well, I hope so. Girl, there are bigger fish to fry, if you get my meaning. This town is full of those who have money and those who don't, but money's easy to get if you know the right person. And you will get to know the right person in this business."

"So, have you fried your fish?"

Donna laughed. "You're funny, Angelica."

"I wasn't trying to be."

"Let's say I wouldn't be living in that fab Manhattan pad if I didn't know the right people. My work speaks for itself, though. My degree and my training have not gone to waste. I know how to play the game because I've watched some of the masters at work, and if you want something bad enough, you do what you have to in order to get what you want."

"I may have lived in Fayetteville, North Carolina, but I know what I like."

"Let's catch the subway. Sometimes I like to feel New York the way it touches everyday folk."

Angelica walked briskly, trying to keep in step with Donna. Donna was an intriguing person, and Angelica could not quite put a finger on her pulse. It would all unravel soon, and she hoped that in the days ahead she would be trading her small condo in Fayetteville for a high rise in Manhattan.

They entered the station, walked down the stairs and purchased metro cards. Angelica wasn't feeling the subway, but Donna seemed right at home.

At Donna's direction, they jumped on the train headed for SoHo. The train was crowded with business types headed to places unknown. The people seemed disinterested, deeply into themselves. There were no friendly hellos or the smiles that she was accustomed to in North Carolina.

The train lurched and pulled into a station to let people on and off. A young woman carrying packages and a briefcase got on and held onto the pole in front of Angelica. As the train began to pull out of the station, the woman held the pole tightly with her hands and wrapped her thighs around the middle. Her bags were trapped between her feet and the bottom of the pole. The strap of her purse was slung over her shoulder. The movement of the train made her body swing along the pole like she was dancing on stage, and as the woman sought to hold on, Angelica had a flashback of her life before Hamilton.

Angelica was a lot like the woman holding the pole. She held the pole like she owned it, making love to it with gestures that aroused the gentlemen who stared at her partially clad body. They begged her to take it all off. The woman at the pole had done this many times before because she moved with the train, squirming and leaning up against the pole when the moment called for it.

"You all right?" Donna asked Angelica. "You seem to be in a daze."

"Thinking about life," Angelica said.

"Well, get ready, because the next stop is ours. We'll have a light dinner, enjoy some jazz, and meet some people I've asked to join us."

"Oh," was all Angelica could say.

They got off at the next stop, Angelica following Donna like a lost puppy. Dusk had fallen quickly, but the feel of the nightlife was overtaking Angelica. And she liked how it felt.

"Why do they call it SoHo?" Angelica asked.

"Because it's south of Houston Street. It's not just that, though. This is the place where artists come alive—galleries full of artwork and boutiques that sell cutting-edge fashions. Here's the place."

The music floated outside. Laid-back business types sucked on draft beer, trying to relieve the stress of the week, and others sipped martinis to set the mood for the rest of the evening.

Angelica followed Donna to a table in a corner where three very attractive ladies sat. They could have easily been the women in the portraits that hung on the walls in Donna's studio. Their makeup was flawless and the weaves on their heads cost at least a thousand dollars a pop. Broad smiles were on their faces as the two approached.

"Hey, sweetie," Donna said to each woman in turn, while pecking each with a dainty kiss to the lips. "This is my cousin, Angelica. She's the one I was telling you about."

Angelica extended her hand and sat down. She would not be placing any kisses on anyone's lips or jaws.

"Hey, Angelica, I'm Jazz. This is Madeline to my right and Coco on my left. Glad to meet you."

"The pleasure is mine."

"Angelica flew in from North Carolina," Donna offered. "She'll loosen up after a while."

"We're fashion divas," Jazz said while the others laughed, including Donna. "Your cousin is a model's gift to the big time."

"That's what I hear," Angelica said. "It appears she is very successful."

"So why have you come to the Big Apple?" Jazz asked, her accent thick and deep. Her facial features seemed exotic. Angelica figured her to be West Indian.

"To get away from my past," Angelica said with a frown. These women were beginning to annoy her, and she hadn't been in the place five good minutes.

"So what is your past?" Coco asked, opening her mouth for the first time.

Angelica looked from Coco to Donna. She wasn't sure what Donna had shared with these ladies, but her past was none of their business.

"My past is just that—my past," Angelica responded. "I need a drink."

Donna waved the waitress over and ordered two martinis. Angelica let out a small sigh. She wasn't used to someone taking control over her every movement. She was a grown woman capable of ordering her own drink. In fact, Angelica was not very comfortable with the little group that was assembled. Maybe she was tired. Tomorrow would be a new day.

"They have wonderful sandwiches here, Angelica," Donna said. "I think I'll have a beef sandwich au jus."

"Order two," Angelica consented.

"Angelica, these ladies are part of the project I was telling you about," Donna began. "We are going to do a photo shoot for a new magazine. I'm really excited about it because I'm the exclusive photographer for this magazine, and the monetary reward is more than generous."

A smile trickled across Angelica's face. For the first time tonight, she had something to smile about. "That's great, Donna," Angelica said. "And you're willing to take a chance on a non-model."

"Well, my contract said that I had to have a set number of women in the shoot. I happened to be talking with my mother and aunt on three-way when they told me you had been released from prison. I remembered how you loved to dress in the finest and command attention at every family event I ever attended. Then it came to me that you might be the person I was looking for."

Angelica sat in silence. The waitress placed her drink in front of her followed by her food. Her privacy had been violated with Donna's announcement. The fact that Angelica had just gotten out of prison didn't seem to faze the ladies, though—Donna had probably given them her bio long before her plane landed in New York. It sucked, and Angelica wished she were back in Fayetteville in her own condo—a place she had left without even telling Margo she was leaving.

The cafe was crowded, and everyone seemed to be having a good time. It was hard to hear at times, but the light jazz put Angelica in a melancholy mood. She had tuned out Donna and her friends and turned to get a better view of the two brothers who sat a couple of tables over. They glanced over a couple of times, but Angelica failed to keep their attention.

Turning around, she saw Donna slide her hand over Madeline's arm. It might have been an innocent gesture, but it reminded Angelica of the way Ms. Macy would handle the new inmates when they came to quad L.

"So what kind of ad are you shooting?" Angelica asked Donna, making an attempt to belong.

"There will be several, which is why the pay will be lucrative. Angelica, you will not make as much as the other girls because they are on union scale, but you will make enough to be independent."

"When do we start?"

"On Monday. You have the whole weekend to rest up because we're just getting started. I hope you've got on your dancing shoes."

"I'm ready."

10

Ding, dong. Ding, dong.

"Hold on, Ivy, someone's at the door."

Ding, ding.

"Malik," Margo said upon opening the door. "What are you doing here?"

Margo blushed. "Checking on my favorite girl."

"I've got my daughter Ivy on the phone. We were about finished. Come in and make yourself comfortable."

"Okay," Malik whispered.

"Hey, Ivy, I'm back. It was Malik checking on me."

"I think he likes you, Mom."

"We've been friends a long time. We're like brother and sister."

"Okay, tell me anything. You better go on and get you some because Dad ain't gonna be any good when he finally gets out of prison."

"Ivy, don't talk like that. I'm your mother, for goodness sake. Anyway, I'm in this marriage for the long haul—for good or for worse. And it's your daddy we're talking about."

"Mom, you have every reason to be with someone else."

"Bye, I've got to go. I'm not going to put up with any foolish talk like that."

"Why are you whispering? Is Malik still there? Mom, you aren't foolin' nobody. Talk with you later."

"Bye, sweetie."

Margo hung up the phone, and her stomach started to flutter for no reason. She walked into the living room where Malik had made himself comfortable on the couch—a remote in one hand and the newspaper in another. Fire began to burn in Margo's stomach and then radiated downward. Surely this wasn't happening at Ivy's mere suggestion.

Blowing air from her mouth, Margo sat across from Malik and pretended to look at the program on television.

"How is Ivy?"

"She's doing fine. She worries about me all the time," Margo said softly. "I don't think she or J.R. will ever come back home to live—they love it in Atlanta."

"Well, at least Winston and Winter aren't far," Malik said as he surfed the channels.

"Yeah, they've really bonded since they moved to Raleigh two years ago and are making all of that good money in the Research Triangle Park. Their college education paid off. Keeps them out of my pockets."

Malik looked up from the television. "What's wrong, Margo? You seem distracted and awfully quiet for the chatterbox you are."

"Am I? I answered all your questions."

"Have you eaten anything? Maybe we can go and get a bite."

"Not tonight, Malik. I'm feeling a bit tired."

"What if I run and get us some Chinese? You haven't eaten; I can tell."

"Don't go out for me."

"Maybe you didn't hear, but I'm hungry, too."

"All right. Maybe some Chinese."

"I'll be right back."

Margo was glad to put some distance between herself and Malik.

Why did Ivy's suggestion make her feel like she had been cheating? Was this a suppressed desire? She had to be careful. She had made a vow to Jefferson and the Lord, and two wrongs didn't make a right—even if she was having feelings for the handsome man with the six-pack, wavy hair, and hands that made her feel safe. Margo shook her head to erase the thought from her mind and then fell to her knees.

Lord, I ask You to take the temptation, if that's what it is, away from me. I am Your child, and I have committed my life to You. You have been so good to me, Lord, and I won't let anything compromise the love I have for You and my getting into Your kingdom. If this means telling Malik that we can't hang out all the time, that's what I'll do.

Margo was puzzled about one thing. Malik had not mentioned Angelica and she had not been able to reach her the past couple of days. That would be the first question for Malik when he returned. Angelica seemed excited about working with Malik, but Margo knew that Angelica always had a silent crush on him.

There was a knock on the door. It was impossible for Malik to have gone to the Chinese take-out that fast, but when she opened the door, there he was, smiling and holding several white plastic bags full of good smelling food. Margo was suddenly hungry.

"Take a seat and I'll fix it for you," Malik offered. "You've had a long day, and you deserve a little pampering."

"You're not my husband, Malik," Margo said, throwing up her hand at him and then letting out a giggle. "Stop trying to give me orders." She giggled again. "Maybe I'm going to have to keep you at bay because you're getting a little bit too comfortable."

Malik laid the spoon down on the table and turned around and looked at Margo.

"What are you trying to say, Margo? I know you've been awfully quiet tonight, but if you don't want me here, say so."

"No, Malik, it's not like that at all. I guess I was thinking about Jefferson and what my life has become," Margo waved her hands, "and I guess I let my confusion get the best of me."

"What are you confused about?"

"Did I say confused? See, that's what I mean, Malik. My head doesn't seem to be screwed on straight, and I say words I don't mean."

"So try saying what you mean."

"I don't know what I mean."

"Perhaps what you're trying not to say is that you're feeling something for me like I'm feeling for you."

"Malik!!!"

"You are not a dumb blonde, Margo. You know exactly what I'm talking about. Sending Angelica to my place to try and knock me off my equilibrium. Nice try."

"Speaking of Angelica, where is she?"

"Don't try to change the subject, woman. Angelica isn't the subject of this conversation. Why don't we eat our food before it gets cold? It'll probably give us enough energy to continue the conversation you started."

Margo batted her eyes and sat back down. Malik may have won round one, but she and Jesus were going to win round two.

Malik fixed the plates and brought one to Margo. No words were exchanged as they ate their food. Soon, the only noise came from a Target commercial that was playing on TV.

"Enough of this," Malik exclaimed, putting his plate on the coffee table.

Margo's startled face turned in Malik's direction as she wondered what would come next. Her chest heaved in and out as she watched Malik get up and come toward her. Before Ivy's call, she and Malik were fine. It was as if Ivy had pulled the mask from her face and exposed her to the world. And her heart was admitting what her mind had blocked out—that she might be...could be a little infatuated with this man.

Malik sat next to Margo and put his arm around her. Margo moved to the far end of the couch. "What are you doing?" Margo asked.

"Surely you had to know that I have feelings for you. Why do you think I come around all the time?"

"Malik, you have always come around. I thought you were looking out for your best friend's wife."

"I was, but then I began to look out for myself. There were many days, Margo, when I'd get close to you and smell your hair, and I would literally have to run home and take a cold shower."

"The best thing you could have done."

"But I have fallen in love with you."

"I'm a married woman."

"Whose husband committed adulterous acts with your next-door neighbor and your 'so-called' best friend."

"And so, are you willing to commit adultery?"

"My wife is dead."

"But my husband is not. And for your information, Angelica told me she did not have a relationship with Jefferson."

"That's her story. Do you know that she tried to seduce me at my shop? Margo, she unbuttoned her jacket and exposed—"

"Too much information. She's always had a crush on you."

"What do you really know about her? Her jailhouse cot was barely a week cold before she was up to her old tricks again."

"Where is Angelica? I've called her number several times the last couple of days and didn't get her. Has she shown up for work?"

"I fired her."

"Fired her? She was volunteering her services."

"It didn't work out, and I haven't seen her since. You know what happened the last time she went missing."

"She wasn't missing. She was out of town."

"Yeah, lying in the lap of some criminal while helping to serve death warrants on Hamilton and Jefferson."

"I'm tired, Malik. I don't want to talk about Angelica, Jefferson, or Hamilton. I don't want to talk about us."

"If you want me to leave, I will. I've resisted the urge to be with you for a long time because I respect the sanctity of marriage. I understand what it means to not covet another man's wife. I understand what it means to not commit adultery, but I want you in the worst way.

"I can't explain what you do to me when I'm around you. You are a beautiful and smart woman, Margo. You are a successful realtor. You have a beautiful home. There are so many qualities about you that mirror my beliefs. Yes, I know it is wrong, but I don't want to be right."

"Did you ever love Toni? You seemed to be very happy."

"Yes, I loved Toni very much. She was special to me, and she made me complete. We were very happy together. And, since I'm telling the truth, there were days when you were going through stuff with Jefferson before the trial and right afterwards that's if you had let me in, I would have dropped everything for you."

Margo covered her face with her hands. She had been so consumed with everything that was going on with Jefferson that she had no inkling Malik felt this way about her.

"Maybe it's time for you to go home, Malik. I think we both need some space to sort things out."

"What is there to sort out, Margo? I'm laying it all on the line. I'm in love with you."

"Please don't say that. You'll ruin our friendship."

"But I do, Margo. If you want me to go, I'll leave, but I can't help the way I feel."

Margo's eyes were tight, but she offered a little smile.

"I love you too Malik, but as a brother. We can't have a relationship because I'm married to your best friend."

Tears formed in the corners of Malik's eyes. Before he knew it, he was catching them with the back of his hand. This surprised Margo. She went to him and hugged him tightly.

"I'll always be your friend, Malik, but I love Jefferson. It is until death we do part."

"Okay, Margo." Malik sniffed. "I have to respect you because you have always been that special kind of lady. That's what I have always liked…loved about you. I'm going to miss seeing you often."

"It might be advisable to change your church membership."

"Ouch. You're serious." Malik waited for Margo to say something, but she didn't. "Well, I guess I'll be going, but it will never stop the way I feel about you."

Margo stood at the door and watched Malik get into his car and drive off. Her heart was heavy because she did not want Malik to leave. If she was going to remain committed to her vows to God and Jefferson, Margo could not entertain Malik in her home or be with him on fun occasions. Although Margo had asked the Lord to keep her from harm and danger, her flesh was weak. And while just about any man would do for her because it had been five years since she felt a man's touch on certain parts of her body, Malik was the one she had fantasized about in her dreams.

The mobile phone was inches from where she stood, and Margo attempted to reach Angelica for the fifth time.

11

S leep eluded Angelica. She lay awake, wondering what her day would be like. Soft fingers combed through her hair as she envisioned changing into expensive garments by top designers in the fashion world. She hoped that one day her name would become a household word that would command millions of dollars for her services. Angelica saw herself stroll- ing the catwalks of New York, Paris, and Milan—the buyers not only checking out the latest fashions but also admiring her beauty. And later, there would be television ads promoting her new line of clothing.

Donna was up early, chatting on the phone. It was four-thirty a.m., and Angelica decided to get on up. She walked into the living room where she found an assortment of cameras strewn through- out it.

Donna had certainly carved her way into the industry. The week- end had been fascinating, to say the least. Hobnobbing with Donna's rich friends and rolling up on Diddy and his crew at a lower Manhattan nightclub was the crème de la crème for Angelica's first few days in the big city. Fayetteville was now a distant reminder of the past, although Angelica knew she needed to call Margo, who had left several messages, to let her know she was all right.

"Anxious to get started, I see."

Angelica jumped. In the shadows stood Donna, who had walked quietly into the room and disturbed Angelica's thoughts.

"Yes, so excited I can't sleep."

"Well, Angelica, this may make or break your career—that's if you desire one in modeling."

"Donna, if I haven't said it already, I'm grateful for this opportunity. I won't disappoint."

"Oh well then, be ready at six. We have an early morning shoot at eight. Hope to be done by noon for the first set. Dress casual."

"I'll be ready."

∞

Ari brought Donna's car to the front of the building, and she and Angelica jumped into it. The city was abuzz, and Angelica marveled at all the people who were already up and about so early in the morning. A bagel hung out of Donna's mouth as she maneuvered into traffic.

New York noise was so different from the sounds of Fayetteville. Angelica sat back as Donna cursed every other car and talked about the pathetic driving, even though she wasn't qualified to vent because she jerked forward and put on brakes as much as the next person. There was a moment when Angelica almost jumped from the car as they entered Times Square and saw the *Good Morning America* crew on the marquee. Before she went to jail, she always watched Diane and Robin in the morning with a cup of coffee. That's what she needed right now—a good ole cup of gourmet coffee.

It was another twenty minutes before Donna finally pulled in front of a warehouse near a dock.

"This is it. Let's move it."

There was nothing glamorous about the grayish-looking build-ing that stood all by itself. It was an elongated building with no windows, and grass grew wildly around it. A lone Porsche sat in the parking lot next to it, but other than that, Angelica could neither make heads or tails of where she was nor identify the building that held no sign.

Dragging her fleet of cameras, Donna approached the building with Angelica at her side. Almost immediately, three females exited the Porsche that sat in the parking lot, and Angelica recognized Madeline, Coco, and Jazz. They did not look as glamorous as they did on Friday night—no makeup and their hair was either straight or pulled back into a ponytail. They wore high-fashion leather jackets in colors of red for Jazz, black for Madeline, and butterscotch for Coco, and they each wore a pair of jeans that looked like they had been spray-painted on. Before the group entered the building, another car drove up.

Upon entering the building, Angelica felt surprised. She wasn't quite sure what she expected; however, there was a makeshift lobby off to one side and a large stage, decorated with some type of props she could not readily see. It must be the place where they would do their photo shoot.

A couple of guys passed by with curling irons and other gadgets in leather holsters that were strapped around their waists.

"As soon as the crew gets set up," Donna said, "you will go to wardrobe to choose your outfits and then go to make-up."

It was hard to keep the smile from Angelica's face. This was for real. She was getting ready to plunge into the world of high fashion without even an interview, much less a portfolio, and what was really puzzling to Angelica was that she was a lot older than the other girls but, like Tina Turner, her body was still in fabulous shape. She would remember from now on not to come made up because there would be someone to do that for her. Madeline, Coco and Jazz already knew that.

The door opened and three unfamiliar females walked into the room. They seemed rough around the edges and not very attractive. Being a model was all about the look. If you happened to have the total package, oh well.

The three newcomers found Donna and kissed her on the cheek and the mouth the way the others had done Friday night. Angelica believed in welcoming a friend, but all that kissing was getting on her nerves. As long as no one tried to do it to her, she would tolerate it, but she didn't have to like it. Artists were strange people to her.

A very tanned male with streaked blond hair escorted the ladies to a back room. Clothes racks littered the room, and there were shelves that housed several hundred pairs of shoes. Out of the corner of Angelica's eye something else caught her attention. Grown-up toys were also on display. She dismissed it when Donna came into the room.

"You all have one hour to get ready for the first photo shoot. The lighting must be just right."

"We'll be right there," Coco shouted, digging through the racks to get the choice pieces.

"Okay. And Angelica, after you've gone through make-up, you'll stay put until you are called," Donna said.

"You got it," Angelica responded.

"André will pick out the outfit you will wear. See you in a few." Donna left the room.

Ooh's and ah's erupted each time André held up a piece of fabric.

Absent were the beautiful couture designs that made Givenchy, Chanel, and Christian Dior household names. Instead, there were pieces of leather with large brass buckles that had to be manipulated onto the body. This was not quite what Angelica had envisioned and she wasn't certain about exposing her goods to the world. She may have played hard as a young woman, but the only exposing she was inclined to do was next to a warm, sexy man whose abs of steel would fold themselves around her body. And there was no one in the building who remotely resembled the description of the man she envisioned being with forever and ever.

André handed Angelica a brown thong, a short-short, brown leather skirt with slatted pleats that stopped at the top of her thigh, and a leather-padded bra that would leave her midsection bare. Angelica stared at the items in her hand and wondered what she was supposed to do with them. The photo shoot was taking a bizarre turn, and the runway lights Angelica hoped to see were clearly nonexistent.

12

Margo placed her coat in the closet and then went to the living room and took off her shoes. She went over to the couch, fumbled through the mail that she laid there on her way into the house, and moved her purse so she could sit down. Several bills were in the stack, but what caught her eye was the envelope in the shape of a greeting card that was scribbled over in Malik's handwriting.

She pulled the envelope from the rest and stared at it for a moment. Margo missed Malik but knew she had done the right thing by telling him that they needed time apart. Prayer kept her anchored, and she felt safe that she had her Jesus to help get through times when she felt a wee bit lonely. Margo looked at the envelope, tore it open, and pulled the card from its holder.

A black and white picture of a black man and woman looking into each other's eyes was on the cover. Margo stared at it as if it was a picture of her and Malik. She stared at it as if trying to understand what the couple was sharing. Hesitantly, Margo opened the card and guided her eyes to the text. It read *Love is in the eye of the beholder. In your voice, I hear it. In your smile, I see it. In your touch, I feel it…You are the things I love.*

Margo closed the card and her eyes, holding the card to her chest. Malik had somehow crawled into her system, but it was a direct result of the loss of her beloved Jefferson, the man she truly loved. Malik offered security and the comfort of a good friend at a bleak time in her life—nothing more, nothing less. Margo had to admit she had let her guard down, though, and now Malik wanted more, more than she was willing to give.

Placing the card back in the envelope, Margo got up from the couch and went to the kitchen. The phone began to ring, and she hesitated, hoping she wouldn't have to hurt Malik's feelings again. She looked at the caller ID, but did not recognize the caller. Out of curiosity, Margo picked up the phone and answered.

"This is a collect call from," the recorded operator said, after which a live voice came on the line, "Jefferson Myles. Do you accept the charges?"

"Yes!" Margo said, dancing in a circle. She covered her mouth with her free hand, excited by the sound of Jefferson's voice.

"Margo?"

"Yes, Jefferson. It's me."

"How are you doing, baby?"

"I'm doing fine…great. How about you?"

"I'm doing fine. I have some news…pretty good news at that."

"What is it Jefferson? What is the news?"

"I have a parole hearing in a few days. My attorney thinks I have a good chance at being released."

"Oh my God!" Margo exclaimed. "Could this be true? I've got to tell Ivy, JR, Winter, and Winston."

"Don't say anything yet, Margo. Let's wait until after the parole hearing. Then we'll know if a celebration is in order. I do feel good about this, baby."

"Oh, this is wonderful news, Jefferson. Extra prayers tonight for everything to go right. I miss you."

"I miss you too, Margo. I don't deserve you, but I'm thankful to

God that I still have you in my life. I love you, and I'm going to do everything in my power to prove it to you."

"You don't have to prove anything to me. God has shown me through His love that we are going to be all right. I haven't abandoned you or our marriage. You are the love of my life. I want you to wow that parole board and hurry home to me, to the family."

"What did I do to deserve you? I've got to go, baby, and I can't wait to see you again."

"I can't wait either," Margo said, tears sliding down her face.

"I'll call you with the news, regardless of the outcome. I love you."

"Okay, Jefferson. I'll be here waiting. And I love you, too."

Margo heard the phone click. She held the phone close to her bosom until the busy signal annoyed her enough to hang it up. Good news was what she needed, and although Jefferson had asked her not to say anything, the first person she thought about telling was Malik.

The card was lying on the kitchen counter. Margo picked it up and tore it into pieces. There was no room for another person in her life, and the moment she had waited for might be only days or a few weeks away. Margo decided against telling Malik her news. She grabbed the phone again and called each of her children. God was in the motion of answering her prayer.

13

A freak, that's what she looked like. In another life, Angelica had worn revealing clothing or no clothing at all—depending on who was telling the story. When she pole danced and the lust-filled men were yelling for her to take it off, Angelica was in a zone. The itsy-bitsy bikini she wore was only a tease to the gyrations that caused men to pull twenty-dollar bills out of their wallets and place it in her G-string.

The outfit she wore now didn't feel comfortable, and it seemed tasteless for a magazine spread. Maybe it was because she expected to be wearing a glamorous gown and four-inch diamond stilettos. Something was wrong with this current picture; no, it didn't feel right at all.

Angelica paced as she waited to be called. It seemed odd that she was the only one left in the room. It gave her time to think, if nothing else, but her mind was clouded and no reason could get through.

"Angelica." It was a voice from a loudspeaker. "Please proceed to Stage II."

Stage II? Angelica had no idea where to find it. She opened the door and left the room to venture through the hallway. She hadn't noticed it before, but on the wall were little hangers with the words Stage I, Stage II, and Stage III hanging from each one. She found Stage II, opened the door, and walked onto a stage that made her bottom lip drop.

The room looked like a jungle. Fake palm trees and antelope-skin rugs were scattered throughout the room as well as light colored straw meant to resemble the brush in Africa. Black, white, brown, and cream colored material was draped on the walls of the stage. What made Angelica recoil was not the large brass bed in the middle of the room with leather bands attached to it by chains, but the real male lions that were housed in brass cages beside it. The lions looked as if they would welcome a human meal if the opportunity presented itself.

"Take your places," Donna spoke.

Angelica remained still, not sure where her place was. Jazz climbed on the bed and was followed by one of the other women that came in late. Madeline and Coco moved to each post of the bed while two other women took their positions behind them.

"Angelica, you will get on the bed with Jazz and Ciara," Donna said, pointing the way with a long-lens camera resting on the other arm.

Angelica looked at Donna as if she was crazy. *Get on the bed with these women and do what?* Angelica was thinking.

"You need to move it, Angelica," Donna prodded. "Time is money."

Angelica moved toward the bed in no hurry. There was complete silence as the rest of the group waited for her to take her place and receive the next order from Donna.

"Angelica, you will lie in the middle of the bed with your legs slightly bent, and Jazz, you will get beside her and lift her hair and put it to your nose while you drop your other hand to her stomach. Ciara, you will be on the other side of Angelica. We will take several frames. You will take your hand and caress her face, finally giving her a passionate kiss. André, place Angelica's hands in the cuffs."

"What kind of magazine is this?" Angelica questioned, pushing Andre`s hands away and scooting off the bed.

"Do you not need a job?" Donna asked.

"I thought this was supposed to be a modeling job," Angelica countered.

"What do you think this is? You are posing, modeling, whatever you want to call it. You are wasting my time. Now get back to your post."

"No female is going to be kissing on me. You all act like a bunch of lesbos."

The air was thick and very quiet on the set.

"Oh, hell no," Angelica screamed. "Oh, hell no! You have misrepresented yourself, Donna. This may be your gig, but it isn't mine."

"Fine, get the hell out," Donna screamed back. "Just remember, you no longer have a job and you will not have a place to live. If you can't pay your way, you have no place to stay."

Donna picked up her camera and began to click away, giving orders that her subjects, minus Angelica, obeyed. Angelica stood by, disgusted at what she saw, closing her eyes during acts that a heterosexual being such as herself found most repulsive. She would have left, but she had no way out of the jungle she found herself in, and she had to pray that Donna would at least give her a ride back to her apartment so she could collect her things. Angelica's eyes flew open at the roar of one of the lions.

∞

Silence was deafening. Angelica would have felt better if Donna had cussed at her or something. Completely ignored, Angelica looked out of the window and watched as the busy streets of

New York conducted their business—taxis escorting tourists to one of the many Broadway plays and busy restaurants welcoming early evening customers for dinner. It would be easy to fall in love with this city, but Angelica had already hit her first obstacle in less than a week, and without a job and a place to live, her empty condo in Fayetteville, North Carolina was looking pretty good.

"You and your stuff have twenty-four hours to be out of my house," Donna finally said without looking in Angelica's direction.

"We should talk about it," Angelica said.

Silence ensued, and Angelica left it at that. She had no idea where she would go and what she would do for money. She had enough money to stay in a hotel for a while, but she needed a job if she planned on staying in the Big Apple. Her plans did not include running back to Fayetteville, at least not this soon. Margo, Malik, Jefferson, and Hamilton were better off without her.

14

It looked like Mother's Day as Margo sat in church flanked by all four of her children—Ivy and JR, and twins Winter and Winston. Margo lifted her hands and sang louder than the other parishioners, her children glancing from time to time to make sure she was all right. Margo was happy because she was sure the Lord was about to answer her prayer.

A side door opened and Malik walked in and found a seat. After a moment, he gazed around the room until he spotted her. A look of surprise registered on his face upon seeing the entire Myles clan. He faced the front and bowed his head.

"'Tis another day that the Lord has made," the pastor said. "We should rejoice and be glad in it. Oh, the Lord is good *all* the time. All the time the Lord is good."

"Yes," the congregation sang, cheering the pastor on.

"Sister Myles, please come down front."

Margo jumped up and made her way to the front of the sanctuary. She felt Malik's stare as she passed in front of him. Neither Malik nor anyone else was going to steal her joy today.

"Sister Myles has a testimony she would like to share today. Go on, Sister Myles, and tell us about the goodness of the Lord."

"Thank you, Pastor. Church, if I haven't told you individually, I'd like to take this moment to say thank you for all your prayers during one of the most stressful times in my life. The last five years have not been easy for me or my children, but through the grace of God, we are doing fine.

"A couple of days ago, I received a call from my husband, and he reports that he is up for parole in a few days. Jefferson's attorney believes he has an extremely good chance of being released from… prison, soon. I rejoice because of your prayers; my prayers are about to be answered. I owe everything to God, and I can't thank Him enough for all He has done in my life and what He is doing for my family. I ask that you continue to pray for us. Thank you, Pastor."

Clap, clap, clap, clap, and clap. The congregation praised the Lord right along with Sister Myles.

"God is good, isn't He saints?" Pastor said.

"Yes, He is," the congregation blurted out.

"Sister Myles, we thank you for your testimony. We will be in prayer for Brother Myles' early release. Hallelujah!!!" Pastor shouted.

Malik continued to look straight ahead. It was obvious to Margo that the news had stung him. It was hard concentrating on Pastor's sermon for wondering what was on Malik's mind. Why should she worry? The Lord was about to answer her prayers, and her husband would finally be home where she could pamper him until he got enough. Jefferson didn't need to worry about a job right away; she had sold four houses in the last few weeks.

Church was over and some of the members came over to give Margo a hug and offer words of encouragement. After the group dispersed, she looked around for Malik. There was no sign of him. Margo shrugged her shoulders. She had hoped to receive congratulations at the news about his best friend, but obviously the news was not good to him.

She corralled her group together and exited the church. Her children seemed to enjoy seeing everyone. It had been years since they had visited. Ivy pulled her mother to the side.

"Mom, you are so obvious."

"What are you talking about, Ivy?"

"Malik. You've got a thing for Malik. I saw how you watched him today. I bet you don't remember a word that Pastor spoke because you were tuned in to Malik. Mom, don't deny it."

"Shut up, Ivy. You're always thinking with your mouth. Malik is your dad's best friend and that's it. You need to keep your wandering mind in check. Do you hear me?"

"Straight up, but I know what I saw. You can't fool me."

"What are you talking about?" Winter asked, walking into the middle of Margo and Ivy's conversation.

"Nothing," Ivy said.

"Your dreads are squeezing your brain, Ivy," Winter said. "It was obvious you were talking about something because your hands were moving a mile a minute. It probably has something to do with Malik." Margo and Ivy exchanged glances. "What I tell you? Anyway, everyone in the family knows that Malik has been more than attentive to Mom."

"All right, hold on Winter. You and Ivy need to get it straight right now. My eyes and heart are only for your dad. Any ideas or illusions you may have conjured up in your brains about me and Malik are false. Now, let's get out of here and go to dinner."

"Hello, Margo," Malik said. Margo jumped and turned around to find Malik in her space. Ivy and Winter each put a hand over their mouths to stifle a laugh. Margo looked like a thief that had been caught.

"Good afternoon, Malik. Good Word today."

"Which one, Pastor's or yours?"

Ivy and Winter turned and continued to giggle at the sight of their mother.

"Of course, Pastor's. He sure did preach today."

"Why didn't you tell me about Jefferson? Don't you think I deserved to have received the news privately, instead of during a congregational announcement? We're like family."

"Jefferson asked that I not tell anyone yet."

"So you make a public announcement? It will probably be printed in the *Fayetteville Observer*, tomorrow's edition. I thought we were better friends than that."

"We are, Malik. Bad judgment on my part."

Malik smiled at the girls. "Sorry for the intrusion."

Margo stared at Malik as he walked away. "As I said, Mother," Ivy chimed in, "you need to come clean with yourself. The Bible says you can't have two masters."

Winter roared with laughter.

"Enough! Go pull Winston and JR from their friends, and let's go eat."

"As you say," Winter said, still laughing.

∞

Malik jumped in his car and drove away. *How could Margo humiliate me like that in front of God and witnesses?* It had taken courage to tell Margo that he loved her. Spending all that time with her wasn't just for show and tell. Now his heart ached for what he was so close to claiming but was now cut off like a major detour on a heavily traveled road.

Jefferson didn't deserve Margo. Hadn't he spent endless hours begging and pleading for Jefferson to see the error of his ways—to leave that married woman alone and save his marriage to Margo? All the lying, cheating, and fornicating Jefferson committed should have been sure grounds for divorce, but wonderful Margo, loving Margo, forgiving Margo would stand by her man, no matter what she had been through or how long it took for her life to mend.

Malik drove blindly down the street, distancing himself from the last image of Margo and his hurt ego. He stopped for the light and watched what appeared to be three generations of women cross the street, the young mother holding the hand of her daughter on one side and that of what appeared to be her mother on the other. His chance at fatherhood had been lost when Toni was killed along with their unborn baby, but he'd settle for being Margo's friend, lover, and confidant.

He shook his head to erase the new image that had forced its way into his subconscious. Angelica's lips were touching his, and he was fighting, resisting the temptation to touch hers.

Honk, honk, honk!!

"Hold your horses," Malik shouted at the car behind him. "I know the light is green." Malik put his foot on the gas and headed down the street. He pulled into the parking lot of an Italian restaurant called Carrabba's to get a bite to eat and be alone with his thoughts.

15

Donna pulled the car to the curb and jumped out, retrieving her camera equipment before placing her car keys in Ari's hand. She looked back at Angelica, who seemed to be taking her time getting out of the car, and then disappeared through the door to the building.

Ari extended his hand and helped Angelica from the car. He got an eyeful as he let his gaze travel the length of her body. Angelica squeezed his hand, and she felt his fingers pulsate.

"This might be the last time I see you," Angelica offered.

"Already tired of the penthouse?" Ari asked.

"Things are not right up there. Weird things," Angelica replied.

Ari began to laugh. "Yes, Miss Donna has a lot of strange visitors to her house. Don't tell her I said it. I thought you were another one of her lesbian friends. They have some wild parties up there. I've been to a few and had a great time."

Angelica crinkled her nose. "No, I'm not like that, Ari. Donna is my ex-husband's cousin, and she was supposed to be hiring me for a modeling job. Imagine my surprise when I got to the set this morning—women kissing women and posing in lewd positions."

"Oh, you're talking about that gay magazine Donna is shooting."

"You know about that, Ari?"

"Yeah, Donna and I are tight. Like I said, I've been to some of her wild, girl parties. It's not a place for the timid or weak of heart."

"It sounds disgusting."

"For some it might be. I kept the party going and was there to dance with the ladies if they wanted to. No one was intimidated by my presence, and I certainly posed no threat."

"Well, since I can't play the game, I've been given twenty-four hours to gather my things and remove myself from the premises," Angelica said with a sigh. "If Donna had given me a week, I would have been very appreciative. I guess she wants me out of her sight."

"Tell you what," Ari said, "let me park the car and meet me downstairs in fifteen minutes. I may have a temporary solution to your problem."

"Thanks, Ari. I'll see you in a few."

∞

There was no sign of Donna when Angelica entered the condo. She went to the room she had called hers for the last few days and began pulling clothes out of closets and drawers, folding them and placing them in a pile. She looked around the room and then focused on the black and white pictures that adorned the walls. All were of women, beautiful women, Donna's women, but Angelica would not be one of them.

Angelica turned to find Donna standing in the crack of the door that was slightly ajar. At first there was a battle of the eyes, each one daring the other to speak. Then it was their body language—Donna's stance was defiant, saying *I have the upper hand; don't mess with me*, while Angelica's stance was more agile and said, *So you played me; I've got nine lives and you will see me again*.

"You will not last a day in this city," Donna began. "This is not a place for losers. I don't know what you expected when you arrived here, but I was doing you a favor, doing my family a favor by offering you a job in the first place."

Angelica clapped sarcastically. "Nice speech, cousin Donna. I didn't ask for your help, and if I had known what I was getting into, I wouldn't have agreed to come to New York. You sold me a bill of goods. Couldn't be honest and upfront with me. So, because I had an attitude today and refused to subject myself to what I felt to be repulsive, you have exercised your right to dismiss me from not only a job that I had already dismissed myself from but also the refuge you promised while I'm in New York. You didn't even have the decency to allow me a few days to at least find a new job and pay for my stay."

"Mighty fine speech yourself, but listen up, sister, you won't be able to find a job in this city that will pay you enough money to afford the room you are staying in. You may need to call your brothers to see if they can help you because your eviction notice still stands."

Angelica looked at her watch. Twenty minutes had passed. She told Ari that she would be there in fifteen. "I've got to get some air," Angelica said.

"You have less than twenty-three hours and counting." Donna left the room, leaving Angelica to ponder her predicament for a moment.

Angelica looked at her watch again and headed for the door. Once in the elevator, she breathed a sigh of relief. The confrontation with Donna was not as bad as she had expected, and she hoped Ari would have some good news.

Exiting the elevator, Angelica looked around but didn't see Ari. She walked outside and, after not seeing him, walked back into the lobby and paced. She was anxious again, and Donna's words, *You have less than twenty-three hours and counting,* haunted her.

She paced for five minutes more and decided to go back up to Donna's.

"Hey, Miss Angelica, I wondered where you were."

"Ari, I've been waiting over five minutes for you."

"You didn't come down when we discussed, and when you didn't show up, I had to park one of the residents' cars."

"I'm sorry, Ari. My nerves are on edge. I don't know what to do."

"Look," Ari said. "Why don't you stay with me until you get on your feet? My place is not fancy, but it will offer a roof over your head. And it's near the subway."

"I...I couldn't. I shouldn't. I..."

"What other choice do you have? No strings attached."

Angelica walked to Ari and placed a quick kiss on his cheek. "Thank you for being my savior."

"I'm off in another thirty minutes. If you get your things down here by then, you can leave tonight."

"I won't be late, Ari."

"All right. It's been a long day," Ari said.

The elevator closed. Angelica thanked God out loud for the miracle. She was only a half hour away from being distanced from the hell she had brought upon herself by accepting Donna's invitation. Yes, she knew it was hell because the pain was worse than any menstrual cramps she had suffered growing up, and they had been awful.

Angelica moved swiftly inside the condo and retrieved her belongings. She placed the key Donna had given her on the coffee table and headed toward the door with her two suitcases in tow.

"So, is Ari rescuing you from the evil cousin?" Donna asked.

Angelica turned around and faced Donna, who stood at a diagonal on the dining room door—her right elbow touching the top part of the doorframe and her feet placed on the floor in the middle of the door opening. Donna seemed to have a thing for standing in doorways; in fact, she looked like one of the portraits that hung in the den that she had so beautifully captured with her camera lens.

"You said it yourself, I had less than twenty-three hours to remove myself, and I'm doing just that," Angelica replied.

"Well, for someone who doesn't know anyone in New York, you move mighty fast." Donna smiled. "I'm surprised. You have twenty-two hours and thirty minutes."

"Why, Donna? I would not have treated you this way."

"Do I have to answer that, Angelica? You cost me a lot of money today, and I don't take kindly to losing money. You're a little old for my taste, but I wanted to help you. Adele Macy said you were feisty and would give the magazine debut the extra *umph* it needed."

Angelica dropped her bags to the floor and stared at Donna, who did not move from her position.

"Ms. Macy?"

"Yeah, Ms. Adele Macy from the North Carolina Correctional Institution for Women." Donna smirked. "We're home girls. Twenty-two hours and twenty-eight minutes."

"So, Ms. Macy is spying on me. Why? I don't understand any of this and I don't want to. I thought you brought me here as a courtesy for being Hamilton's ex-wife…because you were doing a favor for your family."

"Hamilton may be my cousin, but there is no love lost. He's getting what he deserves."

Angelica picked up her bags. "Thanks for the memories."

"Anyway, Adele contacted my mother looking for my phone number. She told Mommy about you getting out of prison."

A puzzled look crossed Angelica's face. "Why would she call you?

Why would she call your mother to tell her about me? What's going on here?"

Donna moved from her position and quickly reached the door to the condo before Angelica.

"You can run, but you can't hide. You're going to have to pay for your sins. At every corner, every train depot, at every fork in the road, there will be someone observing you. You won't get away."

"I don't know what you're talking about, Donna, but I'm glad to be getting up out of here."

"Twenty-two hours and twenty-five minutes," Donna sang and slammed the door just as Angelica cleared it.

∞

Donna's taunting disturbed Angelica. What did it all mean? How was Ms. Macy involved? She had done her time and paid for the crime she had committed—stupidity. While in jail, her betrayal of Hamilton and Jefferson had haunted her day and night. She had gotten what she deserved, but now Angelica wanted to be a productive citizen and possibly right some of her wrongs. So far, she had done a lousy job of it.

Angelica looked at her watch. She had less than a minute to get downstairs. Donna's words still ate at her. Was Ari one of the corners she had to tread? Right now she needed a place to stay, and Ari's offer was a blessing in her time of need. Or was it? She couldn't think about that now. Finding a job so that she could become independent would be her chore, and Angelica vowed she'd do it.

The doors to the elevator opened and Ari was waiting like the perfect gentleman. He took her bags and told her to wait while he brought his car around. Ten minutes later there was a honk, and Angelica went outside. A Jaguar sat out front, and Ari was at the wheel.

A look of surprise registered on Angelica's face. Ari opened the door to the Jag like he would if he were on duty and shut it once Angelica was inside. Angelica silently mouthed, *Eat your heart out, Donna.*

They rode in silence away from Manhattan. After a few moments, Ari turned on the radio and light jazz hit the airwaves. It took another few minutes before Angelica relaxed; Donna's words about someone watching her still resounded in her ears. Angelica looked over at Ari, who seemed to be enjoying the music.

"I guess you think I'm some kind of bimbo," Angelica said to Ari while looking straight ahead.

"Why would I think that?" Ari responded. "You're a beautiful woman who's in a dilemma. I've seen it many times. Now, I don't go opening my doors to everyone who falls prey to Ms. Donna Barnes Reardon, but your need seemed urgent enough that I had to help."

"Thank you, Ari. I really appreciate it. I don't go off with people I don't know, but, as you put it so eloquently, I was desperate."

Angelica began to laugh and so did Ari. "You should have seen your face," Ari said. "You reminded me of the Statue of Liberty, waving her torch for someone to stop." They laughed again, and Angelica really relaxed.

"So tell me about yourself, Ari," Angelica prodded.

Ari looked at Angelica. "What do you want to know?"

"Whatever you are willing to share."

"I was a poor immigrant's son. Our family came from Greece back in the 1950's. My family owned a little restaurant in Queens, and I worked there until I finished high school. Broke my Papa's heart. He thought I would take over the business one day, but I didn't see it in my future. I had a sister who took over the business after my parents died. Still owns it."

"So what did you do after high school?"

"I wanted to act. Took some acting classes in town. Actually did some Broadway. I was never in a leading role, but it was a good living because I seemed to always have a job. If I had gotten that break everybody pursues, I might have been a Cary Grant or a Clark Gable. I liked show biz, and it's still a big part of me. Maybe we can catch a show on my day off."

Angelica smiled. "I'd like that."

"What about you, Angelica? What was life like for you before the penthouse?"

Angelica fidgeted in her seat. She hadn't planned on Ari throwing the question back at her. It was uncomfortable, and Angelica had no planned speech for such an occasion. What could she say?

"Life was full for you, huh?" Ari asked. "Don't know where to start?"

"Life hasn't exactly been good for me, Ari. I've done a lot of things I'm not proud of and the stench of it still seems to follow me."

"Couldn't be that bad. A beautiful woman such as yourself probably has had the world eating out of your hand."

"I wish. Nothing as great at that, although I will say that I had everything I wanted, but it came at a cost. In fact, I paid a high price for a delusion of grandeur.

"I was married to a prominent police officer in Fayetteville, North Carolina, where I come from. He was so handsome. Hamilton is his name. He was the kind of handsome your girlfriends would say you have to watch out for because he was too fine to have as a husband and it wouldn't be long before he'd be stepping out on you. I didn't listen because I had to have him." Angelica purposely left out how she met Hamilton in a strip club. "True to everyone's belief, Hamilton not only had affairs with other women, he was an abuser—mental and physical."

"I'm sorry to hear that," Ari said.

"We divorced years later. However, Hamilton was involved in some illegal mess. I became indirectly involved…" Angelica stopped, not sure how much of the awful details of her life she wanted to share.

"You don't have to say any more, if you don't want to."

"Ari," Angelica looked at him, "I want to be honest with you. You seem like an honest individual. As I said earlier, I did some horrible things that include sleeping with my best friend's husband, and I compromised her husband and my ex-husband, Hamilton."

Ari squirmed in his seat.

"I embezzled funds from my girlfriend's husbands' accounts—he owned a financial securities firm—for the head of an underground organization. I'm ashamed to say that I was the girlfriend of this underground figure, although Hamilton and Jefferson—my girlfriend's husband—did not know it. Fast-forwarding, this underground figure put a hit out on Hamilton and Jefferson and I tried to warn them. I was with Jefferson when he was hit and, much to my chagrin, his wife, who was once my best friend, found out. More than that," Angelica hesitated, then sighed, "I was sent to prison for my part. I was released a few weeks ago. Yes, I'm an ex-convict, released early for good conduct, but I'm a good person, Ari. I'll understand if you want to drop me and my bags off at the side of the road."

"It won't be necessary," Ari said, looking straight ahead.

Ari pulled into what appeared to be a quiet neighborhood in Queens. There were no loitering people or children playing in the streets. He pulled his Jag in front of a modest, single-dwelling brick home. Absent were the spacious yards she was accustomed to in North Carolina. There was a lot of concrete with little or no yard. Houses were close together, each one unique in its own way—a row of similar but eclectic houses that were postcard perfect.

Ari continued to be the perfect gentleman, retrieving her bags and leading the way inside. Angelica followed behind him. Ari disappeared into a room, leaving Angelica to herself. The living room was airy and decorated with French provincial furniture that was covered in plastic. Lots and lots of plants—spider, devil's ivy, mother's tongue, African violets—were scattered throughout, and a modern entertainment system stood against the wall full of pictures of loved ones and a twenty-seven-inch color TV that sat in the center.

Ari reappeared. "I'll show you to your room. Your bags are already there. I hope you will be comfortable."

"Look, Ari, I do appreciate what you are doing, and I hope I haven't caused you any inconvenience."

"Not at all."

"You've been awfully quiet since I spilled the beans. Not quite the bio you expected to hear, but I wanted to be upfront and honest with you. I'm not the shallow person people believe that I am, and if I can get on my feet, I'm going to prove it to all the naysayers in my life."

"I believe you, Angelica. Why don't you sit down and make yourself comfortable? Would you like something to eat? I can warm up some leftovers from yesterday."

"No, Ari, I'm not very hungry. I know you've had a long day. Why don't you relax, get settled in and pretend that I'm not here? I'm going to sit here and thank God for sending you."

Ari sat down. "I'm glad to help. No strings."

16

He rubbed his wrists, the weight of the chains gone, he hoped, forever. Passing the cage-like cells of his neighbors for the last five years, Jefferson raised his fist high and gave a salute along with a smile that showed he was convinced he would be free.

Aided by a walker, Jefferson was taken to a room where he met his attorney, Stacy Greer. Stacy had been with Jefferson during his trial and conviction five years before. She believed that it would be an injustice for Jefferson to remain in jail for twenty years, especially since he had tried relentlessly to get out of Operation Stingray and distance himself from the organization. But he had to pay for what he had done—stealing money from his clients. His wife Margo had to pay twice, once with Jefferson's absence and the other with their savings, which was nearly all that they had.

In the front of the eggshell-colored room was a ten-foot-long table. At the table sat three people with microphones in front of them, the parole board that consisted of an all-white, two women-and-one man panel. A shorter table sat across from the long table, and this was where Jefferson and Stacy sat.

At exactly two-thirty, one of the women on the panel brought the meeting to order and announced that the proceedings were for the parole hearing of Jefferson Myles versus the State. The woman stated the particulars of the case, evidence that might render an unfavorable parole judgment, reasons for immediate release, and Jefferson's history while incarcerated. Jefferson and Stacy sat and listened as the information was shared, argued, and sifted through. After thirty minutes, Jefferson and Stacy were asked to step outside, but inside of five minutes, they were asked to return.

"Jefferson Myles," the man spoke this time, "please stand." Stacy stood with Jefferson. "We have reviewed the evidence in your case, the nature of your request for parole, and have rendered a verdict."

Jefferson stiffened at the latter part of the man's statement. He swallowed hard and focused his eyes on the bearer of his fate.

"Mr. Myles, a unanimous decision has been made in your case." Jefferson thought the guy was never going to let the verdict roll from his tongue. "You are free. Welcome back to society."

"Oh my God, oh my God. Thank you, thank you, thank you," Jefferson said, and then turned to hug Stacy, whose tears were already running down her face.

The panel nodded as if it weren't a big deal and Jefferson ought to be glad that it was his lucky day.

Jefferson didn't care what they thought now. He was free…a free man who could go home to his wife and his family and try to start afresh. Jefferson raised his hand high. "Thank you, God. You do answer prayers."

"Let's go and call Margo," Stacy insisted. "She will definitely want to hear this piece of news."

"I'm ready," Jefferson cried. "I'm ready."

∞

Margo paced back and forth in the house she once shared with Jefferson. Winter had come down from Raleigh to be with her to offer support if the news was negative, and to be whatever Margo needed if the news was positive. There was no quieting the rumbles in Margo's stomach. She prayed for good news.

Winter brought her mother a cup of tea to help calm her nerves. She rubbed Margo's back and sat down next to her mother, her own nerves stretched to the limit already. The day was far spent, and no telephone call had come. Margo wasn't able to depend on the television news because they had said very little about Jefferson or the possibility of his parole.

The clock chimed three times and the two women looked at it, their hopes all but dashed. At three-twenty, the phone rang, but neither of the women had enough courage to pick up the receiver and hear the news. After the fifth ring, Winter answered the phone.

"Winter?" she heard Jefferson say after she said hello.

"Dad?"

"Yes, it's me," Jefferson said, his voice light. "Where is your mother?"

"She's right here." Winter winked and handed Margo the phone.

"Jefferson?" Margo whispered, trying to hold back her excitement.

"Margo, baby, I'm free!" Jefferson wailed. "Five minutes ago, they made the announcement."

"Oh my God. Oh my God!" Margo kept repeating. She jumped to her feet and grabbed Winter and hugged her until Winter pushed her away. "That's wonderful, Jefferson. I've prayed for this day. God does listen. How soon before you come home?"

"It will be several hours. I'll have to out-process, but Stacy will bring me home."

"I wish I was there with you," Margo said.

"I don't want you to have to see this prison again," Jefferson said. "We will celebrate when I get home. I want to hold you and never let go."

Margo was choked up. The words wouldn't come out for the sobs. Finally, Margo caught her breath. "Hurry, baby. Hurry home."

"I will," Jefferson said. And the line went dead.

"Let's hurry and get you processed out," Stacy said. "This was a great victory." She hugged Jefferson.

"Thanks, Stacy. This day would not have happened without you. I owe it all to you."

Stacy smiled, grabbed Jefferson's arm and slowly paraded him out of the room, moving as fast as the walker would allow.

∞

Margo flopped down on the couch, overcome with emotion. Winter scooted down next to Margo and rubbed her mother's back to offer comfort. Winter closed her wet eyes and then looked toward the ceiling and said a *thank you, Lord*.

Several minutes passed. Margo wiped the tears from her face and reached over and squeezed Winter.

"Okay, enough of this," Margo said. "We've got to have a celebration. Winter, call your sister and brothers, I'll call Pastor, and…"

"What about Malik?" Winter smirked, trying to hide a smile. "You know how upset he was because you didn't tell him that Dad might be released."

"Let me worry about Malik, Madam All-up-in-my-business."

"Mother, I'm only saying you have to consider telling Malik. You might want to invite him to the celebration, too." Winter got up and turned away so her mother would not hear her giggle.

An embarrassed looked crossed Margo's face, followed by a scowl. "I'm telling you, for the last time, that Malik is your father's friend as well as a friend to the family. I appreciate him checking on me while Jefferson was away. That's all there was to it."

"Okay, Mother. Don't get upset. I'm not mad at you if you had a teeny-weenie little crush on Malik. It was probably good for your ego. I love my dad, but remember, he wasn't perfect."

"And two wrongs don't a right make. Remember that, young lady. It'll take you far in life. Now, get up and go do what I told you to do. I'll handle the party arrangements."

"At your pleasure, Mother dear."

Margo continued to sit on the couch and watched Winter leave the room. Now left to her own thoughts, Margo realized this was the day she had waited for, prayed for…for five long years. God had honored her prayers. Thoughts of Malik swirled in her head while mixed emotions settled in her stomach. Whatever it was that tried to cloud this moment, she had to suppress it. This was not the time to start having feelings for another man or even think about another man. Her attention needed to be fully focused on Jefferson's release and his return to her and the children.

"Got you to thinking, huh?"

Margo looked up at Winter. "Don't be smug, little girl. I can still spank that behind of yours."

"All right, Mother. I've called everybody to let them know about Dad. Wasn't sure when you were planning to have this party."

"Today. I want banners to welcome Jefferson home. Gosh, I've got to get up from here. I've got to order a cake and get some refreshments."

"Mom, are you serious? Only Winston and I will be here."

"No, I've got to call the Pastor, church members and Malik. Hand me the phone, Winter. I can't waste any more time. I've got so much to do in so little time. We're going to have a celebration!"

Winter watched her mother. She was like her mother in so many ways, although she was her father's child.

17

Angelica sat up in bed and scanned her new surroundings. She tossed and turned throughout the night but had been able to doze off for at least a few hours. She was appreciative of Ari, even though she really knew nothing about him, except for what he had told her on the ride to the house. Now she hoped not to lose too much sleep over it because it beat being homeless.

She listened to see if she could hear Ari stirring. The house was quiet save for the noise outside—the hustle and bustle of New York City getting ready to start the day.

She found her watch and looked at the time. It was five-thirty in the morning. It was time for her to get up, but she didn't feel comfortable roaming about the house. She'd wait until she heard Ari moving about.

Thoughts of yesterday rushed to Angelica's head—a day that had gone so wrong. Angelica wasn't sure what she had done to deserve Donna's wrath, but Angelica was sure about one thing, and that was if her "so-called" career was going to get a jumpstart by posing with a bunch of lesbians, it was indeed over. She didn't want their mouths or hands to touch her. Now she was left with the task of finding another job.

Macy's was right in the middle of Manhattan. There were other retail shops where she could apply for a position as well. The only thing about working in a retail environment was that it would not pay the kind of salary she needed, and she needed a lot of money in order to secure the financial independence she desired.

For a fleeting moment, the woman in the subway holding onto the pole with her assorted packages flooded her memory. Angelica immediately shook the thought from her mind, but as quickly as she had erased the thought, it resurfaced and stayed, offering a vision of the freedom that she sought.

"No!" Angelica said, hoping Ari didn't hear her. Each time she tried to suppress the vision, it would return with a quickness, filling her head with promise of a new life, a life Angelica had hoped to never see again.

The knock at the door diverted her attention. She pulled the covers up to her neck and said, "Yes?"

"Angelica, it's Ari."

"Who else would it be?" She laughed.

"Take your time about getting up. I'm fixing myself some breakfast. Nothing special, but I'd be glad to whip you something up, too."

"No thanks, Ari. I don't usually do breakfast."

"Okay. I'm going to be leaving in an hour. If there's anything I can get you…"

"I'm getting up," Angelica said, cutting Ari off. "I'll ride in with you, if you don't mind. I think I'll put in some applications today."

"Wonderful. I'll wait on you. I only go in early because I don't have much to do since I've retired. I make a little extra cash, and it keeps me occupied."

"Well, I'll be ready in a jiffy."

Angelica flew out of the bed at lightning speed. Today was a new day and a chance to get it right. She rushed through the shower, made her face, and put on a chic blue-and-white seersucker pantsuit. She pulled her hair into a bun and darted out the room to where Ari was waiting.

His eyes roamed, but his lips stayed sealed. Angelica was a beautiful woman, but he had lived too many years and had seen too many things to jeopardize his present station in life. He let his eyes do the talking and relished the little time they would be together. Angelica would offer female company—someone to have a pleasant conversation with and maybe share a laugh or two. "Ready?" he asked.

"I am." Angelica offered a smile.

Angelica sat with her head thrown back in Ari's car and listened to his chatter. He talked about his life in New York and some of the crazy exploits he and his buddies carried out as teenagers. While Angelica listened with one ear, she watched as cars, taxis and New York City landmarks whizzed by.

Silence caused Angelica to look away from the scenery and turn toward Ari. He looked straight ahead, offering no further conversation until he said, "We're in midtown Manhattan. Where would you like to be dropped off?"

Angelica became alert and watched again as they passed building after building.

"You can drop me off at Macy's. It might be too early, but I can walk around until it opens."

"You may also want to go to Greenwich Village or SoHo, if Macy's doesn't pan out. You can get there by subway."

Angelica thanked Ari and looked straight ahead. She glanced his way again.

"Thank you again, Ari. I know I've been distant this morning, but I have a lot on my mind. Getting a job has consumed a lot of my mental energy. I don't want to inconvenience you any longer than I have to."

"You're not inconveniencing me," Ari said. "In fact, it's nice to have a warm face to talk to in the evenings."

Angelica twitched her mouth that settled into a smile. She enjoyed Ari's attention, and he was a good-looking man with a good-looking body. There was no room for a man in her life at this time, although she momentarily thought about Malik and the kiss she placed on his lips. Ari would always be a special friend, an angel in her time of distress, nothing more and nothing less.

"We're here," Ari said, taking Angelica from her thoughts. "What time would you like to be picked up?"

Angelica had not given any thought to being displaced while Ari was at work. He did not offer her a key to his house and she was not going to ask for one. That would make life simple because she had no plans to stay at Ari's for long.

"Give me your number," Angelica said. "I'll call you and we can work it out."

"All right." Ari wrote his cell number on the back of a card and handed it to Angelica. He smiled at her and Angelica jumped out.

She breathed in the air and looked around her, trying to decide which way to go. Macy's looked threatening, but she was going to march in there and complete an application. She was going to become a working girl and brave all the elements of a New York City life.

18

Drapes were pulled back as the restless and impatient group began to peek out the window and pace the room, waiting for the arrival of the honoree. A large "WELCOME HOME, JEFFERSON" banner hung across the fireplace. Margo assured the group that Jefferson would arrive shortly—getting into prison was easy, but getting out took a little longer.

Winter heard it first, running to the window to peek out and then catching a glimpse of the car that pulled into the driveway.

"They're here!" Winter shouted, backing away from the window and falling in line with the other well-wishers.

Margo was a ball of nerves, her fists scrunched up as her excitement mounted.

"*Sshhhh,*" Margo hissed at the crowd so they would lower their voices and not spoil the surprise. It seemed so strange, hearing the knock on the door, but Margo moved posthaste, her smile almost larger than her face.

The moment of truth. Margo pulled open the door, and there stood her man, Jefferson Myles, the one she had promised to love, cherish, and obey until death they did part. Stacy Greer stood next to him, happy for this moment, as did the twenty or so well-wishers who waited patiently to give hugs and say their welcome. Jefferson looked worn and had lost weight, but his healthy smile let everyone know that he was eager for the moment that had arrived. He was aided by a walker—a reminder of the car crash five years ago that had put him in a wheelchair—but rigorous therapy and the desire to walk again wrought the miracle Margo saw before her. Margo went to Jefferson and kissed him and then held him as he did her. Stacy closed the door behind them.

"Welcome home!" the anxious crowd shouted, then clapped for what seemed like forever.

Hugs, kisses, and even tears were passed around, each one thankful for the return of their brother. Margo was overcome as she saw Winter and Winston embrace their dad, accepting him back where he belonged, knowing that he had paid the price for his mistakes.

Jefferson held Margo around the waist as the well-wishers continued to share how they prayed for this day. Every other second, Jefferson stole glances at his soul mate, grateful for this courageous and steadfast woman who did not give up on him with all of his faults, insecurities and human frailties. He was going to do right by Margo, although he would never be able to make up the time he had stolen from her.

A frown formed on Jefferson's face. "Where's Malik?"

The question caught Margo off guard. She was aware that Malik wasn't there, however, she had hoped that, with all the celebrating, Jefferson would be caught up in the moment and not give a thought to the whereabouts of his best friend. It was best that Malik stayed away, and Margo could never allow Jefferson to find out that Malik was not happy with his homecoming.

"He must be working late. He knows about the party," Margo replied.

"I've got to call him. If you can get his number for me, sweetie, I would appreciate it."

"May I get everyone's attention," Pastor said. Margo was thankful for the timely interruption. She would eventually have to get Malik's number, but Pastor's announcement would give her time to regain her composure.

"I'd like to say," Pastor began, "that we are thankful this evening for our brother Jefferson Myles' return home."

"Yes!" the group yelled in unison.

"Brother Jefferson, we have prayed continuously for the day you and Sister Margo would be reconciled and resume your life together as husband and wife."

Margo saw Winter nudge Winston.

"This is a time of rejoicing," Pastor continued. "God saw fit to give our brother another chance, a chance to be restored...a chance to reclaim his life. We're happy for Sister Margo and Brother Jefferson and this family, and we're asking God to be with them, nourish them, give them peace and understanding and love for each other that will stand the test of time. We are denouncing the enemy that comes to seek, kill, and destroy, and we ask that this family continue to be covered with Your wings of protection.

"Now bless this food and let it be nourishing to our bodies. Amen. Let's eat."

Margo fixed Jefferson a plate and the others followed. This was the happiest moment of Margo's life, next to the day she and Jefferson were married. She stayed close to him all night, wanting the celebration to be over so she and Jefferson could have a private celebration of their own.

He stuffed another chicken sandwich in his mouth and then

turned and smiled at Margo. "Don't forget to give me Malik's number," Jefferson said.

∞

The room looked familiar. Jefferson sat on the edge of the bed and ran his hand across the smooth silk comforter. He scanned the room, reacquainting himself with his surroundings. It felt good to be home, however, the last time he had seen this room—his and Margo's bedroom—their lives were turned upside down.

Jefferson was appreciative of all the good wishes Pastor Dixon and the others had given him tonight, but this was the moment he had looked forward to more than any other during the last five years—being alone with Margo again.

A tear rushed down Jefferson's face. Seeing the faces of two of his children and embracing them made his uncomfortable journey back home easy. He had hurt them too, and Jefferson wasn't sure they had forgiven him.

It was Malik's absence that bothered him most. Malik had visited him only a few times while he was in prison. In fact, Jefferson could count the times on one hand. He understood Malik not wanting to come to the prison because it conjured up memories of his father who was serving a life sentence for armed robbery and murder, but his absence tonight was puzzling. Jefferson would try and call him once more before the night was over.

The bathroom door clicked and Jefferson looked up. Margo emerged wrapped in a purple towel from head to toe. Jefferson tensed, not sure what to do or say. Even wrapped in all that cotton, Jefferson could still see the hourglass figure which had made him fall for Margo in the first place. She was still the beautiful woman he had married years ago, and now his body ached for her.

Jefferson felt like an awkward young buck trying to get his mack on. It had been more than five years since he had touched a woman, and now this was his wife, Margo. He remained planted on the bed, following Margo with eyes that were full of longing and anticipation. Jefferson offered a smile when he saw that Margo had done so.

"Welcome home, Jefferson," Margo said.

"It's good to be home. So many nights I lay awake in that prison cell angry with myself for all the pain I brought upon this family and how I had hurt the most important person in my life. Margo, baby, I'm so sorry..."

"*Sshhh,*" Margo said, placing a finger over her lips. "Let's not talk about it now. I'm glad you're here."

"Thanks for the welcome home. It was good to see everyone, but I'm glad they're gone. I've been looking forward to just you and me."

Margo flinched. "Me, too," she said and then looked away. "Why don't I help you get your clothes off and get you settled into the shower?"

"I can do it." Jefferson looked up at Margo and smiled. "You're still beautiful, Margo."

Margo blushed. She sat on the bed next to Jefferson with her towel still pulled around her. "We're going to make it."

Jefferson smiled again and placed a quick kiss on Margo's lips, surprising her. With the aid of his walker, Jefferson got up and went into the bathroom as Margo looked on. When the door closed, Margo let her eyes fall to the floor. She clutched the towel that was still wrapped around her, and with her free arm circled her upper torso. She closed her eyes and whispered a prayer.

∞

They lay side-by-side without touching. Their eyes were wide open, each with a different view. Margo stared at the wall, while Jefferson stared at the white cotton gown that was draped over Margo's back. He reached out to touch Margo, but at the last minute, pulled his arm back. Her body was stark still, but his subconscious fear of rejection made him withdraw.

"Are you asleep?" Jefferson asked, a slight tremble in his voice.

"No," came the feeble reply.

"Margo, I'm sorry I wasn't there to protect you. For the past five years, all I thought about was you. I love you, Margo, and if I could erase all the ugly things that brought us to this day, I would. I can't, but I want a life with you. I understand that it may take some time for you to respond to me, but I want us to try. I need you."

Margo did not turn to face Jefferson. She held her pillow tight and shut her eyes. What she remembered was that Malik had been there to protect her for the past five years. He had come to her rescue more times than she could count. When Margo was locked out of the house, Malik was the one who called the locksmith and came by to make sure she would be all right. Malik was her dinner companion when she desired to go out for a bite to eat, and he was her confidant when she needed a friend. While she waited patiently for Jefferson to return home from prison, Margo had unconsciously fallen in love with Malik. What was she going to do?

19

Frustrated, Angelica headed for Greenwich Village, hoping that she would have better luck. No one was hiring; the seasonal help had been selected weeks ago. She needed a job that paid benefits and would give her a comfortable cash flow so that she could do all the things that made her happy.

Her employment adventure this morning left her exhausted and, as the train passed from station to station, Angelica had a thought. At the next stop, she jumped off the train, climbed the stairs and went to the other side to catch the northbound train. Time was not on her side, and Angelica headed back to midtown.

Angelica got off the train and hailed a cab. Once inside, she pulled her hair out of the bun and instructed the cab driver where to go. Within minutes, the cab pulled to the curb and Angelica jumped out, confident that she would have a job by the end of the day.

Outside, the sign posted on the building read Club Platinum. Angelica slipped inside and met the dark. She was guided by a light that spilled from the inside of an office around a corner. The click of her heels announced her arrival long before anyone saw her, and when she entered the open door, Angelica put on her seductive smile and switched her hips with her ponytail following.

The two men looked up and photographed Angelica with their

eyes. One of the men sat behind a desk, while the other stood next to him, both dressed in designer suits. It was obvious they were the owners and not some run-of-the-mill overseers handing out orders at the request of the boss.

"May I help you?" the man sitting behind the desk asked, his elbows resting on the desk while his eyes gave Angelica his full attention.

"Yes, you may. My name is Angel…Angel Barnes," Angelica said. She even liked the sound of Angel—a name she was called while in prison. "I'd like to dance. I need a job."

The man looked at her again, looked back at his partner for support, and then turned back to look at Angelica.

"What is a classy chick like yourself doing in this joint? And, you appear to be much older than the girls we hire to dance here."

"Look, I can dance. I'm willing to audition for you now, if you like. I've stripped before, and I was darn good."

"How long ago was that, Angel? Ten, twenty years ago?"

The other gentleman laughed.

There was a seriousness in Angelica's eyes that the man behind the desk recognized. "Lady, I don't know why you're here, but I'm going to let you audition to see if you've got what it takes. This work is not glamorous, and the filthy-rich men who come in here spending their money won't have much respect for you. They'll eat you alive and sometimes treat you like the night women who are a dime a dozen. The only difference is that you're inside and they're on the street."

"I can handle myself, Mr.…I didn't catch your name."

"Peter Ward and my partner, Gerald Lloyd." Peter pointed to the other man.

"I don't care what the customer thinks of me, Mr. Ward. I'll be using them to get what I need."

"All right, Angel. Do you have something you can dance in?"

"No, I hadn't..." Angelica stopped short. She thought better of sharing the reason she was there. This was the last place she wanted to be, but it was the only place that would get her out of the hole she had been dropped into. Donna hadn't crossed her mind until then, but if things went well at Club Platinum, there would be no time for Angelica to think about what her life would have been like if she hadn't walked off the job. In fact, it was already yesterday's news.

"Gerald, find something for Ms. Angel to wear. And Angel, after you've put on the bikini, please go to the stage; it will be lit for your audition. We'll see you in fifteen minutes."

"Thank you, Mr. Ward. You will not be disappointed."

Angelica followed Gerald Lloyd to a tiny room and changed into the bikini he gave her. It was skimpier than the outfit she had on yesterday, yet it felt right. While most of her body was exposed, only she and the pole would make love to each other and the only thing touching her skin would be the Hamiltons, Lincolns and Washingtons that half-drunk men would ease under her G-string, not the repulsive fingers of another female. She looked in the mirror, took out a tube of lipstick from her purse and repainted her lips. She squeezed her lips together, checked herself in the mirror and proceeded to the stage.

On the stage were three poles that were affixed to the floor. A long-ago memory rushed into Angelica's mind. She was a much younger woman then, and her stage exploits got the attention of the man who became her husband and took her away from the life because he didn't want any other man laying eyes on her body. Angelica smiled at the memory and, for a fleeting moment, wondered how Hamilton was doing.

"Ready?" Peter asked, startling Angelica.

Angelica faked a smile, but she would do what she had to do. "Any music preference?"

"Do you have 'Golden' by Jill Scott?"

"Gerald," Peter shouted, "see if we've got 'Golden' by Jill Scott and put it in the player."

Before too long, Jill Scott's voice boomed through a set of speakers that were on either side of the stage. Angelica sauntered over to one of the poles and reached up and caressed it with her right arm. Her body followed, now parallel with the pole, and within seconds Angelica's body began to move like a belly dancer's. So smooth was her rhythm that it was hard not to be mesmerized…to be caught up in the lure of the sensual fantasy that was being played out on the stage.

Her ponytail fell back as Angelica wrapped one leg around the pole and extended the other in the air, her head pointed toward the floor. She swung her body around the pole, performed a sultry move and then brought her body upright, making love to the metal like it was made of human flesh. All of a sudden the music died, and Angelica came out of her trance. She was annoyed that her audition had been interrupted.

"When can you start?" Peter Ward asked, looking back at Gerald and giving him a wink.

Angelica started to hesitate but in the next breath said, "Immediately."

"Be here at six-thirty this evening. You're going on tonight."

Angelica smiled. "Salary?"

"You can make up to five thousand dollars a night—depending upon what kind of night you have."

"I can live with that," Angelica said. "Thank you, and I'll be here at six-thirty."

Peter and Gerald watched Angelica disappear into the dressing room to change.

"She's a pro," Peter whispered. "A revenue goldmine. When word gets out about our find, there won't be a soul left at Club Amazon."

Gerald laughed out loud. "Goldmine!"

Angelica heard them laugh but ignored it. The job was a stepping-stone on the course she was charting for herself. She walked toward the exit, giving an extra jiggle to remind the owners why they hired her.

∞

Overcast skies awaited Angelica when she exited Club Platinum. She walked to the corner to catch a cab, but took a moment to reflect on what to do next. Angelica looked at her watch. It was two-thirty in the afternoon, four hours away from show time. What would she tell Ari? She needed a place to stay, but she didn't want him all in her business. If he'd give her a key to his house, the matter would be resolved. The wheels in her head began to click.

She pulled her cell phone from her purse and dialed. No response. She clicked off, then dialed the number again.

"Hello," said the voice at the other end.

"Ari, this is Angelica."

"Hey, love. Something is going down at the condos. Police cars are lined up out front. Can only talk for a second."

"Okay, well, I got a job!

"Great, Angelica!"

"Problem is I'm working the night shift."

"The night shift? Where at?"

Angelica was in no mood to play twenty questions, and she owed Ari nothing but the rent she would pay him for her temporary shelter.

"Ari, my shift begins at six-thirty, and I need to go to the house and freshen up. Is it possible to get a key to your house?"

There was a moment of silence. "Sweetheart, I'm not in the habit of giving out my key. You seem like good people, but I've known you for less than a week."

"So why did you invite me to your house? Look, I've been straight with you from the beginning. My time is temporary, but I will pay rent until I get on my feet. Right now, I need a means to access my things so I can freshen up."

"All right. Come by your cousin's condo and I'll give you my spare key. You may not be able to get close to the condos because of the cops. If you have any trouble, call me on my cell and we'll work it out. I've got to go."

"Thanks, Ari. I owe you."

The line was dead.

It was easier than she thought. Angelica waved down a cab and headed for the condos. It took less than five minutes to reach the street where Donna lived, but as the cab got near, she could see that up ahead the street was blocked off and there seemed to be a lot of commotion going on.

Angelica dialed Ari's cell phone and asked him to meet her down the street. When he arrived, his face was ashen. Ari handed the key to Angelica and, without a word, he turned and walked away. Angelica looked in her hand and smiled. Ari was having a bad day, but she was on the road to recovery and possible success.

20

M alik sat in the restaurant parking lot, rehearsing what he would say to Jefferson. This was his frat, his boy, yet he felt like he was meeting a complete stranger. He should not have been surprised when he received the call from Jefferson, who asked why he was not at his welcome home party. Now he waited with dread in his heart all because he had fallen in love with his best friend's wife.

The parking lot was filling up. "Avalon, Maxima, Honda, Camry, Altima, Saturn," Malik said out loud, playing a childhood car game. "Mercedes, Margo's Mercedes," Malik said.

He sat up and watched as the driver of the Mercedes pulled into a parking space. A few moments passed before the door to the car opened. There he stood, all six feet of him. Then he noticed the walker. Malik had almost forgotten that Jefferson had been in a wheelchair. He had not visited Jefferson in the last six months. He couldn't do it. Malik could not tell much about the way Jefferson looked from where he stood. This was the moment he regretted. He got out of the car and waited.

Jefferson walked slowly toward Malik until recognition set in. "Malik, that you?" Jefferson asked.

Malik offered a half smile and offered his hand. "Hey man, you look good." Jefferson looked malnourished and tired about the eyes. *Prison food is supposed to be good*, Malik thought.

"It feels like a million dollars." Jefferson paused. "I wish I had listened to you back then, Malik, but the last five years have taught me more than I asked for, and I can say that with all honesty. I never want to see the inside of prison again."

They dropped their hands, and Malik looked at Jefferson.

"I'm glad you're home, buddy. Why don't we go on in? We can catch up in there."

"Lead the way," Jefferson said.

Jefferson followed Malik into the restaurant, and the waitress seated them. Sadness was etched on Malik's face as he watched his friend push the walker in front of him and then maneuver into his seat. Jefferson seemed in full control of his handicap, though, moving about as if he didn't have one at all.

"What's good on this menu?" Jefferson asked Malik.

"Almost everything," Malik responded. They laughed.

"I was sorry to hear about Toni and the baby." Malik tipped his head in acknowledgment. "I know it was tough on you. I hated I missed your wedding."

"Toni was a beautiful woman. Our day was special; our life was special. It still hurts, man, but I've got to move on."

"Well, what's the good word? What's been happening in Fayetteville since I've been gone?"

"Not a whole lot has changed. They're bringing in about twenty thousand troops to Ft. Bragg. It has to do with all these base closures throughout the country."

"This would have been a goldmine for me."

"What are you going to do, Jefferson? Margo is doing well with the real estate, but your business…"

"My business is dissolved," Jefferson began. "I probably will be unable to work in securities again. For sure, it will be hard to get bonded. While I sat in prison, Malik, I thought a lot about what I was going to do when I got out, but I'm not sure what that will be. I do know that I am going to enjoy my family." Jefferson hung his head.

"You know Angelica is out of prison. She's been out almost a month."

Jefferson did not speak. "Humph. That's a memory I'd like to forget. Is she in Fayetteville?"

"I'm not sure where she is. She volunteered to work for me, and after one day on the job, I had to let her go."

"What happened? She came on to you, didn't she?" Jefferson laughed.

"Man, that woman is something else. That's exactly what she did. Started taking her clothes off right in my shop."

"Get out of here, Malik! In your shop? You know she used to be a stripper."

"Yeah, you told me."

"So, are you seeing anyone?" Jefferson asked.

Malik looked at Jefferson with suspicion. He had not expected the question so soon. As he prepared to respond, a waitress approached their table. Grateful for the interruption, Malik quickly gave the waitress his order. Jefferson followed and then stared at Malik.

"So, you're keeping the lady a secret?" Jefferson continued.

"Wha...wha...oh no. I'm not seeing anyone at the moment. It hasn't been a year yet since Toni...died."

"Sorry, didn't mean to bring it up. My last memories of you were of Malik the ladies' man. Always had a woman at your beck and call. I guess Angelica thought she had another chance. How is it that she ended up at your place of business?"

Malik recounted how Angelica showed up at the church and Margo offered Angelica's services and said that they should forgive her.

"So Margo has forgiven Angelica," Jefferson said matter-of-fact. "I don't trust her."

"I don't either," Malik agreed. "Angelica had the nerve to tell Margo that she did not have an affair with you."

Jefferson looked at Malik and then turned away. He sighed and rubbed his chest, as if remembering another moment he cared to forget.

"Look, hopefully she's gone forever," Malik interjected. "Margo has tried unsuccessfully to call Angelica, so it's evident to me that she doesn't want to be bothered. We have not heard from her in over a week or so."

"Thanks, man, for taking care of Margo in my absence."

Malik flinched. "It was nothing. We're best friends, frats. Brothers always take care of family."

"Well, I want you to know that I appreciate it, and I'm sure Margo felt secure, knowing there was someone around she could trust."

"No problem, man."

"It's going to take some time before Margo and I become romantic."

"What do you mean?"

"Frat, she seemed happy to have me home, but also somewhat distant. I couldn't put my finger on it, but it's as if she has something on her mind. She turned away from me in bed."

"I'm sorry, Jefferson. It's not necessary to share the intimate part of your life, if you don't want to."

Jefferson wrapped Malik's fingers with the back of his hand.

"You're like a brother to me, and I feel I can share anything with you. I'll need you to get through this."

"I'm here for you, but maybe you need to talk with Margo about how you're feeling. She's the one who needs to know."

"Has she been seeing anyone?" Jefferson asked.

Malik's eyes widened. "Frat, what would make you ask that question? A few Sundays ago in church, she talked about your possible release. She seemed happy."

"Just a feeling, Malik. Just a feeling."

"You may be reading Margo all wrong. Give her some time. I'm sure that, with you now at home, some of the memories of the trial and even your affair with Linda may have come rushing back. She'll be fine. Excuse me a minute; I'm going to the men's room."

Malik found the men's room and fell against the wall. He walked from one end to the other, peeping to see if anyone else was in there. When Malik realized he was alone, he raised his hands in the air and let out a mini scream to release the pent-up anxiety. All of Jefferson's questions about a new person in his life were getting next to him. Sleep had eluded him, and it had been a while since he had had a decent meal. Malik resisted the urge to admit to him that there was someone else in his life.

Jefferson's sudden confession about his and Margo's sexual relationship made Malik wonder. Malik knew in his heart that Margo felt something for him. It was the way she looked at him when they had been together. They had a carefree friendship before...before the day Ivy called and spoke to Margo. Yes, that was it—the day that Ivy called. But what did Jefferson's confession mean? He had to find out. Malik hit the stall with his fist. He was in love with Margo...smitten, for lack of a better word. There was no way he could turn down the heat in his heart or slow the palpitations that were coming a mile a minute. He had to do something about it, even if it meant being guilty of the same crime Jefferson had committed. Malik shook his head. Somehow, adultery wasn't so dirty when it concerned him.

21

Angelica's day was looking up. In less than twenty-four hours, she had lost a job and then become gainfully employed. There was not much difference between the two, but one appealed to her more than the other and she was no longer at the mercy of Donna Barnes Reardon; she didn't care if she was Hamilton's cousin.

Arriving at Ari's, she used the key he had given her to let herself into the house. It was peaceful here. For the first time, Angelica took a real look around the place. It was warm and homey—had the touch of a woman from long ago. Everything was simple but tasteful. A large crucifix with the figure of Jesus affixed to it hung in one corner of the living room.

Time was ticking. Straight to the shower was where Angelica went. The water rolled over her body—the pulsating water made her come alive, causing her to rehearse the performance she was going to give tonight's patrons. Angelica swung her head to the left, then to the right, twisting her neck as she did. She swiveled her hips from side to side and lifted her arms in the air. It was so natural, as if she had been doing this all her life.

Angelica quickly toweled her body off and looked for something to wear. She hadn't emptied her suitcase, and hopefully she would find something she didn't have to iron. Since there was no clock in the room, Angelica picked up her cell phone to check the time. "A call from Ari." Angelica was too hyped to call him right now. It was now four o'clock, and in two and a half hours she would be performing live on stage again.

Rummaging through her suitcase, Angelica found a nice jean outfit, complete with rhinestones that ran up the sides of her pant legs and studded the pockets of her jacket. She looked at herself in the mirror and decided to let her hair flow freely. Angelica released the ponytail from its band, and her reddish-black mane fell to her shoulders. A few curls would give pizzazz to her limp hair.

The taxi ride to Club Platinum was uneventful. Angelica wanted to call Ari and share the details about her new job. She felt comfortable talking to him because he did not judge. It was at that moment that Angelica remembered Ari was acting a little strange earlier in the day. She would make it her business to talk with him before he left for work in the morning.

Confidence made Angelica walk into the club as if she was the star of the joint. Angelica was met by Gerald Lloyd, who introduced her to Desiree. Desiree was the head stripper, the one who made the schedules and passed out the costumes the dancers wore. It was not hard to sense that Desiree was not feeling her by the scowl on her face and the way she handed Angelica the piece of costume she was to wear. Angelica took the outfit and proceeded to a work station that was pointed out to her. Once there, she ignored the haughty stares the other ladies gave her.

Dressed in a revealing, gold-sequined bikini top and thong, Angelica waited her turn. It was a revolving door as dancer after dancer went on and returned after her twenty-minute set. After an hour and a half, her name was called.

"Angel," Desiree said with a frown in her voice. "You're on."

Angelica walked proudly with a little sway in her hips. The small chatter that could be heard in the room ceased, and Angelica poured it on. Now on stage, the music began to play for her. Angelica nearly skipped to the pole and caressed it like it was her forever lover. Then she heard the announcer.

"Give it up for Angel!"

She heard clapping and, for the first time, Angelica looked at the crowd. The place was filled. Men in business suits, men in casual wear, and men who looked as if they didn't have a nickel in their pockets were there.

Angelica danced her heart out, occasionally jumping on the pole, wrapping her legs around it, and twisting her upper torso until the audience roared. She slid from the pole and performed some Tina Turner moves. When the men covered the edge of the stage with their dollar bills hanging from their hands, Angelica moved toward them. She let them place the money in her G-string first, and the rest was either placed in her hand or in the cup of her bikini top. It was intoxicating, and Angelica continued to deliver as she heard screams for an encore. When she ended her set, whistles and loud clapping met her ears.

"Angel, come back Angel," someone screamed.

"We want Angel," another screamed.

"Angel, please dance for me. I love you."

Angelica was exuberant as she returned to the dressing room. All eyes were on her.

"So, where you from, Angel?" asked a tall, dark girl with distaste in her voice. She could not have been more than nineteen years old, and came to stand in front of Angelica.

Angelica looked at her as if to say, *You need to move out of my way.* "Are you talking to me?" Angelica replied.

The other women moved closer. "It don't look like I'm talking to no one else in the room," the girl said, pointing her finger in Angelica's face.

Angelica gathered her money together and looked at the young girl who dared to get in her face. "It's not important, uh, uh…"

"Kiki."

"Kiki, it's not important who I am or where I come from, and I don't owe you an explanation. But I'm going to satisfy your curiosity." Angelica waved her finger in Kiki's face. "I'm another person trying to earn a paycheck. I don't want any trouble, and there won't be any if you move out of my way."

"Listen here."

"Kiki," Desiree said. "Leave Angel alone. She just got hired on today. She's not bothering you."

"Well, ain't she kinda old to be dancing?" Kiki asked.

"Not by the sound of the crowd out there," Desiree said as she eyed Angelica. "Instead of you running your mouth, you should be getting ready to go on."

The ladies dispersed, and Angelica went to Desiree. "Thank you."

"No problem." Desiree shuffled off and Angelica went to her station to regroup. She had to go on two more times, after which her first night would be over. It would be nice to share her excitement with someone. At that moment, she thought of Margo.

Margo probably hated her for the way she breezed in and then breezed out of her life. It certainly wasn't the way to rekindle a friendship, but it was probably for the best.

Angelica completed her next two sets and breathed a sigh of relief. She looked at her watch. It was one in the morning.

It was getting expensive riding a cab back and forth from Queens to Manhattan, but hopefully it wouldn't be long before she could find a place of her own that was closer to work. Angelica sat back in the cab and closed her eyes. She let the day pass in front of her. *It went well*, she thought. No real complaints about her first day except for Ms. Kiki who needed to be taught a lesson about respect.

Sleep was what she needed, and Angelica was grateful that Ari would be asleep when she arrived at his house. She was going to take a shower and head straight for the bed. Angelica paid the cab driver, skipped up the three steps to the porch and headed inside the house.

The house was dark. Angelica stumbled forward without turning the lights on in order to get to her room. Before she made it to the bedroom doorway, the dining room light was switched on, making Angelica jump and cover her mouth. Ari was standing near the other entrance to the dining room, looking at her with disdain.

"Ari!"

"Angelica. Where have you been? I've called you several times, and you have not called me back."

Angelica wanted to brush Ari off, but something in his tone changed her mind. "What is it, Ari? Sorry about the phone calls, but I was working and had to turn it off."

Ari looked thoughtfully at Angelica. "Something happened at the condo today."

"Yeah, I remember you mentioned something was going on, and…uh, yeah, all the police cars outside."

"Did you stop to wonder why the cops were there?" Ari asked.

"Look, Ari. I'm sorry for not calling. I found a job, and I was trying to make sure I had everything I needed to get started. I know it's not always about me, but today it was."

Ari seemed to appreciate her answer. Then he blurted it out. "Donna was found dead in her apartment."

Angelica was not sure she heard Ari correctly. "Donna who?"

"Donna Barnes Reardon. You were probably the last person to see her."

"Donna? NO!" Angelica's hands flew to her face. "She was alive when I left last night, Ari. You saw us come in. The only thing I did was pack my bags and leave." Angelica found a seat at the dining room table and rested her hand on her head. "No. Why? How?"

"Those are the questions the police are asking. What happened with you and Donna yesterday that you needed to leave in such a hurry?"

Angelica looked up into Ari's eyes. "What are you trying to say…that I did it? I wouldn't hurt a fly."

"You do have a sordid past."

"If I had something to hide, I would not have shared those few tidbits of my life with you. Donna asked me to leave, and I did as she asked."

"I don't know how she died," Ari said absently. "Privileged information. I guess we'll have to wait for the morning news. So, tell me about your new job."

"It's not important. Just a job."

"A job that keeps you out until the wee hours of the morning?"

"I'm going to bed, Ari. I'll see you whenever."

"You've got until the end of the week to find someplace else to live," Ari said and left the room. Angelica watched him disappear—her mouth wide open.

22

Jefferson watched Margo as she went about her day, stuffed in her blue jeans and pink linen shirt. Three days had passed since he arrived home, and he and Margo had yet to make love to each other. Margo had said all the right things, even looked into his eyes when she said she wanted him and their marriage, but each time Jefferson attempted to reach out to her, to hold her, she would pull away. Jefferson had hurt her terribly and he probably didn't deserve this second chance. However, he was grateful to the Almighty for intervening on his behalf, and he was going to do whatever it took to gain Margo's trust so that they could resume their life together.

Margo moved effortlessly through the house, picking up pieces of paper and straightening pillows. Jefferson caught her smile when she looked in his direction, he offering one in return. Something hit him as he watched the graceful movement of Margo's body, still lean and hourglass perfect after four kids and a thirty-year marriage. He recalled Malik's demeanor when they were at lunch and he talked about Margo in an affectionate way—it ate at him.

"Why don't you stop and sit next to me for a while?" Jefferson asked sweetly. "You've been at it all morning."

"I guess I'm at a point where I can stop. I want to get this done before I have to show a house this afternoon."

Jefferson patted the place on the couch next to him. "Take a break, Margo. The house looks nice. Whatever you don't get done, I'll take care of it."

Margo walked slowly to the couch and sat down. She turned sideways until her thigh was completely on the couch, bending her knee and sitting on her lower leg. Jefferson placed his arm along the back of the couch, resisting the urge to embrace his wife.

"What is it, Margo? What is it you're afraid of?"

"Afraid of? What do you mean?"

"You seemed to look forward to my coming home, but now that I'm here, you are as far away from me as we were when I was in prison."

Margo reached and tugged at the edge of Jefferson's sweater, knotting the end of a thread that was threatening to unravel. She moved her hand from the sweater to the back of his hand, brushing it with her own and finally squeezing his fingers tight. Jefferson looked deep into Margo's eyes, searching for the answer he sought and praying that rejection wasn't on the way.

"It's going to take some time. Five years has taken a toll on me, but I waited because I wanted to."

"Do you love me, Margo?"

She continued to hold his fingers and hesitated before answering. "Yes," came the lone word.

Jefferson swallowed hard. "I'll take whatever you can give me now."

"Just give me time," Margo repeated. "I thought it would be easy…that we could go on with our lives, pick up where we left off. Not so."

"I had lunch with Malik yesterday," Jefferson said.

Margo flinched, and Jefferson noticed. "How did you get there?" Margo asked.

"I drove the Mercedes while you were out showing houses. My legs are getting better all the time."

Margo withdrew her hand. "That's good, Jefferson. God is so good."

"Malik told me that Angelica is out of prison. He said that you forgave her."

"I did, but something is not right with that woman. I want to trust her, but she gives me every reason not to. I was willing to help her get a job and be her friend again, but she up and disappeared to God knows where without even a thank you."

"Angelica is not worth wasting your time on."

"Why do you say that?" Margo searched Jefferson's eyes. "She seemed resourceful when things weren't…"

"No, Margo. Let's not rehash this. I'm sorry I brought Angelica into our conversation. She is no longer part of our lives, and I want it to stay that way."

Margo reached over and kissed Jefferson on the lips. The kiss lingered longer than she had planned, but it seemed to please Jefferson.

"I hope I can expect to receive more of those kisses." Jefferson began to tremble. "Your lips felt good, Margo, and if you let me, I'd like to make love to you."

"I can't do it right now, Jefferson." Margo jumped up from her seat. She turned and looked back at Jefferson sitting on the couch, a boyish innocence radiating from him. "I want to, but not now."

"Will you hold me?" Jefferson begged. "I need you, Margo. I need you."

Margo looked at him. He wasn't the strong tower she was used to. Jefferson seemed weak, almost timid, and she hated a begging man, but he was her husband and she did love him.

Margo sat back down on the couch and wrapped her arms around Jefferson. She held him to her bosom and gave him a big hug. Holding Jefferson made her think about Malik. *What is this sudden feeling I'm having for him? My covenant is with Jefferson and God.*

But Margo felt like King David in the Bible who coveted the wife of one of his finest soldiers, after which he put the soldier on the front line of battle to be killed. But Jefferson put himself on the front line of battle with no thought that Central Prison would be his address. His absence made Margo long for another man, although she had never realized it. She hugged Jefferson tight, even though it was Malik who claimed her thoughts.

23

Angelica was unable to sleep. Images of Donna Barnes Reardon invaded her dreams. Donna's hand with its twisted pointer finger was stretched to the limit, narrowly missing Angelica's nose by a centimeter. *Get out! Get out!* Angelica heard Donna say. *Get out, you miserable freeloader.*

Angelica tossed and turned all through the night. Her sheets were pulled from the mattress as if a savage beast had been in the room. She rolled to one side and then the other. Unable to will herself to sleep, she sat up in the bed and waited for her eyes to focus.

Birds chirped outside her window, but the noise was irritating. Angelica ran to the window to try and scare them away.

Slowly, night gave way to day. Angelica lay down on the crumpled up sheets, balling up her pillow to form what looked like a bird's nest, and laid her head on it. Before she knew it, she was fast asleep.

She bolted upright, not sure where time had gone. The sun was bright as it forced its way into her bedroom. She got up and tiptoed, listening for signs of life. Hearing none, she ventured outside the room on her tippy toes, her back hunched over and her eyes darting in different directions like a predator hunting its prey. When she was sure that she was alone, she let her shoulders relax and then air escaped through her lips.

Quiet was sometimes a lonely feeling, but this morning it was a welcome relief. Ari was gone to work, and she didn't have to face his accusing stares and unspoken accusations, although she had nothing to worry about.

Sunlight flooded the dining room. As Angelica started to cross the length of it, there it was in bold black letters, DONNA BARNES REARDON, PHOTOGRAPHER TO THE STARS, FOUND DEAD IN HER MANHATTAN APARTMENT, on the front page of the *New York Times*. Angelica gasped and reached for a corner of the table and held onto it, looking at the newspaper once more, bringing herself face to face with a blaring press photo of Donna. It was real because the papers didn't lie about the demise of the city's elite— or at least Donna thought she was. Angelica couldn't move and continued to brace herself on the table as Ari's conversation in the wee hours of the morning came rushing back to her.

Finally able to move, Angelica sat down in one of the dining room chairs. Donna was dead, but how did she die? Angelica inched her hand to where the paper lay, hesitating a moment before picking it up. At first she couldn't see anything for the blaring headline, but right there in paragraph one was the answer, stark and to the point.

Manhattan's own Queen of Photography was found murdered yesterday in her Manhattan apartment. A close friend, who asked to remain anonymous, found her in her studio with her neck slashed and called the police immediately.

Angelica trembled and raised her hand to her throat as she read the words again, *with her neck slashed*. She wondered which one of Donna's three companions found her: Jazz, Coco or Madeline? The paper shook violently in Angelica's hand until she finally set it on the table, unable to read anymore. But her curiosity got the better of her, and she grabbed the paper and forced herself to read more.

There was an apparent struggle between the victim and her assailant. Camera equipment was strewn throughout the room, and one of Ms. Reardon's award-winning photos that hung in her studio was slashed. This appeared to be the work of a cold-blooded killer.

The doorman, Ari Parrias, said that Ms. Reardon entertained lots of guests. They came and they went. He did recognize a female friend of Ms. Reardon who entered the apartment at approximately four in the afternoon.

Angelica put the paper down. "Thank you, Ari, for not mentioning my name." The last time she spoke with him, he was visibly upset and throwing accusations her way. *Why would she want to hurt Donna? Why would anyone else want to hurt her?*

∞

The cab drove up and she was on her way to her second night on the job. Angelica enjoyed the applause of the crowd—and the men that threw tens and twenties her way. There was an air of freedom in dancing before the gawking men and making the pole a slave to her gyrating body.

The cab driver stared at her in his rear view-mirror. Angelica hurled him a makeshift kiss and turned her head and watched Queens roll by. New York was not as intoxicating as she once felt. She had not even been in the city long enough to give it a failing grade, but something about it made her uncomfortable, like she didn't belong.

The cab finally arrived at the club, and Angelica paid her fare and walked in. Tonight she wore a black, form-fitting dress that hit four inches above the knee and showed enough cleavage to get someone's interest. A one-inch, patent-leather belt circled her waist.

A look of surprise enveloped Angelica's face. The music was jumping, and it was not even time to start the show. She took a peek beyond the curtain that led into the main entrance of the club where all the entertainment was held, and a couple dozen men were sitting at round tables engaged in heavy talk. A rather well-built man offered a toast. "Aw, a celebration," Angelica said to no one, backed away from the curtain and headed toward the dressing room.

As Angelica entered the room, the reception was lukewarm. "Hey, Angel," said several of the girls as Angelica walked toward her locker.

"Hey, yourself," Angelica said, throwing an appreciative smile their way. These girls didn't judge, at least not openly, and it kept things in perspective because Angelica was only there to make a paycheck like the rest of them.

"We've got ourselves a nice crowd tonight, Angel," Desiree said. "The money is going to be goooooooood. And the way I heard you were working your thang last night, you might have a down payment on a nice automobile when you're through."

Angelica laughed and patted Desiree on the arm. "I'm going to put it on them, girlfriend."

The others turned to look at Angelica and Desiree as they filled the room with laughter.

"Can't be that funny," Kiki said, rolling her eyes.

"It was to us," Angelica said, looking back at Desiree, who started laughing again and slapped Angelica five.

"Get this, you too old to suck a momma's tit, wanna-be stripper.

Those men," Kiki pointed toward the club, "want a fine, young tenderoni such as myself. Day-old bread won't do. You might as well leave now because the only thing you'll be counting tonight is change." Kiki dropped a penny on the floor for emphasis.

There was no breathing or moving in the room. The air was thick, and the music that played in the other room seemed louder than ever. Angelica put her hands on her hips and twisted her lips into a scowl.

"Normally, I wouldn't stoop this low to an uneducated, brainless bitch like you. You wished you knew what I know. I can turn tables around your sorry ass, and I've made men faint at the sound of my name. I'm the last of the real diva pole queens. Sweetie, I bet you've never picked up five Gs from one person on a single dance. You need to watch me work."

Kiki sneered at her, but Angelica had turned and walked away. Kiki was livid.

"What are you heifers looking at?" Kiki shouted at the group. The others dismissed Kiki with a swing of their hands. She walked off in a huff, eyeing Angel with a carnivorous stare. "We'll see about that," Kiki said under her breath.

"Show time in thirty minutes," Desiree shouted. "Tonight's line-up: Michelle, Foxy, Toya, Lovey, Misty, Arnell, Kiki, and Angel."

"Oh, no!" Kiki shouted. "I'm not going in front of the old bag."

"'Fraid I'll clean up what you couldn't get?" Angelica said.

"I ain't afraid of an ole goat like you," Kiki roared back. "I'm not going on before a has-been. You have heard of saving the best for last." Kiki pointed her finger at Angelica.

"You stupid, simple-minded, little bitch. You can go last because no one is going to be interested in a newborn infant, especially after I give them what they came for. Savor the flavor because you'll be the one counting the change tonight, honey. Not another word from you."

Kiki tried to speak but Angelica threw her hand up and everyone else ignored her.

Michelle, Foxy, Toya, Lovey, Misty, and Arnell had completed their sets and were gleaming with sweat and dollar bills.

"There's enough Benjamins to go around. This crowd is in the giving mood," Misty said.

That was great, Angelica thought. She suddenly remembered Ari's words about being out of his house by the end of the week. It frightened her, but payday was around the corner.

"Angel, you're on," Desiree called out. "Shake what your momma gave you, girl."

"I'm already shaking it, Desi," Angelica said. They laughed.

Angelica felt the energy. She looked out into the crowd, and the room was filled to capacity—men in business suits, casual players in polo shirts, and men off the street looking for a good time and a couple of beers. They came in a variety of colors and ethnicities—white, black, Hispanic, Italian, Puerto Rican, you name it. They were there to have a good time and fantasize about how hot it would be to roll with the beautiful women who danced on stage.

A white, felt cowboy hat sat on Angelica's head. She wore an off-white midriff bolero and an ultra-short matching skirt that consisted of one-inch strips that were attached at the waist. Underneath the cowboy costume, rhinestones trimmed Angelica's skimpy, shimmery gold top that circled the outermost parts of her breasts, while a G-string wrapped her bottom like gold ribbon on a Christmas package. Her four-inch, gold pointed-toe stilettos made her feel like the queen diva she knew she was.

As the music played, Angelica sashayed to the center of the stage, enunciating her hips as she did so, her body glistening under the glare of the stage lights. Whistles from the men teased her on, and she made up her mind that she was going to give them the thrill of their lives.

The intro finished playing, and Angelica reached for the pole as the drummer's cymbal crashed. The beat was sultry and pulsating, and Angelica's hips made quick jabs in and out, eventually taking the pole between her legs and sliding down the length of it. Her body gyrated until she was on the floor, and then pulling up swiftly, she let go of the pole and rubbed her hands seductively against the length of her body. At the urging of the crowd, Angelica made seductive movements with her body and dropped her shoulders back, letting the bolero slide off her shoulders and down her arms. In one swift move, she snatched at the side of her skirt that was held together with Velcro. She pulled it from her body and threw it out into the crowd. She turned and looked at the pole, bending her body at the waist, shaking her heart-shaped buttocks in the air. The applause and the roar of the crowd pushed Angelica to the edge.

Standing upright, Angelica's body rippled and screamed at the crowd that begged her to do more or take it all off. Angelica sensually licked her lips and wiggled her tongue, then jumped on the pole midway, extending one leg upward with the other wrapped around it. She brought one arm out to the side and spun around the pole, finally pulling herself upright. She danced with the pole like it was her lover, making grown men howl for more.

Finally releasing the pole, Angelica switched her way to center stage and let her body rip.

"Take it off, Angel," someone screamed. "Take it off."

"I love you, Angel," said another.

"Shake it, baby. Shake it for meeeeeee!"

Angelica moved closer to the edge of the stage, her body still gyrating in the faces of her adoring fans. Money seemed to fall from the sky as bills in all denominations were either placed in her G-string or dropped to the floor. Then, in one swift move, Angelica removed her top and mayhem broke loose.

Men scrambled over each other, trying to get up on the stage to touch the golden-bronze goddess. Dollar bills continued to rain as Angelica continued to dance. Alarm showed on Angelica's face as the crowd continued to advance, and she looked at Gerald Lloyd to see if it was time to cut it off. Getting no sign from Gerald, Angelica looked back into the crowd and saw the money that was being flung her way. She needed a place to live and she only had three days left at Ari's. This was the payday that might make it happen, so all thoughts of abandoning her out of control admirers were set aside. Angelica moved to the edge and stooped down to scoop up the paper bills. She stopped short when five crisp one-hundred-dollar bills were placed under her chin.

"You're beautiful. How about a private dance?"

The voice was familiar and so was the face, although it had been a long time since she had seen or heard from him. Angelica tried to cover her breasts with the handful of paper money she held in one hand, but the five one-hundred-dollar bills distracted her from her sudden embarrassment.

"Robert Santiago," Angelica said slowly.

"Oh my angel, you remembered. I'm flattered. So it's Angel now?"

"It's my stage name."

"Dinner afterward? I would love to catch up for old time's sake."

"I'm not sure it would be a good idea."

"I'll make it worth your while." Santiago placed the money in her hand. "I'll be waiting."

Angelica stared after Santiago as he disappeared into the crowd. She picked up the few bills that remained on the floor and blew the crowd a kiss. The set was complete, and the crowd was calling Angel's name.

Angelica nearly ran to the dressing room, passing a smirking Kiki. Flustered, she placed her night's take on the table and caught her breath, leaning her head on her open palms with elbows planted squarely on the table. She jumped when she felt cold hands on her back.

"Girl, you rocked the house," Desiree said. "They're still screaming your name. Kiki went out there and they were shouting, '*We want Angel. We want Angel.*'"

Angelica turned to face Desiree.

"Are you all right, Angel?"

"Yeah, Desi, I'm fine. I just saw a ghost."

"What do you mean you saw a ghost?"

"Someone from my past that I've tried to forget." Angelica pulled the five one-hundred-dollar bills out from the pile of crumpled bills.

"Damn, that's a big tip. Put that out of sight," Desiree whispered. "Don't let anyone know you have it. You want to talk?"

"Not right now, Desi. Maybe later."

"I'm here for you, girl, but you know you've got to go back out there. They are emptying their pockets for you."

"Yeah, I know," Angelica said half-heartedly. "I delivered, and they paid. I was on a high, you know. Wanted to show that simple-minded Kiki how a real pole dancer did it. Never expected to see him again."

"I can give you a ride home tonight, if you like," Desiree offered. "If it will make you feel better."

"I appreciate it, Desiree, but I'll take a cab. Don't want you to have to go way out of your way. I'll be all right." Angelica paused. "Thanks for being a friend."

"Girl, you're all right in my book," Desiree said. She patted Angelica's back. "I knew you were special the moment I first laid eyes on you."

A look of surprise covered Angelica's face. She looked up at Desiree and smiled. They both turned toward the commotion at the entrance to the dressing room.

Kiki was arguing with Gerald Lloyd. Her hands were flying in the air and her mouth was going a mile a minute. Gerald was up in her face, and his fingers were swishing back and forth like windshield wipers. Kiki took her hands and pushed him in the chest, and, then walked in Angelica's direction, Gerald walking right behind her.

Kiki threw her hands in the air. "You owe me, bitch. You went out there and stole my money. I've got a baby who needs milk and Pampers, and your old ass is in here cuz you ain't got nothing else to do."

"Ignore Kiki, Angel," Gerald Lloyd said. "She's having a bad day."

"I don't need you to talk for me," Kiki screamed. "She's gonna pay for this!"

"It's all right, Mr. Lloyd. I can handle this." As Angelica stood and stared at Kiki, Gerald Lloyd backed away. "Poor, poor, Kiki. Didn't make enough money to buy her baby some milk?"

Kiki raised her hand.

"I wouldn't do that if I were you," Angelica said, throwing her hand up to block Kiki's hand. "Next time, you'll be careful what you ask for. Last is what you wanted, and last is what you got.

You have no one to blame but yourself. I told you before you got in my face that you were no match for me. You're cocky, ignorant with mush for brains, and if you had only listened to the advice this old ass gave you, you would have fared much better.

"I believe there's hope for you Kiki, but before you go around attacking people because of your inexperience and insecurities, use your head for something other than a coat rack. You'll be better off."

"I'll sue you first. Those men out there were my customers."

Angelica peeled off a twenty-dollar bill and pushed it into Kiki's hand. "Get your baby some milk and Pampers."

Kiki stared at Angelica with tears welling up in her eyes. She slapped the money away, walked to the restroom and slammed the door.

24

Tonight's payday made Angelica a very happy woman. Not only would she be able to afford first and last month's rent, she could also buy a whole lot of other things. Her five hundred-dollar tip was tucked deep in the crevice of her bosom, and her employers at Club Platinum would be none the wiser.

She called for a taxi and chit-chatted a moment with some of the other girls who had taken a liking to her. They begged for Angelica's secret because a payday like hers meant freedom for them...freedom to make the kind of choices they wanted—where to live, what stores to shop in, and even the choice of a higher education, if they wanted it. They listened intently to Angelica's colorful monologue on how to please a man with your body without being touched. Finally, Angelica waved goodbye and headed for the door.

Upon opening the door, cold air rushed into Angelica's face. It was three-thirty in the morning, but she felt alive. Facing Ari wouldn't be a chore this morning because she could leave his house tomorrow if she chose to do so.

A set of headlights crawled down the street but, to Angelica's disappointment, it wasn't the cab. The black car pulled to the curb, and the passenger door flew open. Out stepped Robert Santiago, his gold diamond ring shining under the moonlight.

"Thought I forgot, didn't you?"

"Well, I hadn't thought about it since we first spoke," Angelica replied.

Santiago laughed. "I bet you didn't forget the thousand-dollar tip I left you. If I check with the owners, I can almost guarantee that you didn't turn it in. See, I know you, Angelica. You lust for money like most men lust for women."

Angelica stood on the curb, unable to find a word to say. Santiago was amused but not for long. "Come on, let's hop in the car. I don't like long drawn out conversations standing outside in the cold when I have a warm comfortable place to do that sort of thing.

"I really ought to go home. I have a lot to do tomorrow."

"Like what?"

Angelica stared at Santiago. She had been free of him for the last five years, even if she was in a prison cell, and she wasn't about to let one evening send her back into his clutches if she could help it.

"I'm sorry, Angelica. What you have to do is none of my business. I want to take you for breakfast and some small talk."

"I'm sure there aren't any places open at this time that serve breakfast."

"You're in New York City. Nothing ever closes."

Santiago guided Angelica by the arm and led her to the car. "By the way," Santiago said, "I like Angelica much better than Angel. Angelica has a ring that pulsates down my spine."

A sigh slipped through Angelica's lips. She couldn't believe that she was allowing Santiago to manipulate her. No, she wasn't putting up a fight because she knew the power of his reach. Angelica had seen Santiago in action. Maybe breakfast was all he really wanted, and then she could be on her way to making her own success, whatever it was, all by herself. She slipped into the car, with Santiago right behind her.

The car was spacious. A smoked-glass partition separated the back from the driver, and a well-stocked mini-bar faced the couple where they sat.

"How about some champagne?" Santiago asked.

"All right," Angelica whispered.

"You were working it tonight. But why, may I ask…a strip club?"

"If you really want to know, before I became Hamilton Barnes' wife years ago, I used to be a stripper. In fact, that's where we met."

Santiago passed Angelica the drink and cocked his head to get a better look at her. "You certainly haven't lost your touch."

"Some things you never forget."

"Truer words were never spoken. You know, Angelica, I adored you once. I know that it wasn't a match made in heaven, but you were special to me. My princess. Remember?"

Angelica swallowed hard. She had no desire to recount the past, especially the part where she betrayed him. "Yes, I remember."

"You would do anything for me then. Manipulation was your game, and you did it well. I hated that you ran out on me like you did. Don't worry, you'll have an opportunity to redeem yourself."

"Redeem myself?"

"No need to worry about that now. Enjoy the ride. We'll be at our destination in about twenty minutes. We'll have a nice meal, small chit chat, and then I'll take you home."

"Whatever. I'm here now."

Santiago placed his arm behind Angelica and watched the New York night roll by. They drove in silence. A long expanse of bridge lay before them, and when they had crossed over, Long Island lay before them like a mystical city under the stars.

Santiago pulled his arm to the front and tapped on the glass partition. He motioned to the right and the driver pulled in front of a storefront building. The area surrounding it was all but empty, however, and Santiago smiled and turned to Angelica. "This is it, El Conuco—the best Honduran food outside of The Republic."

Angelica looked nervously about her, got out of the car and followed Santiago into the small but clean family-owned restaurant. A wide smile radiated on the faces of the old couple inside. They were of Latin decent and seemed very familiar to Santiago.

"Angelica, this is *mi tio*, Jorge, and *mi tia*, Maria. This is my uncle and aunt," Santiago said, addressing the frown on Angelica's face. "They are the first persons I stayed with when I came to the United States from Honduras. Nothing like family."

Santiago uttered a barrage of words in Spanish to Maria, and before anyone could count to three, a skillet and pots were hitting the stove.

"In another few hours, they would have been up to start the day," Santiago said. "Uncle Jorge and Aunt Maria have owned this little restaurant for almost thirty years. Life has been good to them, and they love it when I come around, give them a few dollars, and bring some big spenders. They have been my only family since the day my mother and father were killed in Honduras. I owe them so much more than I've given them."

"They seem to be very nice people," Angelica said. "To fix you breakfast in the middle of the night…"

"They would do anything for me. Now, let's talk about you. What are you doing in New York?"

Angelica cringed as she suddenly thought about Donna lying in some morgue. At some point and time, she was going to have to make contact with someone about Donna's death. Whom, she did not know. The last thing she wanted to do was share any of it with Santiago. She fidgeted in her seat, and tried to think of something to say.

"I wanted to start a fresh life far away from North Carolina," Angelica said softly. "Not much in N-C. I figured I would have a better chance in great big New York."

"So your fresh start is stripping at a nightclub for a bunch of lust-filled men?"

Angelica looked directly at Santiago. She sensed he was fishing for something but could not put her finger on it. Why was he so interested in what she was doing with her life?

"I needed some quick money to get me started."

"I thought you owned property in North Carolina or something."

"My brother, Edward, sold my home and used some of the money for my trial. The rest…he is overseeing. He doles it out to me when I need it." She wasn't about to tell Santiago about leaving her condo she recently bought in Fayetteville.

"It's your damn money, isn't it?"

"Oh, I'm sure I can get some anytime I need it, but coming to New York was a sudden move for me, and I didn't have time to consult my brother about it."

"So you came to New York without a real plan. Seems rather odd to me."

"Well, I had actually been asked to model for a magazine, but I found out that I really wasn't cut out for the business. Too demanding."

"Modeling would have been much more respectable than what you're doing."

Angelica was becoming irritated at Santiago's line of questioning. Again, why should he care? It was her life, not his. She only consented to go to breakfast with him, not become part of his life.

"Why does it matter to you what I'm doing?" Angelica asked.

"Curious. There's so much more to you, Angelica. It doesn't seem to be your style."

"Do we really ever get to know everything about someone—the real truth?"

"So, what should I know about Ms. Angelica Barnes that I don't know?"

"You probably already know all there is to know about me."

A pained look crossed Santiago's face. It frightened Angelica, but she refused to let him see it. He placed his chin on his hand and continued to look at her as if he had disappeared into her soul. Angelica could feel his footsteps on her heart, searching and looking for the thing that made her tick. The footsteps were so hard that she could feel her blood running from them.

She needed to get far away from his quiet probing because she had no idea what was going through his mind. The demons of the past were starting to haunt her, and his words came flooding back to her, *You'll have an opportunity to redeem yourself.*

Santiago was getting ready to say something when Aunt Maria shoved two steaming plates in front of them full of scrambled eggs, sausages with grilled onions and peppers, hash browns and hot biscuits.

"That's breakfast," Santiago finally said after a period of silence.

"Way too much for me at this time of morning," Angelica said. "Gracias," she said to Aunt Maria whose wide smile acknowledged her thanks.

"You can take home what you don't eat and have it in the morning." Santiago rattled off more Spanish to Jorge and Maria. They rattled something back, nodded their heads and exited the room. For the first time in a while, Santiago smiled at Angelica.

They finished their meal with so many unanswered questions still lingering in the air.

"I'll take you home, now," Santiago said. "I enjoyed our short time together."

Although Santiago was a perfect gentleman, Angelica still questioned his motive. She wanted to believe that his seeing her at the club was a shock to his system, and he wanted to commune with an old friend. She may never know what he was thinking, but she hoped that their repast satisfied any curiosities he had about her.

The driver was waiting for them outside. They got in the car. She really did not want Santiago to know where she lived, but she had little or no choice.

"So, you live alone?" Santiago asked.

"No," Angelica was quick to say. "I'm staying with a friend temporarily. I hope to have a place of my own soon."

"Why not move in with me? I have a beautiful place outside of the city. A beautiful woman like yourself would certainly add a certain amount of elegance to the place."

Angelica's lips remained sealed. She looked straight ahead as a bad feeling began to mushroom. Santiago's world was not her world. She did not belong. Anonymity was what she truly wanted, but exposure is what brought him to her. This is what he meant about redeeming herself. No, she couldn't live with him.

"Think about it," Santiago said. "You don't have to give me an answer right away." Santiago looked straight ahead. "I know all about you—your whereabouts, what you've been up to, and I know you have nowhere else to go."

The whites of Angelica's eyes bulged from their sockets. Her chest heaved in and out as she digested what Santiago said. She turned her head to stare at him, unable to comprehend the madness that was erupting before her. Santiago stared back.

Angelica's frown turned to anger. "Have you known all along that I was here in New York? What is this, Santiago? I don't have time for games."

"Neither do I. You owe me, Angelica. I've waited five long years for you to repay your debt, and you can start by giving me the five one-hundred-dollar bills I gave you. You won't be needing them, because somehow I already know that your decision to move in with me will be a yes, and if so, you won't need to take off your clothes to a room full of drunk, lecherous men for your survival."

"I hate you."

"You'll love me more in the morning."

The rest of the ride was in silence until they neared the street where Ari lived. It was six in the morning, and day was breaking. As they started to turn down Ari's block, Santiago spotted a police car at the end of the street, sitting at the stoplight. Perspiration formed on Santiago's forehead, although it was cool in the car. He instructed the driver to pull to the curb and told Angelica to get out. He would be in touch with her later.

Angelica stiffened. Why were the cops in this neighborhood at this time of morning? She wondered if they were casing Ari's place and compiling information on her because of Donna's death? She shuddered and exited the car, glad to be away from Santiago. Her knees began to wobble and her hands started to shake. Angelica's feet felt like lead—too heavy to lift and climb the few stairs to the porch. She managed the climb and turned her head in time to see the police move on as the light changed. And then from out of the shadows, the lone black car with Santiago in it pulled away from the curb, turned the corner, and drove out of sight.

25

Several days had passed since Malik had had lunch with Jefferson. Malik couldn't erase the picture of the broken-down man who had sat before him. This was the man he held in high esteem, a man he would've walked, ran, swam, and pole-vaulted to the ends of the earth for. He and Jefferson were fraternity brothers, Omega Psi Phi, bound together like a ball and chain, trying to emulate the successes of their brothers William "Bill" Cosby, Reverend Jesse Jackson, the late astronaut Ronald McNair, and Michael Jordan.

Something else had Malik bound. It was not the fraternity brother he held in high esteem. Friendship had its place, but there was something, someone more demanding of his time, thoughts, and dreams.

Had his life come to this, moping around like a lovesick puppy? Malik had not been able to eat or sleep because his head was rocked with daydreams of Margo Myles, his fraternity brother's wife. It frustrated him that he allowed so much time to pass while he cultivated an unsuspecting Margo for a future that had no guarantees, and when the moment came to release his pent-up feelings to her, she reacted like he was an unwanted stalker. In his soul, Malik felt Margo's presence, and he was going to find a way to reel her in because she was a catch worthy of his time.

But the bars of the cell that were supposed to house Jefferson

Myles at Raleigh's Central Prison for another fifteen years were suddenly opened, and his dutiful wife Margo, who stood by his side for his eventual return, now welcomed him home with open arms. Jefferson reminded Malik of the story in the Bible of Daniel in the lion's den and the three Hebrew boys, Shadrack, Meschack and Abindigo, who were thrown in a fiery furnace yet God delivered each one. For sure, Jefferson had nine lives; there could be no other answer.

The bell on the front door jingled—a fixture Malik had mounted on the door at Margo's suggestion. He pulled himself out of his daydream to face the customer that dared to interrupt his thoughts.

His mouth fell as he watched the beautiful woman in the red linen jacket, white linen slacks and white silk blouse walk through the door. Malik scrambled to his feet and tripped on a cord that he hadn't taken care to secure to the floor.

"Margo, what are you doing here? Is Jefferson with you?" Malik punctuated his words.

"No, I'm alone. I had to show a house this afternoon, and since I was in the neighborhood, I thought I'd drop by to see how you were doing."

"I'm much better, now that you're here," Malik said with a smile that stretched the width of his face.

"Look, Malik, I don't want to beat around the bush." Malik's smile began to fade. "My husband is home now, and I really want to make it work. I don't know how since…since I can't stop thinking about what you said the last time we were together…"

"Can you be feeling what I'm feeling, Margo? I won't apologize for the way I feel about you. I've been in love with you for some time now. I was afraid to say it any earlier than I did for fear you would react the way you did."

"Malik, I don't know what's going on inside of me. I want to make love to my husband, but I can't because you keep getting in the way. I hold Jefferson, but I'm thinking about you."

Malik stood in front of Margo and looked into her eyes. "Oh, Margo, I've prayed for this day. God, I know it's wrong, but I can't deny how I feel about you. And I do want you."

"Maybe you're lonely because of Toni. We've both been without our loved ones, Malik. We're probably reacting to pent-up needs that we've been deprived of for so long."

"Margo, I loved you before Toni and I were married."

"Malik! I know you loved Toni. You told me so not more than a week ago."

"I did love her, Margo, because you were forbidden to me. I was a good husband to Toni, and she was a good wife. I miss her dearly. But there is still you."

Margo sighed and tried to move away from Malik. He grabbed Margo and wrapped his arms around her. With little effort, Malik kissed Margo passionately on the lips. And to his surprise, she responded, withholding nothing. Their tongues mated greedily, neither letting the other go. Malik held Margo tight, not wanting the moment to come to an end, but it did with Margo gasping for breath and then wiping her mouth before releasing a smile.

"I've got to see you again," Malik said to Margo, unable to contain his good feeling.

"I don't know…I'm not sure, Malik. God's going to punish me for this."

"Don't back away, now. I've waited a long time for this, and I'll wait as long as it takes—a week, two weeks, so long as I can touch your lips again."

"It's wrong, Malik, but I do feel something for you. I better go. I told Jefferson I would be back in a few hours."

Malik smiled. "Margo, I love you."

Margo smiled back and turned and left the way she had come. Malik watched the door close behind her, and this time when he slapped the wall, there was hope in his heart because the woman he loved was beginning to feel the same way.

26

Angelica quietly tiptoed into the house. She hurriedly crossed the living room and then the dining room like a thief. It was still dark in the house and Ari would be stirring at any minute.

The grandfather clock began to chime, startling Angelica. She fell against the wall, recovered and prepared to move on. On the fifth chime, Ari, fully dressed, appeared in the doorway to the dining room and jumped when he saw Angelica's figure pass in front of him.

"Halt," Ari said.

Angelica stopped in her tracks. She was disappointed that she and Ari's relationship had faltered before it got started. "You talking to me?" She slowly turned and faced Ari. *God, he was so good-looking, even in the dark.*

"What are you up to, Angelica? Why are you creeping in here like you've stolen something?"

"Didn't want to disturb you."

"I gave you a place to stay because I cared. You're beautiful. I like beautiful women, but I don't like to be taken advantage of. I've tried to help you, but I'm not sure what went wrong."

Angelica eased into a seat. "Ari, sit down. You're a good man and you've been more than kind to me. I appreciate all that you've done, and for that I'll be forever grateful."

Ari sat down. "What's up with you, then? What happened between you and Donna? What kind of work are you doing that keeps you out until six in the morning?"

"One question at a time. I'll answer them all since it doesn't look like I'll be getting any sleep."

"I need some explanation, Angelica," Ari said. "It pisses me off when I don't know what's going on right under my nose."

Angelica touched Ari's arm lightly. "You'll be late for work."

"I can get someone to work in my place. We need to talk."

"Okay," Angelica said, sitting back in her seat.

"Where have you been all night?"

"Ari, I'm…I'm working…I'm a stripper. I work at a club in Manhattan. Of course, the hours are late, but the money is good… very good."

Ari's silence made Angelica uncomfortable. She lowered her eyes and continued.

"I needed to make some fast money so that I could get out on my own. I have some money, but I needed the security of a job. Not that I'm proud of it, but I used to be a stripper years ago, and I guess I haven't lost my touch." Angelica smiled. "I don't want to be a burden on you, Ari, and I believe I have enough money so that I can be out of your hair sooner rather than later."

His voice was serious. "You don't have to go," Ari said.

"That's not what you told me yesterday."

"I've changed my mind. What about Donna?"

"What about Donna?" Angelica asked.

"What happened between the two of you?"

"Donna was angry because I refused to do the photo shoot she set up. All those lesbians; I was not about to compromise myself in some rag magazine like that. I'm sure Donna thought I was ungrateful since she was doing me a favor, but I had visions of walking a top-model runway—not posing in compromising positions. She told me to get out of her house, and I did. Donna nearly slammed the door on my behind when I walked out to meet you."

"I believe you, Angelica. I'm surprised the police haven't questioned you yet. I'm sure it won't be long, now, before they show up."

"There was a cruiser sitting at the light when I got home. Scared the crap out of me. Have you heard anything else, Ari?"

"No, only what has been printed in the papers. To date, they have no motive, no murder weapon, and are still talking to acquaintances. The arts community is baffled by Donna's death."

"It's a shame. I can't fathom who would want Donna killed, but I sure as hell didn't do it. I couldn't hurt a flea."

"Rest assured, the police will be coming around soon to ask questions."

"You seem so sure about that Ari."

"They questioned me yesterday. I told them you had been staying with Donna right before her death."

Angelica's face froze in time. It looked as if she stopped breathing. She slowly rose from her seat and wrapped her arms around her chest and began walking in circles. Then, she threw her hands up. "You told them about me, Ari? What did you say?"

"As a doorman, I see a lot of people come and go. They asked me questions…pointed questions, that I had to answer. We have surveillance cameras on the premises, and all the cops had to do was watch them to know if I was telling the truth or not. On the day of Donna's death, you both walked into the building together."

Angelica exhaled and fell back into the chair.

"If you didn't do anything," Ari said, "you won't have anything to worry about."

"I didn't kill Donna, Ari. You've got to believe that. I didn't have time to do all the things the paper said happened."

"Plus, you were as cool as a cucumber. I know you didn't do it, but who did? Do you want me to stay around today, in case the cops show up?"

"Would you, Ari? I don't mean to sound desperate, but I'd feel better if you did."

"Look, why don't I fix us some breakfast, while you take a hot shower and get comfortable," Ari said.

"No breakfast for me, Ari. Maybe a glass of juice."

"I can manage that; now go on and take your shower."

Angelica looked at Ari. He was a decent man, and he only did what any other citizen would have done. He'd known Donna a lot longer than he knew her and was probably loyal to Donna's memory. She wasn't mad, just glad that Ari prepared her for the unexpected. She got up and went over to the bathroom.

The warm water relaxed her. So many things were running through her mind—Donna, Ari, the cops and Santiago. Santiago was the last person Angelica had counted on rekindling a relationship with. In fact, she had hoped he had fallen off the earth in some great big black hole never to be seen or heard of again. Was it a chance meeting? She would never know, but the last thing she wanted was to be back in his clutches.

Finally shutting off the water, Angelica emerged from the shower, feeling like she could conquer the world, until she heard a knock on the door. Grabbing a towel, she wrapped it tightly around her body.

Knock, knock. "Angelica," Ari called, "the cops are here."

Angelica froze. She wasn't sure what time it was but it seemed awfully early for the police department to come calling. "Give me a minute, Ari. I've got to get dressed."

"All right. I'll tell them you'll be out in a minute."

"Thank you, Ari."

Angelica took her time. *What kind of questions would they ask her?* Nerves replaced the good feeling. She finished drying off and went to her room and put on a pair of jeans and a blouse. She looked in the mirror and decided not to put on any make-up but brushed her hair into a ponytail. She blew air from her mouth, looked once again in the mirror, pressed her blouse down and opened the door to face the music.

When Angelica entered the living room, Ari was talking to two middle-aged, white men dressed in plain clothes. They each had a notepad in hand and stopped talking when they saw Angelica. It was obvious they were admiring her as their eyes roved over her body.

"Ms. Barnes?" one detective asked. "My name is Detective Michaels, and this is Detective Henderson," Detective Michaels said, pointing to the other gentleman before they flashed their badges. "We're with the Homicide Division of the NYPD, and we'd like to ask you a few questions about the death of Donna Barnes Reardon."

"Okay."

"How do you know Ms. Reardon?" Detective Michaels asked.

"She's the cousin of my ex-husband," Angelica replied.

"I understand that you were living with Ms. Reardon as recently as two or three days ago. How did you come to live with Ms. Reardon and how long did you live with her?" Detective Michaels asked.

Angelica sneered at Detective Michaels, not liking his tone of voice or the questions he posed. She looked at Ari and turned away.

"Donna invited me to come to New York because she said she had a job for me—a modeling job. I was very excited about the opportunity to do something different and get away from North Carolina."

"So when did you come here from North Carolina, Ms. Barnes?" Michaels asked, while Detective Henderson was writing feverishly in his tablet.

"I've been here a week," Angelica replied.

"I understand you were no longer living with Ms. Reardon at the time of her death, but just now you stated that she invited you to stay with her. What prompted you to leave her so soon?"

"Well, the modeling job that Donna promised me turned out to be quite the opposite of what I was expecting."

"What do you mean, it wasn't what you expected, Ms. Barnes?"

"Detective Michaels, the job Ms. Reardon wanted me to pose for was for a gay magazine. There is nothing gay or lesbian about me. I was asked to pose and participate in a scene that was tasteless and not part of my lifestyle."

"What do you do for a living, Ms. Barnes?" Detective Michaels continued.

Angelica looked at Ari for support. "I'm a dancer."

"What kind of dancer?" Michaels asked, giving Angelica a real once-over.

"An exotic dancer."

"I see," Detective Michaels said. "But you never told me why you no longer were living at Ms. Reardon's residence."

Angelica licked her lips and sighed. "Donna became upset when I told her that I wasn't participating in her photo shoot. She told me that if I wasn't going to work, then I would have to get out of her house—that night.

"And what did you do?" Michaels pushed.

"I left."

"What time did you leave?"

"It was…"

"It was six-fifteen," Ari replied. The detectives looked at Ari with amusement, but he was not amused. "I'm a doorman, for God's sake," Ari said, shaking the smug looks off the detectives' faces. "I ought to know when the residents come and go."

Detective Michaels spoke up, "You remember the precise time of each and every resident as they come and go?"

"Well, some of them come and go like clockwork. I can set my watch to their movement," Ari said smugly.

"So what made you remember that Ms. Barnes left the building at precisely six-fifteen?" Detective Michaels asked Ari.

"Because I had offered to give her a place to stay, and at that precise time, I loaded her things in my car to take to my house."

"So, is it your presumption that Ms. Reardon was alive when you left the apartment building?"

Ari was getting perturbed with Detective Michaels. He had come to question Angelica, but somehow he was caught up in the dragnet and was answering all of the questions. "Yes, I believe Ms. Reardon was alive. She and Ms. Barnes had arrived at the house approximately a half hour before Ms. Barnes and I took off. Ms. Barnes got her things together, and I met her down-stairs."

"She slammed the door on me," Angelica jumped in, not want-ing to be upstaged by Ari. "I got the hell out of there, thankful for Ari's offer to stay with him."

"Well, do you know, Ms. Barnes," Detective Michaels continued, "who would want to kill Ms. Reardon?"

"Although she was my husband's cousin, I didn't know her well. I was even surprised by the invitation to come to New York, thinking my bad luck had turned to good. I met a few of her friends my first few days here, but all of them seemed to adore her." Angelica made a face.

"What was the face for, Ms. Barnes? Did they or did they not adore her?"

"I think they were all lovers. They kissed each other on the mouth like they were, like, I can't find the word for it. It was nasty and disgusting. I can't stomach females kissing females or men kissing other men. It's not right. If God meant for it to be, he would have made Steve out of Adam's rib instead of Eve. Get my drift? I don't think any one of them had a murderous bone in their body, though."

"What about you, Ari, keeper of the door?" Detective Michaels asked.

Ari wanted to punch the detective in the mouth. "It could be one of a number of people," Ari snapped. "Ms. Reardon was a happy woman. She liked to party. I never heard her argue with anyone or throw anyone out of her apartment. I wasn't on duty when this horrible thing happened to her, and in my heart, I wished I had been. The perpetrator might have been found by now. I truly cared for Donna. She was like family to me."

"You seem to know a lot for being a doorman," Detective Michaels said as he shot Detective Henderson a glance.

"I've been invited to some of Ms. Reardon's parties," Ari offered. "Some of New York's elites would attend. I mostly observed, enjoyed the music, danced every now and then and enjoyed the eats—nothing more."

"As an observer, did you ever get a sense that some of the folks on the invite list did not like Ms. Reardon?" Detective Michaels asked.

"Not once. Of course, I only attended a handful of her parties."

"Ms. Barnes, tell me, what state would you say Ms. Reardon was in the last time you saw her?"

"Detective Michaels, I believe she was glad my ass was out of her house. I barely cleared the doorway before the door was slammed, as I said before. I was happy to be out of there, but I would never wish anything ill toward Donna."

"You got all of that, Henderson?"

"Yep."

"Don't think about leaving the city any time soon," Detective Michaels said. "I'm sure you'll see our faces again." He nodded. "Let's go, Henderson."

Angelica and Ari watched them leave the house. She dropped on the couch and let out a big sigh. It was mind-boggling, but she was glad the interrogation was over.

Angelica looked up. "Who do you think did it, Ari?"

He came and sat next to Angelica. "I wish I knew. They will have to answer to me. If the police don't find the killer, I will."

There was something about the woman who sat so close to Ari. He had been with some of the most exotic women in the world, yet there was something about this caramel-colored diva that made his insides erupt. It could be in the way she switched her hips when she walked or the generous curves of her body that rippled in all the right places. Such things would make any man fall to his knees and beg for her attention and then some.

For a moment, Ari imagined Angelica dancing with a pole, caressing and teasing it with her body, while a room filled with men craved what they couldn't have, letting their imaginations run wild and keeping their aroused groins in check. Ari reached over and pulled Angelica close. The fragrance from the lilac scrub she used when she showered oozed from her body. He inhaled her fragrance once more and brought his lips to her neck.

Her head flipped back as Ari's lips dotted every inch of her neck. Angelica pulled her ponytail out of the way so that his lips wouldn't miss a spot. She turned slightly to the right so that she faced him.

Lifting Angelica's legs, Ari placed them over his. He lowered his face to hers and sealed her lips with a kiss. She responded in kind, linking her arms around his neck. Savoring the flavor of Angelica's lips, Ari moved again to her neck while her body pulsated with every touch. Her hands caressed his head like she was creating a master watercolor piece—slowly and gently. His thick lock of hair twisted this way and that as her body answered to the touch of his lips.

"Let's go to your room," Ari said in a whisper, not wanting to interrupt the mood.

Angelica seemed to hesitate, but before she could answer, his lips were on hers and his hands wandered over her body, exploring her, making her testify to the power of his touch. She sat up, and Ari scooped her off the couch and headed for her room.

With his foot, Ari pushed open the door to Angelica's room. It was simple but inviting. A mahogany bed and double dresser with an attached mirror took up most of the room. An old, yellowish quilt covered the bed. Ari gently laid Angelica on it and sat next to her, unbuttoning his shirt. Unable to peel his eyes away from her, he pulled his shirt off and reached down and kissed her again.

Angelica responded to his advances, helping Ari to take off her shirt. He nibbled at her ears and planted kisses on her chin, snaking along her neck until he fell into the bottom of the ravine that lay between her twin mountains. He breathed in her scent and languished in the ravine as if he'd been given a potion to make him sleep. She lifted his head and pouted her lips, and he kissed her again, passionately.

Wasting no time, Ari removed the rest of his clothing and helped a helpless Angelica remove hers. His breathing became labored as he stared at her nakedness, his head moving up and down her body, stopping to analyze a small mole adjacent to her navel like a person with a trained eye.

Angelica looked up and smiled at him, her arms lying lazily by her sides. She could feel the heat from Ari's body as he continued to X-ray every inch of her, and immediately she knew she wanted to feel him, all of him.

"You are beautiful, Angelica. You have the body of a twenty-year-old—perfect in every way."

"Thank you," she said softly, accepting Ari's compliment.

Ari kissed Angelica and felt her muscles contract as he explored her twin peaks, kissing and squeezing as if he held the controls of a brand-new PlayStation game. Then down the slopes of Aspen he continued, kissing and feeling his way through the sweet terrain until he descended upon the Bermuda Triangle that sucked him under without remorse. Unable to wait any longer, Ari filled her well to the brim with his throbbing manhood.

Angelica shuddered and shook violently—her head turning from side to side—her body a volcano erupting from the pleasure that Ari gave her. She looked like a flight of geese flapping their wings, excited about the flight down south. Then, from the belly of Ari's soul came a blood-curdling yell, his own body giving up the ghost after the ride of his life.

His body collapsed onto hers, sweat glistening on his back.

Angelica's toes were curled tight as if they had latched onto something they didn't want to let go of. Moans of pleasure and satisfaction enveloped the room, chasing away the stillness of the morning. Both enjoyed the tender moment and lay in each other's arms for the next hour.

Finally, Ari lifted his head, finding Angelica asleep. He kissed her gently and then rose, taking his clothes with him before disappearing from the room.

Angelica stirred—the weight of Ari's body now gone. She opened her eyes and focused them, letting out a little sigh when she realized where she was. She closed her eyes again and relived the last few hours in her dream. Ari was a wonderful lover, and she found herself wanting him again.

27

Jefferson walked back and forth, pushing his walker in front of him. Being cooped up in the house with nothing to do was getting the better of him. His livelihood—the business he had built from the ground up, the business he had cultivated and grown to be the premier minority business in the city of Fayetteville and which had garnered him the title of Black Businessman of the Year, was no more. Myles and Associates had been sold to another up-and-coming black businessman.

Jefferson pushed the walker from the kitchen to the window in the family room. He pulled back the drapes and looked out. He dropped his eyes, and then the drapes, at the sight of what was once Blake and Linda Montgomery's house. Old wounds he'd rather leave dormant tried to resurface.

He had thought very little about Linda or Blake since going to prison. He felt some responsibility for Blake's death, although it was police Lt. Hamilton Barnes who had orchestrated his murder and was still in Central Prison paying the time for the crime. And Linda…Linda was a mistake that he would probably have to pay for the rest of his natural days on earth.

He had thought having someone new in his life would invigorate him. Linda was at the right place at the right time, ready, willing, and more than able. But in the end, Linda betrayed him because she couldn't deal with the ghost of her dead husband. Little did Jefferson know that his brief romance with Linda would unleash a holy war against him—a war that caused people to be killed, igniting headlines with a scandal that would rock Fayetteville for years and years to come, and that would cause him to come close to losing the best thing that ever happened to him. This war eventually sent him away to prison for twenty years but, by the mercies of God, he had gotten out in five.

Looking away, Jefferson wondered where Linda had gone. A new set of neighbors inhabited the house next door—people who were unfamiliar, people who he could not boast as friends.

Jefferson looked at his watch. Margo should have been home over an hour ago. Maybe she stopped to pick something up for dinner or was showing another house to a client. He wanted her near—near enough to see her, near enough to smell her fragrance, and near enough to feel safe, believing that their lives were destined to be intertwined forever.

A twinge of reality made Jefferson slump down in the nearest chair, toppling his walker over as he did so. He had been home over a week, but he had yet to make love to Margo. Pain and guilt engulfed him, and he knew that it was going to take more than a thousand *I'm sorry's* to heal the hurt that he had inflicted upon her.

Something was not right. Jefferson could feel it deep in his gut. Malik seemed estranged, distant, like he was trying to avoid him, and Malik's not showing up for the welcome home party didn't help. Jefferson simmered on that thought, letting his mind wander, pushing away thoughts that he didn't want to entertain.

"I believe Malik has feelings for Margo," Jefferson said out loud. He didn't like the sound of what he said as his words vibrated against the walls. Jefferson balled his fists and struggled to stand up straight, bending over to pick up his walker while holding onto the edge of the chair. "He better not touch Margo," Jefferson said, his nostrils flaring. "He better not touch her."

Not sure what to do next, Jefferson walked toward the door. Maybe it was time to pay Malik a visit. Jefferson picked up his wallet and his keys from the coffee table and headed for the door. He was about to open it when he heard the key turning in the lock. He backed up before the door opened.

"Were you on your way out?" Margo asked, surprised.

"Yeah, I need some fresh air," Jefferson lied.

"Why don't I get you something to eat, and then we'll take a ride? You've been cooped up in here all day. Sorry I was late, but I'm poised for another sell. Gotta keep the money coming in."

Jefferson relaxed and then tensed at her statement. What was Margo trying to say—*that she had to work extra hard because he wasn't able to support her?* Yes, he was a felon, but he had paid his dues to society and, somehow, he was going to land back on his feet.

"Margo, we need to talk."

"What about, Jefferson?" she said hesitantly.

"Us, sweetheart, us."

"Jefferson, you've got to give me some time. I know this is about us not being able to make love…"

"Whoa, Margo. Let's not get excited. Yes, things are a little tense right now and, yes, our not being able to make love to each other is one of our problems, but I was hoping to share my feelings with you…and get an understanding of what you're feeling."

"What brought this on, Jefferson?" Margo asked accusingly.

"Baby, I'm not used to sitting around doing nothing. I hate that I'm not taking care of my family the way I should be, that… that you're the one who is getting up every day, going to work, and paying the bills. I can't go on like this."

Margo reached out to Jefferson. "Let's talk." She dropped her purse on a nearby chair and helped Jefferson sit on the couch before sitting down herself. "Tell me what's on your mind."

"I feel like I'm losing you," Jefferson began. "I can't put my finger on it, but since I've been home, you don't seem to be the same person who was eager to see me."

"I'm trying, Jefferson."

"I know I don't deserve a second chance, but I prayed every night I was in that jail cell that, if God returned me to you, I would love, cherish, and take care of you until the day I die." Jefferson grabbed Margo's hand. "I don't know what I'd do without you. Please say you won't leave me."

Margo pulled her hand from Jefferson's and stood up. "Why would you say that?" She sighed. "I do love you, Jefferson. I'm having a harder time than I thought possible."

"Is there someone else?"

"Someone else?" Margo shot back, stuttering on the two words.

Jefferson looked deep into her eyes. "Yes, someone else? It's been five lonely years, or has it?" Jefferson pinched his lips together and then sighed. "I've asked myself over and over again why you seemed to be turned off to me. A couple of things popped up in my mind, but the overwhelming thought is that there's someone else.

"I know five years is a long time to wait, especially since I hadn't been the ideal husband before I went to prison. My thoughts were only on making this right, and I thought you felt the same."

"I do want us to be a family again. Lord knows I prayed long and hard for you to come home," Margo said.

"Then what is it, Margo? Tell me so I can toss these negative feelings I'm having in the trash."

Margo let out a deep sigh. She circled her waist with her arms and paced as she contemplated what to say.

"You're going to wear a hole in the carpet," Jefferson said, not taking his eyes off of Margo.

Margo sat down, tension written all over her face. "I have not been with anyone, Jefferson. Had not thought about it…"

"Until recently?"

"Are you trying to put words in my mouth? I wanted you to hold me, I wanted to make love to you as soon as you came through the door, but thoughts of the past—you and Linda, you and Angelica, washed over me and I couldn't erase the images of you being with them. You've got to believe me, Jefferson. I'm not as strong as I thought I would be. I…"

"Is it Malik?" Jefferson continued to stare at Margo.

"Malik? Why would you say Malik?"

"Why not, unless it's someone else?"

"You've got some nerve. After all the dirt you've done!" Margo shouted.

"Seems like I struck a nerve," Jefferson said calmly. "I'm only trying to understand what the rift is between us."

Margo stood. "You have too much time on your hands, sitting around conjuring up these fictitious stories about me and Malik. I've been a one-man woman all the years we've been married, even when things were rocky. I've been doing a balancing act, trying to maintain a household that we had become accustomed to while you were serving time, and the weight of the world has been on my shoulders. Can you understand that, Jefferson? You changed the nature of my life, but I've dealt with it, so excuse me if I have some reservations when it comes to giving my whole self to you again. You're still my husband; I'm being cautious. Can't help it. I've gone through so much."

"Maybe I should move out and uncomplicate things."

"Don't try reverse psychology on me, Jefferson. This is not the time. I've gone through too much. I've sacrificed a lot, and if it wasn't for Malik, there were days that I might not have made it."

Margo stopped and looked straight at Jefferson, who was staring back. What she was trying to conceal—any connection to Malik—had spewed out in less than two minutes.

"So it is Malik." Jefferson moved his eyes away from Margo's. For the first time in a long time, tears formed in his eyes. He balled his hands into a fist and then released them and reached for his walker.

"Baby, Jefferson, I love you," Margo pleaded. "Nothing has happened between Malik and me. We've been so close, and...well, we couldn't help feeling some connection. But that's all it is...a connection, nothing more."

"Have you slept with him, Margo?"

Margo stepped back at the sound of Jefferson's voice.

"No!"

"Has he touched you?"

Margo's eyes darted around, trying to find the right words.

"No," was all that came out.

"Look at me, Margo. Did Malik touch you?"

"No...yes, he kissed me." Margo was breathing hard. "And I kissed him back."

Jefferson pulled himself up and leaned on the walker. He stood there a minute but didn't say a word. He picked up his keys and shuffled to the door, opened it, and slammed it behind him.

Margo raced to the door, her tears falling fast. "Where are you going?" she called out to Jefferson upon opening the door.

"Don't worry about it. Right now, I want to be left alone."

Margo closed the door and grabbed the sides of her head. She shook her fists at the sky. She went back into the family room, picked up the telephone and dialed. She listened as the phone continued to ring, and after the tenth ring, she slammed the receiver down.

28

Jefferson drove blindly out of the subdivision and into heavy traffic. He wasn't sure where he was going, but he knew it had to be far away from Margo. Anger controlled his brain and his foot as he realized that he was going twenty miles over the speed limit. He could not afford a ticket or any run-in with the law, so he eased off the gas and pounded the steering wheel.

Passing an Arby's restaurant made Jefferson realize he was hungry. He moved over to the right lane, turned at the next intersection and doubled back through the parking lot until he was at the drive-through window. At window number one, he paid for his food and advanced to window number two.

Three feet away, the door to the entrance of the building flew open...and déjà vu. He couldn't believe his eyes. Linda Montgomery passed in front of him. She was engaged in an animated conversation with another woman. Still slender, she wore white cord jeans and a red polka dot knit shirt that came to the top of her jeans. Her hair was full and curly like she had gotten a perm. She and the other woman walked to a black Mercedes Coupe, got in and left.

It brought back memories of the night Linda was riding in his Mercedes on Fuller Street— the night her husband had followed them, the night that changed his life forever. Blake Montgomery's death flashed before him, flooding him with memories of infidelity and why he was now sitting in the drive-through window at Arby's instead of at home with Margo.

He had a sudden impulse to follow Linda…to find out where she lived, or perhaps find out what path her life had taken. But as immediate as the thought was, he dismissed it quickly because his heart belonged to the one woman he truly loved, Margo. There were obstacles there, and he needed to deal with them—and he would.

"Would you like ketchup with your order?" the server asked, handing Jefferson his bag.

"No thanks. Have a good day." Jefferson drove off and headed into town.

Seeing Linda again made Jefferson conscious of the need to insure that his family remained a unit. Mistakes were made, and he had made plenty of them, but now that he was home and trying to put his life together, no one was going to disrupt it—even if they were brothers.

Jefferson made a series of right and left turns and drove down a long street, passing in front of SuperComp Technical Solutions. He circled the block and found a park down the street from Malik's business. Mindless of the slight incline, Jefferson maneuvered the walker until he was in front of the building. This was a mission he was not about to abort.

There was little activity when Jefferson entered the building. A customer lingered, leisurely browsing at the selected display of computers and peripherals. A sign hung from the ceiling that called attention to the latest technology in operating systems, VISTA.

The customer looked up as Jefferson ambled forward and then went back to browsing. Forging ahead, Jefferson stopped when he saw the backside of Malik, who was gathering brochures. This was his best friend, the person he trusted. Never in a million years would he have thought that Malik would make a move on Margo—that he'd have the audacity to do so. Not Malik the advisor, the scolder, the one who tried to make him see reason when he was stepping out on Margo.

All thoughts aside, Jefferson approached Malik, who turned around with surprise written on his face. There was a kind of fear in Malik's eyes as he looked at him and, without asking a question, Jefferson knew that the fear was riddled with guilt.

"We need to talk," Jefferson said. He looked straight at Malik without batting a lash.

"Jefferson, it's good to see you. I'm with a customer right now… maybe we can talk later."

"I'll wait until you're finished. I'm sure I need to upgrade my system."

Malik nodded and continued to pull brochures while watching Jefferson at the same time. Jefferson shuffled around the store, pretending to be interested in other things. Ten minutes passed, then fifteen, and it appeared Malik was in no hurry to scoot his client along. Tired of standing, Jefferson found an empty chair near the back of the store and plopped into it.

SuperComp had become a thriving business. When Myles and Associates was still in business, Malik had set Jefferson up with some of the best accounting and bookkeeping software that money could buy. Bored with sitting, Jefferson stood up and walked over to Malik's work area. Jefferson could feel Malik's eyes on his back. It felt like daggers trying to tear through the arteries in his heart because Jefferson's heart was hurting. Wild ideas passed through his mind. Where were Malik and Margo when they kissed? Were they standing next to his desk or at the front of the store as she said goodbye?

Nervous hands began to sift through papers and files on Malik's desk. Jefferson had crossed the line, but he wanted answers—any kind of answers that would give him an excuse to put Malik out of his misery. Fingers lifted the edge of a greeting card that sat under some papers. A picture of a beautiful bouquet of roses adorned the front, and when Jefferson opened the card, only the author's words stared back...the card was unsigned.

Before Jefferson had a chance to read the card, a heavy hand sat on top of his and closed it.

"What do you think you're doing?" Malik asked, removing Jefferson's hand from his desk.

"Sounds like you've got something to hide, bro," Jefferson responded while staring straight at Malik without flinching.

"I'll talk with you in a second—as soon as I'm finished with this customer."

Jefferson rose and looked back at the card that sat on the desk. Instinct told him to grab it and keep walking, but that would defeat the purpose of his coming in the first place. Instead, he walked among the rows of ink cartridges, jump drives, wireless adaptors and cables that lined shelves or hung from them. He looked up when he heard the bell ring at the front door and Malik walking toward him. Jefferson leaned on his walker, bracing for the confrontation that was about to happen.

"So, what is it you want?" Malik asked. "Apparently, you aren't here to purchase a computer since you were snooping in my things."

"Malik, you and I go way back. We've been friends for a long time. I counted you among the top five of my most devoted and loyal friends. However, I've noticed a difference in you since I've been home. I don't know what it is…a kind of disconnect when it comes to me, and I don't know where it's coming from. No, I don't know where this attitude of yours originated, but my intuition tells me it has something to do with *my* wife.

"I want you to know, Malik, that I didn't sit in that prison day in and day out without feeling remorse for the things I did to Margo. She's the only woman I've ever loved and will ever love, and I prayed to God that when I got out, I would right my wrongs…that I would do everything in my power to see that my family recovers from this awful event in our lives that I created."

"What makes you think that Margo wants the same thing?"

"Oh. Is that what she told you when you had your arms wrapped around her, kissing her and telling her you could do things for her that I couldn't do? Huh, you sorry ass hypocrite?"

"Don't come in here accusing me of things because you're a no-good son of a bitch."

"Margo told me herself, this very afternoon that you kissed her and she kissed you back. I've come to serve you notice, lover boy. Stay away from my wife. You got it? MY wife! Margo is my wife, and don't you ever forget it. I have no intention of going back to prison, but put your hands on my wife again…"

"Is that a threat, Jefferson?"

"Call it what you want, Malik, but you've heard what I said." Jefferson gritted his teeth and went eyeball to eyeball with Malik. "Don't you ever forget what I said."

Jefferson pushed past Malik and walked out the door. Malik grabbed one of the hangers that held the ink cartridges to the board, yanked it, and knocked cartridges to the floor.

"You don't deserve Margo!" Malik shouted at the closed door. "And I'm not scared of you, Jefferson. I will have Margo." But there was no one in the room to hear those words.

29

Ari cracked open the door and found Angelica tucked deep beneath the warm comforter. There was little movement, save for her breathing, which was marked by little shifts of her body as she inhaled and exhaled. Ari smiled. He knew he wanted more of her.

He closed the door to the room and headed for the porch to retrieve the morning paper. The air was brisk when he stepped onto the porch, but it was what he needed in order to cool the hormones that had been awakened in his body. Ari picked up the paper and noticed a long black car slow when it neared his house and then continue to move forward. Ari shook his head. *What could such a person be looking for in my neighborhood?* Ari wondered. He dismissed it and went inside.

After finishing the paper, Ari went to the kitchen and made a piece of dry toast. He washed it down with coffee he had brewed earlier that morning and then went to check on Angelica again. She was still asleep.

The sight of her, the touch of her, excited him. Ari wanted to lay with her and make love to her again, experimenting and exploring every inch of her body. He was smitten hard, and he felt like an alcoholic who needed his bottle or the junkie who needed his fix now! No, he couldn't wait to make love to her. He couldn't wait to kiss her tender lips. He couldn't wait to unleash the animal he was when one of the seven deadly sins lay in front of him. Men had fought and lost wars over the scent of a woman and what lay between her legs.

He paced throughout the house, finally venturing into the living room. The paper he was reading was in disarray, and he picked it up and folded it. Ari went to the window and peered out. He was getting antsy because he was not used to being cooped up in his own house during the day. Waiting on the people at the high rise gave him a high as well as the opportunity to see many celebrities, oftentimes being extended an invitation to one of the fabulous parties they gave. He stopped and stared. A car that looked like the one that had passed the house earlier passed again, this time slowing down almost to a crawl.

Could it be Donna's killer? Nerves replaced the feelings that had him riding on a cloud for the past few hours. Ari had to wake Angelica because something strange was going on, and he wasn't able to comprehend what he felt.

Before Ari had a chance to move from his trance-like state, Angelica appeared in the room. She was all smiles. For a brief moment, Ari forgot about the car that seemed to be circling his house and smiled back at Angelica. Pink cotton pajamas covered her body and, with her hand on her hip, Angelica waltzed over to Ari, put her arms around his neck and kissed him deeply in the mouth. Flushed, he responded to her call, and within minutes they were having a re-enactment of their earlier performance, adding a little flavoring along the way. They were too far gone in their lovemaking to respond to the knock on the door.

Arms slumped over the side of the bed, Ari cocked his head. "Did you hear that?" he asked Angelica.

"No," she slurred under the influence of their lovemaking.

"There it goes again. Someone's knocking on the front door.

The damned doorbell isn't broke. I'll get up and see who it is."

"Do you have to?" Angelica begged, her voice just above a whisper. "I don't want you to leave."

"I don't want to go," Ari assured her. "But if I don't answer this door, whoever is there is going to knock it down. Don't go anywhere; I'll be right back, sweetheart."

"Hurry," Angelica said, throwing Ari a kiss.

Ari jumped in his pants and grabbed his shirt, putting it on as he moved to the front of the house. He couldn't imagine who was determined to see him, especially when everyone knew he was always at work during this time. He peeked out the front window and moved back abruptly. There it was again—the long black car that had been circling the neighborhood for hours.

Curiosity was getting the best of him, and Ari hurried to the door and opened it. A medium height, medium build, dark-skinned man dressed in a black suit, white shirt, and black tie stood on the porch. Ari looked past the man to the car that sat in front of the house, not sure what to think.

"How may I help you?" Ari asked.

"I'm looking for Angelica Barnes," the man replied.

Eyebrows arched in suspicion, Ari took another look at the man. "Your name?"

Looking back at the car and then at Ari, the man stared at him pointedly. "Tell Ms. Barnes that Mr. Robert Santiago would like a word with her, now."

Ari stretched his neck like he was working out a kink. "I'll see if Ms. Barnes is available to come to the door." And he shut the door, leaving the man on the porch.

As Ari approached Angelica's room, she appeared but stopped when she saw the frown on Ari's face.

"What is it, Ari? Who's at the door?"

"There's a gentleman standing on the porch who says that a Mr. Robert Santiago wants to speak with you, and he is insistent that it be now."

Angelica's hand flew to her mouth. "Oh, God no."

30

Angelica rushed back into the room, slid into a pair of jeans and then put on the blouse she had on when the detectives had come to the house. She hated Santiago, but most of all she hated herself for allowing him to manipulate and use her the way he did. Her mind raced back five years when he had attempted to kill her ex-husband, Hamilton, and Jefferson Myles. It was crazy, and she was almost a victim as well. Death might have been a welcome vehicle if she hadn't wanted to live.

Frustration was written all over Ari's face. Angelica couldn't deal with it at the moment; she had to get rid of Santiago. She was frustrated, too, because she had been the recipient of some of the best lovemaking she'd had in a long time. Ari was tender and romantic. He knew what buttons to push and when to push them. Whispers of sweet nothings were music to Angelica's ears, but the icing on the cake was the way he rocked her body with passion like they were the last two people on earth.

She avoided Ari's gaze and moved past him toward the front door. Sweaty palms opened the door, and the dark-skinned gentleman dressed in a chauffeur's uniform still stood on the porch with an expressionless look on his face. Before Angelica could speak, he said, "Mr. Santiago is waiting for you in the car."

"Did he say what he wanted? I've got to get ready for work in a few hours."

"I don't make it my business to ask why, and you shouldn't either." Angelica rolled her eyes, but the gentleman ignored her. "I do know that his patience is wearing thin."

Angelica looked toward the car. The windows were tinted and she couldn't see inside. All of a sudden, the back passenger window began to roll down, and there sat Santiago with a frown on his face, staring directly at Angelica. She walked down the few stairs from the porch and headed for the car, with Ari staring behind her. Ari shut the door hard, but no one turned around.

The driver escorted Angelica to the other side of the car, opened the door, and motioned for Angelica to get in. The car was soon in motion.

"What is this, Santiago? Why couldn't you have called me?"

"You might not have answered, and what I came to say, I had to say it in person."

"Well, talk."

"You're awful cocky for someone who got a lot of my money last night."

"I don't mean to be. It's just that so much has happened since I've been in New York and I'm on edge. I really wanted this to be a fresh start."

"Why don't you let me help you with that fresh start? There's a room ready for you at my house and you can call Club Platinum and give them your resignation."

"I have a place to stay," Angelica said, her voice shaking.

"You don't belong there. That old neighborhood with its one-hundred-fifty-year-old houses, that's not quite your style, that is, unless there's somebody helping to make your accommodations more comfortable."

"I don't know what you're talking about."

"I'm talking about the doorman that lives in the house you came out of."

"How do you know he's a doorman? He could be a saxophone player."

"My contacts tell me he's a doorman for a fancy apartment building in Manhattan. Nothing gets by me."

Angelica was quiet. She couldn't put her finger on it, but Santiago's knowing about Ari made her uncomfortable—like he was spying on her. *What else did he know?*

"Cat got your tongue?" Santiago asked. "Look, I've missed you, Princess."

Angelica shuddered at the sound of the word *Princess*. She wasn't a princess...just a slave that did his bidding. In the end, she got a few trinkets and five years in jail.

"I want you, Angelica. I want to make love to you. You were a valuable asset to me once."

"I've put that life behind me, Santiago. Memories of prison have done that for me."

Tension was in the air. The driver kept his eyes straight ahead as he drove from Queens to Harlem, Harlem to lower Manhattan, and then over the bridge into Brooklyn. There was total silence for the next fifteen minutes, as they glided through Brooklyn, except for the constant tapping of Santiago's fingers.

"Niko, turn the car around and head for Queens. The lady is going to get her things, and then we'll head into Long Island."

"Santiago, I'm not going with you. I want to live a simple and uncomplicated life, and being with you will make that difficult."

"Drive!" Santiago yelled at the driver.

Beads of sweat formed on Angelica's face. She knew that Santiago was ruthless, but she had never heard him raise his voice. She sat back in her seat, afraid to move and unsure of the consequences if she chose to do something other than what he wanted.

A little music would have made the ride to Ari's house more bearable, but the only thing she could hear was her heart beating. And she was glad for small favors.

They reached Ari's house in record time. Santiago barked for Angelica to hurry and get her things without loitering. She wanted to run, but where would she go? It would not be fair to Ari with all that he had done for her to intrude on his generosity any longer.

Angelica found Ari sitting in the living room and watching TV. His eyes followed her as she strolled straight to her bedroom without a word, and then he went back to watching television as soon as she was out of sight.

She returned moments later with the straps of her Hobo flung over her shoulder, followed by the suitcases that had accompanied her to New York. She stopped where Ari sat and looked at him.

"Ari, I care about you. Today would have been the happiest day of my life, if…if," she sighed, "Santiago had not shown up here."

"Who is he? Why are you going with him?"

Ari was almost pleading for the truth. It made leaving harder than she'd anticipated because part of her wanted to be with this man.

"I'll have to explain later, Ari. All I can say is that my past has come to haunt me, to make me pay for my sins."

"Don't bother. I've done all that I could do. In some ways, I wish I had never laid eyes on you. It's plain to see how you can seep into a man's soul without even trying, but I should've known it would be hell to pay, falling for you. Go on to your…your demon, your past…or whatever it is. Just don't call me again. I'm through. I'm through with you, Angelica." He raised his hands and shooed her away.

"Ari, I'm so sorry. Believe me when I say I want to stay. I…I want to stay with you, Ari. Believe me."

A loud knock at the door startled them.

"Go, Angelica, and leave me alone."

The tears flowed, and she turned and left without another word. Ari went to the front window and peeked out, in time to watch Angelica get into the car. A frown formed on his face; something was not right.

31

Weeks had passed since Margo had last seen Malik. She brushed her lips with her finger as a repressed memory of the day Malik kissed her ushered forth. It was an exciting moment that ignited sparks throughout her body—something she hadn't felt in a long, long time.

Weeks had passed since she and Jefferson had slept in the same room as well, although they were still under the same roof. His mood was somber as he rummaged and piddled around the house in a deep funk, knocking things over and slinging a few choice words about what he'd do to Malik.

Margo wasn't sure what it all meant. Part of her wanted to embrace her husband and heal the wound, close the rift that had already torn them apart. However, there was the other part of her that threatened war—a battle between good and evil where she would take what belonged to one and give to another, making her ready to taste and see if life was truly greener on the other side.

Margo jumped. She wasn't sure how long Jefferson had been watching her. She hadn't heard him come into her bedroom—their bedroom—and then she noticed that he was standing straight without the aid of his walker. Surprise registered on her face.

"Thinking about him?" Jefferson asked as he leaned against the door frame.

"When did you stop using your walker?" Margo asked, ignoring his question.

"Living under the same roof, but you don't have any idea what's been going on with me."

Margo sat down on the cedar chest in front of the bed. "Jefferson, I remember a moment when I begged and pleaded for you to love me. You had my undivided attention. I would have done anything for you because I loved you that much. Remember? But you didn't want me."

"Why are we rehashing this, Margo? I've told you over and over again how much I love you. I've asked for forgiveness more times than I can count. You told me that you were going to be by my side through it all, and it was that acknowledgment that gave me the strength to survive that hellhole. I've paid the price, but I will never forgive myself for what I've done to you."

"What are you going to do with the rest of your life? I can't stand by and watch your daily pity parties, Jefferson. They've gotten old. It's time to get up off your duff and do something with yourself."

"So, is this about my not being able to provide for you or is it an attempt to find some excuse to leave me for someone else? It's not enough that my wife won't sleep with me…make love to me, but humiliate my manhood? Do you think Malik can provide for you better than me?" Margo didn't answer. "Well, maybe you should be with him. Yeah, go be with him. I can't do anything for you. I'm a broke, jobless ex-con."

Jefferson turned to leave. In his haste, his left foot didn't move as fast as the rest of his body, and he fell to the floor. He grabbed his knee and began to rub it when he felt a warm pair of hands on top of his own.

"I'm not going to leave you, Jefferson. You're my husband and will always be. Let's get you up from the floor and get some ice on that knee. We'll work this out somehow."

Jefferson looked up. "Do you mean it, Margo?"

She looked past him with a vacant look on her face. "Yes, I mean it."

32

She was a prisoner in Santiago's sprawling mansion. It was tucked away on Long Island in the Hamptons, far enough away from the grind of the city but close enough to be there in under an hour. A tall, wrought-iron fence circled the property, and a security guard manned the gate that gave entry. The stone house was surrounded by lush greenery as well as a variety of flowers that reminded Angelica of Santiago's place in North Carolina. A long stone pathway intersected with a circular driveway and led to the house. For some it was the breeze from the ocean, for others it was the view that made it a spectacular piece of real estate.

Thirty rooms she counted in all: nine bedrooms, nine bathrooms, a large gourmet kitchen, a formal living and dining room, an entertainment center, a movie theater with high-backed velvet seats, a workout room with every conceivable piece of gym equipment, two nine-by-ten, walk-in closets that held Santiago's leisure and casual clothes in one and the other his suits and formal attire, an indoor basketball court with its own bathroom facilities was accessible by way of the workout room, and in the lower level of the house were two rooms for the hired help along with the washroom facility.

The house in the Hamptons was a place Angelica would have died for if her companion had been anyone other than Santiago.

It was reminiscent of the homes she saw in her daydreams, and for sure she would have been the perfect fit. But it wasn't her home, and she wasn't even sure why she was there or what Santiago was planning.

She was forced to quit her job at Club Platinum much to the disappointment of Gerald Lloyd. Angelica liked her freedom and the idea of making a nice sum of money for a few hours of dancing with a pole while she intoxicated her nameless admirers suited her just fine. But it was Ari she thought about all the time—his kindness and her disappointing him.

She had last seen him staring into Donna's coffin. Angelica wondered if Ari blamed her for Donna's demise. Her attempt to speak with him was met with contempt, but at least she tried. It was difficult getting to the funeral because Santiago refused to let her go—maybe he thought she was going to run—but he gave in in the end.

Many of Hamilton's family members crowded the small cathedral—some she recognized and some she didn't. It seemed as though the area's entire gay and lesbian community was there as well as many notable celebrities that Donna had either worked with or had some ties to. The police still didn't have a suspect in custody. It was a shameful act of cowardice, and Angelica hoped that whoever killed Donna would pay dearly.

Needing something to do, Angelica went to the exercise room. Dressed in a purple pair of spandex tights and exercise bra, she walked into the room and examined each piece of equipment until she came to the Bowflex machine. She straddled the bench and placed her arms around the metal bar, applying pressure as she lifted the twenty-pound weights.

Angelica rested as her mind raced, contemplating what she was going to do and how she was going to get away from Santiago. He barely spoke to her, yet he was insistent that she be with him. Something was looming on the horizon; Angelica could feel it deep down. It frightened her—the not knowing, all the secrecy that seemed to surround Santiago's daily activities—but the not knowing was the price she was paying for selling him out the last time they were together.

She did four sets of ten lifts and then she heard voices. They were coming from the basketball court. Whoever it was must have come in through a side door. Easing down the metal bar, Angelica stiffened and listened to the voices that were getting louder. She could hear Santiago's above the others. He cursed at his companions and threatened to reduce their pay if... Someone picked up a basketball and began to bounce it hard on the floor, drowning out all conversation. Angelica wanted to get up and peek, but she remained frozen to the equipment and prayed she wouldn't be discovered.

The ball stopped hitting the floor and the muffled voices began to fade. Angelica hadn't seen any more than two people at any given time with Santiago—his "goons" she had called them. Operation Stingray was dead as far as she knew, but she was smart enough to know that if Santiago was purchasing and selling weapons in North Carolina, surely he was doing that or something similar to it in New York. There was no evidence of his wrongdoing in this house where she was so free to roam, but somewhere there was an answer, and her mind said the answer lay at the restaurant she had visited the first night she had laid eyes on Santiago again.

She sat for five or ten minutes before deciding to get up. Crossing her leg over the bench, Angelica was about to stand up when Santiago appeared. He moved toward her without a word, coming to sit at the end of the bench. He lifted her leg and brought it back over so that she was straddling the bench once again, except that he now faced her.

"Looked all over the house for you," Santiago said. "You hiding out?"

"No, I wanted to get some exercise," Angelica assured him. "Not much else for me to do."

"In time, my Princess. I've been so involved with a project I've been working on, and I've been inattentive. Forgive me."

"Santiago, I've been your captive for over a month. You made it seem urgent that I come with you right away, and yet I've barely seen you the whole time I've been here. What are you up to? Why am I here? I know I don't mean anything to you."

Santiago gave Angelica a puzzled look. "Captive? Are you trying to say that I kidnapped you?"

"I didn't have a choice, now did I?" Angelica roared back.

"No one held a gun to your head, Angelica."

"It was invisible, but I felt it in my back."

Santiago laughed. "You mean everything to me, Princess. Things will get better soon, you'll see. How about I take you to dinner tonight at El Conuco? Uncle Jorge and Aunt Maria would love to see you again."

Something smart wanted to come out of Angelica's mouth, but she thought better of it. She needed some air and, maybe, she would find a clue to what Santiago was doing. "I'm overdue for some fun, although I thought we might do something else, but dinner at your family's restaurant will be fine."

"Well that's settled," Santiago said, inching his body toward Angelica's.

Her stomach crawled up in knots as he crept toward her. He

rested his large hands on her thighs and massaged the length of them—his diamond-encrusted rings sparkling. Angelica shivered as Santiago's hands glided from her thighs to her waist and, when he reached for her breasts, she blocked his hands with her own with such force that they hit the bench pad with a thud.

Santiago grabbed her hands and pinned them behind her. "If you won't give it, I'll take what's mine."

"That's rape."

"No, because you're going to consent to every minute of it."

"I hate you!" Angelica screamed. "Your ass should be the one in jail. I don't know how you've gotten away with your mess all these years."

"And I should have had you killed for running to the police after all I'd done for you. I let you live, and now you're going to repay me for the ill you've caused me."

Angelica sighed and relaxed. Santiago released his grip on her.

"Now, that's better." He pulled her to him and kissed her on the lips. Angelica did not respond, but he continued until her lips parted and she felt in the moment.

Santiago smothered her with kisses and lay her down on the bench. Heavy breathing mixed with lustful moans filled the room. Rough foreplay caused the steel bar that was suspended overhead to shift to the left, then the right, but it didn't deter the heat of passion that had consumed the former foes.

Rough hands tore the clothes from Angelica's body. Santiago held her breasts and sucked them like he was a baby who was taking milk from his mother. Unable to quench the fire in his groin, he pulled off his clothes and took what his body couldn't resist. To his surprise, Angelica accepted his passion with the same intensity.

It was Ari's face Angelica saw when Santiago entered her. She tried to substitute the moment she had with him for the one she was presently having, but realization took over and reminded her that the thing that had set her on fire was the enemy. In an instant, survival became Angelica's number one goal, and if it meant sleeping with the enemy, so be it until she was able to come up with a plan. She would outwit the fox before it consumed her whole.

Santiago looked like a man in a drunken stupor as he rode the last tidal wave to ecstasy. Sweat rained from his body, sending heavy droplets down on Angelica. She wiped them away in disgust, wanting it all to be over.

"Take me," he screamed as his cell phone began to ring. He tried to ignore it, but Angelica's body was already relaxed and thankful for the interruption. Santiago reached for his pants, retrieved his cell phone and immediately pulled himself away from her.

After missing the call, Santiago made another. Angelica watched as he listened and saw a broad smile cross his face.

"We're done for now," Santiago said. He picked up Angelica's clothes and laid them next to her. "Clean up. We're going out to dinner."

Santiago put his clothes on and left the room. Angelica picked up her clothes from the bench and rolled them in a ball. She was angry with herself for letting Santiago have his way so easily, but the truth of the matter was that she was afraid of him.

She slid into her things and went to her room. A hot shower would erase the scum that had infiltrated her body.

The vibration of her cell phone made Angelica jump as it danced across the dresser. She picked it up and smiled when she recognized Edward's number. There was nothing like a friendly voice to talk to, especially since she hadn't spoken to her brother in weeks and he had no knowledge of her predicament.

"Edward! This is a pleasant surprise."

"The phone system works both ways, Little Sis. How have you been?"

"I can't complain," Angelica lied. "I've had better days."

"Well, I've got some bad news."

"What kind of bad news? Something happened to Michael?"

"No, thank God."

"Well, what is it then?"

"Hamilton is dead, Angelica. He was murdered."

"Hamilton? Dead?" Angelica dropped the phone and sank to the floor.

33

A chill ran through Angelica's body. All around her people were dying, but she hadn't expected to hear Hamilton's name in that context. True, she and Hamilton hadn't been husband and wife in more than seven years, but she still felt a connection to him.

The phone call from her brother left her numb. Hamilton had been murdered. The details were sketchy, but it was believed that another inmate had done the deed. Her brother would fill her in as soon as he was able to obtain more information. There was nothing left for Angelica to do but head to North Carolina. Hamilton was her ex-husband, and she still considered herself family.

Angelica wasn't sure how she was going to get to North Carolina. It was too expensive to catch a flight on such short notice, but she was going to find a way. Rubbing her temples, it came to her. She would drive, but she needed to get a car. She knew the person to call. Ari would get her what she needed, but it would be up to her to get beyond Santiago's net. And she would run away for a second time from the demon that made her life a living hell. She decided to call Ari tomorrow, as soon as Santiago left the house, but now she looked for something to wear.

Going to the restaurant was the last thing she wanted to do, but she pushed her present emergency to the back burner. The one thing she didn't want to happen was for Santiago to get wind of her mood so that he would start asking a lot of questions. Hamilton's death was her secret passage out of the house and away from him.

A knock on the door took her out of her reverie. She smoothed down the fabric on her black dress that hit just above the knee and then went to the door and unlocked it. Santiago stood there looking handsome in all black, setting off his fine Latin features, especially his coal-black wavy hair. Angelica pretended not to notice.

"You look amazing," Santiago said as he stood in the hallway while his eyes roamed the length of her. "We may have to go somewhere swanky with the way you look."

"Oh, I can change if I'm overdressed," Angelica said, not wanting to extend her evening with Santiago beyond dinner.

"No need to change. I've got to tend to a little business with Uncle Jorge, and it might take awhile."

Her ears lifted at that bit of information. Angelica wondered what type of business Santiago had with his uncle, especially since his relatives had been running a successful restaurant for over thirty years. If her heart weren't so heavy with Hamilton's death laying on it, she'd probably do some investigating of her own.

"Well, I'm ready whenever you are."

A brisk wind met them as they stepped out into the late spring night. Angelica adjusted her wrap and stood quietly next to Santiago as they waited for Niko to bring the car around. He was not alone. Hamilton's two goons were in the car—one sat in the front, the other in the back. Both were dressed in black leather jackets with turtleneck sweaters and slacks underneath. They had a sinister look about them, and they tipped their heads when Angelica got in, careful not to let their stares linger too long.

Santiago uttered something to them in Spanish and then introduced them to Angelica. "This is Sammy," Santiago said of the man sitting next to Angelica, "and up front is Dominic. Old friends of mine."

Angelica leaned over and whispered to Santiago, "I thought we were going to dinner alone?"

"Sammy and Dominic are catching a ride. They have other business in town," Santiago responded. Satisfied, Angelica sat back with her hands on her lap.

Light rain began to fall. The pitter-patter of the raindrops pierced the silence in the car.

"Something on your mind?" Santiago asked Angelica a few minutes later. "You're distant, too quiet. I like my women noisy." Angelica remained silent while the goons laughed at Santiago's lame joke.

The drizzle became buckets of water, and cautious drivers slowed their vehicles on the slippery asphalt. Another Spanish conversation between the three men resumed. Santiago caught Niko stealing glances at Angelica. "Keep your eyes on the damn road," Santiago shouted at Niko as the tire hit a wet pothole and the car swerved to the left. Niko recovered and pulled it straight into the lane.

"Hell, what you trying to do, Niko? Get us killed? I'm gonna…"

"Chill out, Santiago," Sammy said. "Give the boy a break. It's nasty outside. We want to get to where we're supposed to be safely. Everything's cool, man," he cautioned.

"Yeah, yeah, yeah," Santiago said, releasing a huge sigh.

Santiago looked from Sammy to Angelica. He laid his hand on Angelica's thigh and patted it, and while she wished she had a fork to pierce his hand, she played along because plans for her getaway were formulating in her mind. She didn't want to give Santiago any cause not to trust her.

Twenty minutes later, they pulled up alongside El Conuco. Niko pulled the car to the curb, but left the motor running. Sammy and Dominic stayed behind while Santiago and Angelica got out of the car. Maybe Angelica was wrong about his being involved in some unscrupulous activity, but nothing explained the twelve-thousand-square-foot house Santiago lived in that sat on a few prime acres of land. She had yet to determine what his real occupation was because he never appeared to be going any-where fast or at any given time. Whatever he was up to, she wanted no part of it.

Before they entered El Conuco, the scent of food flooded their nostrils and spicy Latin music met their ears. Angelica was sud-denly hungry, and a good homegrown meal would satiate her stomach and keep it still while she internalized her grief. Regardless of what Hamilton had done to her, she was unable to imagine him lying out on a cold slab in somebody's mortuary.

To Angelica's amazement, the place was full. It was a Wednesday night, but it proved that people either didn't have time to or preferred not to cook. Angelica faked a smile when Aunt Maria hugged her and Uncle Jorge showed all thirty-two pieces of porcelain in his mouth. They seemed to be a nice couple, and it was quite obvious they adored their handsome nephew.

"Whatever the lady wants," Santiago said, placing a juicy kiss on Aunt Maria's cheek. "She needs some cheering up...hasn't gotten used to the Hamptons."

"We got what she needs," Aunt Maria said. Angelica's eyes bulged. *Was that Aunt Maria speaking halfway decent English?*

Aunt Maria continued with an accent, "Girl, what's not to love in the Hamptons? I go over once a week and clean the house for Roberto, and then I go out and sit on the deck, if the weather permits, and catch the sun. Sometimes I stay over if I drink too much tequila and can't make it back to town. When Roberto is gone, Jorge and me housesit for him; and we have the run of the house. That's the only time the oven gets turned on, except when we've catered a party or two."

Angelica listened intently. It explained why she hadn't seen any domestics at the place, although she hadn't seen Uncle Jorge or Aunt Maria either. Santiago always brought food home or took her out. She pondered this. Santiago relied on them for a lot of things, but she'd bet her last dollar they relied on him as well. There was nothing thicker than blood.

"His place is beautiful," Angelica said. "I love the view of the ocean and the spaciousness of it all, but lately I've been missing my family, and I'm feeling lonely."

"Her cousin was murdered a month ago, and she's been under the weather," Santiago said, watching Angelica out of the corner of his eye. "I'm going to see to it that she gets what she needs to make her happy again."

"Well, let me take your order," Aunt Maria said with a wide smile. Uncle Jorge tapped his finger like Angelica had seen Santiago do earlier, and then he disappeared.

Santiago took the liberty to order their food and then excused himself. Angelica watched him go through a door off the kitchen— the same one Uncle Jorge had disappeared through. She played with a book of matches that had El Conuco written on it, tossed it in her purse, and gazed around the room.

There were two waitresses who saw to it that everyone was taken care of. People chatted around Angelica as if they had no cares in the world. A snappy number rolled over the loudspeaker, and several couples hopped on the floor in the rear of the restaurant. Their bodies were engaged in a salsa dance that included smooth fancy footwork. Other patrons joined in, clapping their hands to the spicy Latin beat.

Angelica was sipping on a Margarita when she noticed a black man in braids dart into the restaurant and out the back where the others had gone. There was something different...strange, like he didn't belong there, yet familiar. She sat up straight and searched her brain for why he aroused her curiosity. Sitting back in her chair, Angelica caught her breath. He wore an old Army field jacket that was too big—it was the man who got on the bus outside of Central Prison.

What would he possibly be doing at Santiago's family's restaurant, of all places? Was he working for Santiago? Maybe he was following her, but why?

Angelica felt sick. Her food had not come yet, but she had to get out of that place. She didn't know what was going on at El Conuco, but she was getting the hell out of there.

She scrambled from her seat, went to the counter and asked the waitress to get Aunt Maria. Aunt Maria was flying from the kitchen uttering something in Spanish when she saw Angelica. "What is it, Angel?" Aunt Maria asked.

Angel? Did Aunt Maria know I worked in a strip joint? Angelica dismissed it.

"Would you please let Santiago know that I'm sick and that I need to go home now, please?"

Maria looked at Angelica as if she were a nurse, trying to determine the cause of her illness. "Wait a minute, Angel. I don't think he can come right now. Diego," Maria called to the cook and then uttered something in Spanish. Maria turned to Angelica, "I'll be right back."

Maria returned and told her the driver would meet her outside in five minutes. Angelica thanked Maria and offered her apologies about dinner. She went to the table, grabbed her things, and headed out the door.

Headlights blinded her as she stood near the curb, but the car stopped and Niko got out and opened the door for her. They road back to the Hamptons in silence. All the while, Angelica's brain processed what she had observed. Something was not right, but her mind wouldn't let her find any order to her mishmash of discoveries.

34

A ngelica sat on the couch, toying with her cell phone and feeling glad Santiago had left. He was in an ill mood, partly because he didn't take kindly to her leaving the restaurant last night and because something hadn't gone according to plan. He was shouting obscenities at Sammy and Dominic when she waltzed into the kitchen to find something to eat. Santiago sneered at her and then announced that the three of them were leaving. It didn't matter to him that she didn't feel well last night; he didn't ask how she was doing or even bother to check on her. Angelica didn't care. It was time for her to make her break.

Lifting her cell phone, Angelica dialed Ari's number. She felt awkward but hoped he would answer. Weeks had passed, in fact, it was a month to the day since she had seen or spoken to him even if the moment was brief at Donna's funeral. *And now Hamilton. What did it mean?*

Thinking back to the day she left Ari made her realize what had probably caused him to wash his hands of her. She didn't want to go with Santiago, but she knew the power he wielded and that her death warrant would probably be imminent if she didn't go. It was Ari's look of disgust that had hurt her the most. He was a good lover, and she was beginning to feel more for him than she had planned to.

The phone continued to ring until Angelica ended the call. She threw it down on the couch and grabbed her sides, contemplating what she would do next. She didn't know how long it would be before Santiago returned, and she had to activate a plan before it was too late. She picked up the phone and dialed again. This time, Ari answered, obviously annoyed.

"What is it, Angelica? I thought I told you not to call me again. I'm busy."

"Ari, when I get an opportunity, I'd like to explain all of this."

"Don't bother. I don't care what you've done, whom you've been with, or any sordid story of your life. I don't give a damn. Got it?"

There was a moment of silence. "Ari, I need your help."

"I'm done helping, Angelica. Helping you has caused me nothing but heartache and grief. I can't believe that one woman can wreak so much havoc in a person's life. And to think, I really felt something for you. How could I have been so blind? A fool I was, but not any longer. Good-bye."

"Ari, please don't hang up. I really need you. I'm in trouble."

"You're always in trouble. What's new? You were in trouble the moment you set foot in New York, and you're not going to drag me down into any more of your desperate situations. Donna would probably be alive if you hadn't shown up."

"Don't blame Donna's death on me, Ari. I appreciated her giving me an opportunity. She may not have been my best friend, but I would never have killed her."

"So what is it you want, that you had to call me to help you? Where is that big, bad boyfriend of yours?"

"I promise to explain all of that to you, but right now I've got to get out of New York."

"Leave New York? Where are you going? What's so urgent that you have to leave now? What if the police come to question you again?"

"Settle down, Ari. I don't have much time. My ex-husband was murdered, and I need to get to North Carolina. I need you to rent a car for me. It would be much cheaper than trying to get a plane ticket. I don't have any transportation to get around, and Santiago has made it next to impossible for me to leave his place without him. Please, Ari, I need you to do this for me."

"Why should I do this for you, Angelica? I can't get involved in your mess. You didn't hear me when I said I hated being used."

"You're the only person I can trust. I wouldn't ask you, Ari, if I didn't need you."

"I'll get the car, but I'm not going to pick you up at that man's house. I don't even know where he lives."

"How long do you think it will take for you to get the car?"

"I've got connections. It won't take long."

"I'll call you later. Santiago just pulled up; I've got to go. I'll have a plan when I call back."

Ari sighed. "This is the last time, Angelica."

"Thank you, Ari. I owe you big."

Angelica quickly ended her call and hid the cell phone deep between the cushions on the couch. She picked up a magazine and pretended to read. She heard the front door open and shut but continued read. She felt his presence and then his breath as he descended upon her.

"Feeling better?" Santiago asked, acting as if nothing had happened as he pecked her on the neck from behind.

She shifted her body so that she was out of reach. "I'm okay, a little bored."

"Being here is much better than shaking your ass down at that awful place."

"You were there. It must not have been that awful."

"I don't make it my business to frequent joints where whores prefer to work inside instead of on the street. No matter what anyone says, strip clubs are high-priced whorehouses, with fore-play without sex."

"Go to hell, Santiago. I'm no one's whore. I was making an honest living. It might not be the most prestigious profession, but I applied for it like any other job, took a test, and got the position. It's not becoming of you to try and put me down."

"I don't have to put you down, you do that all by yourself, Angelica. It wasn't a coincidence that I ran into you at Club Platinum. I knew you were going to be there."

"Santiago, how would you have known that I'd be there? I haven't seen you in over five years—before I went to pri... prison."

Santiago took off his long leather coat, laid it across the back of the couch, and came around and sat down next to Angelica. He lifted her chin, but she would not look back at him. He took his hands away, got up and went to the bar. He poured himself a stiff brandy, walked back to the couch and sat down.

"Bad memories, huh?"

"I don't want to go there," Angelica said with a huff. "It's my past, and I want it to stay there."

"I hear your boy Jefferson is out of the joint, and Hamilton," he hesitated, "Hamilton will probably die there."

Angelica shot a menacing look at Santiago. Did he already know about Hamilton? If he did, who told him? At that moment, a cold chill ran through her body again. Of all the people who should have been in prison, Santiago was the only one still walking around and living the life. Something was wrong, but her first thought was on getting out of there.

"Look, I thought you might want some company, maybe take a drive somewhere."

"I'm not in the mood right now." Angelica jumped up and began walking in circles. "Santiago, you've changed. I don't feel..."

Santiago stood and grabbed Angelica's arms to make her stand still. "I'm getting tired of you, Angelica. Nothing about me has changed. You've changed. I thought you wanted the finer things in life. It wasn't beneath you before to get what you wanted any way you could."

"Prison made me rethink my priorities." Angelica pointed her finger at Santiago. "I'm not going back there…for you or anyone else."

"You were going to turn me in for what…that good-for-nothing ex-husband of yours that couldn't run a police precinct if he tried? He certainly didn't give a damn about you. Huh? And Jefferson… he didn't think any more of you either. I hear he's back with his wife. Poor misunderstood Angelica."

"Are you through?" Angelica said through clenched teeth. "Your time is coming."

"I'm out of here. I don't know why I'm bothering with you. You'll come around because you owe me."

With that, Santiago summoned his two bodyguards and had Niko bring the car around. He looked back at Angelica, who had slumped down on the couch.

"Don't wait up for me. Make yourself useful…do something constructive instead of sitting around making butt impressions on my couch." Santiago laughed and walked out of the door.

There was no time to waste. It was hard to say how long Santiago would be gone. He seemed preoccupied and distracted, like something big was about to go down…maybe something big like having Hamilton killed. That something big had already happened. No, Santiago couldn't be involved, Angela reasoned with herself. A bad feeling began to burn in the pit of her stomach, erupting like hot lava from an agitated volcano, its inferno oozing up to her chest. Then fear washed over her, drowning what little bit of sanity she had left.

There was no way for Santiago to know that she knew Hamilton was dead. Hell, she didn't know if Santiago knew. She was making assumptions because that was all she could do at the moment, but her moment of sanity took over. She was going to walk off of this compound and go to North Carolina.

Angelica pulled the cell phone from between the cushions and punched in Ari's number. He answered on the first ring, and before he could say anything, Angelica started in. "Hey, Ari, this is Angelica. Were you able to get the car?"

"Yes, a friend of mine has secured one. How do you propose we get it to you?"

"We don't have much time."

"I gathered."

It was crystal clear to Angelica. She was going to get her purse and walk out. Only two bodyguards had been seen with Santiago at any given time and both had left with him. There was the guy sitting at the booth at the entrance to the house, but she would distract him and then get in the car that Ari sent for her.

"I have an idea that I think will work," Angelica said before sharing it with Ari.

"Too dangerous," Ari said. "You've got to come up with a better plan than that. You risk the car being seen, and I don't want my friend to take any bigger risks than he's already taking. I don't know why I'm doing this for you anyway."

"You care about me," Angelica said very matter-of-factly.

"Don't fool yourself. I would never be in love with a fool."

"Who said anything about being in love?"

"We're wasting time," Ari said. "We need to move or forget it."

"You love me, Ari," Angelica said in a seductive tone. "I heard it in your voice. If it makes you feel any better, I feel something, too. I can't say it's love, but it sure feels like something close to it."

"What's your plan?" Ari interrupted. "We need a better plan."

"I hid a piece of mail in my bag that has Santiago's address on it. Let me get it so I can give you the address."

Angelica went to her room, got her bag and retrieved the envelope. She gasped when she looked at the names above the address.

"What is it?" Ari asked with concern.

"This piece of mail is addressed to Santiago's aunt and uncle. Maybe they're fronting for him. He is still a fugitive."

"A fugitive? What kind of mess are you involved in?"

"Later, Ari. I know for sure I've got to get out of this house."

She gave Ari the address to the house. There was no other recourse than to go with her first idea, if she intended to leave right away. Angelica would wait until she received a call from Ari's friend, who would drive the car. He would park as close to Santiago's residence as he dared. He would call her at ten-minute intervals.

"You have thirty minutes to get to the car, unless I hear from you," Ari said. "After that, consider our task done."

"Thanks, Ari. I wouldn't have asked if I didn't have to. I knew I could depend on you."

"This is the last time." He hesitated. "Good-bye and good luck."

Fear gripped Angelica again and sent beads of sweat dancing on her forehead until the sweat broke into a waterfall and leapt from her face onto the floor. *So Uncle Jorge and Aunt Maria weren't so innocent. They didn't have to want for anything because their nephew was greasing their palms while they kept him hidden from the feds. His time would be soon.*

It dawned on Angelica that she had not been careful. What if there were cameras in the room recording her every movement? If there had been, Santiago would have known about the phone calls, and he and his goons would have returned to the house by now. She casually walked to her room and got a few belongings that she could easily tuck away in her bag and that wouldn't cause questions to arise.

35

The housing market in the U.S. was taking a plunge, but neither Margo nor the real estate company she worked for felt the effects. In fact, sales couldn't have been better. An estimated twenty thousand military troops and their families were expected to converge on the Fayetteville area in the next two years, and real estate deals were for the asking.

Margo sat in her office, preparing showings for two of her clients. She had sold over two million dollars in property this month and made a nice piece of change doing it. She picked up the photos of the homes she would show that afternoon and thought about how happy the families would be if and when they decided upon any one of the dozen properties she had chosen for them to look at.

She glanced at the picture of her family that sat on a corner of her desk. Those had been good times—times when she knew what a happy home meant. Over the past few weeks, she was trying to make it a home again. She and Jefferson were back to sleeping together, but her body wouldn't respond to what her brain chose to ignore.

Glancing at her watch, Margo shoveled the photos and specs together and put them in a file folder. Thankful for the privacy screen that surrounded her office space, she grabbed her purse, took out a tube of lipstick, and painted her lips. Before she had time to bring her lips together to make sure they were covered, she heard voices and then a face soon peeped into her cubicle.

She froze upon seeing him. Avoiding Malik had been easy, except on Sundays while at church. They would turn away from each other, if one happened to look in the other's direction, especially since Jefferson was attending every week.

Eyebrows arched, Malik approached and stared at Margo as if she was the goddess Venus, the one responsible for love, beauty, and sexuality, not to mention marriage, procreation, and domestic bliss. Still holding the lipstick, Margo sighed and looked away.

"You're beautiful, Margo," Malik said, his stare searing her flesh and going through the garments she wore.

"You shouldn't have come here, Malik," she whispered. "Jefferson may show up anytime, and right now I've got to see a client."

"When will you be finished?" Malik asked, not willing to let go so easily.

"I don't know. It could take a couple of hours or more. And I've got another client to see after that."

"Why don't you cancel…reschedule your late appointment? I need to see you, Margo. It's been weeks since we've talked, since we…"

Margo put her fingers to Malik's lips.

"You've got to forget it, Malik. I'm trying to make a life with my husband. I promised that I would stand by him."

"Did he stand by you, Margo? Think about all the time you lost while he was sitting in prison, unable to support you because he comprised his right to be with you. Embezzling from your own company and having an affair with your married next-door neighbor shouldn't qualify you for a second chance."

Margo stood up. "Listen to you, Malik. The pastor spoke

about forgiveness on Sunday. You're better than Jefferson. Please, please don't try and put me in a position to choose between you and my husband."

"Oh, so I might stand a chance?"

"Cut it out, Malik, and leave. I'm going to be late."

"Is something going on that I should know about?"

Margo and Malik jumped at the sound of Jefferson's voice. "No, Jefferson," Margo managed to say. She looked like a ghost. She wasn't sure what he might have heard. "I'm on my way to meet a client."

"I hope he isn't it," Jefferson said as he controlled the urge to do harm to Malik. "I received a call about an hour ago from my attorney."

"What is it?" Margo asked.

Jefferson kept his eye on Malik, who had yet to move. "Hamilton was murdered today in Central Prison."

Malik and Margo reacted at the same time.

"My God!" Margo said.

"Damn," was all Malik could come up with, although he had relaxed a bit now that he was sure Jefferson hadn't heard his exchange with Margo.

"Do you know who did it?" Margo asked.

"Another inmate. They believe Hamilton had a mark on him."

Margo dropped down in her chair. "I don't believe it. No matter how awful Hamilton was, he didn't deserve to die that way."

"Someone believed he did, and it has me a little worried." Jefferson scrunched his face. "Do you mind if I speak with my wife alone?" he asked Malik.

"I was on my way out anyway," Malik said and walked away.

"I don't like him, Margo. I don't like the sight of him, and I best not catch him hanging around you again. Today was his lucky day because I didn't feel like a fight with Hamilton on my mind."

"Jefferson, I can't keep him away from here. This is a public place," Margo said and sighed. "You have nothing to worry about; I'm not going anywhere."

"I'm not worried about that right now. I'm afraid, Margo. I have to find out who killed Hamilton. Robert Santiago is still out there somewhere, and this sounds like him. Why now? Why today?"

"Hamilton's death may be entirely the work of someone else. He probably pissed someone off in prison—you know he could do that well. I think you're reading more into it, Jefferson. Try and relax. I wonder where Angelica is? Even though she and Hamilton had a rocky marriage, she loved that man."

"She did."

"Were you ever in love with her?" Margo asked as if it were a routine question. It was quite obvious to her that she caught Jefferson off guard.

Jefferson stared at her. "I've never been in love with Angelica, Margo. She used people to benefit herself, but she loved you more than you believe."

"Well, it's all relative now. I tried to do the Christian thing by her, love thy neighbor as thyself, but she ran off to who knows where, and I'm done being the nice person."

"She's probably somewhere making someone else's life miserable. I'm glad she's out of our lives. But I'm worried, Margo. Hamilton's death has Santiago written all over it. Mark my words."

36

Curtains closed, Angelica sat on the edge of the chaise lounge in the room Santiago had designated as hers. It was strange that he did not insist that she stay in the room with him when she had made such a big protest about not doing it. For the first time in a long time, she held onto her soul—the memory of her morning with Ari not far behind.

Two hours had passed since Santiago and his goons left the house. She had to get out now or she never would. Deep in thought, she jumped at the sound of her cell phone. She grabbed her phone and answered it, pleased it was the call she was waiting on.

Grabbing her Hobo bag, Angelica tiptoed from the room as if someone could hear her on the thick carpet. She stuck her head out into the hallway, cautiously, looking first to the left and then the right. Anyone who might have seen her would have thought it was a scene from a movie, *The Great Heist*, except Angelica sought to steal nothing but her way out of the house. Seeing no one, she tiptoed through the lifeless house and out onto the grounds.

Getting past the guard would be the hard part, but she had a plan. Her nerves were in a shambles, but nothing was going to keep her from going through with it.

"Damn," Angelica said as the phone began to ring. That was her first signal. Ten minutes had passed and she had only twenty minutes left to get past the guard. It was now or never.

She walked halfway down the circular drive and pulled out the book of matches she had thrown in her purse while at El Conuco. With amazing swiftness, Angelica tore two matches from the book, lit them and threw them into a nearby bush. A flame erupted and climbed the bush, catching a whole row in one gulp. Angelica ran to the guard and pointed to the fire.

"Fire, fire," Angelica screamed, coughing as she continued to run toward the gate. "Look over there," she pointed.

"Yes, ma'am, I see it," the guard said. "Move to the sidewalk while I call the fire department."

"Maybe turning on the sprinklers will do it," Angelica suggested, looking at her watch.

"Go to the sidewalk, ma'am. I'm calling the fire department and I'll see what I can do."

"All right," Angelica said, walking through the open gate.

She watched the guard run in one direction while she ran in the other, locating Ari's friend in a car sitting off on a side street halfway down the hill. Her lungs were full of air, and she coughed uncontrollably but found enough strength to knock on the window.

The gentleman looked over at the passenger window and unlocked the door. Within seconds, Angelica jumped in the car and put her head down for fear of being seen. This was déjà vu. There was a time five years ago when she was bent down in Jefferson's car and bullets were raining all around them, yet she survived.

"Hello," the gentleman said, trying to keep from laughing at the sight of her.

"Oh, I'm sorry. I'm Angelica. A little paranoid at the moment, but once we're out of here, I'll be all right."

"I'm Nicholas, or Nick, as my close friends call me. Ari and I go way back. Our families were close, and there isn't anything we wouldn't do for each other. But I knew you were Angelica the moment I saw you running down the hill. You *are* exciting, like Ari said."

"Ari said that?" Angelica was surprised.

"He did."

"Well, I don't know whether to be flattered or take that as an insult, but seeing as how I'm all scrunched down in this car, it really doesn't matter. Please tell Ari thank you for me."

"You'll be able to do it yourself. We are going to meet him in Queens, and then we'll take you to Jersey and the freeway to help you start your journey. My car is parked at a hotel in Jersey, and Ari and I will pick it up and ride back to Manhattan. He must really like you."

Angelica was silent. It was hard to believe that he would do all of this for her after the way she had hurt him. If she could ever turn her life around, Ari would probably be the one person she'd like to be with.

There was very little chatter until they reached the outskirts of the city. Planes were flying low overhead, and Angelica knew they were in the vicinity of an airport. Before Angelica could react, Nick followed the signs to LaGuardia; however, instead of going to the passenger/ticketing terminal, they followed the signs to baggage claim. Standing on the median outside of the American Airlines terminal was Ari, dressed in his work uniform.

Angelica smiled, and Ari hopped in the back, beckoning for Angelica to do so as well.

"Ari, thank you," Angelica said softly.

Ari held Angelica's face and kissed her passionately. There was no fighting the urge as Angelica kissed him back. To the casual observer it appeared that CPR was being administered, although there was no clue as to who was resuscitating whom.

"You could have waited until I pulled off," Nick teased.

"No time to waste," Ari said in between kisses. He looked into Angelica's eyes.

"Did you mean what you said when you told me you didn't want to leave and that you were feeling something for me?"

"Yes, I meant every word of it," Angelica said, tears welling up in her eyes. "I thought to myself that, if my life wasn't in such a shambles, Ari would be the man I'd like to be with."

"I've thought about nothing else but you. I don't know what kind of hold you have on me, but I like the way it feels. It has nothing to do with the wonderful sex..."

"Not for my ears," Nick shot back.

"You're not supposed to be listening," Ari said. "Drive the car." They laughed.

"Ari, we didn't have sex," Angelica began. "We made love to each other. I've not felt that way with someone in a long time. You were warm and tender. I felt safe in your arms."

Ari looked at her and kissed her again. They held each other and kissed until they reached their destination.

"I hate to leave you, baby," Ari said with a smile on his face. "I'm sorry I acted the way I did."

"You don't owe me an apology, Ari. I probably don't deserve all that you've done for me, but I'm so thankful that you didn't close the door completely. I hope this isn't the last time I see you. I'm having mixed emotions, but I know I must get to North Carolina."

"This won't be the last time, I promise. Angelica, I feel something for you. It may be love. For sure, whatever it is, it has kept me from eating and sleeping—it's kind of what people say when something gets in your system."

"I'm falling for you, too, Ari. Ever since leaving your house, you have consumed my thoughts. It's not infatuation because I already know what that's like. I do…love you." Angelica put her arms around Ari's neck and cried.

"I wish you would have flown, but you know best. It's time. The days are longer, but I still worry about you on the road. Call me if you need me, but for sure let me know when you've reached your destination."

"I will," Angelica said.

She and Ari got out of the car first. They leaned on the car like love-struck teenagers. They embraced and found each other's lips and kissed like there was no tomorrow. Ari let his arms roll down her shoulders, her back, and her backside, holding her nicely shaped behind until he had to make himself release her.

Nick stepped from the car.

"You need to let her go, Ari," Nick said. "She needs to get as far from New York as soon as possible because, when the boyfriend discovers she's gone, it's going to be hell to pay."

"You're right." Ari turned to Angelica and kissed her lips softly. "This won't be the last time."

Ari reached in his pocket and pulled out his wallet. "Here's a couple hundred dollars to help you on your way. I see you don't have the pretty luggage you brought to New York."

"I can't take this, Ari. I've got money left from the time I worked. You've done so much for me already," Angelica said as she tried to hand the money back to him.

"When was the last time you worked, Angelica? You may need it for an emergency. You can repay me later." Ari smiled.

"Thank you," Angelica said and kissed Ari again.

"Okay, here are the papers for the car and an atlas should you need help navigating," Nick said. "It was a pleasure meeting you, but we really must go."

"Thank you," Angelica said and got in the car. Nick and Ari got into the other car and Angelica followed them to the New Jersey Turnpike. Angelica waved when they turned off, crying softly as she headed away from the bright lights of New York.

37

Several fire trucks had trampled the grounds. The fire-fighters were able to contain the fire to a relatively small area, considering the size of the grounds and the amount of foliage surrounding the house.

"What happened?" Santiago screamed as he jumped from the car and pounced at the guard.

"The lady came out screaming that there was a fire, and when I went to investigate, the shrubbery was burning pretty good."

"Where is Angelica? Did she go back into the house?"

"I told her to stand on the sidewalk while I contacted the fire department. I tried to see if I could put the fire out myself, but the blaze was going pretty good. In less than five minutes, the fire trucks were here, though. The lady may have gone back into the house."

"Freakin' fire trucks! Those firemen are going to pay to have this place landscaped. Look at that, Sammy. Look at the freakin' mess they made! I don't care if they were coming to put out a fire, they should have used the damn driveway instead of crushing my blooms and leaving tire tracks all over the place."

"I'll take care of it, boss," Dom said. "I've got a friend that works with the union. We'll get it straightened out."

"Do that. Now I want to be alone for the rest of the day." Santiago went into the house, leaving Sammy and Dominic to their own devices. Dominic and Sammy walked to Dom's car that sat in one of the four garages that was attached to the house and then drove off.

Santiago went to Angelica's room. Not finding her there, he went to the rec room, the scene of their last sexual encounter. Skipping down the stairs two at a time left him out of breath, but not seeing Angelica in the room caused his adrenaline to flow at a rapid rate. He peeked into the indoor basketball court, but no luck. The house was big; she must have wandered to a corner where he had not yet looked.

Anger rose in Santiago's bowels as he rushed from one room to another. He thought maybe Angelica had walked to one of the other houses in the neighborhood. It was at that moment Santiago began to see the light. How did the fire begin? No one said how the fire started. He knew; Angelica staged the fire in order to get away. But she couldn't have done it all by herself.

Santiago hit the wall with his fists. "No one screws me over and gets away with it," he hissed out loud. "She wouldn't go back to Queens, but the doorman has to know where she went."

Anger turned to rage. Santiago picked up his cell phone and immediately dialed Sammy.

"Sammy, you and Dom come pick me up. We have a job to do. Now!"

Santiago slammed the phone shut and knocked over a lamp and the contents that sat on a nearby end table to the floor. "Somebody's gonna pay!"

∞

More than a month had passed since Angelica sat behind the wheel of a car. After fifteen minutes and a steady dose of jazz flowing through the radio, she felt reacquainted with driving and sailed down the road.

Angelica shook her head as she thought about the last image she had of Ari. What a handsome guy. She regretted that their time together was so short because she was having more than "feelings" for him. Ari showed her how much a man could care for a woman—something she didn't know much about. What made her shiver was the thought that he had been there for her, even when she didn't deserve it. She owed him so much.

She moved effortlessly down the turnpike, her mind somewhat at ease. The taste of freedom did wonders for her psyche, and she whispered a short prayer, thanking God for her release. What she didn't have was a plan once she returned to Fayetteville, and the thought of calling Margo was out of the question for now.

Although it was spring and it would be light outside longer, there was no way she was going to drive straight to Fayetteville. Angelica picked up her cell and dialed.

"Thompson, Smart and Fisher," the voice at the end of the line said.

"May I speak with Edward Thompson, please?"

"One moment, please," the voice replied.

"Edward Thompson."

"Hey, big brother."

"Hey, Sis, I'm sorry I haven't called you with more information."

"That's okay. Guess where I am?"

"New York?"

"No, Edward. I'm heading your way. I may need somewhere to sleep tonight, and then I'm going to Fayetteville."

"Sure, Sis, but how are you getting here?"

"I rented a car, for goodness sake. You're a brilliant attorney. That should have been an easy one for you."

"You know what I mean, Angelica. You didn't have a car, you were upset about Hamilton, and sometimes I don't know what's up with you."

"Edward, I'm going to tell you something that I've kept hidden from you. You're not going to like it, but I had no other choice at the time."

"Well, spit it out. Nothing surprises me when it comes to you."

"Edward, I was staying with Santiago."

"Say what? Santiago? How in the hell did that happen?"

Angelica sighed. "I ran into him at a nightclub. He all but threatened me to come stay with him."

"I knew you sounded strange when I spoke to you a couple of days ago."

"Edward, I was afraid of him. He wasn't physically abusive in any way, but mentally, yes. I even had the nerve to think that he may have had something to do with Hamilton's murder, but I know that's far-fetched."

"It really isn't far-fetched, Angelica. Another inmate did the killing, but my sources believe it was a hit with orders that came from outside of Central Prison. Do you know what that means, Angelica?"

"I'm in danger?"

"Hell yes, little sister. Santiago isn't going to let you get away this time."

"But we don't know that he did it or that he even knows Hamilton is dead."

"I'm betting Santiago knew long before you knew. How much longer until you get to D.C.?"

"I've only been driving about two hours—another two hours, I think."

"You're going to stay with me tonight. We'll turn the car in tomorrow, and I'll drive you down to Fayetteville. That way, I'll feel better knowing you're safe. We'll have to get a hotel since your condo is rented. I'll see if I can find out the date and time of Hamilton's funeral."

"You know they say, death comes in threes—first Donna, then Hamilton—who's next?"

"Look, I've gotta go. Drive safe and give me a call when you get to D.C. We'll hook up then."

"Thanks, Edward. I feel much better since I've talked with you."

"Okay, Sis. Talk with you later."

Angelica flipped the lid on her phone. Just when she felt safe, Edward gave her reason to feel insecure. She looked into every car that passed by, hoping that the evil she left behind hadn't caught up with her. Nerves shook her self-confidence, but she gasped as the steering wheel began to shake and the car felt strange as it rolled over the asphalt.

She took her foot off the accelerator and moved over in the right lane and then onto the shoulder. When she was able, she got out of the car, walked around it, and discovered the culprit—a flat tire.

Angelica grabbed her head. "Why me, Lord?" She was out on Interstate-95 without a credit card or AAA. She had enough money to fix it plus the two hundred dollars Ari gave her. She lowered her head.

She went back to the car and got her cell phone. She hated to call Edward again, but she had no choice. As she was about to dial his number, a red pick-up truck pulled off the highway. Angelica froze still with thoughts of Santiago in the back of her mind.

A middle-aged white man with two front teeth missing jumped from the truck. Angelica stood there, not sure if this man was going to rob her and take her car. Before she had a chance to assess him further, he stood in her space wearing a crooked smile.

"Ma'am, you need some help? Saw you off to the side of the road."

"Well, yes," Angelica said, sizing the man up. He seemed harmless. "I've got a flat tire, and I don't have Triple-A."

"Shoot, it may take Triple-A three or four hours, before they get here. If you have a jack and a spare, I'll change your tire for you. Won't take long at all."

"Listen, I don't know what I have because this is a rental vehicle. I'm trying to get to…." Angelica hesitated. She didn't know this man from Adam. He could be working for Santiago—well, even though she doubted it, she wasn't going to give him any more information than was necessary.

"Look, I'll get my jack out of my truck. Check the trunk to see if there's a spare, and if there is, I'll have you back on the road in no time."

Lucky for Angelica, there was a spare in the trunk of the car. She was racing against time, and if the man with no teeth was willing to help her get to where she was going, so be it.

"What's your name?" Angelica asked.

"Larry, Ma'am. I promise I'll have you up and running in no time. You're mighty lucky it isn't a donut."

"Huh?" the one-syllable word rolled from Angelica's tongue.

"A donut is a temporary tire. If you were planning on going anywhere far, I wouldn't recommend it. But since you got a spare that matches the other tires, you're good to go."

"Yeah, yeah, yeah. I know what you're talking about. Can you hurry?"

"Look, Ma'am, this service is free. And it's not like you're at the Daytona 500 where they can put on a tire before you can spit. Relax, I'll have you on the road in no time."

Like a pro, Larry dismounted the old tire and replaced it with the spare. He unhooked the jack from the car, knocked the dirt from his hands, and gave Angelica a toothless grin. "You're all ready to go."

She grinned. "Thanks, Larry. How much do I owe you?"

"Nothing, Ma'am. I was glad to help a pretty lady. Now take care of yourself."

"I will." Angelica jumped in the car and was on the road again. She wasn't sure why she deserved it, but God was surely looking out for her.

38

Long, well-manicured fingers examined the gun, extracting the clip and shoving it back in its chamber. Satisfied with the inspection, Santiago placed the gun inside of his slacks, pulling his tan cashmere sweater over it. He glanced at his likeness in a hall mirror, making faces as he did so. He patted his hair and ran his hand down the length of his sweater, feeling for the gun for added assurance.

"No one plays me for a fool," Santiago said to the reflection in the mirror that pointed back when he did. "No one."

Santiago reached for his leather coat when the phone began to ring. He uttered a few choice words and told the caller he'd meet him outside in a minute.

Snapping the phone shut, Santiago went to Angelica's room once more. He surveyed it and shook his head. While it appeared that her belongings were still there, she was not and apparently hadn't thought it necessary to share her whereabouts with anyone else. *Where was she?*

Santiago stepped out of the house as Dominic pulled up. Sammy jumped out and opened the back passenger door for Santiago. Santiago slammed the door, and the trio was off.

"Where to, boss?" Dominic asked.

"I want you to drive to Queens. I would have had Niko take me there, but I didn't want my car to be recognized. Once we get into Queens, I'll direct you to where I want you to go." Santiago lifted his right hand and felt the gun. Hopefully, he wouldn't have to use it.

The trio drove in silence—Sammy and Dominic sensing Santiago's mood. It seemed that there was some urgency to the task they were about to undertake, although they didn't know what it was yet. Santiago barked orders—a left turn here, two right turns there—and then he told Dom to pull over to the curb. Dom and Sammy looked at each other in the rearview mirror and waited for the word.

Upon Santiago's orders, all three scrambled from the car. Dom and Sammy hung back at the bottom of the steps, while Santiago climbed them to the porch and rang the doorbell. After one minute of knocking and no answer, Santiago became enraged and beat on the door—still no answer.

He motioned to Sammy and Dominic, and they jumped into the car.

"Dom, take me to Manhattan. I'll let you know where to go once we get there." And they were off again.

Thirty minutes later, Santiago motioned for Dominic to pull over to the curb beyond the next traffic light and in front of a twenty-five-story apartment building on Manhattan's east side. A tall, olive-complexioned man dressed in a traditional doorman's uniform stood in front of the building.

Ari stood tall, almost like the building where the residents he doted on lived. He never saw or had time to react to the two gentlemen that jumped from the car that sat idling in front of the building. He had barely turned around from bidding Ms. Faraday a good day when he was hijacked from his post.

"Put me down," Ari shouted at the men.

Sammy and Dominic said nothing but pushed Ari through the car door that stood open. Sammy and Dominic jumped into the car and took off.

Ari stared at the man that sat next to him. His eyes scanned Santiago's face with interest. A slight grimace passed over Ari's face as if there was some recognition upon examination. But he sat quietly, waiting to find out what was so important that he was plucked from a busy New York street for it.

"This will be painless and you can return to your little perch outside the building in a few minutes if you cooperate," Santiago said with a stoic face. "Where is she?"

"Where is who?" Ari asked with a puzzled look.

"You know who I'm talking about. I know it was you who helped Angelica to leave my home…her home."

Ari looked at Santiago as if he were mad. "What in the hell are you talking about? I haven't seen Angelica in weeks."

"You're lying!" Santiago screamed. "You know and you're going to tell me now." He pulled Ari by the collar until Ari's face was inches from his.

There was no smile on Ari's face. In fact, it was hard as stone— like clay that had been fired in a kiln under 400-degree heat. The fine line that formed his lips was etched on the lower part of his face, and his eyes were blank like they were drawn on his face by the hand of a five-year-old child.

In slow motion, Ari took the palm of his hand and placed it over the one that had his collar in a chokehold.

"Don't you ever put your hands on me again," Ari said with authority.

Santiago let go, but placed his face less than an inch from Ari's. He reached down and lifted his sweater to reveal the gun that was concealed under it. He brandished it in Ari's face and then stared menacingly at him. "Tell me what I want to know."

"I can't tell you what I don't know," Ari replied.

Whoop. Santiago slammed the butt of the gun into the side of Ari's face. Ari clutched his face—a small trickle of blood leaked between his fingers.

"You going to tell me now, old man?"

"Angelica is getting as far away from you as she can…you evil manipulator," Ari said. "And I remember you. Oh yes, I remember you, now. Came to see Donna the day she died. I would bet my last dime that you killed her."

"You talk too much," Santiago said in a gruff voice. "I don't like people who run off at the mouth."

Before Ari knew what happened, Santiago hit him in the face again and then punched him in the stomach. Ari began to wretch. Dom looked at Santiago in his rearview mirror.

"Drive to the spot," Santiago barked. He looked at Ari, holding himself and punched him again.

Somewhere outside of the city, Dominic drove. Dusk turned to dark. At some remote area amid a forest of trees, Dom pulled over. There was no reason for dialogue—it was apparent that Dom and Sammy already knew the drill.

They got out of the car and pulled a doubled-over Ari out. Though he was already unconscious, they beat him unceremoniously until Ari seemed to have given up the ghost. Satisfied that the lesson had been taught, the duo jumped in the car while Santiago looked out of the window, keeping Ari's body in view until they drove out of sight.

"Don't mess with me," Santiago said to himself aloud and put the gun back in its hiding place.

39

Angelica felt more at ease as she pulled into D.C. Even though she and her brothers didn't always see eye to eye, they were there when it mattered. She was closer to Edward, the attorney, than her brother Michael, the doctor. It might have been because she needed Edward more than she should have, and while he could not keep her out of jail, it felt good to have someone you knew and trusted on your side.

Washington, D.C.—with its many one-way streets and those that could tangle you up for hours if you weren't sure if you were supposed to be going N.W. as opposed to N.E. or S.W. as opposed to S.E.—was enough to make you pull out your hair. Angelica hadn't driven in D.C. in years, and now the confidence with which she rode into D.C. was beginning to fade. Luckily for her, the phone rang and it was Edward, instructing her where to get off I-95/I-495 so he could meet her.

Angelica's face lit up when she saw Edward and immediately followed him in the rental car to his place. Edward seemed truly glad to see his sister, and they hugged each other and walked arm in arm to Edward's expensive condo.

After settling down, Edward poured himself and Angelica a glass of wine.

"You look good, little sister. You never cease to amaze me how you continue to rise from the ashes."

Angelica looked from behind the glass of wine to stare at Edward. "What do you mean, Edward?"

"Sweetie, it was a compliment. You are so resilient. All the things you've been through, you don't seem to let it stop you from moving forward with your life. You weather one storm after another and, as the title of Maya Angelou's famous poem suggests, and still you rise."

"I really want to get my life together, Edward. It seems that trouble seems to follow me like flies to a picnic. I don't even ask for it, but when I look up, the dark cloud is swarming over me. I can't seem to shake the dark side of my life. I'm trying, Edward. God knows I'm trying."

"Sis, you are going to be fine. Hearing you say that you want to turn over a new leaf leaves me no alternative but to help you in every way I can."

Angelica looked at Edward with so much love in her eyes. "Oh, Edward, that's the nicest thing anyone has said to me in a long time...well, almost."

"What do you mean by almost?" Edward snickered.

"I did meet a nice man in New York. Edward, he truly cares about me. In fact, if it wasn't for him, I wouldn't have been able to get out of New York."

"You plan to go back to New York after the funeral?"

"I'm not sure what I'm going to do. I know it would be a death sentence to go back there now, with Santiago looking for me. He gives me the creeps. Sometimes I feel like he's following me."

"Well, big brother is here to protect you now. We're going to get rid of the rental car tomorrow morning, and we'll strike out for Fayetteville after that. Hamilton's funeral is temporarily set for Saturday; however, I believe the family is waiting for you to get there to complete the arrangements."

"How is that? I've been estranged from that family forever. They must know that Hamilton gave me his insurance policies and things to hold. Maybe we can get Jefferson to go over Hamilton's investments."

"Is that a good idea? My sources tell me that Margo and Jefferson are trying to work on their marriage, and your asking Jefferson to help with Hamilton's finances might be misconstrued."

"Remember, Edward, I'm no longer up to my old tricks. I want to take care of business and be left alone."

"I'll give Jefferson a call, and see if we can't set something up. I'll be with you."

"Great. Now I'm tired. I had a long day. Today was like a page out of one of James Patterson's mystery novels."

"Glad you're here, Sis. You're in good hands."

Brring, brring, brring. Angelica hesitated at the sound of her cell phone ringing. She had ignored several of Santiago's calls, but maybe he would go away if she answered.

"Don't answer that if it's Santiago," Edward cautioned. "He's a smart guy. Your call could be traced, and he might have the resources to do it. I think we are going to have to get the police involved because, if we don't, we may be letting ourselves in for a showdown that we'll all regret."

"You're right," Angelica said.

Brring, brring, brring, the phone began again. Angelica looked at the number closely and realized it was Ari.

"This is the gentleman I told you I met in New York," Angelica said to Edward, her face lighting up. "Hello, Ari," Angelica said with excitement in her voice.

"An...An..."

"Ari, are you all right?"

"San...San...tiago," the voice at the other end said.

"What about Santiago, Ari? Where are you?" Angelica saw the concern in Edward's eyes.

"Beat... me... up...left to die. Wanted to know where you were. Says I helped...you. He...he killed Donna."

Angelica's heart sank. "Oh my God. Where are you, Ari?"

"I don't know. Left to die. San...ti...ago and his goons snatched me...in front of the apartment building. Don't know if I'm going to make it."

"Don't talk like that, Ari. You're going to make it. I'm going to call the police and Nick. Hang in there, Ari, if not for yourself, for me. I need you."

"Beeeeeeee care...ful. Santiago is dangerous. He...he had a... gun."

"Don't worry about me; it's you I'm worried about. We're going to find you."

There was a long silence. "Ari!" Angelica shouted. "Ari, can you hear me? Hang in there, baby."

The cell phone shook violently in Angelica's hand. "It has already started, Edward. I guess Santiago tried to find out from Ari where I was, and when he didn't tell him, he beat him up. He's out there somewhere hurt and by himself." She closed the phone, and the line was dead.

"Give me the phone," Edward said. "I'll call the police and put things in motion. I need to call that Captain Petrowski in Fayetteville to let him know that we're on our way there and Santiago may be coming that way, too. We need all the help we can get."

"Great, Edward. In the meantime, I'm going to call Ari's friend Nick to see if he can help find Ari. Maybe they can trace his location through my cell phone."

"Sounds like we're racing against time. Hopefully we can find

Ari before it's too late for him. We're going to the police tonight, though. We have to stay a step ahead of Santiago and maybe set a trap he never saw coming. As soon as we talk to the police and all our calls are made, we are heading to Fayetteville. I'll have someone pick the rental car up and turn it in. Let's go."

"I'm on it."

Angelica called Nick and shared what she knew. She could hear the fear in his voice when she told him what Ari had said. Guilt consumed her because, if it weren't for her, neither Ari nor Nick would have been involved in her mess. Angelica's only hope was that Ari would be found before it was too late.

"I just got off the phone with the police and they want us to come to the station now, if we have any hopes of saving Ari," Edward said.

"Let's go," Angelica said, grabbing her purse.

Edward raced to the police station, maneuvering around slow moving cars with reckless abandon. When they arrived, Angelica recounted the sordid story of her past and the details of Ari's abduction and what led to it. She also shared her speculation about who may have murdered her ex-husband, Hamilton, and his cousin, Donna. If there was a tie-in, she didn't know since she was merely making an assumption based on the thoughts of others.

Angelica gave the police Ari's cell number and a description of what he looked like. The information was dispatched to the New York Police Department. They also offered to share the information about Santiago with the Fayetteville Police. Angelica was thanked for a job well done.

Glad to have that behind them, Edward and Angelica headed back to his house to grab their things. There was one other piece of equipment Edward needed before they headed to Fayetteville.

While Angelica fiddled with her face in the bathroom, Edward reached into a hidden compartment in his dresser and withdrew a revolver. Quickly, he put it in his briefcase underneath a batch of papers and locked the case. Feeling better about things, he was ready to face what lay ahead.

40

Nothing had changed since Angelica left Fayetteville. She couldn't say that about the turn of events in her life—Donna, Hamilton, and now Ari. It was as if she wore a neon sign that said "I'm bad news and if you get close to me something terrible will happen to you."

She and Edward got a hotel room somewhere in the middle of town, Edward had suggested that they get double beds so that he could be close to Angelica in case Santiago should roll into town.

"You know Hamilton's folks are waiting on you to finish the arrangements."

Angelica walked around in circles with her arms folded across her chest. "Edward, I really don't want to go. Those people hate me, and I think they blame me for Donna's death because I was living with her."

"Well, you're going to have to, Little Sis. I'll be with you. I'm going to call Jefferson when daylight comes and see if he can meet us sometime today—get all of this over with."

"Do what you have to do. I wonder if they found Ari yet? I can't believe Santiago would stoop so low as to harm Ari to get to me."

"I hope the police find Santiago before he hurts another soul. Angelica, I fear that if they don't, you will be in grave danger."

∞

Embezzling funds from his corporation had cost Jefferson more than a twenty-year prison sentence that was reduced to five. It cost him his livelihood and a marriage that was crumbling at a fast rate right before his very eyes. Several million dollars of stolen property marked him as a man not to be respected, causing him undue stress and liabilities which, if it had not been for Margo, could have put the family in ruins. Jefferson understood Margo's distrust of him in some ways; it tore at his heart that while he thought she would accept him back with open arms, she had rejected him, although she had led the church congregation and others to believe that she wanted him home and was willing to do whatever it took to get their family back on track. Seeing Malik at Margo's real estate office earlier served as a reminder that his indiscretions were still costing him.

Quiet invaded the house. For the first time since coming home, Jefferson ventured to the little area that they called a bar and poured himself a stiff drink. His mind was in knots but not because of Malik. He had another worry that caused him great anxiety—Santiago. Memories of a not so distant past flooded his mind. *How did I end up in this mess*, Jefferson reasoned with himself.

The wet drink trickled over his fingers as he dodged the memory of the hail of bullets that had rained on his Mercedes. He grabbed his glass with his other hand to keep from spilling its entire contents. Jefferson was deathly afraid of Santiago, and he still carried the scars of a near-fatal crash.

The ringing of the phone brought him back to reality. He rushed to the phone, anxious to talk to someone, anyone who would take his mind away from the thoughts that were trying to rob him of his sanity.

"Hello," Jefferson said, not recognizing the number.

"Jefferson, this is Edward Thompson, Angelica's brother."

This was not the voice Jefferson was anxious to hear. It was not soothing, and the last thing he wanted to talk about was Angelica.

"Yes, Edward. Are you in town?"

"Yes, Angelica and I arrived early this morning, a little ahead of schedule. Do you have some time today to go over Hamilton's papers? It looks like we may have to bury Hamilton, and we'd like to have all our ducks in a row so we can move expeditiously, if possible."

Jefferson hesitated. He hadn't anticipated seeing Angelica so soon and wasn't sure he wanted to see her at all. Edward's voice brought him back to the moment.

"If it's not convenient…"

"No, no," Jefferson said. "My mind was on something else, but sure…this afternoon is fine. How about in a couple of hours?"

"Sounds good. Why don't we meet at O'Charley's, say two o'clock, it's open and public."

"I'll be there."

"All right, see you later," Edward said.

Jefferson hung up the phone and looked at his watch. He had an hour and a half before he would meet them. Why not? Many of his days and nights were spent alone. If Margo wasn't showing a house, she had other things she was involved in that kept her away from home. It seemed she consumed much of her time finding ways to stay away from him.

Jefferson let out a small sigh as he continued to think about his state of affairs. He needed a job. It was the only way he would add some civility to his life. Maybe it would be best if he and Margo led separate lives. It certainly seemed to be what she wanted. He shook the thought from his head temporarily.

He hobbled to his bedroom. Every day, strength was returning to the muscles in his legs. There were times he still needed to use his walker, but today he was going to show Angelica and Edward that he was a whole man and that he had truly come back from the dead.

Jefferson marched into the large walk-in closet and pulled out a pair of starched jeans, a white long-sleeved shirt, and a blue Polo blazer. After laying his clothes on the bed, he ran through the shower, splashed on a little of his favorite after-shave and sang a song while putting on his clothes. A song had not split his lips in a long time, and while he was only going to see Angelica and Edward on business, Jefferson felt like he was back in the saddle.

Checking his watch again, Jefferson picked up his wallet and looked around the house to make sure he wasn't forgetting anything. It wouldn't take him long to get to the restaurant, but he wanted to arrive a few minutes early so that, if he did have to struggle to the door, he wouldn't be the object of their stares. Ten minutes later, Jefferson was out of the house and on his way to O'Charley's.

The air was brisk, but it felt wonderful as Jefferson rested his arm in the frame of the open window. The radio was tuned to Foxy 99; Jefferson's head swayed with the music. He wasn't sure why a simple drive to a restaurant to meet with the woman he despised invigorated him, but he reminded himself that this reunion was strictly business.

The parking lot was relatively light and Jefferson pulled into one of the free handicapped spots that were available. After exiting the car, he looked around to see if he recognized any familiar faces. Seeing none, he headed inside and requested a table for three.

Several couples entered the restaurant. Jefferson's eyes darted into the parking lot, anticipating the arrival of his lunch companions. Then he saw her—dressed in a white, form-fitting pantsuit, set off by a golden-yellow blouse with a pronounced fly-away collar. She seemed taller than he remembered, but once she entered the restaurant along with her brother Edward, he saw the sleek pointed-toe stilettos that encased her feet. Her hair was brushed back into a ponytail, and diamond studs dotted her ear lobes. He resisted the desire to stare.

"Hello, Jefferson," Angelica said, nodding her head slightly with an arrogance Jefferson remembered well. She extended her hand to him.

"And a good afternoon to you, Angelica, Edward," Jefferson replied, patting Angelica's hand and then letting it go.

Angelica made a full scan of the man she last saw sitting in a wheelchair at the county courthouse. "It's been a long time."

"Yeah, a very long time."

Pleasantries over, the trio followed the hostess to a table at a nearby window. Jefferson expressed his condolences and shared with Angelica and Edward that he feared Hamilton's death might be the work of Santiago. It was Angelica's revelation that gave more meaning to what Jefferson feared and multiplied his anxiety. With Santiago looking for Angelica, he would constantly have to look over his own shoulder. Edward shared that the local police were already alerted that Santiago might find his way back to Fayetteville.

They each ordered a salad and continued their light conversation. Jefferson felt Angelica's eyes dart in his direction, but he resisted the temptation to look back. Even though she was as beautiful as she ever was, he refused to fall into her clutches again. Jefferson hadn't forgotten the moments he'd spent with her, compromising his marriage and his reputation, but they were just that, moments of the flesh, and although his life with Margo was on shaky ground, she was the only woman he'd ever love. They finished their lunch and agreed to go back to Angelica's hotel room to look over Hamilton's will and the other documents.

41

Traffic was heavy for late afternoon. Margo drove toward the center of town to get a bite to eat. She had completed a mound of paperwork back at the office, and instead of going home, she opted for time by herself to reflect and think.

Her mind was conflicted. It seemed she couldn't turn off thoughts of Malik, although she felt an obligation to her husband to make their marriage work. Playing over and over in the back of her mind was yesterday's scene at the office. There couldn't be any more near misses between Malik and Jefferson. Margo was fascinated with Malik, but his obsession for her was making her crazy because he was bent on her making a decision between him and Jefferson sooner than she thought she was ready. And then there was her conscience that wouldn't allow her to entertain an adulterous proposition such as leaving her husband for another man, especially since she had made a pact with the Lord that she was His and Jefferson's.

As she drove on, Margo silently asked the Lord to forgive her fornicating thoughts. A good Christian wouldn't entertain thoughts of the flesh, even though Margo was weak. There was nothing left to do but tell Malik that she was committed to her husband, and they needed to do what was right. She couldn't risk both of them going to hell.

Margo pulled into the parking lot of Logan's and proceeded to get out. In doing so, she faced O'Charley's and the surrounding parking lot. Her mouth flew open as she saw Jefferson leave the restaurant with a woman that looked very much like Angelica.

Anger replaced surprise. Life with Jefferson was not good, but Margo hadn't expected to see him with Angelica after he had sworn that he wanted nothing else to do with her. *What a liar*, Margo thought.

She jumped back into her car and turned on the ignition. As soon as Jefferson pulled out, she followed them at a safe distance. She hadn't expected them to stop so soon. They drove around the bend and pulled into the parking lot of a hotel that sat on the backside of the restaurant and a Sam's Club.

She couldn't believe her eyes. Right out in the open, before God and all of Fayetteville, Angelica was getting out of Jefferson's car. No, he didn't run to her side of the car and open the door, but the mere fact that they were about to enter a hotel was reason enough to follow them and pump their bodies with bullets from a gun she wished she had. Instead, she watched as they disappeared through the double doors of the hotel lobby entrance, dropped her head on the steering wheel and cried.

With tears still flowing, she lifted her head and proceeded out of the parking lot unaware that Edward had passed in front of her and parked his car near the front of the hotel. There was no need to delay her decision about what to do with her marriage. It was settled. Whenever Jefferson returned home, his things would be waiting at the front door or on the sidewalk. She didn't care which. This would be the last night they would share the same address. The hunger pangs would have to wait. There was one stop Margo had to make before she headed home.

Horns blared as Margo weaved in and out of traffic, cutting off two or three victims of her reckless driving. She honked back, oblivious to the fact that she was the culprit that was deserving of those honks. Ten minutes later, Margo jerked the car to an abrupt stop in front of SuperComp Technical Solutions.

With her purse swinging at her side, Margo rushed from the car as if it were on fire. She was a woman on a mission, but not to purchase a computer or any other piece of electronics.

Surprise registered on Malik's face as he saw Margo making her way toward him. There was alarm on her face. "What's wrong, Margo?" Malik asked, assuring his customer that he would return in a moment.

"I need to talk to you," she said, "but not here."

"Why don't you go into my office, and when I'm finished with this customer, we can go wherever you want," Malik suggested. "It'll take a few minutes."

Margo waited ten to twenty minutes before Malik returned. The wait was driving her crazy. She couldn't let go of the last image she had of Jefferson and Angelica entering the hotel. The more she thought about it, the angrier she became.

"To what do I owe the pleasure of your company?" Malik started, shuffling a few papers on his desk and looking around for his jacket. "After yesterday, I thought you were too busy to see me."

There was no response from Margo. For the first time since she arrived, he stopped and took a good look at her. "What's wrong?"

"Angelica is in town."

"And why do you care? She's probably here because of Hamilton."

Margo looked at Malik. He was thinking like a man, but she didn't care. She needed someone to talk to. "I followed Angelica and Jefferson to a hotel this afternoon. And to think that bastard had the nerve to tell me that Angelica meant nothing to him and he was glad she was out of his life. I believed him."

"I tried to tell you earlier that that scheming witch was no good.

I've never trusted her and could see straight through that demented mind of hers the moment she was back in town. With all of Jefferson's professing to be in love with you, the first thing he does the moment Angelica rides back in town is to go sniffing like a hound. I told you he didn't deserve you."

"Okay, that's enough. Can we get out of here?"

"Wherever you like. We'll take my car."

∞

Margo followed Malik to his car and got in without looking back or at him. Malik put the car in gear and drove away.

"Where would you like to go?" he asked, not sure of Margo's mood.

"Why don't we go to your place; I want to talk."

"We're on our way, Ma'am." Malik patted her thigh. Although she didn't brush his hand away, Margo looked straight ahead.

They rode in silence until Malik turned abruptly, hit the remote to raise the door to his underground garage and entered. It had been awhile since Margo was last here, and her body began to tense.

Malik opened the car door. Margo followed him through a door that led into the foyer off to the right of the living area. Malik still maintained his love of art with new pieces by Poncho and Charles Bibbs merged in with the old ones that hung on the walls. The rooms were cozy, and Margo scanned them as she walked from one to another. She even managed a slight twirl as she also surveyed some of the African art pieces.

"Beautiful," Margo said, finally sitting on one of the oak bar stools that flanked the high-top counter that separated the kitchen from the living room.

"You're beautiful," Malik said as he walked and stood in front of her. He took her hand and gently kissed her fingers. "Let me take your coat."

He watched as Margo graciously slid from the stool, one foot dropping to the floor and then the other. Malik moved behind her to catch her coat as it slid from her shoulders as if in slow motion. He sniffed her fragrance as he dragged her coat across his nose and then briefly shut his eyes. Intoxicated!

After hanging up her coat, Malik invited Margo to sit with him in the living room. Margo began to share what she was feeling—the feeling of déjà vu. Margo's lips moved but Malik was in a trance, smitten by the woman standing next to him.

"Make love to me, Malik."

42

Stunned was Malik's word of choice. He was not sure he had heard her correctly. Three days ago, not even two minutes ago, Malik hadn't thought he would own this moment. The woman he secretly admired, the woman he yearned for, the woman he had fallen in love with, had asked him to make love to her. He had waited what seemed a lifetime to hear those words, and now that they were spoken, he stood in front of her like a bump on a log. His pulse raced as the stark reality of what Margo said penetrated his brain. Looking at her, as she continued to stare at him, told him that the time was now if he ever planned on making this woman his.

Malik resisted the urge to swiftly scoop Margo up and take her straight to his bedroom and make love to her. He would take his time and savor the moment, giving her what he knew she needed in time.

"I love you, Margo," Malik said.

He brushed her hair away from her face and kissed her lips. Margo leaned into him and kissed him back full on the lips. Their tongues mated, and before long, Malik's body lay alongside Margo's, the arm of the couch giving them support. Hungrily, they savored the taste of each other's lips.

"I want you!" Malik cried out.

"I want you, too," Margo responded.

Malik gently lifted Margo from the couch. He kissed her again as he hurriedly crossed the room and took her up the stairs to his bedroom. For the first time since Margo arrived at his place of business, Malik noticed her magenta, long-sleeved dress that hung right at the knees and defined her curves. She wore a smart pair of black pumps that accentuated the firm muscles in the calves of her legs.

She wrapped her arms around him, and they found each other's tongues again. He embraced her and their bodies locked, making cylindrical designs in the carpet as they tap-danced in place during the mating call. Finally, Margo kicked her pumps away, dropping a couple of inches shorter than she was previously, and Malik found the zipper that opened possibilities yet to be discovered.

Margo wiggled out of her dress, exposing her lacey magenta underwear. A sexy teddy covered her bra and the high cut of her bikini panties accentuated the curves of her hips. Malik licked his lips as he watched Margo and removed his clothing at the same time.

Margo walked seductively, slowly dragging one foot in front of the other until she was directly in front of him. She gazed at the length of his body and threw her arms around him, rubbing her body against his. Now she had seen what others only imagined.

As much as Malik enjoyed Margo's flirtatious advances, he was extremely surprised at her forwardness. He understood the reason she was with him, but he hoped that their being together was more than charity work. Malik loved a feisty woman who brought the passion with her—it cut down on half the work he had to do, but he was serious about his love for Margo, and he wanted this moment to be more than a one-night stand.

"Are you sure about this, Margo? I don't want you to have any regrets."

"I'm here, Malik. This is where I want to be—with you. Since the day you told me you loved me, I've been in constant turmoil with my feelings. It wasn't until you said you loved me out loud that I realized I might have repressed my own feelings for you. But it also scared me because I wasn't ready to announce to the world that I might be in love with another man when I had promised myself that I would be there for Jefferson."

"What about Jefferson?" Malik asked, his tone serious.

"What about him?"

"Our confessions of love for each other mean that you'll have to choose between me and Jefferson. It will be a difficult decision, but I'm sure you'll make the right one."

"Well, I wouldn't want my reputation tossed around like it was in a bargain basement sale. My mind is already made up, Malik. Now, are you going to make love to me?"

Malik stared at this woman, who had thrown him off his elliptical course. She had his rapt attention, and he wasn't going to waste any more time wondering what made her decide to make him a happy man. He took Margo's hand and guided her to his bed with the overstuffed pillows that beckoned their bodies to become one.

Making love to Margo wasn't as easy as Malik thought. The casual foreplay led him to believe that she was ready to make a serious commitment and they would be rumbling in the tumbler for a long while, but his heart sank when Margo seemed content to only lie with him and make small talk. It certainly wasn't what he envisioned as making love. Malik wanted Margo for far more than what lay between her beautiful legs, but a sampling of what he expected to receive on the regular would be a good start.

She shared feelings about Malik that had lain dormant all the years he had spent time with her. If only he had known then what he knew now, he would have been more aggressive. Malik let Margo ramble until he was no longer listening, closing the doors of her lips with his own. She moaned.

Malik took Margo's shoulders and squeezed them gently, slowly moving his hands down the length of her arms. He continued to taste her tongue as he did so, and she responded in kind, letting out a satisfied moan every few seconds. So far, so good. Malik grazed her breast then guided his hand down over her tiny waist and up the hill to an ample helping of hips and lingered a moment, satisfied when Margo spent another healthy moan.

Malik felt Margo's hand move down the middle of his chest, circle his left breast and then the other. Feeling better about his route of travel, Malik lifted the edges of her lacy panties in the back and ran his hand along her smooth posterior, squeezing until she moaned again. There was no mistaking how aroused he was, and surely Margo knew it as well.

Suddenly, Malik shifted his body so that Margo was underneath him instead of on her side. Her eyes were still closed when he took a second to peek, and he took the opportunity to move in for the kill.

He slipped the straps of her bra from her shoulders and gently kissed the tops of her breasts as her hands moved to cover the tips of them. Whether she was shy or embarrassed, Malik was determined to cure Margo's nerves. She clung to her breasts and shivered slightly but relaxed as Malik took control. Soon he was back to exploring, stopping to give her an occasional tongue lashing that she seemed to take with pleasure.

It was only a matter of minutes before their love for one another was consummated. Margo was better than Malik had ever dreamed, and although they were resting from a first go-round,

Malik was ready for round two, three, maybe four. He was sure that Margo enjoyed it as much as he did. She seemed content as she lay in the hollow of his arm.

"What are we going to do now?" Margo asked Malik.

"What do you mean? If you're ready for me to make love to you again, I'm ready. It was wonderful." Malik kissed Margo on the lips.

Margo sat up. "What are we going to do about Jefferson?"

"We're going to tell him that we're in love with each other," Malik replied.

"Are you in love or did you…did we…merely satisfy some lustful feeling that we have been harboring for sometime?"

Surprise registered on Malik's face. Surprise became concern. "Margo, I love you. This wasn't some conquest to put a notch on my belt. I want us to be together for the rest of our lives. It may be wrong, but Jefferson doesn't deserve you."

"Doesn't mean it's right."

"Listen to me. I'm the one who loves the woman who deserves much more than what she is getting. This is not a game to me, Margo, and so you know, I'm playing for keeps."

"Oh, Malik, I don't know. I promised Jeff…"

"Don't you feel the same way, Margo? When you came here, you gave me the impression that you had come to a decision about your life with Jefferson. It was music to my ears because I've waited a long time for you to come to the realization that we were meant to be together."

"Malik, there is no doubt that you have been there for me the five years that Jefferson was in prison. In fact, you've made me feel like a whole woman."

"That didn't happen until today. Shhhhhh," Malik said, bringing his finger to his lips. "Let me make love to you again. Let me take care of you. I love you," he whispered in her ear, fondling and pressing his nose up against her hair. "Your hair smells so good. You may not know this, but every time I was near you, I'd smell your hair. It always smells like honeysuckle."

Margo smiled. "You may not have known this, but I remembered the times you would get close to me and smell my hair. I often wondered what I would do if I had someone who was that attentive to me. Jefferson used to be that and more, but something happened in our lives to push him off track. Yes, Malik, I remember—I believe it was then that I began to lean on you."

Malik held her and began to caress her again. It was hard to tell what she was thinking with her eyes closed and no expression on her face, but he sought to make Margo his. It certainly wasn't a bad position to be in. She was his friend, and Margo had come running to him, asking him to share his bed and to make love to her. If it was time Margo needed, he could more than accommodate her request.

No, it wasn't a conquest. Malik smiled as he made love to Margo again. Through all the emotions and good feelings, he failed to see the tears that threatened to seep down the sides of Margo's face.

43

Anger and frustration enveloped Santiago like a dark, nasty cloud that announced the onset of a terrible storm. He and his goons had combed the city and come up empty-handed. Angelica was nowhere to be found, and it infuriated Santiago that she had so easily slipped from his clutches.

Underestimating Angelica's prowess had caused him to lose time, money, and the energy he had invested to make sure that his vengeance was carried out in the methodical way that he had planned. Aside from the few unexpected glitches, his plan was falling in place. Soon the breaches of trust in his fallen empire that had been dubbed Operation Stingray would be eradicated once and for all.

Five years was a long time to wait, but now that his new team had been properly organized and trained, it was only a matter of time before he, like King David in the Bible, would kill the giant pain in his ass with one shot from his sling. While it was proving to be more difficult than he expected, one down was not bad.

Needing to calm his nerves, Santiago went to the wet bar and poured himself a brandy. He swished the drink in the snifter and brought it to his lips. Taking a sip, his mind reflected on the room where Angelica slept. He walked to it, opened the door and surveyed it once again.

Had she planned on returning or was freedom more important

than a few pieces of Louis Vuitton luggage, clothing, and other personal effects? Santiago threw the brandy snifter to the floor, its contents splashing and wetting the carpet. He screamed for Sammy and Dominic, though they could not hear him. Angry that no one responded, he left the room and slammed the door.

He found his cell phone where he had left it and dialed Dom's number. "Get ready. You, me, and Sammy are going to take a trip down south."

Santiago slammed the phone shut. He knew where to go. *The bitch had found out about Hamilton, and she went running.* What amazed him was that she found a way to do it. Courage—he had to give it to Angelica. Well, her end was near, and her boyfriend wouldn't be able to help her because his body was probably decomposing where he and the boys had left him.

Smiling for the first time, Santiago rushed to the vault where he kept his arsenal of weapons. He'd take two or three assault rifles and a Glock for himself.

He held the gun in his hand, took off the safety, and pointed at the target he used for practice. *Pop.* "Bull's-eye." A hearty laugh erupted from deep within. Santiago released another shot. "Bull's-eye. That was for you, Angelica. You're gonna wish you had never double-crossed me. Ask Donna."

Santiago's laughter was so loud that he didn't see Sammy and Dominic walk in with puzzlement in their eyes. Turning around at last, he saw them at the entrance to the vault and pointed the gun in their direction.

"Whoa!" Sammy shouted. "What's up with you, man?"

Santiago laughed harder now. He put the gun down and placed the safety back on it. "A little practice, boys. Good for my psyche."

Sammy looked at Dom. "Understand, boss," Sammy replied, the fear finally released from his eyes. "Dom and I are ready to ride."

44

The front door shook like a mild earthquake. The tears that had fallen from Margo's face hours earlier had long since dried, but anger had replaced them. She pulled the belt from around her trench coat and, after slipping out of it, threw it on the nearest chair.

"You're a cheater and a liar!" she said, throwing her pointed finger in Jefferson's face.

He held out his hand. "Hold it, Margo. What are you talking about?"

"I saw you, Jefferson. I saw you with that slut, Angelica. Yes, I followed you to the cozy hotel. I guess you figured if you were out in the open, you would blend in."

"Margo, it wasn't what you think."

"Don't interrupt me!" Margo screamed. "You told me you didn't love her…that you didn't want anything to do with her. Made me believe that I was all you wanted. The moment that wench moved onto your radar, you went sniffing and running like a basset hound; you couldn't resist. You make me sick!"

"So why didn't you come in and find out what was going on?"

Margo raised her hand and swung it at Jefferson. He grabbed her arm and held it in mid-air. He looked like a trainer giving his student an exercise tip. "You, you…"

"You aren't a good detective," Jefferson said, his eyes trained on Margo as he let her arm go. "It's apparent you didn't stay long enough to see Angelica's brother, Edward, come to the hotel as well. Now what do you think happened?"

"Don't try to play reverse psychology on me, brother. Tell the truth for once," Margo hissed. "You were in the hotel with her."

"You're doing all the accusing. Sounds to me like you've gathered all the facts and come to some kind of conclusion that I'm sure is incorrect."

"Don't get smart with me, Jefferson. I'm not playing with you."

"Angelica asked me to review some documents and account information Hamilton had given her for safekeeping. Edward had put them away while Angelica was in prison, and it turns out that Angelica will realize a small fortune. Hamilton had inherited all of his mother's assets after she died some years ago, and although he and Angelica were divorced, Hamilton trusted Angelica with his finances. He didn't have a great relationship with the other members of his family. When he was in the hospital before they carted him off to prison, he had Angelica go and retrieve the papers from his house.

"Nothing happened between me and Angelica. She, Edward, and I reviewed the documents and I advised them on what to do. I may not be able to practice, but I still know my money."

Margo bit her lip and tugged at her dress. She sighed heavily, ingesting what Jefferson had said. She began to sway unconsciously from side to side, tapping each foot on cue. There was no way to know whether Jefferson spoke the truth, but she wanted to believe him.

This bit of news stripped the venom from her heart. She had wanted to be angry because it justified what she had done, running straight away to Malik and crying crocodile tears on his shoulders. Now she felt like a fool because she used what she thought was Jefferson's deceit to fall into the arms of another man and give up her goodies—her hidden treasure—without a second thought. Maybe she was in love with two men, she admitted to herself—and just gave her puddin' away. Damn that Jefferson.

"Since you have nothing to say, I'm going to help Angelica finish the funeral arrangements. You can come if you like. It seems it was a good thing Angelica came to town because Hamilton's family members weren't interested in him—only his assets.

"Now, sit down. I have something to tell you," Jefferson continued.

Margo began to hyperventilate. After all of Jefferson's relating what had gone on with him and Angelica, there was a strong possibility he was going to tell her he had had enough and was leaving. This wasn't the moment she had visualized. Jefferson had taken her anger and turned it into something else. That pissed Margo off, but this was not the moment that made her realize Jefferson was her heart. Maybe she wanted to make him suffer like she had suffered. Malik was there—a convenience at the moment—but she could never love him the way she loved Jefferson. Margo knew she had not been the wife Jefferson had hoped to come home to, but from this moment on, she was going to do everything to right the wrong.

"What's going on?" she finally asked.

"Remember when I told you that I believe Santiago may have had something to do with Hamilton's death?"

"Did you find out who killed Hamilton?"

"No, but to fill you in on Angelica's whereabouts, she was in New York. And guess who she was living with?"

"Santiago?"

"Not by choice. I'll fill you in on the whole sordid mess later, but I'm sure and she's sure that he'll be looking for her."

"That's why you need to separate yourself from her, Jefferson. I don't want anything to happen to you."

A frown formed on Jefferson's face. "You don't mean it, Margo. I know you're in love with Malik. I feel it every time I'm around you...*when* I see you. It's that look of disgust you give me. Oh, it hurts, and maybe I don't deserve you, but I'm not going to be the one to leave. I meant what I said about loving you for the rest of my life."

Margo bent her head down and then back up. She was unsuccessful in trying to keep the tears from falling. She went to Jefferson and placed her hands on his shoulders.

"While you may not want to believe what I'm going to say, it's true. I've never stopped loving you. I've been a little mixed up. I'm convinced that seeing you again made all the pain that I thought was gone reappear. But at this very moment, I can stand here and tell you that, even with all we've been through, you're the man I love, and I want to be with you forever."

Jefferson grabbed his wife and held her tight. Tears fled from Jefferson's eyes as he continued to squeeze Margo. He pulled back, looked at her and whispered, "I love you." Finally, he kissed her passionately and she responded in kind.

A moment turned into minutes until Jefferson picked Margo up from the floor.

"Let me make love to you," he said.

Margo hesitated but knew she couldn't back away now. She felt the eyes of God looking down at her shame. It wasn't even an hour ago that she was getting out of one man's bed, and now she contemplated getting into another, even if it was her husband's.

The marquee from Heaven was blaring bright: Sister Margo is a bona fide Ho! She hadn't given herself to a man in the last five years, yet now, in all of two hours, her credibility and sterling reputation were called into question. Her page in God's Book of Life was marked with a blemish. But she loved her husband.

"I want all of you," she replied.

Jefferson kissed her as he brought her to *their* bedroom. Lust may have followed them, but there was nothing but love in the room. Jefferson helped Margo remove her dress. Margo helped Jefferson unbutton his shirt. When they were completely naked, they held each other, massaging each other's souls and letting forgiveness roll away, allowing love to take complete residence in their bodies.

They took their time and kissed, turning the heat up a notch as the minutes rolled by. Discovery was a beautiful thing because they both rediscovered the sensual side of what their lives had been and what kept them together all those years. Thirty years was a long time, but their romance was as hot as it ever was.

They took their time, exploring and learning each other's bodies again—inch by inch. Margo's groans were music to Jefferson's ears, and the love and gentleness Jefferson gave to Margo as he took his time with her all but confirmed that Jefferson really did love her.

Passion took them to another level. Although Jefferson took his time, he was like a drunken fool, tasting, cuddling, sucking and kissing every inch of Margo's body, unable to get enough. Likewise, Margo became the woman Jefferson once knew—the one who knew how to tend and fan the flames of his desires and return the love in ways that would make a man beg the Lord for divine intervention because he couldn't take much more of what the sister had put on him.

Guilt riddled Margo's body when she finally lay next to Jefferson, spent from a long-awaited reunion. She wondered if Jefferson had felt as she did at that moment—the moment after he had made love to another woman. Making love to Jefferson was as good as it ever was and hadn't been hampered by his being in prison the last five years.

Gathering up courage, Margo looked at Jefferson. "I need to share something with you."

"Shhhh," Jefferson said, holding his second finger to his lips. "Let's not spoil the moment. Whatever it is, I forgive you."

Her courage evaporated as quickly as she had gathered it. For now, she'd let sleeping dogs lie, but somehow secrets always had a way of coming to the light and manifesting themselves. Margo closed her eyes. "Welcome home."

45

Angelica pulled the sheer curtains back as she surveyed the hotel parking lot. An hour or two had passed since Jefferson left, leaving her in an upbeat mood. Although Edward had her money tied up in assets that she was unable to get her hands on, Hamilton's death had left her better off than she had expected.

She turned toward the desk where her brother sat making sure that everything was in order. Legal minds thought that way, and Angelica was glad to have Edward in her corner. There was going to be a fight on her hands, though, when Hamilton's other surviving relatives received the news that they weren't going to get a damn thing. There were a couple of aunts and a host of cousins to contend with, and Angelica was sure they weren't aware of the majority of Hamilton's assets, which was why he passed them on to her for safekeeping. Hamilton's mother's sisters were well aware that she left him practically everything, and they would certainly be standing in the wings with their crusty hands out.

"Jefferson looked good," Angelica said.

"Aged a little bit and I noticed the limp in his walk," Edward retorted. "I hope you're not thinking of playing with fire again, especially since you're at a good place in your life to move on and get away from the hell that has been your past."

"No, Edward, I was really thinking about Margo and how gracious she was to me when I first got out of prison. She probably won't speak to me since I ran out on her generosity. It's plain to see that Jefferson is still and always will be in love with her. I'm ashamed of all the mistakes I've made in my life. But I'm scared, Edward."

Angelica put her arms around Edward's neck and laid her head on his. "I'm afraid of Santiago. I'm afraid that he's going to try and kill me. I haven't told you this, but I haven't slept a wink since I've left New York."

Edward pulled Angelica's arms from around his neck and made her sit down on the edge of the bed. "Sis, I love you. I'm not here to judge you on your past mistakes, but I'm going to help you move on to a new life with new aspirations. The Fayetteville police are informed about Santiago, and hopefully it will be only a matter of time before he is caught. Stop looking back and embrace the future. We need to get to the funeral home to finalize everything."

"Thanks, sweetie. You've been a jewel. When all of this is over, I'd like to see Michael. I know he hates me, but I have to let him know that his sister is trying to start a brand-new life, even though I've had a painful start."

"He'll come around soon, Sis. Give him some time."

"I am going back to New York when this is over," Angelica said, changing the subject.

"Oh, the guy you met. Angelica, you can't let a man rule your head. What about your brand-new start?"

"This is not 'some guy', Edward. He is caring and loving. If I were to be with someone for the rest of my life, it would be with Ari."

"How do you know? Weren't you living with Santiago?"

"Donna, Ari, Santiago…I've lived with everybody, Edward. I

bounced around like I was a carefree balloon with no home to call my own. Wherever I landed at a particular moment, I accepted it and went on with the program, giving little or no thought to tomorrow. My life has so many layers, and most of it, I'm sure, has been because of one bad decision after another." Angelica looked up at her brother. "I'm going to get it straight one day."

They both jumped when Angelica's cell phone began to ring. Her fingers were shaking as she tried to retrieve it from her bag. She glanced at the number and smiled, hurriedly opening it up to retrieve the call.

"Hey, Ari," Angelica said softly as if she was in a library full of people. "How are you doing?"

"Much better than yesterday. I wanted to hear your voice…to know that you're all right."

"My brother Edward is with me. He makes me feel safe. We're getting ready to go to the funeral home to finalize the arrangements for Hamilton." Angelica sighed. "All of this makes me numb, and I hate that you have to be in the middle of it."

"I was lying here thinking about how un-dramatic my life was before I met you. Guess what?"

"What, Ari?"

"You added a little spice to my life. Not that I didn't have fun hobnobbing with Donna's bourgeois friends. Anyway, I wanted to tell you that the *New York Times* had a little article about Donna. It said they have a lead in her murder investigation, but they were not releasing any details yet."

"My God," Angelica said thoughtfully. "That's good. I hope they catch the killer soon. Anything about Santiago?"

"No, but I recognized him as being at Donna's apartment on the night that she was killed."

"Are you sure, Ari? When did you realize it?"

"The day he and his goons kidnapped me from in front of the apartments, one of the guys threw me in the back seat with your Santiago. Mean son-of-a-gun. I got a good look at his face when he was questioning me about your whereabouts, and it clicked."

"You've got to tell the police, Ari. They need to know as soon as possible."

"They know; I'm their lead in the case. If I didn't tell you, an undercover cop has been monitoring my room in the event Santiago should decide to show up. I doubt that he will because he was obsessed with finding you. He probably thinks I'm dead, especially since I haven't returned to the house."

"I'm glad you're doing better. Be sure to let me know if you hear anything, and I'll let you know if anything transpires on this end. I love you," Angelica whispered.

"Why are you whispering? You don't want big brother to know that you might have a thing for me?"

Angelica laughed. "I told him that I might return to New York when this is all over—and not because I left my things. I'm sure Santiago has thrown them out in the trash."

"Well, I hope you do. I'll talk to you later." And the line was dead.

Angelica flipped the phone down and turned to look into Edward's inquiring eyes.

"You've got it bad, huh?" Edward asked.

"He's the best thing that has happened to me in a long time. But Edward, he said he recognized Santiago as being at Donna's house the night she was murdered, and he has told the police."

"I only hope the cops are out there doing their job."

"My nerves are shot," Angelica said, throwing her hands in the air. "I need a drink, if I'm going to get through Hamilton's funeral and have to deal with a murderous lunatic who's walking around free when he should have been locked up a long time ago. I can't believe the feds were never able to find him."

"We don't know where Santiago has been. I'm surprised that he showed his face to you."

"Vengeance. I believe it has always been a part of his plan to get rid of me, Jefferson, and Hamilton when he thought no one was looking or no one cared." Angelica slumped in the nearest chair and sighed.

Rescuing her from her thoughts, Edward sat next to her on the arm of the chair, took her hand and rubbed it. "It's going to be over soon. You can bet your bottom dollar on that."

Angelica smiled at Edward. "I hope you're right. Now let's go so we can get this over with. I don't want to be around Hamilton's folks longer than I have to."

"I'm with you, Little Sis."

46

The steady stream of hot water temporarily soothed the guilt that consumed Margo. Her mind raced to her fling with Malik, hoping the suds from the body wash would erase her infidelity. She convinced herself that running to Malik's doorstep was done in the heat of the moment—a sincere need to have the ears of a friend help her understand why Jefferson had a need to see Angelica. Instead, she found herself succumbing to the source that had plagued many of her dreams—a fantasy come true. And while she had enjoyed all of Malik's attention, her mind was on Jefferson.

Stretching her neck upward, the water ran down and eased the tension there. A smile passed over her face as she thought of Jefferson. Everything was right with their lovemaking, and Margo wished she could erase the few hours beforehand that now made her feel dirty and guilty. Many of her friends said she was an idiot for taking him back, but she loved some Jefferson Myles. He was her man, and she was going to love him until the day she died.

Shame was driving her crazy. How was she going to tell Malik that it was over before it started? Tears welled up in her eyes. She had to put an end to this and soon. After today, she knew that Malik would be relentless in his pursuit of her, and the last thing she needed was for Jefferson to find out that she was no better than him.

"Oh, God, what have I gotten myself into?" she sobbed.

Just then, the door to the bathroom flew open. "Are you all right, Margo?" Jefferson asked. "I thought I heard you crying."

"Were you listening at the door?"

"No, but you were loud enough to be heard throughout the whole house. That's why I came in."

"It's okay, baby. I was crying tears of joy."

Glad that she was on the other side of the frosted glass of the shower door, Margo wiped her eyes with her hands. The last thing she wanted was for Jefferson to know what had been running through her head and that she was feeling guilty over having sex with his best friend. She turned the shower off, but didn't come out. Before she could offer up another explanation, Jefferson opened the door to the shower, walked in with his clothes on and kissed her.

Wet from head to toe, Margo kissed him back, glad to be in his embrace. She wanted to believe that everything was back on track, that their life together was on the mend, and they would not be touched again by the ugly forces on the outside. They embraced until Jefferson left, overcome by the steam.

"I love you, Margo, and always will. I'm going to go and meet Angelica and Edward at the funeral home, and I'll be right back when I'm done. I'm going to fix dinner for you tonight. So get pretty; I won't be long." He blew her a kiss and was gone.

Margo walked out of the shower, grabbed a towel and wrapped it around her. Wet hair and all, she walked into her bedroom, lay down on the bed and drifted off to sleep. Dreams began to invade her subconscious: she naked in Malik's bed, deep in the passion of lust, and he partaking of her body as if it was his last supper. Then the dream switched to her and Jefferson: she giving him what she wanted him to have; and then wanting to give him more, except that the twinge of guilt edged its way in, cutting off the emotion that no longer let her be free. She smiled, though, as her mind revisited Jefferson making love to her. He was ravenous and greedy, devouring her body with joy.

Deep in her subconscious, she heard a phone ringing, angry that it sought to disturb her. She needed this time to rest, to relax her mind and shake her head out of the confused state it was in. Jumping this time, she sat up. Her cell phone was ringing, and it might be Jefferson.

Without looking at the caller ID, she answered, "Jefferson?"

"Jefferson? This is Malik, Margo. You haven't forgotten already how special our day was, have you?"

"Malik...oh, I'm sorry. I had dozed off, and I guess the phone startled me."

"How do you feel? I know how I feel—on top of the world. If I was with you now, I'd make love to you again."

Margo listened in horror. What was she going to say to Malik? There were no magic words she could summon that would put an end to the catastrophe she had created. Courage to deal with it at this moment was lost on her, so she would have to do her best to keep Malik at bay until the right moment presented itself.

"I can't talk right now, Malik. Jefferson is in the other room, and I don't want to risk him overhearing me."

"Have you decided when you're going to tell him?"

"Tell him what?"

"Margo, what's wrong with you? We agreed that Jefferson needs to know how we feel about each other. It's only a matter of time before he knows for sure because, at this moment, I don't want to be without you."

"We're moving too fast, Malik. I can't just up and tell him out of the blue."

"I'll be there with you when you tell him. There is no way I'd let you do it by yourself. He might get violent."

"Okay, let's talk about it later. I need to get off the phone."

"Can I see you tomorrow? You can come over to the house."

"Tomorrow is not good. I've got houses to show all afternoon."

"In the morning?"

"I've got a business meeting."

"Margo, if it wasn't for what happened between us this afternoon, I'd think you were trying to avoid me."

"No, Malik," she lied. "Tipping out on Jefferson was new to me. Vengeance isn't in my blood."

"You were tipping out on a no-good adulterer who still can't keep his thing in his pants."

"So what does that make me—a good adulterer? Malik, you're not making sense."

"What I'm trying to say is that Jefferson has hurt you time and time again. Even though he told you he was a different person, he's still up to his old game. He hasn't changed. He wants you to think that way because he has nothing left but you. If you weren't there for him, his sorry ass would be out on the streets. I can't believe he and I were once best friends."

"What if Jefferson didn't meet Angelica for what I thought?"

"You said yourself, you saw them go into the hotel. How much more convincing do you need? Look, sweetheart, I know that today was different and new for you because you've been a good and virtuous woman all of your life, but today was special in every way and we could have many more days like this. You would never have to worry about me cheating on you, ever."

Margo sighed into the phone. "I feel…this was not right." She wanted to say she felt dirty.

"The first time is always the hardest, but I promise that your second time, third, and on down the line will be nothing but ecstasy. I'll let you go now. I'll call you tomorrow. Sweet dreams."

Margo shut the phone without saying goodbye. The right moment might never come but, for certain, she had to put an end to this nightmare sooner rather than later.

47

She thought there was going to be a reading of the will. All of Hamilton's relatives had assembled at the funeral home. It appeared that all of the arrangements had been spelled out, down to the casket, services, and final resting place. Even the mark-up of the obituary was laid out regally. One of Hamilton's nieces had a friend with a great deal of desktop publishing experience who created a fabulous memento of the deceased with fancy fold-out pages and pictures of each stage of his life. All this crew needed was the money to pay for it all.

Scrunching her face, Angelica, with Edward by her side, looked into the sea of greedy piranhas. They looked back at her with disdain but didn't voice how they felt because they knew she had what they needed to make Hamilton's home-going celebration one to remember. She could hear the individual whispers and see fingers pointing, *'There she is…There she is.'*

"Hello, Angelica," Aunt Dot said, approaching Angelica from behind. Aunt Dot was Donna's mother. Donna looked so much like her, but she had a lot of her father's features, too. Donna's and Hamilton's fathers were brothers, both of whom were now deceased.

Angelica wanted to reach out to her and console her. Living the wild lifestyle as Donna did had probably put her in harm's way. She wanted to tell Aunt Dot how sorry she was about Donna's death and how much she appreciated Donna extending the offer for her to come to New York, although it didn't pan out. Instead, she uttered, "Hello," and offered a reassuring smile.

Aunt Louise moved in behind Aunt Dot, making sure no additional plans were being made without her knowledge. Aunt Louise was Hamilton's mother's sister and was the one who called herself being in charge of Hamilton's celebration. She was a short woman who dressed to the gills, and in her hand was a lacey handkerchief; Angelica was sure it was for effect. Aunt Louise probably hadn't cried one tear after finding out Hamilton had been killed.

"Angelica, glad you and your brother could make it. All we need is the insurance policy to make this happen."

"Good to see you, too," Angelica said to Aunt Louise in a sarcastic tone of voice.

Aunt Louise paid Angelica no mind and continued on with her instructions. Aunt Dot used the moment as an excuse to mingle. She wasn't particularly fond of Aunt Louise.

"I know many people in this town, and because they know me, they've gone ahead with the arrangements, certain they would receive their money," Aunt Louise said. "The services will go on as planned day after tomorrow, Saturday, at eleven o'clock, and the wake on tomorrow. It will be held at my church on Raeford Road."

"I guess there was no need for me to come down tonight!" Angelica exclaimed.

Aunt Louise put a smile on her face. "Yes, dear, you are still part of the family. You and Hamilton seemed to be even closer after your divorce. And we still need to take care of the financial part of this," she hinted.

Not giving Aunt Louise any satisfaction, Angelica asked to speak to the undertaker. Just as Aunt Louise was about to direct her to the undertaker, Jefferson walked in, looking as fresh as ever. He had always been there for her, and she quickly cancelled the thoughts that began to roam around in her head. Whenever Jefferson was in her presence, Angelica felt a vibration between her legs. He was smart and had been one of the most successful black entrepreneurs in the city of Fayetteville. That had always turned her on, but he was a married man who was devoted to his wife now. Her thoughts momentarily turned to Ari.

Eager to have the business before them completed, Aunt Louise pulled aside the assistant who had helped them make the arrangements. Angelica asked if she could speak with the assistant alone—well, with Edward and Jefferson but minus Aunt Louise. She wanted to get all of the expenses she was going to pay for straight from the horse's mouth. No hidden agendas were going to get by her.

Aunt Louise huffed and left the room but stood outside, hoping to catch any discrepancies that went against what she had already planned. When the trio filed out, followed by the assistant, Aunt Louise gazed into each person's eyes, hunting for clues that the funeral wouldn't go on as planned. Seeing none, she relaxed, following alongside the group. Before they rejoined the rest, Aunt Louise turned and grabbed Angelica's hand.

"Is everything all right?"

"You darned near depleted his life insurance policy with all of this unnecessary stuff, but since this is what you want, it is done."

Aunt Louise relaxed. "Good. I'm sure Hamilton had some other assets that should go to the family."

"I don't know about that, Aunt Louise. If there are any, they'll probably be tied up in probate—that is, if he didn't have a will. Now, I would like to have a look at the obituary, if you don't mind.

After spending all that money, I'd like to know that my name appears somewhere on the program. Also, who will be sitting in the five limos you ordered?"

"For sure, you and your brother will have a spot. I don't know about that other gentleman. I'll get the program for you."

Angelica grinned. I guess she let Aunt Louise know that she wasn't in charge of her. "Thank you, Aunt Louise, and you don't have to worry about Jefferson needing a space in the car."

Aunt Louise looked back at Angelica and gave her a shifty-eyed grin before mumbling something that Angelica could not hear. Within minutes, Aunt Louise returned with the program, which Angelica took and read in its entirety. Pleased to see her name, even if it was at the bottom bunched up with "*and a host of other relatives*," she smiled.

"One last thing, Aunt Louise."

Aunt Louise gave Angelica a *We've got what we needed from you, and now you can leave* look, and stood tall in all of her five-foot-four glory. "And that would be?"

"I would like to purchase the flowers that will rest on Hamilton's casket," Angelica said very tactfully.

"No, honey, that has been reserved for the family. The family spray was one of the items listed for the service."

"But who's going to pay for it?" Angelica asked.

"It was on the list, and it should have been paid for when you took care of everything."

"Well, Aunt Louise, I took it off. I felt that, with all the money you were spending, or should I say Hamilton was spending on himself, I deserved to give my ex a little something. Can't take my name off the obituary; I've already approved it to go to press."

"I'll be!" Aunt Louise shouted. "No wonder Hamilton divorced your behind. Such a contrary spirit."

Angelica laughed. It was infectious and Edward and Jefferson joined her.

"I guess we're through here?" Edward asked.

"Yes, and I won't be going to the wake tomorrow," Angelica offered.

"Fine by me."

"Look, I'm going to get home since you don't need me," Jefferson said.

"Maybe we can all go out and get something to drink," Angelica said. "We can celebrate Hamilton's life our way."

"No," Jefferson said. "I promised Margo I'd come right home. We have dinner planned. Angelica, you ought to stop by and see Margo before you leave."

Angelica was caught by surprise. She knew that Jefferson didn't mean it any more than she believed man had landed on the moon, regardless of what NASA claimed though their scientists had a record number of pictures to back it up. If Margo wanted to see Angelica, she could have come to the funeral home with Jefferson.

"We'll see," she lied. "When was the last time you talked with Malik?"

"Gotta go," Jefferson said, not offering any further explanation. He shook Angelica and Edward's hands and left the way he came.

Angelica watched Jefferson's back disappear into the parking lot with her mouth hanging open. "I think I hit a nerve, Edward."

48

The telephone call from Malik left Margo disturbed. Unable to rest, she got up from the bed and went into the bathroom. She looked at herself in the mirror, half expecting the devil to be waiting for her. Seeing her own reflection, she grabbed the sides of her head and shook it, as if to erase the accusation of infidelity her image rendered.

"Get yourself together, Margo," she said to herself out loud.

She found the blow dryer and dried her hair, after which she massaged her body with scented lotion. It seemed to revitalize her to the point that she decided to fix dinner for Jefferson. Not sure how long Jefferson would be, she hurriedly put on a pair of jeans and a tank top and then went to the kitchen and put on her little maid's apron.

Lying in the refrigerator were a couple of salmon steaks she had planned to cook yesterday but had gotten home too late to do so. She would grill them and fix some garlic mashed potatoes to accompany them. Opening the refrigerator again, she reached in the vegetable compartment and pulled out a head of romaine lettuce. She grabbed four eggs and quickly put them on the stove to boil. One small tomato Margo planned to use for something else found its way under the rinse water and then was sliced for the salad. Crème Brûlée would be their dessert, if she had enough left from when she had made it a couple of days ago.

With the salmon broiling and the eggs on boil, Margo rushed to find one of her best linen tablecloths, which she placed on the dining room table. Next, she pulled out a few pieces of her Noritake china and set places for two. Rounding out the setting was her best crystal stemware, used only during special dinners. She opened the blinds that hid the floor-to-ceiling beveled windows that stretched the full length of the dining room and, pleased with the way the room looked, she closed the French doors so that she could surprise Jefferson when he came home.

In half an hour, all was ready. Not expecting Jefferson anytime soon, she was surprised when the front door opened. Jefferson was toting bags that he struggled to carry since he wasn't using his walker. His nose sniffed as he moved closer to the kitchen and then he let out a smile when he saw Margo in her maid's apron.

"What have you done, woman? I'm supposed to be cooking dinner for you, not the other way around."

Margo looked at the clock. "You weren't gone long. I was going to jump into something other than my jeans."

"You're fabulous as you are. Would you mind helping me with these grocery bags? I think I've been on my legs too long today. I've got a real bad ache."

Margo took the bags and peeked inside them. "You were going to fix me filet mignon? We can save my meal for tomorrow."

"No, I'll save mine for tomorrow. It smells good now, and I'm famished."

Jefferson watched Margo as she scurried around in the kitchen and then carried dinner into the dining room. Her attitude had changed drastically, and he wasn't sure why, although he wasn't going to complain. Something must have happened between her and Malik. He'd find out soon enough; he was glad to have his wife back.

When invited to do so, Jefferson followed Margo into the dining room. His face lit up upon seeing Margo's good china and crystal set out for the two of them. He put his arm around her shoulders and fought back tears.

"Reminds me of the last Christmas we had before all hell broke loose," Jefferson said.

"It does, doesn't it? Only thing, Linda won't be showing up tonight and Blake is already dead."

"Let's not allow those memories to spoil this wonderful dinner you've prepared." Jefferson looked at Margo. "That was a long time ago, Margo. It's just you and me now." He thought about telling Margo that he believed he saw Linda the other day at Taco Bell, but telling her would cause a setback in healing the wounds that were still painful. It wasn't worth the risk.

Jefferson said grace, and he and Margo enjoyed a wonderful dinner together. They chatted about local and world events and stole glances at each other as if they were on a first date. Nothing was going to spoil this evening.

"I want every day to be like this, Jefferson. I want to share my day with you, ask your opinion about things, and have great sex with you."

Jefferson stared back, not knowing what to make of this one-hundred-eighty-degree turnaround. He felt blessed and happy that Margo was ready to make their marriage work, but the timing was strange given her attitude only a few days earlier. He smiled, however, not wanting her to think anything was wrong. It was more than her believing that he and Angelica had done no wrong—much more. There was definitely more to the story than he was hearing.

"I'm happy, Margo. I've waited for this day a long time. Why don't we skip the Crème Brûlée and get some real dessert?"

Pop! Pop! Pop! Pop! Pop! Pop! CRASH! Pause. *Pop! Pop! CRASH! Pop! Pop! Pop! Pop! CRASH!*

Jefferson and Margo dropped to the floor and crawled under the dining room table. Margo covered her ears in an attempt to drown out the noise.

"Stay down, Margo!" Jefferson shouted. "Sounds like an automatic weapon. I think the windows in the living room were blown out."

Margo was visibly shaking. She moved close to Jefferson.

"I've got my cell in my pocket," Jefferson said. "I'll call 911."

"The alarm is going off; the police are probably on their way," Margo cried.

"Just in case, I'm going to call anyway. Someone tried to kill us."

Within minutes, the Fayetteville police arrived.

"Police, anybody home? Police."

Jefferson and Margo stayed hidden under the dining room table. Even though they heard the sirens, they couldn't be sure that it wasn't the enemy attempting to pull them from their hiding place so they could finish them off. The police called out again.

"In here," Jefferson shouted, making the decision to crawl from under the table.

"Are you all right?" the officer asked as he moved into the dining room, looking out of the undraped window to see if any perpetrators were hiding.

"We are now," Jefferson offered. "My wife and I were eating dinner when all of a sudden we heard what sounded like firecrackers and then broken glass hitting the floor. Whoever it was used a semi-automatic. It lasted for no more than ten seconds, but it was the scariest ten seconds. We're grateful that we weren't killed."

"Let's move from this room. Even though I didn't see anyone outside, we can't be certain no one is hiding out back. I'm going to draw the blinds so that the inside of your house won't be so exposed."

Margo broke down. She was frightened out of her skin and held onto Jefferson for dear life. Her body began to shake, and she began to cry out loud.

Jefferson held Margo in his arms. "I'm going to protect you, baby. Please don't cry. The police are going to get whoever did this to us."

"Do you have any idea who might have done this?" the officer asked, ignoring Margo.

"I can make an assumption," Jefferson replied. "I didn't see anyone, so I can't back my theory with proof. If at all possible, I'd like to speak with Captain Petrowski in Homicide. He needs to be made aware of this because it lines up with my theory."

"I'm calling him now," the officer stated. "I suggest you good people find somewhere else to sleep tonight. You'll also need to board up your house to keep the curious and the robbers out."

"After I talk with the Captain, I'll take care of that," Jefferson replied.

"Some of my men will be walking around outside and inside to see if they can find any clues as to who did this. Don't touch anything in the living room until we've finished in there."

"You don't have to worry about us. We want whoever did this to be caught posthaste." He turned to Margo. "I need to call Edward and Angelica to warn them about what happened."

"If she hadn't brought her narrow behind back to Fayetteville, this wouldn't have happened," Margo said as the tears continued to roll. She laid her head on Jefferson's chest, still sobbing. "Why us? Why us, Lord?"

He speed dialed Edward's number, and he answered on the first ring. "Edward, our house was hit tonight."

"Hit, what do you mean?" Edward asked.

"Someone tried to kill us—shot a round of fire power into our house, shattering our living room window. I'm sure it's the work of Santiago or someone close to him. If we had been in the living room, it would have been messy."

"Jesus, Jefferson. That lunatic Santiago is playing for keeps."

"It scared us to death, got Margo half out of her wits. Angelica needs to know right away."

"I don't want to upset her right now. Hopefully, this can keep until Hamilton's funeral. I have reinforcement, if I need it."

"I think it's important that she knows what she's up against, Edward, so she can be on guard. That's all I'm saying," Jefferson admonished. "After I speak with Petrowski, Margo and I are headed to a hotel. I thought about skipping the funeral Saturday, but with Hamilton being an ex-cop, Santiago wouldn't dare show up there with a church full of police officers."

"You're right. Let me know if you hear anything else," Edward said, his voice strained. "I can't believe it's come to this. The feds should have nailed Santiago a long time ago."

"I guess the war wasn't big enough. Talk with you later, man. Petrowski just arrived."

"Later."

∞

"Who was that on the phone, Edward?" Angelica asked, sitting up in the bed.

"It was Jefferson. He wanted to know if we made it back to the hotel safely."

"Seems kind of odd, don't you think?"

"Why would it seem odd?" Edward asked, looking at Angelica strangely.

"Because he was in such a rush to be with his wife. And from the sound of it, you and I getting back to the hotel all right was the last thing on his mind. Tell the truth, Edward. What's up? What didn't you want to upset me with now?"

"Somebody tried to kill Jefferson tonight."

"Oh my God!" Angelica cried, grabbing the sides of her face in disbelief. "Is he all right?"

"Whoever it was shot several rounds into the house but, thank God, Jefferson and Margo were in another room."

"Edward, I'm scared. I don't feel safe here anymore. What if someone comes here and tries the same thing?"

"Calm down, Angelica." Edward reached for his briefcase and opened it. "If anyone tries to come through that door, they will have me to reckon with." He brandished the revolver, checking the safety. "They'll have to kill me first."

49

"Good evening, Mr. Myles."

"Captain Petrowski."

Captain Petrowski shook Jefferson's hand. "Good to see you on the other side of the law."

Jefferson dropped Petrowski's hand and motioned for him to have a seat. He dismissed Petrowski's little innuendo about his tour of duty in prison because he had more important things on his mind. "Any word about Santiago, Captain? My gut feelings tell me this is his work."

Formalities out of the way, Captain Petrowski shared with Jefferson most of what he knew.

"We have questioned several inmates at the prison who might have witnessed Hamilton's murder. We still have not come up with anything concrete. The Highway Patrol has been sweeping Interstate 95 for the last two or three days, but our dragnets haven't netted anything yet. We've got the city pretty well surrounded, with double duty the day of the funeral.

"We've received word from New York that suggests Santiago could very well be tied to the murder of a well-known photographer by the name of Donna Barnes Reardon. Coincidentally, she is the cousin of Hamilton Barnes."

"I wasn't aware of that," Jefferson said thoughtfully, wondering why Angelica hadn't mentioned it to him. Brushing his curiosity aside, Jefferson looked at the Captain. "When did this happen?"

"A month ago," Captain Petrowski responded.

When was Angelica going to tell him? She'd been sleeping with Santiago for some time, and surely she had to have known about Hamilton's cousin. He balled his hand into a fist and slapped it into his other, pissed that he had to hear this bit of news from the Captain.

"Is there something wrong?" Captain Petrowski asked, noting Jefferson's agitated state.

"Wrong? Santiago is a madman, and I'm afraid he'll do whatever he has to do to eliminate Angelica Barnes and me. I'm frustrated because he's still running around when he should have been in prison years ago." Petrowski looked away because he wanted Santiago more than anybody and hated that he had slipped through his fingers. "And to see my wife paralyzed with fear when those shots were fired into my house tonight...hell, I'll admit I'm scared."

"Wherever you choose to go tonight—I'm sure you won't be staying at your house—we will have security for you."

Without knocking, a police officer that had been outside gathering evidence rushed into the house.

"Captain, we've got a witness who saw someone shooting at this residence from a car. We've got a tag number and it's from New York."

"Get an ID on it now," Petrowski barked. "By the way, good work!"

"Thanks, Captain. Already working on it."

50

Sleep escaped Jefferson. It gnawed at him that Angelica had not shared the bit of information about the murder of Donna Barnes Reardon, Hamilton's cousin. She had to have known because she was right there in New York when it happened. Maybe she wasn't aware, given that she had been Santiago's prisoner, but this was a serious matter, and it was hitting mighty close to home.

It pissed him off more that he and Margo had to uproot and leave their home for an undisclosed place because of what he feared was near. He had not been as close to God as he should have, but he was certain that Margo's direct connection to the Father was what saved their lives. If Jefferson was a praying man, his single prayer was that God would strike Santiago dead and rid the city, state and country of a horrifying and treacherous menace.

Unsure if they were in Fayetteville or a neighboring city, Margo and Jefferson had been placed in an unmarked police vehicle and whisked away to an undisclosed location. The only thing Margo and Jefferson knew for sure was that they were holed up in a hotel suite that offered a temporary shelter away from home.

He held Margo close, satisfied that she had finally drifted off to sleep. Even her snoring was music to Jefferson's ears because Margo's fear was greater than his own. Uncomfortable with security protecting their privacy, they were grateful for their protection nonetheless. Jefferson considered sending Margo to Atlanta to stay with her brother or with Ivy and J.R., but when Jefferson approached her with the idea, she pulled rank and insisted that she was going to stay by his side.

Patting Margo, Jefferson eased from underneath the covers and sat on the edge of the bed. With his elbows on his knees, he placed his forehead on the ball of his knuckles and contemplated what he should do. It was still a good idea to remove his family from harm, but he wanted to do something to make this nightmare end.

Noises in the hallway made him look up and turn his head toward the door. Cautiously, he got up and tiptoed toward the door. Reaching the door, he stretched his ear to see if could hear what was going on. Muffled words were traded but none that Jefferson could decipher. Again, he heard footsteps that seemed to be retreating—and then quiet again.

A thin layer of sweat formed on his face. Jefferson moved from the door and went to the bathroom. He relieved himself and took a face cloth and washed his face. Leaving the bathroom, Jefferson breathed a sigh of relief but was startled when he saw Margo sitting up in the bed.

"What is it, Jefferson?"

"Can't sleep. I still hear the shots in my head from earlier this evening. I see Santiago's face mocking me—telling me that my time is up."

"Stop it, Jefferson," Margo pleaded. "We can't give into the fear or it's going to swallow us up."

"I'm trying, Margo. God knows I'm trying not to worry. We came so close tonight...so damn close. We could have been lying in the morgue alongside Hamilton. I keep asking myself, why? Why now?"

"We don't know the answer to that but we have to trust that the police will do their job. We have more security protecting us than they do at Fort Knox. Unless Santiago has a well-trained network, I believe the feds and the police are in a good position to apprehend him before he does anymore harm."

"Why didn't they stop what happened to us tonight?" Jefferson asked with a tremble in his voice.

"Santiago had to make a move. Unfortunately, we were the targets. You know what happens when a criminal becomes anxious to carry out his mission; he sometimes becomes careless and sloppy. His desire is so strong to get revenge that he will stop at nothing to carry it out. It's only a matter of time before he's caught."

Jefferson looked at Margo. He wasn't sure where the confidence she exuded came from, but it was what he needed at this moment. Margo exercised such control over her emotions that it surprised him.

"I love you, Margo. Even at three o'clock in the morning, you're so full of wisdom."

"I didn't say I wasn't afraid of the big bad wolf, but I can't allow fear to control my destiny. Come and sit down next to me." Margo waved Jefferson over and patted the bed. "Give me your hands; we're going to pray."

Jefferson sat next to Margo and put his hands in hers. He looked at her with a smile, said nothing and closed his eyes.

"Dear Lord, Jefferson and I have come to You as humbly as we know how, asking once again for Your help. There's a crazy, mad man roaming the city who wants to kill my husband and others. I know there's nothing too hard for You, Lord, and I ask that You would put Your loving arms around us and protect us from all hurt, harm, and danger that threatens to kill and destroy our family. I know that we don't always deserve Your love and blessings, but I ask that You do this for me…for us.

"My husband is a good man, Lord. He's paid for his mistakes and he wants to do the right thing. Please forgive us for those things we have done that weren't right in Your sight and restore us to good standing with You. You are an awesome God, Creator of all things. You would not have put the sun, moon, and stars in the heavens if you didn't love us the way you do.

"Again, I submit my request humbly to You because You're the only one I know who can get us out of this jam. These things I ask in Your name, Amen."

Jefferson opened his eyes and kissed Margo. "That was beautiful. How did I get so lucky to have the best woman in all of the universe?"

Margo turned away and wiped the tears that had converged at the corners of her eyes. *God, forgive me for my transgressions*, she prayed silently. She opened her eyes and fell into Jefferson's waiting arms. With all the firepower that surrounded them, standing guard to take out the enemy if it should decide to raise its ugly head against them, Margo and Jefferson made love, after which they settled into a restful sleep.

∞

Jefferson's body shook. He woke and sat straight up in the bed. Loud noises resounded in his head—*rat-a-tat tat, rat-a-tat tat, rat-a-tat tat, rat-a-tat tat*. His dreams would not retreat and release him to the real world. Santiago, surrounded by his death squad with automatic weapons, stood only several feet from his defenseless body, spraying him over the city street without an ounce of remorse.

"Uh, uh, uh, uh, uh." Jefferson struggled to catch his breath, reeling from the dream. He clasped his throat with his hand and then dragged it down to his heart, letting it lay there for a moment until his heartbeat became normal.

Margo's body shifted. Not feeling Jefferson next to her, she sat up in the bed. Adjusting her eyes to the darkness, she reached out to him. "What's the matter, baby? What's, what's wrong?"

"Go back to sleep, Margo. I'm restless…couldn't sleep."

Margo sighed. "I feel guilty because that was the best sleep I've had in a while. Tell me what's on your mind."

Sighing, Jefferson looked back at Margo, contemplating if he should share his dream, and voted against it. "I want this to all go away," he finally said. "Do you mind if I turn on the TV? I need a distraction."

"Go ahead, but turn it down low. I can't stand loud noises early in the morning."

Finding the remote, Jefferson switched on the television. The morning news with John and Barbara flooded the screen.

"We have a breaking news story out of Fayetteville," Barbara said. "Denver Grey is live in Fayetteville now."

"Thank you, Barbara," Denver said. "We've learned that last evening, around nine o'clock, the home of Jefferson and Margo Myles, in the Jordan Estates subdivision here in Fayetteville, was riddled with bullets gangland style by unknown assailants as they drove past the home. An eyewitness to the event was able to obtain the license number and identify the make of the car. The Myleses, in the meantime, were taken to an undisclosed shelter under police protection.

"Many may remember that, five years ago, Jefferson Myles, a well-known businessman in the city, was involved in a covert organization called Operation Stingray and convicted of embezzlement. Mr. Myles was recently released from prison. Operation Stingray—headed by then leader Robert Santiago, who is still at large—was an underground organization that purchased stolen weapons from Ft. Bragg Army Base and then sold them to a rebel group in Honduras.

"The police have made a positive ID of the license plate and have the name of the owner of the vehicle, which they will not release at this time. They do say, however, that Mr. Robert Santiago, who has eluded police dragnets for five years, may be linked. There is some speculation that the murder of former Lieutenant Hamilton Barnes, who was killed at Central Prison earlier this week and was also a member of Operation Stingray, may be the work of Robert Santiago. Mr. Barnes will be laid to rest tomorrow.

"We will continue to update you on this news story as information becomes available. I'm Denver Grey reporting to you live from Fayetteville. Back to you, Barbara."

Silence gripped the room, save for the newscasters' continuing coverage of other local news stories. Jefferson sat glued to the television, as if in a trance, without batting a lash. Margo heard the news as well and sat up in the bed, now fully alert. Slowly, she lifted her hand and touched Jefferson's shoulder.

"Did you hear what they said?" Margo asked.

"Didn't miss a word. Santiago is written all over this atrocity. And you know what, Margo? I don't feel any better with all those policemen sitting outside. He'd shoot all of them to get to me."

"Why didn't he try to take your life while you were in prison, as you believe he did with Hamilton?"

"I've been thinking a lot about that. As I try and analyze this thing, I believe it all begins with his wanting to get even with Angelica." Jefferson jumped from the bed.

"What is it, Jefferson?" Margo asked in alarm.

Jefferson continued to pace the floor with his thumb under his chin and his index finger across his nose. "That's it!"

"That's what?"

"Santiago wanted to control Angelica, to get her in his clutches. She owed him after she ran out on him to warn Hamilton and me that there was a hit out on us. I believe that Angelica wasn't playing the game he wanted her to play, so he had Hamilton killed to put the fear of God in her, and after she ran out on him, he was out for blood."

"But why you, Jefferson? You had nothing to do with Angelica."

"Everything connected to Angelica and Operation Stingray is tainted. Santiago has declared war and is making every effort to see that we pay for the demise of that group, although only Hamilton, Angelica, and I did time for our part in Operation Stingray."

"It always comes back to Angelica. When will men come to their senses about the likes of that woman?"

"Margo, Angelica was trying to start her life over. If you ask me, it was almost as if she was drawn to New York by Santiago. I know it sounds far-fetched, but I wouldn't put it past that master manipulator to have pulled something off like that."

"You're sounding like those soap operas now—too good to be true. But, baby, I'm beginning to think like you. Humph. You may not be far from the truth, not far at all."

51

embers of the Fayetteville precinct that Hamilton Barnes was affiliated with filed into the church to bid farewell. Their shields of authority hung over their left breasts on their dress blues, and they looked liked an elite brotherhood. Sergeant Carl Broadnax, who was now Lieutenant Broadnax, brought up the rear.

Fear gripped Angelica as she filed into the church, followed by Edward and a host of Hamilton's relatives. She wore a charcoal-gray suit with black embroidery along the collar, pockets, and cuffs, charcoal-gray stilettos with a black suede heel, and a matching hat that looked as if it was sliding off the side of her head. Her eyes spotted Lieutenant Broadnax and Captain Petrowski, as they watched the crowd, scanning them for clues or some subtle message that would lead them to the killer or killers of the dearly departed. She almost stopped when she saw Margo sitting next to Jefferson, obviously surrounded by police officers. Angelica could have used one of Margo's hugs today.

As Angelica approached the front of the church, she saw him for the first time—stretched out in his dress blues with his name-plate "Barnes" placed over his breast without the shield that was the policeman's badge of honor. Some say he didn't deserve to wear the policeman's uniform, but Aunt Louise fought tooth and nail for her nephew to wear the uniform that had been a large portion of his life. In the end, even the police department gave up fighting the feisty, short woman who was going to have it her way or else.

In death, Hamilton still looked good. His hair seemed blacker than before but thinner, and he seemed very much at peace…at last.

From the tops of the few businesses that surrounded the church, sharpshooters were poised to respond to any strange activity they saw. Plainclothesmen with bulletproof vests were embedded among the mourners inside, equipped with firepower should they need it in the House of the Lord.

Various people came to the pulpit and expressed their condolences, but it was Lieutenant Carl Broadnax's soliloquy that captured Angelica's heart and caused her to temporarily forget the fear that had consumed her the past few days. Lieutenant Broadnax looked straight into the hearts of the people who were assembled and spoke about a man who loved the badge, the uniform, the honor among brethren, and the code that bound the men and women of the police force together. He said that Lieutenant Barnes loved life but loved protecting the city's residents more, and he had a laugh that was contagious whenever he talked about having tucked away the city for the night after a day went by without incident.

"There were many times that we did not see eye to eye on cases we were working on," Broadnax continued, "but I couldn't help but love this man because, even with all of our differences, he gave me a chance to realize my dream to become a police officer, and we had the utmost respect for each other. It is with profound sadness I find myself here today. No matter what you thought or knew of Lieutenant Barnes, he had a heart—a giving heart, and… and I loved him."

Tears welled up in Lieutenant Broadnax's eyes, and he looked down upon his sleeping brother. He took his hand and saluted Hamilton. "My brother, farewell."

It was too much for Angelica. A nurse rushed to her side as she broke down and wept openly. Edward rubbed her back to try and calm the pain she was feeling, but she continued to cry out loud. There was a moment of silence until the ushers were able to subdue Angelica, their fans moving in rapid succession. A soloist was next and sang "His Eye is on the Sparrow," which caused Angelica to weep again. Aunt Lucille threw Angelica a look that said *You can cut the phony crap now*, but that didn't stop Angelica from bawling. And after the preacher laid out a message that should have had everyone on their knees, it was time to say good-bye. It was the end of an era.

∞

Pallbearers were lined up like pins in a bowling alley. Tension flooded the church as plainclothes officers moved into position, pivoting left and right while scanning the mourners for any possible disruptions. Giving the minister the go-ahead, the funeral procession moved down the aisle as the mourners looked on.

Angelica acknowledged different ones with a nod of her head until her eyes latched onto Margo's. Margo seemed to look straight through her soul. She saw Jefferson take Margo's hand and thread his fingers through hers, at which Angelica dropped her head and moved on.

They laid Hamilton to rest in a goodbye fit for a king—maybe a king of a small nation or king of a city block, but nevertheless, it was beautiful in every way. *Hamilton would have been pleased*, Angelica thought, *since he always thought highly of himself*.

"Hamilton sure looked good," Aunt Louise said as she took her seat in the limo.

"Looked like he was sleeping," Aunt Dot added, putting her tissue in her tiny purse.

"It was a nice service. I'm glad that Angelica has stopped all that crying. It was getting on my nerves," Aunt Louise said, crinkling her nose and glancing at Angelica from the corner of her eye.

Angelica ignored them. She found that, by not giving Aunt Louise any ammunition to get on her soapbox, she would be left alone.

"Edward, I'm not in the mood for the repast. I can eat something at the hotel," Angelica said in a low voice.

"All right, but you might want to stop by the fellowship hall for a few minutes and say a few words to some old friends."

"Old friends like whom, Edward? I'm really not up to the Barnes clan this afternoon," Angelica whispered, not wanting Aunt Louise to hear.

"I think it would do you some good if you spoke to Margo. Might ease your conscience where she is concerned."

"I don't think I can face her. She gave me a second opportunity, and I failed miserably. I'm not up to being hospitable or faking the funk. As much as I want to, today is not the day."

"Well, it looks like they are taking us back to the church anyway and we don't have a ride to the hotel."

"Oh, Edward, use your imagination. I'm sure you can call a taxi if you want to."

"Too late. Look who's standing at the curb. Don't part your lips to say it."

Angelica sat in silence as the limo pulled in front of the church. On the curb stood Margo and Jefferson, talking to several other people—the plainclothesmen close by. The day had gone off without a hitch, and everyone seemed to be in a more relaxed mood.

Edward offered his hands as Aunt Louise and Aunt Dot filed out of the limo. He extended his hand to his sister, and Angelica finally got out.

"Margo, Jefferson," Angelica began, "I'm glad you were able to come to the service. I'm so sorry about what happened the other night at your place."

Edward shook Margo and Jefferson's hand. "We're lucky to be alive," Jefferson responded. "I'll feel a lot better when they catch Santiago."

Edward rubbed his right side. "I've got something for him, should he decide to ride up in here."

"You packing?" Jefferson asked. "It's a wonder the cops didn't throw you out of the church today."

"I guess since I came in with the family, they didn't think to check me for hardware."

Margo continued to stare at Angelica, who turned her head slightly in light of the awkward silence. Angelica wished she had stayed in the car, not relishing this moment at all. She tugged at Edward's sleeve so they could move to the fellowship hall, say a few thank you's and be on their way. Ignoring her, Edward continued to talk to Jefferson.

"How are you doing?" Margo finally asked, a coldness to her tone.

"Could be better, Margo. I've been through a lot these last couple of days."

"I know what you mean. I can't even go home—in fact, I'm afraid to go home because of some crazy lunatic that tried to kill us."

"Look, Margo, I'm sorry."

"Why are you apologizing? You didn't do anything."

"Ladies," Jefferson cut in, "maybe we should go into the fellowship hall. It might be much safer than being out on the street."

"Can I say this while I have the courage to do so?" Angelica asked. Jefferson looked at Margo and then at Edward and back at Angelica.

"Sure," Jefferson said.

"Margo, I know you don't think much of me. I don't blame you. I'm sure you're wondering why I left Fayetteville without saying a word. I was offered a job in New York, and since my assignment with Malik didn't work out, I was ready to go. You know how I am. I make rash decisions without thinking them through, but I felt I needed to get as far away from Fayetteville as I could—get away from the memories that seemed to haunt me and wanted to destroy me in the process. I fled on the first thing smoking."

"When it didn't work out in New York, I didn't want to come crawling back. I couldn't face you after you had extended a peace offering to me and I defaulted. One day, when I've finished chasing my shadow, when this whole mess with Santiago is over, I'd like to sit down and tell you about it. I so badly wanted a brand new start, but the old keeps overshadowing the new."

"Maybe someday we can sit down and have that talk," Margo said. "Now we better go inside. I think our shadows are getting pretty anxious because we're making ourselves targets for whomever is trying to rattle our cages."

"Good idea," Edward said, pulling Angelica along.

"After you," Jefferson said and kissed Margo on the nose. "I love you."

52

Five four-by-six tables were filled with Barnes' family members and close friends, Angelica and Edward included. More friends of the family occupied the other tables in the fellowship hall as they joined them in a meal that consisted of fried chicken, country ham, mashed potatoes and gravy, macaroni and cheese, snap peas and green beans, and buttered rolls. A slideshow of the highlights of Hamilton's life played out on a giant screen.

Jefferson and Margo sat close to Angelica and Edward at their request and melded right into the family. Even though Hamilton's life had been heavily tarnished, he had been a friend of the family. Margo recalled the times in her memory that she had drooled over the handsome man, although privately, but in all of her dealings with Hamilton and Angelica, she never thought that his end would be so tragic.

Margo excused herself to go to the restroom. It had been a long day, and now her body sent an urgent message to care for it. Crossing the room, she saw familiar faces and acknowledged them but stopped cold in her tracks when she saw Malik standing at the end of the row.

If he had been at the service, she didn't see him. Margo looked back at Jefferson, who was busy biting into his chicken and conversing with Edward. She was not ready to face Malik or be reminded of the unthinkable thing she had done with him.

His smile made her wet herself as she fought the nerves that racked her body. How was she going to tell him that she made a mistake and that her heart belonged to Jefferson? She was angry for so easily giving herself to him, but she knew without a doubt who held her heart.

Malik stepped in front of her. "Hey, Margo. How are you feeling?"

"Like I really have to get to the restroom."

"You go on; I'll wait for you to come out."

"I'm with my husband, Malik. This is not a good time."

"When is a good time? Look at him. He can't seem to get enough of Angelica. Dragged you by his side so he could…"

"Stop it, Malik. Angelica and Edward asked us to sit with them. I've got to go. I'll talk with you later." Margo left Malik standing there with a puzzled look on his face.

Margo closed her eyes and breathed in and out. Encounters with Malik had to be avoided because she was afraid he wouldn't understand that she really didn't want to be with him. With her shoulder, she pushed into the stall and hugged the wall until her urgency made her dance in place until she found relief. She washed her hands and exhaled, praying to God that Malik had gone to his seat.

Slowly opening the door to the restroom, she peered out. Not seeing Malik, she tried to make a mad dash back to her seat. Before she got two feet, a hand grasped her arm, making her flinch. Margo turned and looked into Malik's quizzical face.

"Take your hands off of me, Malik."

"Margo, what's wrong with you? I want to talk with you. I grabbed your arm because you were moving so fast, and I didn't want to miss the opportunity to speak to you again before you waltzed to your seat."

Margo looked at her arm and up at Malik. "Malik, we have to talk, but this is not the time or the place."

"You're making me crazy, girl. I want you so bad. The other day was so wonderful, I could make love to you right here."

"Malik, not now. I guess you aren't aware that Jefferson and I were almost killed the other night."

"What are you talking about? Almost killed?"

"A drive-by. Someone riddled our house with bullets. It's only by the grace of God that we're alive."

"I'm sorry, Margo. I haven't looked at the news…oh my God… are you all right? Do the police know who did it?"

"No, they don't know for sure, but they have some idea—in fact, a pretty good idea."

"What can I do for you?"

"There's nothing you can do for me or Jefferson. We're under police protection, and that's as good as it gets until they make an arrest. It's been a scary ordeal."

"You know you can stay with me. All you're going through is probably because of all the mess Jefferson created. I've told you over and over, he doesn't deserve you."

"I'm staying with my husband, Malik. I love him, and I'm not going to leave him."

"Does he know that you slept with me the other day?"

"Not unless you propose to tell him."

"You've disappointed me, Margo. I didn't come to you, you came to me. You gave yourself to me. You allowed me to touch your husband's jewels."

SLAP!! All eyes turned away from the slideshow that played

Hamilton's life over and over. No one was sure what had tran-
spired, and murmuring was heard throughout the crowd. Stunned,
Malik cradled his jaw with his hand while looking at the stranger
who had laid one on him. Margo walked away in a hurry, leaving
Malik for a second time, only this time nursing his aching jaw.

Margo saw Jefferson moving toward her as she hurried to
distance herself from Malik. A frown was drawn on his face, and
when he reached Margo, his frown turned to anger as Malik
came toward them.

"Jefferson, not now," Margo pleaded.

"Well, tell me something," Jefferson said, looking between
Margo and Malik.

"Your wife slapped my face," Malik said, staring Jefferson down.
"Do you want to know why?"

"Because you deserved it, you imbecile? Malik, I've given you
more warnings than you deserve about staying away from my
wife, but this is the last time I'm telling you."

"And what are you going to do?"

"It's fortunate that you won't find out tonight because this is
neither the time nor the place. Don't push my nerve because if I
have to go to prison again, I will if you mess with my wife."

"Maybe the two of you deserve each other. You know, she's not
a saint either."

Margo begged Malik with her eyes to keep her secret. She
hated him and wished she could make him disappear. She hated
herself even more for succumbing to a lust of the flesh in a
moment of weakness, no matter how many times Jefferson
might have been unfaithful to her. But it was the painful moment
between two former friends that left everyone's tongues wagging;
it didn't take clues to help them figure out what Malik was trying
to say.

Jefferson was silent as he followed Margo back to their seats. Margo looked at Angelica as her eyes asked what had happened. Ashamed, Margo folded her hands and placed them over her mouth, her elbows glued to the table. She dared not look at Jefferson, for fear that his accusing eyes would convict her—and rightfully so. A reprieve came her way when one of Hamilton's cousins got up to talk about what a good friend he had been.

53

One after another, they single filed to the front of the room, sharing good times about cousin Hamilton, Uncle Hamilton, my nephew Hamilton, and my good friend Hamilton. Laughter was the best medicine as it took some of the sting away from the final service, with each person trying to outdue the next in the stories they told. The crowd began to dwindle, and the few police officers that remained began to relax as the home-going for Hamilton was coming to a close without incident.

Angelica walked over to Lieutenant Broadnax and extended her hand. "Your words touched me, Carl. They were beautiful. I wished Hamilton could have heard them."

"You know, Angelica, the lieutenant and I were at odds about a lot of things, but I truly loved him. Hated that things went down the way they did for us five years ago, but I took an oath to uphold the law, and I was doing my job."

"I know." Angelica brushed his shoulder. "You got someone in your life yet?"

"You remember Ebony?"

"Yes, she was Jefferson's secretary."

"Well, after her mom died, we became very close. In fact, we have a December wedding planned."

"Congratulations, Carl. I'm so happy for you. Please give my regards to Ebony."

"I will, and…we'd love for you to come to our wedding."

Several seconds passed. Angelica did not respond, and Lieutenant Broadnax waved his hand in front of her face. It was not her imagination, but passing in front of her was the man in dreads. She'd recognize his face anywhere. It was etched in her memory.

"Lieutenant Broadnax, don't move. Read my lips. I don't know how this man got in here, but I believe there is a guy in here who works for Santiago. I don't want to set off an alarm or make him aware that I recognize him."

Eyes shifting, Angelica watched the man scanning the room as if he was looking for someone. He eased through the crowd without arousing suspicion. Pulled back from his face, his dreads were held together with some type of elastic band. He wore a black, double-breasted suit, a tie and a white shirt. *Santiago is clever*, Angelica thought. *Dreads looks like one of the mourners.*

People continued to file out of the fellowship hall, although there were still groups clustered together, engaged in deep conversation. Angelica continued to follow him with her eyes when Lieutenant Broadnax began to speak.

"I need to call Petrowski and let him know that we have what seems to be a penetration in the building."

"Look natural," Angelica cautioned, tapping Broadnax's chest with her hand. "I don't want to give him any indication that we suspect him of anything."

Broadnax removed her hand and made a quick call, never looking back to personally eyewitness the intruder. He hung up and looked at Angelica. "It's not going to look normal if I keep standing here talking to you. I need to move around so that, if I need to make a move, I can get into position."

"I'm sorry. My nerves have got the best of me. My brother, Edward, has a gun on him. I need to let him know what's going on."

"That wouldn't be a good idea, Angelica. Let the police handle this."

"Letting the police handle it has allowed the enemy to get into our camp. That man is looking for me; it's my life on the line."

"Please, Angelica, don't do anything stupid. You could jeopardize everything. Just play along."

Angelica let out a sigh and then panic gripped her as she lost sight of the man in dreads. She looked to the left and to the right, and then she felt it in the small of her back.

"Don't move and don't scream," the voice said hurriedly. "I'm FBI. I've been working on the Santiago case, and I've been following you because we were sure you would lead us to him. We've made a lot of headway, but I'll explain in more detail later. I've only got fifteen minutes to make my move. The SWAT team outside is working with the bureau."

Angelica tried to turn around. "But why didn't Lieutenant Broadnax know that you all were…"

"Don't turn around, we have to move forward. The Fayetteville police are well aware of what's going down. They were waiting for my signal. That's why no one has pounced on me. I was able to infiltrate Santiago's organization, and be glad I was in place when he decided to take you out. I didn't learn about Hamilton until it was too late. That's why I volunteered to take care of you; I knew that I could save your life.

"Santiago and a couple of his men are waiting outside a few blocks away. If I'm not successful with what they charged me to do, I'm sure they are going to try an attempt on your life. I'm going to walk you to a bulletproof vehicle, in the event something happens."

"But my brother, Jefferson and Margo are here—what about them?"

"Look to your right, Broadnax is alerting them now. They are herding the others to the back of the room. They'll be all right. Right now, we want to catch Santiago in the act. We have enough information on his activities, but since the shooting of your cousin, Donna Barnes Reardon, and Hamilton, things have moved so fast. Since I knew that he was going to make an attempt on your life, we are in a position to take him down. After you put on the bullet-proof vest I have in my backpack, you and I are going to walk out of the fellowship hall."

"But what about all those things you said to me on the bus that day?"

"That was an attempt to get information from you. We let Santiago slip through our hands without a trace, but had high hopes that you would lead us to him."

"That was pretty presumptuous of you because I wanted to be as far away from Santiago as I could possibly be."

"Knowing how the criminal mind works, we were sure he was going to make some kind of effort to contact you—unfinished business. Now we've got to get moving. The plan is that I'll have the gun drawn to your head, and the police will surround me. We hope to draw Santiago from his hiding place. Put the vest on, and let's go."

"And your name?" Angelica asked.

"Agent Walter Hopkins, at your service."

Edward, Jefferson, and Margo stared at Angelica. Her fear returned as the remaining crowd watched from a distance. She and Agent Hopkins moved toward the main door of the hall, and when they reached it, he stopped.

"Act like you're afraid but don't go crazy. I'm not going to hurt you, and the other officers will be holding their guns on me. Drag your feet to make it look realistic—we'll replace your shoes if we need to."

Angelica's face relaxed into a smile. "All I want is my life back."

"Ready?" Agent Hopkins asked Angelica and the officers nearby. They moved through the door.

54

An ocean of orange, yellow, and a hint of magenta blazed across the sky, offering a panorama equal to that over the Polynesian honeymoon island of Bora Bora. Breathtaking was the sun as it slowly made its ascent due west. *It is too beautiful a day to die* Angelica thought, although she had buried a part of her past earlier that afternoon.

With a gun pointed at her head, she felt like death still lingered near, regardless of the amount of reassurances Agent Hopkins had given her. Out in the open, the commotion began as Agent Hopkins threatened to kill her if the police didn't back off. She knew this was staged, but her life hung in the balance, and it made her cry out openly. There was no Edward at her side to rescue her if she needed him, and the thought of being the pawn to catch Santiago sickened her more.

Angelica and Agent Hopkins stood on the top step of the hall with police surrounding them.

"Release the woman, now," blared the voice on the police bullhorn. Agent Hopkins had Angelica by the neck and the gun pointed right at her head. He continued to reassure her under his breath that all was under control.

The standoff was on. Agent Hopkins pointed his gun at the police officers and told them to move back because he was taking this woman hostage. The police would not back down and, for fifteen minutes, Agent Hopkins continued to wave the gun at the officers, who were poised to shoot at any time while he held Angelica tight. Then it happened.

"Kill her. Kill her now, you fool. Kill her or I'll kill you," Santiago shouted from across the street. He moved closer and pointed the Glock. "What are you waiting for? You said you were going to take care of it."

Hopkins pushed Angelica into the sea of officers, who immediately pushed her into a bulletproof patrol car that had been sitting on the side of the church. All of a sudden, gunfire rang out as Santiago pulled the trigger. Twenty members of the SWAT team and Agent Hopkins returned the fire, and Santiago stood still like a robot waiting for its next order, taking a few steps before falling face down on the sidewalk.

Members of the Fayetteville police rushed to the fallen Santiago but dropped to the ground when a round of gunfire cut them off. From the rooftops of neighboring businesses, gunfire poured down until there was no response from the enemy—a deafening silence ensued. The officers who had dropped to the ground slowly picked themselves up from the pavement and went to check on the fallen victims. Soon, the others joined them, and then an announcement was made.

"Three down," said one of the sharpshooters. "No sign of anyone else."

Angelica emerged from the car and walked cautiously toward the group of officers. When Agent Hopkins saw her approach, he put out his hand to stop her from coming closer. This wasn't something she needed to see up close. Her worries were over—Santiago was dead.

The door to the fellowship hall opened, and Lieutenant Broadnax stepped outside. Edward, Jefferson, and Margo were right behind him, all in a hurry to find out what went down. All efforts to restrain the group of people left in the fellowship hall were fruitless as they pushed past Broadnax and spilled outside. A yellow ribbon and a sea of police officers blocked their attempt to proceed beyond a certain point as the police waited for the coroner's office to scoop the dead from the ground.

"What happened...are you all right?" Edward asked Angelica as he ran to be by her side.

"Edward, it happened so fast. One minute I had a gun pointed at my head, the next minute I was thrown to a bunch of muscle-bound cops, who tucked me away in their patrol car. Then the shooting began, and after a couple of minutes, it was all over. Agent Hopkins saved my life, and to think I believed he was one of the bad guys. He deserves a medal for his undercover work."

"Good job, Angelica," Margo said. Margo smiled and went to Angelica and hugged her.

"I needed that, girl. You don't know. My life flashed before me a hundred times, but I'm glad it's all over."

"It's over for all of us," Margo responded. "We have you to thank for risking your life to save ours."

"I'd do it all again," Angelica laughed. "Well, I hope I don't have to do it again. If I wasn't forced to be the sacrificial lamb, I'm not sure I would've volunteered."

Jefferson put his arms around Margo and finally spoke. "I can't believe it's all over."

"From the little Agent Hopkins told me, Santiago probably wouldn't have seen the light of day. Even though he won't stand trial, there was enough evidence to convict him of several murders, including Hamilton's."

"Yeah, I heard about Hamilton's cousin. Well, Santiago won't be around to hurt anyone else," Jefferson said.

"Look, why don't we get away from here and go back to our hotel so we can sit down and talk?" Edward said. "We'll get room service, if you want something to eat."

Margo glanced at Jefferson and then looked quickly away. She puckered her lips. "Everyone has been through so much today," Margo began, "and we've got to get our house taken care of."

"This is Saturday, for heaven's sake," Angelica said. "You're not going to get anything done on your house tonight. Come on, Margo. I want to bring you up to speed with what's happened to me."

"Well…" Margo began.

"Yeah, a few appetizers and some iced tea might do it for an hour or so," Jefferson put in. "Help us to unwind from the day. We're coming."

"The Fayetteville police would have made Hamilton proud today," Angelica added as an afterthought. "He lived and breathed that badge." Before she could say anything else, Agent Hopkins approached.

"Hi, folks, I'm Agent Hopkins. Angelica was a brave woman tonight. I don't know that I would have trusted me, if I were her."

"It was a hard sell, but you left me little choice," Angelica said. "And I'm glad it's over."

"Well, you did a fine job. Helping us to apprehend one of the FBI's Most Wanted was a good thing. One of these days soon, I'll be able to tell you the whole story leading up to this day."

"Do you have any idea why Santiago may have killed Donna?"

"I can't talk about the case, but it may have something to do with Donna kicking you out of her house and not telling him. But it's apparent he found out where you were."

"With Ari…," Angelica mumbled. She pulled herself together.

"Thank you again, Agent Hopkins, for saving my life…for saving all of our lives. I don't know how we can repay you."

"Nothing to repay, Angelica. I was doing my job and I'd do it again."

"Would you do me a favor?"

"If I can," Agent Hopkins said.

"On the day I left the women's prison, Sgt. Macy told me that she would see me again, and because I don't plan to ever darken the doorway to that place, please tell Sgt. Macy for me that Angelica Barnes is never coming back. She gave me and the other girls in Dorm L a hard time. And, Agent Hopkins, she is not quite right—a lesbo who's taking sexual liberties with women, those who want it and those who are forced against their will."

Agent Hopkins pondered what Angelica said. "We may be taking a trip to the women's prison sooner than you think. You may have repaid me by giving me what I need to take down corrupt workers in the system. Thanks again, Angelica."

"Glad to be of service."

55

Nausea floated through Margo's body as the images of Jefferson and Angelica walking into the hotel she now approached herself came back to her. Knowing the whole story did not make her feel better because she now had to deal with the mistake she had made. She hated how Malik had reacted when she told him that she was staying with her husband. Now she knew it would be only a matter of time before Jefferson found out.

She grabbed her stomach as a terrible reality seized her mind. *God, don't let me be pregnant*, she thought to herself as her nerves started to unravel. She was too old to have baby momma drama.

"Are you all right, Margo?" Angelica asked with concern on her face.

Margo looked up, and Jefferson, Edward, and Angelica were in front of her, staring her down. From somewhere, Jefferson grabbed a piece of paper and began fanning her.

"I'm all right." Margo sat up straight. "I guess so much happened today that it all caught up with me."

"Do you want me to take you home…I mean, the hotel? We no longer have police protection since they've killed Santiago."

"No, Jefferson. I'll be fine. If I can have some water or something else cold to drink."

"Coming right up," Angelica said as Jefferson sat next to Margo and held her in his arms.

"Water for the lady," Edward said, handing a bottle to Margo. "Look, I want to thank you guys for sticking with us today. I know the relationship between our families has been rocky, but when it counted, you were there. We owe you a debt of gratitude. And I think my sister can finally get on with her life."

Angelica smiled, walked to Edward and gave him a brotherly kiss on the cheek. "That was sweet, Edward, and I'd like to say I feel the same as my brother. Margo, you are the best, and if I ever get a friend like you again, I'm going to keep her for life. I want you to know that I do love you, and if you can find it in your heart to forgive me, I'd appreciate it so much."

Margo smiled and nodded. She took a sip of water and sat the bottle down.

"Angelica is thinking about going back to New York," Edward said, trying to ruffle the silence.

"So, you liked New York?" Margo asked quizzically.

"It's not that I like New York so much, but I left someone there who is very special to me. I don't know what I would have done if I didn't have Ari on my side. He gave me hope and came to my rescue when I was trying to get away from Santiago. I put him through more changes, but he was my pillar of strength when I didn't have it for myself. I'll never forget how he gave me safe passage out of New York. He means the world."

"He seems awfully special," Margo said. "Sounds like you've found true love."

"I believe I have, Margo. I believe I have."

"Let's see if we can't get a bottle of wine to celebrate!" Jefferson said. "I don't believe in taking a life, but seeing Santiago lying face down on the sidewalk made my heart glad. He was evil, and I can't believe I allowed myself to get caught up in his scheme for the sake of the almighty dollar."

"It's your past now, baby," Margo said. She went and put her arms around him and kissed him passionately. Visions of Malik tried to break through, but she held Jefferson tight to keep the ugly deed she'd done with Malik at bay.

"Uhh, time out, time out. It's getting hot in here," Angelica roared, making the time out sign she'd seen football players do on the field. "You may need to go on home." Angelica winked at Margo and Jefferson.

Margo pulled away from Jefferson and wiped the corner of his mouth. "Hurry back, baby. Don't let Edward keep you out too long."

Surprise registered on Jefferson's face. "I'm back, baby," Margo said before Jefferson could utter a word. "Run along. Angelica and I have a little girl talk to do."

Jefferson didn't say a word but watched Margo with renewed interest. He followed Edward out of the hotel room, but not before glancing back at Margo with a curious frown on his face.

"What's up with Jefferson?" Angelica asked.

"He can't comprehend the new me. You see, it was a little difficult for me to consummate my marriage when Jefferson first came home. As much as I loved him, memories of all the things he had done and how he had treated me flooded back. I wanted to accept him without any reservations, but I found, Angelica, that the wound was open and hadn't completely healed."

"How was it that you forgave me so easily when I got out of jail?"

"Angelica, don't kid yourself. It was not easy, and I'm not sure that I had forgiven you totally. It's different when you live with someone and you see them every day and night. I made baby steps with you because I knew I wasn't going to sleep with you and bear my soul to you."

"Okay. I can accept that because I certainly didn't deserve an ounce of your love."

"But, as a Christian, I'm taught to love everyone, even my enemies. I didn't hate you, Angelica, I hated the things you did and what you represented. I trusted you like a sister—I would have gone to the ends of the world for you. But you disappointed me greatly, for which I thought at one time there was no repentance. But I do love you."

Tears flowed from Angelica's eyes. She took her hands and wiped them from her face. Angelica stood and went and sat next to Margo and hugged her. "Thank you for the hug today, friend, I needed it," Angelica said.

"I can't breathe," Margo said and began to laugh at herself. "Girl, you about squeezed the life out of me."

"Margo, you're the best friend I've ever had and I don't want to lose you."

"Sit up and look at me. Angelica, I'm not perfect." Margo looked away and then back at Angelica. "I've done some things in my life I'm not so proud of, but I know that God forgives me. Now, if God, whom I can't see, can forgive me, why can't I forgive you, who I *can* see?"

"Profound, even though I know it came straight from the Bible. I remember my grandmother quoting a scripture close to that when she would always talk about faith and forgiveness."

"I love you, too, Angelica." She said it. *That wasn't hard,* Margo thought. But she really meant it.

"Not to change the subject, but what happened with you and Malik tonight?"

"Let's change the subject."

"Malik fell in love with you, didn't he? Don't give me that strange look, Margo. The chemistry was there. You all had the chemicals burning out of the Bunsen burner."

"Malik was there for me during the time Jefferson was in prison.

He was like a brother to me—checking on his big sister. I realized it was much more than that right before Jefferson came home.

"I did everything to avoid him, Angelica, but he wouldn't take no for an answer. And soon, I found myself thinking about him." Margo looked straight into Angelica's eyes. "I'm not sure why I'm telling you this, but I think I was feeling more for him than I cared to admit. But it wasn't until a couple of days ago when I saw you and Jefferson going into this very hotel that I did lose it."

"What do you mean, lose it? Wait a minute, back up—when you saw Jefferson and me? You mean the other day when Jefferson was going over Hamilton's papers? Edward was there, too. Didn't you see him? Honey, Jefferson and I were conducting business.

"Margo, I'm ready to settle down again, but I want a real and honest relationship with a man who loves me, who's single, and would like to be with me until the sunset of our lives. That's Ari, my friend in New York. He's a beautiful person. And it doesn't hurt that he can work a girl over, if you know what I mean."

"You haven't changed, Angelica."

"I have, Margo. Long gone is the woman who used a man to get what she wanted. If I have to be all by myself, so be it, as long as life is kind to me and I can smile when I wake up, thanking the Lord for all of His goodness. It's kind of like the pursuit of happiness."

"Boy, what a new-sounding Angelica. I like it, and I pray that God grants you your dreams. Everyone deserves some happiness in their lives."

"I'm glad we've had this moment to reflect, Margo. I've missed you so much. When I was in prison, I thought about you all the time, hoping you would come to see me...that you would truly forgive me."

"I'm sorry that I didn't come," Margo whispered.

"Not to worry, girl. I didn't deserve your love, and now I'm better for it. So, finish telling me about Malik. That man is still fine."

"He told me you tried to push up on him and you exposed your breasts."

"What? Not me! How could Malik say such vicious things about me?" Angelica chided. "But girl, you should have seen his face. Now, any other man would have jumped at the bit to squeeze my melons. Don't fool yourself, my fine brother was tempted, but he pushed the urge to get a free sample to the back of his mind because he had a Jones for someone named Margo."

They laughed.

"How do you know that?"

"Margo, he was so nasty to me. He was mad that you recommended that I volunteer with him. He was so nasty that the pretty melted off his face. I'll say the brother is fine, but he wasn't going to treat me, Angelica Barnes, like that. I didn't need him, even if I didn't have two nickels to rub together at that moment—arrogant S.O.B. But it's all right because I got me a real man."

"Is he as fine as Malik?"

"Baby, he's finer. Now, you and the handsome Malik didn't get busy, did you? Did you…? Oh my God, you did."

"What are you going on about, Angelica? No one said I did anything with Malik."

"But, my sister Margo, you didn't say you didn't. O-M-G. Now I get it. You thought Jefferson was with me so you ran over to the fine brother's house and gave him some. Shut up!!"

"Angelica, control yourself. Look, I can't let on to Jefferson that this happened. It's getting the best of me because Malik believes that I want to be with him."

"Did you give him any reason to believe that?"

"Well, no…maybe. But I told him tonight that I love my husband and that we are going to be together for life."

"Do you really believe that or are you psyching yourself into believing it?"

"I love my husband, Angelica. I love him with all my heart, soul, and…you know."

Angelica let out a guttural laugh. "You should have seen your eyes. I believe you. But you know what you've done; you've messed Malik up. He's not going to give up easily, even going as far as telling Jefferson what he had done to make Jefferson angry."

"I've got to do something to make it right. I do love Jefferson, and I'm going to make it all up to him."

"Do your breasts seem full? Have you felt your womb preparing itself?"

"Preparing itself for what?"

"A tax deduction? Like waaaaaaaaa, waaaaaaaaaa."

"Truthfully, I'm scared, Angelica. I can't believe I allowed this to happen The thought of having a baby at my age frightens me to death."

"Well, you know it only takes one time and one sperm. I sure hope it was good. So were you going to make your husband wear protection?"

"Now, you're talking like the crazy Angelica who used to be my friend. What I do or don't do with Jefferson is off limits to you." The reality, however, was that Margo hadn't thought about it at all, and that wasn't like her.

Angelica smiled. "I'm your friend, Margo. I'm only pointing out the reality of what you've done to spite Jefferson who loves only his wife and wouldn't have come to the meeting if Edward hadn't insisted. I know I've made my bed many times, but Margo, you're much better than me."

Margo let Angelica's words sink in. She was going to have to find a way to tell Jefferson what she had done. Their marriage was on the brink of disaster, but she wanted it to be healthy again. She would have to find a way.

"You know, Margo, I miss Hamilton, in a funny kind of way. When he wasn't doing his dirt, he was the most loving and kind husband. In fact, he was much more handsome than Malik—that's what happened to his womanizing self. Thought he was fine…"

"He knew he was fine, Angelica. You couldn't tell that man he didn't look good. Shucks, I had to give him a couple of quick glances myself." They laughed.

"Wow, those were the days. I can't believe I buried him today, Margo." The tears began to stream down Angelica's face. "I loved him, and he still loved me. We just couldn't live in the same house. I can't believe he's gone. Oh God, help me. Why did You take my husband from me?"

A box of Kleenex sat on the table. Margo pulled a handful out of the dispenser and dabbed Angelica's tears. "It's all right to mourn for Hamilton. He was your husband."

"Excuse me, but I've got to make a phone call."

Angelica stood up, retrieved her purse from the nightstand, and reached in it and took out her cell phone. She retrieved a number and dialed, and in an instant her face lit up. "Hey, Ari, this is Angelica. Santiago is dead, the police killed him. When I'm finished here, I'm coming back to New York. I hope you'll be waiting for me…I love you, too."

56

Quiet peace lay in the room. Sporadic snoring invaded the silence but did not disturb the peacefulness around it. Then a short grunt and a shifting of the covers dared to spoil the tranquility. And in the next instant, Jefferson pushed off the covers, sat up, rubbed his eyes, and then leaned over and looked at the clock on the nightstand. He sighed and reached over and patted the other lump in the bed.

"Baby, we better get up if we're going to church."

"Can we stay in this morning?" said the muffled voice.

"Don't you think we need to let the Lord know how grateful we are for delivering us from the hands of the enemy? Margo, I feel freer than I've ever felt."

"When did you become so holier than thou? And why are you talking so loud?"

"So, are you trying to be a bedside Baptist this morning? Rise and shine. This doesn't sound like you."

Margo sat up. "Baby, I don't think the Lord would be upset with us if we praised Him from our hotel room. I would have to go home and get something to wear, and I can't go there right now. The memories are too fresh in my head."

"The memories are fresh for me too, but to know that it's all over is a blessing."

"How do we know that there aren't more people in this organization waiting out there somewhere to hurt us? Can you be sure that it's all over, Jefferson…that no one else will come after us?"

Jefferson looked at Margo and pondered the question. "No, we don't know, Margo, but my spirit tells me different."

"I like the way you're thinking."

"I'm going to turn my life completely around. You'll see. I need to go to Atlanta and see Mom and Dad, and I want you to go with me. While we're there, maybe we can catch up with your brother, the good pastor."

"He'd love to see you."

"Let's do it. So, what's the real reason you don't want to go to church today?"

Margo's eyes widened. "What do you mean, the real reason? Do I have to play back all we've been through the past couple of days or the last twenty-four hours, to be more specific?"

"Okay, sweetie. I wasn't trying to excite you. The thought had occurred to me that you might be trying to avoid Malik. I haven't forgotten the little scene you both caused last night. Forget I said anything; I'm going to turn on the television."

Margo lay back down and turned away from Jefferson. He watched her, sure she was keeping something from him. In due season, it would manifest itself. In fact, it was time to have a word with Malik because he was back, and whatever was going on between Malik and Margo was about to be loosed. As Malik's last words were coming to him, the weekend anchor team of *Good Morning America* was running their story.

We have a breaking story coming to you straight from the pages of Hollywood. Yesterday, in Fayetteville, North Carolina, the FBI brought down one of the most dangerous and sought after criminals in their files. Robert Santiago, a mob boss, was killed, as were a couple of his associates, as he attempted to have an old girlfriend assassinated at the funeral repast of her ex-husband, former police officer Hamilton Barnes. Hamilton Barnes, a former member of Santiago's operation, was serving a life sentence in Central Prison in Raleigh, North Carolina, for murder in the deaths of Blake Montgomery and Marsha Wilson.

This story began five years ago in Fayetteville, North Carolina, when Operation Stingray, headed up by Robert Santiago, blew apart at the seams. Operation Stingray was a cover for a large theft ring that purchased stolen weapons from Fort Bragg and sold them to a rebel group in Honduras—the birthplace of Mr. Santiago.

Mr. Jefferson Myles, a Fayetteville businessman who was also a part of Operation Stingray, was convicted of embezzling funds from his corporation, Myles and Associates, and using the money to purchase the weapons. All went haywire when Jefferson Myles and Hamilton Barnes were gunned down by Robert Santiago because of internal problems. Both Myles and Barnes survived their ordeals, however, and stood trial for each of their separate indictments, eventually going to prison. Robert Santiago was not caught and eluded police for five years.

We have learned that Santiago is also responsible for Hamilton Barnes' death a week ago while Barnes was a prisoner in Central Prison. He is also responsible for the death of a prominent photographer here in New York, Donna Barnes Reardon, the cousin of Hamilton Barnes. It has been a month since Ms. Barnes Reardon's death, with no arrests made. Such a bizarre turn of events, and it is still not known what the motive was for the murders. One can make a number of speculations.

And, to add a twist to the bizarre tale, the ex-wife of Hamilton Barnes, Angelica Barnes, had moved to New York before Ms. Barnes Reardon was killed. Ms. Angelica Barnes had recently been released from prison for her part in Operation Stingray. We have also been told that Robert Santiago may have been tipped off by Barnes Reardon that Angelica was coming to New York, and eventually she, Angelica, became a guest in Mr. Santiago's home.

We will keep you updated as this story unfolds. Again, Mr. Robert Santiago of Operation Stingray has been killed.

Jefferson sat with a blank stare on his face. The nightmare had not ended. His past kept coming up like yesterday's vomit—a bad taste in his mouth. When would he get rid of it so he could resume the rest of his life?

"You decided to be a bedside Baptist today, too?" Margo asked as she turned over to look at Jefferson.

"No, I'm going to get up. I've got a lot of issues to sort through. Damn, I can't believe that, even in death, Santiago continues to drag me down to the gutter with him. I paid the price for my bad deeds, and now the good old media wants to have a field day at my expense. Margo, I can't take much more."

"What about your sermon this morning about being grateful to the Lord? You were passionate—had me believing that this was truly over and that we could now lead a normal life."

"Tell me about you and Malik."

A long silence ensued, except for the morning newsanchors, who were relating another heart-breaking story about a woman who was moving from one military town to another military town, marrying innocent soldiers without divorcing the previous ones and then having their babies.

"Tell me about you and Malik," Jefferson said again. "I want to know where I really stand in your life."

Margo finally sat up and leaned back on the headboard. She looked thoughtfully at Jefferson and parted her lips, although nothing came out. She wrapped her arms around her waist and breathed deeply, and when she could no longer hold it, the air flew out of her mouth. "I had sex with him, Jefferson."

The *Good Morning America* team faded to black as Jefferson pointed the remote and clicked the television off. He stood up from the bed, put on his robe, and paced the tiny space in the room without looking at Margo. He stopped in front of the lamp, jerked it from its socket and threw it across the room.

"Say something, Jefferson. Be mad at me if you want. You forced me to tell you. Now say something."

"What do you want me to say?"

"Hell, I don't know! But it wasn't like you think."

"Wasn't like I think? What kind of bull is that? You told me you had sex with Malik, and it's not what I think? Hell, I'm not trying to visualize it, but the very thought of Malik touching you anywhere repulses me." Jefferson rammed his hand into the wall. "I could kill him right now."

Margo threw her hand over her mouth. "Stop it, Jefferson. Haven't we had enough killing for one week?"

"Then tell me why, Margo, why? Do you love him? And don't lie to me."

"You got some nerve, Jefferson Myles. I waited for you for five long years. I was a faithful wife every minute of those five years, even though you didn't deserve my love and trust. I loved you in spite of your infidelity and the way you treated me, and I was the dutiful wife waiting for you when you returned."

"So, what happened when I returned? You were the one who told me that you were going to stand by me. And I wanted you to because I never stopped loving you. But from the moment I returned home, things were different...Malik was being different.

His not showing up to the homecoming party should have been a sign. I remember the day at the restaurant; he acted so strange. We haven't had a real decent conversation. It was during that time, though, that I felt something was wrong. I wasn't quite sure what it was, but now I know. That's why you couldn't make love to me."

"But you're wrong, Jefferson. Yes, Malik was falling in love with me, but I never committed to anything. In fact, I asked him to stop coming around. It wasn't until I saw you with Angelica going into the hotel that I did run to him, and…it happened."

"And then you came home and made love to me or was it just sex. Are you telling me that you never thought about being with Malik? Do you know how it felt when you wouldn't touch me, wouldn't sleep with me?"

"Listen to me. Don't make me out to be the bad person. I know *very well* how all of that feels…not to be touched, not being wanted because your flavor for the month was not chocolate."

"Okay, I asked for it. Let's not bring that up."

"Why not, since we're talking about indiscretions? Have I thought about being with Malik? The answer is yes. When I tried to get close to you, it was Malik I'd see. He was there for me during those five years you were gone. I depended on him for a lot of things, except sex. Foremost, he was a friend that I could count on. And when Antoinette died, he was a wreck, and I was there to nurse him back to health. I know you can't understand how we could have such a friendship without it being sexual, but we managed."

"Humph, managed? Do you love him? You never answered the question."

"If I loved Malik, I wouldn't be having this conversation with you. That's why we were arguing last night. I know what I did was wrong, but in my moment of weakness, I gave myself to him, and yes, I led him to believe that I wanted him the way he wanted me. I told him tonight that I loved you, and that you were the person that I was going to spend the rest of my life with."

Jefferson continued to pace with the weight of the world on his shoulders. He was on his twenty-fifth revolution when Margo couldn't take anymore.

"Would you sit down or say something? You are getting on my nerves. If you want me to leave, I'll go."

Click, click, click. Click, click, click went Jefferson's teeth. The noise was aggravating, but he continued to scrape them together. Margo started for the bathroom.

"Please don't leave the room. I'm doing much better than I thought. Malik would have been dead by now, if the thought of being locked up in a prison cell hadn't occurred to me. But you're not going anywhere." Jefferson's countenance changed.

Margo looked up at her husband's smiling face. "What are you getting ready to do? Jefferson, I'm not up to any games."

"I'm taking off my robe."

"For what?"

"For some hot fudge sundae. That will always be my flavor of the month, the year, and the next several decades."

Margo stared at him with her hands on her hips. "What would Jesus say about you having hot fudge on a Sunday, no pun intended, while you should be at church?"

"I don't think He would say never on a Sunday—maybe He'll say *not on His time*. But let me take something from the scriptures. The bridegroom cometh. Is there oil in your lamp? Is it trimmed and burning?"

"You are blasphemous. The Lord is going to strike you down. But if you're offering yourself to me, I'm a taker."

57

Hints of summer were all around. Spring flowers had become enormous flowerbeds of day lilies, mums, impatiens, and hostas. Even the eerie feeling that blanketed the city yesterday gave way to a brilliant sun that would cause many to flock to Myrtle Beach or other resorts if it weren't a Monday.

They walked through the house as they waited for the contractors who would assess and repair the damage. The memory of the shooting had shaken them both to the point that the house on Andover Street was no longer attractive. Other bad memories clouded their desire to stay in the house also, and a "For Sale" sign would most likely be imminent.

"I can't believe Angelica wants to go back to New York. A large part of her life is here," Margo said thoughtfully as she placed a finger in a hole in the wall that had held one of the many bullets that had flown through the front window.

"Can't blame her," Jefferson responded. "Some memories you want to leave behind. I hear she has a love interest waiting for her."

"Ari is his name. She called him while you and Edward were at the store last night. I believe she has finally found true love."

"I'm not sure Angelica will ever know what true love is, but it's her life."

"Why would you say that, Jefferson? It's almost as if you're jealous of…"

"Please don't start speculating about what isn't, Margo. I'm only saying that Angelica bounces around from one man to another… and, I hate to say it, but she keeps messing up other people's lives. She doesn't know what she wants. Men find her attractive, which means she gets lots of attention. When a man whispers in her ear, she believes it's love but the woman really doesn't have a clue."

"So, Mr. Know-It-All, sounds like you've got Angelica all figured out, like you're talking from experience."

"Give me a little more credit than that, Margo. Angelica is transparent as glass—you see her for what she is and use her for what you want if she doesn't use you first—and most times she does."

"That's terrible, Jefferson. I can't believe you're talking about the woman who was once my best friend. We've been with her and Edward the whole weekend, even through this ordeal with Santiago. You helped her with her money matters. Why are you all of a sudden talking down about her?"

"True, but it's the other side of her you really don't know—the part that I want to put distance between."

"You're saying that because she deceived you by getting into your accounts. You only have yourself to blame for that."

"Yeah, you're right, but that's only part of it. Did you know that Hamilton met Angelica in a strip joint? She made her living as a dancer until he took her off the streets."

Margo sighed. "So, she didn't flip burgers at McDonald's or Burger King. She didn't go to college. Sounds like she had hopes of a better future; I hope she made lots of money trying to get there. That was a long time ago, Jefferson."

"Margo, only you would say something like that. You're upset because you didn't have any idea about her past."

"If you knew so much, why didn't you share it with me before now? It's Angelica's past, so let's leave it there. For the record, we've all fallen short with more than a few blemishes on our lives, Mr. Jefferson Myles. No room to talk. Get my meaning?"

"Got it and saved by the bell. The glass man is here."

"Don't try and change the subject. I think Angelica has met the right person this time, and if I was a betting woman, my money says she'll be married within the next year."

"The bet is on, and girl, you're going to lose. Oh, and here comes the other contractor. Thank God. I'm tired of talking about Angelica."

"Suit yourself."

"I'll get the door."

"Don't forget, we have an early dinner with Angelica and Edward today."

"How I wish I could forget," Jefferson said under his breath.

Jefferson's words bounced in Margo's head—*transparent...the other side of Angelica*. There may have been no love lost between Jefferson and Angelica, but there was something that he was not saying—something that only he and Angelica knew about. Of that Margo was certain.

∞

The sweet smell of hickory invaded their nostrils as they exited the car and headed into the restaurant. Running behind schedule, Margo and Jefferson rushed inside and waded through the eclectic sea of people—some standing and others sitting on long wooden benches, waiting to satisfy their hunger. Empty peanut shells littered the floor, while nostalgic pictures hung on the walls in the rustic motif of the restaurant, and fires blazed on long open grills as chefs turned over steaks that were rare, medium, medium well, and well done to the customer's satisfaction.

A hand held high waved them in their direction. *Angelica seems so at peace*, Margo thought. Death sometimes had a way of bringing closure to headaches and heartaches, and Angelica had had enough of both to last a lifetime.

Margo saw Jefferson's eyes move to Angelica's backside when she bent over slightly to pinch the cheek of a cute little baby girl whose mother had squished her into a carrier. A pair of low-rider jeans hugged Angelica's shapely behind, but even the top of her thong was too much for Margo's eyes. The peep show was over in a second, but the real show was about to begin.

A gasp flew from Margo's mouth. Sitting next to Edward like he was the Duke of Earl, was Malik. She grabbed the side of Jefferson's arm, but not without feeling the electrical currents pulsating through it.

It was showdown at the Texas Roadhouse. Shorts-clad waitresses were already linked together in a do-si-do victory dance. Someone had yelled hee-haw before the winner was ever announced, better yet, before the fight had taken place. The two bulls, one named Jefferson and the other Malik, flexed their muscles and stared each other down, waiting for the bell to ring.

"What's up with you all?" Angelica asked, glaring at Margo and Jefferson.

"As much as we want to celebrate your new freedom and return to New York," Jefferson began, "I find it a bit crowded."

"Do you want to move to another table?" Angelica offered.

"What is Malik doing here?" Jefferson asked with disdain. "You didn't mention that Malik was invited to this shindig."

"Sit down," Margo whispered to Jefferson. "Let's have dinner peacefully."

"I asked him to join us," Angelica interjected. "He was already here, and I didn't see any reason why he shouldn't celebrate with us tonight—the more, the merrier. I will admit, though, that I'm not one of Malik's favorite people."

"Come on, Angelica," Malik said. "We're a little like oil and vinegar—we're always going to have our differences."

"No need to move. We'll sit right here," Jefferson said with little enthusiasm. Jefferson did not remove his eyes from those of his former friend. Malik looked away and picked up the menu.

"Everything squared away at the house?" Edward asked sincerely. "Did you get the window fixed?"

"They put the front window in this morning and we have some drywall work yet to be done," Margo said, trying to lighten the conversation and purposely averting her eyes so she wouldn't have to look at Malik.

"I think everyone should get something to drink to lighten the mood," Angelica interjected. "I want to make a toast—to new beginnings and new loves."

Malik shook his finger. "I'd like to drink to that." Margo and Jefferson looked at him strangely.

Angelica picked up her glass from the table, took her index finger and swirled the concoction around. Licking her finger, she took a sip. "Umh, umh, umh. This Jamaican Cowboy is so good. Uhm. The rum and Schnapps in this thing is going to do me in. I'm going to make a toast to myself. May life be greater than it was before, and may true love find me and cover me like a tidal wave because I'm long overdue."

"So, what are you celebrating?" Jefferson asked Malik, ignoring Angelica's toast since he and Margo hadn't had the opportunity to order anything yet.

"Look who's talking? Try turning back a few chapters of your life. But since you've asked the question, why don't you ask Margo?"

Liquid gushed from Angelica's nostrils like fireworks. The intensity of Malik's counter-question caught her by surprise, and the drink she was consuming chose to take another route than the one it should have taken. Her eyes bulged when Margo stood up and began to give Malik a piece of her mind.

Margo stood and faced Malik. "I have seven words for you. I don't know what you're talking about. Whatever you're celebrating couldn't be what I'm celebrating because I'm celebrating new life and new love with my husband. That shouldn't be a foreign language to you because you've heard it before. I don't know what your purpose for being here is or your intentions, but let's get one thing clear, Malik: I, Margo Myles, have dedicated my life to my husband, Jefferson Myles, for the rest of my days, through the good and bad times, through the storm and the rain, and whatever else may come." Margo sat down.

Jefferson clapped while the others looked on.

"Good speech, very good speech, Margo." Malik took a sip of his Beringer. He put the glass down and stared directly at Jefferson. "Maybe you're not aware, Mr. Myles, but only a few days ago, your wife came to me crying. She told me that she saw you and Angelica entering a hotel."

Jefferson's hands transformed into two large fists. He hit the table, but Margo made an attempt to quiet him.

"Umh, looks like I'm getting out of Fayetteville in time," Angelica said with a feigned look of fright on her face.

"And Margo told me she was through with you. Begged me to make love to her."

"Oh my God!" Angelica hollered, covering her face with her

hands. "Malik, this is a celebration. You can air your dirty laundry with Jefferson another time. Right here and right now, it's about me, not you."

"Shut up, Angelica."

"You wait a minute," Edward said, jumping into the conversation. "My sister was kind enough to extend the invitation for you to sit down with us, so the least you can do is be courteous and considerate."

"Man, I'm not mad at you." Malik threw his hands up. "This jailbird doesn't deserve this wonderful woman sitting next to him."

Jefferson jumped up from the table and reached for Malik. Edward pushed him back and looked at Malik. "I'm telling you for the last time, shut the hell up or it's time for you to leave. Jefferson and Margo are happily married, and what they do is none of your business. Margo has already told you that she is committed to her marriage. So chill out, brother. Jefferson, it's all right. He's not going to do anything else." Jefferson sat down.

A huge scowl crossed Malik's face. He looked like an angry monkey in a coconut tree. He was no longer the attractive man that made Angelica and even Margo swoon. Sure, he still had the handsome good looks, impeccable pects, but his attitude had soured to an all-time low, and Margo felt she had been the cause of it.

"Jefferson and I are going to leave," Margo said. "Didn't mean to spoil your party, Angelica."

Before they were able to get up, Malik stood up. "So, you don't care that your wife was with me?" he began.

"If you say another word," Jefferson said while rising to his feet, "you're going to be eating peanut shells."

Out of nowhere, the manager of the restaurant appeared at

their table. "Excuse me please, but other patrons are complaining about the noise at this table. Please keep it down. Thank you." And he walked away.

"Come on, Jefferson," Margo said as she pulled on his arm. "We don't need this. Malik is an angry black man."

"Oh, that's not what you said when I was making love to you. By the way, did you know that Angelica seduced Jefferson when she was still married to Hamilton? He tried to convince me that he ignored her advances, but he committed to the act anyway. And when he finished, he put his shirt and tie back on and came running home to you."

No one knew who threw the first punch. All the hee-hawing came to a screeching halt as Jefferson, Malik, and Edward became a huge tumbleweed rolling on the floor in the middle of the aisle, trading punches with each other after first knocking everything off the table. Everyone in the restaurant was up on their feet and gathered around, some shouting, "*hit him, get 'im,*" and imitating each punch with their own hands.

"Get up, Jefferson," Margo screamed, trying to pull him from the pile. Angelica was at her side, trying to pull Edward from the fracas:

"I want you all out of here, now," shouted the manager, "before I call the cops."

The roadhouse girls began their chant, kicking their heels from side to side and singing their country line-dance song. Soon the whole restaurant chimed in as if it were the entertainment for the evening.

With a swollen face, Jefferson was the first to unravel from the pile on the floor and stand with Margo tugging at him to get up. Next was Edward, dusting dirty peanut shells from his suit. Malik sat up and both Jefferson and Edward punched him simultaneously—one in the chest and the other up-side his head until Malik slumped back to the floor.

"You all ruined my party," Angelica said as Jefferson and Margo moved away from the chaos and exited the restaurant.

"We've had enough for today, baby sister. It's time you headed back to New York or wherever it is you're planning to go."

"Edward, all I wanted to do was celebrate my new life."

"Angelica, you've already had your celebration. You will no longer be harmed by Santiago. Be grateful that you don't have to look over your shoulder every minute of the day in constant fear that…that evil man might get you. If you hadn't gotten out of his house, who knows what might have become of you. Sometimes, I…I want to throw my hands up and…"

"And what, Edward? Throw me to the dogs?"

"I'm sorry, Sis, nothing like that. Sometimes I get so tired of fighting your battles—battles that you create. I love you, Sis, but I want you in your new life to think not only of yourself but of others also—the awkward and sometimes crazy positions you put them in and the consequences of your actions. I'm sure your friend Ari would not be in the place he's in now, if you hadn't helped put him there."

A veiled mask covered Angelica's face.

"Please don't pout, Angelica. Someone should have sat you down a long time ago and had this talk with you."

"I'm a grown woman…"

"A grown woman who's made a mess of her life, but with my help, is going to straighten it out. We'll go back to D.C. first, and I'll call our brother Michael to come join us."

"Thanks, Edward. I love you, big brother. You are my saving grace, and I owe you big. Now let's get out of here."

"Yeah, here comes the manager."

"Who's going to pay for this," the manager asked out of breath.

"He is," both Angelica and Edward answered, pointing to Malik. "He got off easy," Angelica continued, "since we didn't get to order anything but a few drinks. How about you and me find a nice quiet place to eat?"

"You've got it."

58

Music blared from the car radio. Puffed faces stained with tears looked straight ahead as Jefferson and Margo drove away from the restaurant.

"Why did you do it, Jefferson? Why did you rile up Malik and cause a scene that made us look like we weren't intelligent beings? Wasn't it enough that I said I didn't love Malik, but I love you? And what was he talking about...you and Angelica were together?"

Jefferson kept his hands on the steering wheel and continued to look straight ahead.

"Answer me, Jefferson. I'm tired. I'm so tired. When I think I've gotten over a rough spot, here comes another speed bump."

"You don't understand, Margo." Jefferson threw his hands up.

"Please put your hands on the wheel. I don't want to die because *you* don't understand."

"This man was my best friend. We were closer than I am to my own siblings. Been knowing him since college, and we've shared so much of our life together. But he crossed the line. And the nigger had the nerve to think that I was going to share the one thing I held most precious with him. I should've killed him."

"I hate that you and Malik are at each other's throats. I can't believe that it's all come to this."

"So, was he better in bed than me, Margo? Did you tell him how good it was or how happy he made you feel?"

"Shut up, Jefferson. You have no right."

"I could've killed him tonight."

"And prove what…that you're a big man…that you were protecting your possession? Huh! Is that what I am to you, your possession?"

Jefferson's fist hit the steering wheel and then he slammed his foot on the brake and screeched to an abrupt stop just as the light turned red. Tears began to form in his eyes and fell the length of his face. He looked like a grown-up teddy bear looking for someone to cuddle him.

"Stop that crying," Margo huffed. "Those crocodile tears aren't going to get me to melt after having endured tonight's humiliating experience."

"I wasn't going to let Malik stand there and continue to disrespect you."

"And expose your dirty laundry." Margo shook her head and then released a long sigh. "You and Angelica deserve to rot in hell. You slept with her, didn't you? Told me you didn't, but you figured what I didn't know wouldn't hurt me. They say the truth always comes to the light."

"That was a long time ago, Margo."

"That was a long time ago, Margo," she mimicked. "You were unfaithful, and I guess I'm supposed to forgive you of your sins as if nothing happened." She snapped her fingers.

Jefferson sighed. "Does that make you feel better about what you did with Malik?"

"Don't try and use reverse psychology on me." Margo turned and looked out of the window. "Maybe if I had enjoyed it as much as Malik seems to think I did, maybe I'd feel better."

Silence ensued. Jefferson took a chance and glanced at Margo.

Her head was leaning on the passenger door window with her eyes staring at the passing cars.

"Why don't we get an ice cream cone?" Jefferson asked.

"Are you serious? We're having a discussion about the rest of our lives and you want to get ice cream?"

"Yes."

"I was thinking. What if Malik presses charges against you? Do you know what that means?"

"Let him, but I doubt seriously that he'd do it since he openly admitted that he had extramarital sex with you."

It was Margo's turn to sigh. "Let's get ice cream. Maybe this nightmare will go away."

They drove on in silence as contemporary jazz flooded the car. At the next light, Jefferson turned into the parking lot and drove through a maze of cars, finally bringing the car to rest.

"Cold Stone ice cream okay with you?" he asked Margo.

Margo pulled her face away from the window, turned to Jefferson and shook her head yet again. "You know it's my favorite, so why did you ask me that silly question?"

"Hoping I would get a smile from you?"

Her head fell forward and then up. Plastered on her face was a great big smile. "What are we going to do? Our lives have become so complicated. We should be enjoying the best years of our lives—going to plays, concerts, lying out on the beach, but instead we're bickering about who screwed who and which one of us screwed up the other's life."

"Margo, stop. I love you with everything I have. Woman, I know you don't believe this, but I don't care what you and Malik did. I want my wife back, the mother of my children and all my daydreams. I know we can't start from the beginning, but we can start fresh from this time forward, even if that means divorcing all the negative folks who have been a part of our lives. What do you say?"

Pinching her lips, Margo brought her hand to her face to hide the smile that was trying to get through. Doe-like eyes batted their lashes while she shook her face from side to side. "I guess that's why I married you—you're the only one who knows how to break me down. Pulled the shame right out from under me until there's nothing left to say but I love you, too, you crazy, mixed-up man. My mother always told me to stand by my man, but I never knew it would be this hard. But I do love you."

"Whew, I'm glad that ended well. I love you, too, girl. Now let's go and get that ice cream. I want a pint of Chocolate Devotion," he said in a sexy voice.

Like an action figure in the comics, Jefferson sprung from the car and ran around to open the door for Margo in a flash. He lifted her hand like he did so many years ago when Margo was a beautiful debutante at the ball. He bent his elbow and Margo put her arm through it, linking them together forever. They headed for the ice cream bar.

As if there were an invisible partition that didn't allow them to move any farther, they stopped cold in their tracks. Their eyes shifted between a woman and a child that had exited the ice cream bar and were headed in their direction. Now only a couple of feet away, they also stopped and stared back at Margo and Jefferson.

"Jefferson, Margo…"

"Linda," Margo responded, releasing her arm from Jefferson's and dropping it to her side. She looked hard at the slightly tanned little boy who seemed to be about four or five years old. It wasn't his cute crop of curly hair or his handsome good looks that made Margo cringe, but rather his uncanny likeness to her eldest son J.R.

Jefferson refused to open his mouth. He was as astonished as Margo when he looked at the boy while avoiding eye contact with Linda. There was no denying it was his son and that Linda had gotten pregnant those many years ago. He felt the life rush out of him. Prison hadn't been enough, because now he was truly reaping the consequences of his sins.

"Your son?" Margo asked when Linda said nothing further.

Linda glanced briefly at Jefferson and then back at Margo. "Yes, this is Jaylin. Say hi to these nice people, Jaylin."

"Hello," Jaylin said.

"Jaylin?" Jefferson mumbled. "Oh, God, what a mess I've made."

"If you're speaking of Jaylin, God doesn't make messes. I think it's pretty presumptuous of you to think he's yours. He isn't your child. Nice to see you both again. Come on, Jaylin, let's get home before our ice cream melts."

Linda grabbed Jaylin's hand, stepped off the sidewalk and walked to their car without looking back. Suddenly, ice cream was no longer appealing to Jefferson and Margo.

∞

THREE MONTHS LATER

Summer had come and gone. Leaves were beginning to turn along with the temperature, which dropped from a three-month stint of ninety-degree days to sixty-five. Healthy lawns prayed for a little rain, but Margo's lawn begged for strangers to come and stake their claim as the new owner of the house on Andover Street.

Margo walked from room to room, remembering times past. She ran her fingers along the frame of the French doors that separated the dining room from the kitchen. She moved into the room and looked through the floor-to-ceiling, beveled windows that gave a breathtaking view of the saltwater cove and beyond.

She turned and looked at the empty room where her beautiful dining room set with the French Empire chairs circling the table once sat. She remembered the last big Christmas meal she shared with her family and friends. Allen Myles, Sr. said grace in such an eloquent way. After grace, the others sat devouring the succulent turkey and ham she'd cooked, and then came the bad news that Blake Montgomery was dead.

Margo's mind began to race as thoughts of Jefferson's infidelity tried to consume her. Who would have thought her archenemy was her next-door neighbor, Linda, Blake's wife? And now, to learn five years later that Linda had a baby by Jefferson was a bitter pill to swallow.

The memories were too many. She crossed back into the kitchen and then into the family room, stopping at the luggage parked in the doorway. A month-long trip to Europe was what she needed.

Almost as if her arm was ejected from its position, Margo reached for her head. She felt faint, dizzy, and lightheaded. She moved from the room and found the stairs that went to the second floor and plopped down on them.

The moment passed and she was on her feet again. She walked back into the kitchen, hit the answering machine that sat on the counter and listened to Angelica's voice one last time. *Hey Margo, this is Angelica. Ari and I are doing great. We're getting married— sometime next June. I haven't been this happy in years. I sure hope you and Jefferson can come. It'll be in New York. Call me sometime when you get a moment. I know you're busy. Talk to you later.*

The message over, Margo pressed the delete button. Opening a small portfolio, she pulled out a group of papers and fumbled through them.

"Boarding passes for London, Paris, and Germany; passport; and, ahh, separation papers." She looked at the document long and hard and then rubbed her slightly protruding stomach with her hand.

"Jefferson," Margo said out loud to no one, "you were right about divorcing all the negative people and things from your life. It frees your mind and helps you to see things much clearer. Thanks for that tidbit of good information. No more Angelica, no more Malik, no more Jefferson." She put the papers away.

Prying herself away from her thoughts, she clutched the side of the counter as a wave of nausea hit her again. She rushed to the bathroom, leaned over the toilet and regurgitated. She wiped her mouth with the back of her hand before turning on the cold water and splashing it onto her face. Turning the water off, she sighed and looked at herself in the mirror. "I had no desire to be a mother again at forty-eight years old, but I'll be a good mother."

Margo moved quickly to the family room and picked up her luggage so she could put it in the car. She took another glance around the house as far as her eyes could see. The house was empty now—empty of hope, false dreams, and empty promises.

There was no way she was going through another bad storm with a husband she had vowed to spend the rest of her days with because it would probably kill her, even though she was still very much in love with him.

ABOUT THE AUTHOR

Suzetta Perkins is the author of *Ex-Terminator: Life After Marriage*, *A Love So Deep*, and her riveting debut novel, *Behind the Veil*. She is also a contributing author of *My Soul to His Spirit*, an anthology that was featured in the June 2005 issue of *Ebony* magazine. Suzetta is the co-founder and president of the Sistahs Book Club in Fayetteville, North Carolina and is Secretary of the University at Fayetteville State University, her alma mater. Visit www.suzettaperkins.com and www.myspace.com/authorsue or email to nubianqe2@aol.com

BOOK CLUB DISCUSSION GUIDE

DÉJÀ VU

- What was Angelica convicted of that sent her to prison? Did prison reform and prepare her for reentry into society?

- Did Angelica make an assertive effort to reconcile her relationship with Margo Myles? Why or why not?

- Someone was missing from Jefferson's homecoming. Who was it and why were they not there?

- Explain the relationship between Margo and Malik.

- What took Angelica to New York?

- If you live long enough, you will ultimately experience life's bumps and bruises. Sometimes life has a way of repeating itself because we allow ourselves to fall into traps through our inability to control our destiny. Angelica once again falls prey and becomes a victim of her own stupidity—she never seems to learn, but when she finds herself in trouble, she relies on her knowledge of the past. What past profession did she fall back on when she felt she had no other recourse?

- Do you condemn Angelica or applaud her for her actions?

- How does Angelica's past catch up with her?

- Who is Donna Barnes Reardon, and how significant was she in the turn of events in Angelica's life?

- Jefferson and Margo's relationship was strained. Although she welcomed her husband back into her life after a five-year prison stint, other obstacles kept them from re-consummating their marriage. What were the obstacles?

- What event drew Angelica back to Fayetteville?

- What does Margo observe that pushes her over the edge? What does she do in light of that knowledge?

- Angelica is on the run for her life, and so is Jefferson. Will they be able to stop running?

- Do you believe Angelica has found true love?

- What unsuspecting event turns up to haunt Jefferson's past, just as he and Margo have reconciled their differences?

- What is Margo's secret?